~ews of *The Silver Dark Sea*:

~ly beautiful ... poetic, dreamlike prose.'

FRANCESCA ANGELINI, *Sunday Times*

~amedly romantic ... Fletcher is a careful recorder of ~ural world, and *The Silver Dark Sea* is illuminated ~riginality of observation and strong sense of place'

PAMELA NORRIS, *Literary Review*

~derfully redemptive story of love and loss, Susan ~r's prose shimmers like light on water, and she's ~ adept at charting the emotions of her memorable ~ers ... Old resentments are revisited, dark secrets ~ealed, while barricaded, shut-away hearts let in the ~ility of love'

EITHNE FARRY, *Marie Claire*

~her is a powerful storyteller – full-blooded, a bit ~ashioned and with a knack for combining sensual ~atives with a feel for ancient myth and natural ~scape ... Deliciously briny writing'

CLAIRE ALLFREE, *Metro*

~th, flowing and feminine, Fletcher's prose lulls you ~s lyricism and emotional resonance ... [a] fishy, ~mythical tale of love and loss and the depths that grief can reach'

LESLEY MCDOWELL, *Herald*

SUSAN FLETCHER

The Silver Dark Sea

FOURTH ESTATE • *London*

Fourth Estate
An imprint of HarperCollins*Publishers*
77–85 Fulham Palace Road, Hammersmith
London W6 8JB

This Fourth Estate paperback edition published 2013
1

First published in Great Britain by Fourth Estate in 2012

Copyright © Susan Fletcher 2012

Susan Fletcher asserts the moral right to
be identified as the author of this work

A catalogue record for this book is
available from the British Library

ISBN 978-0-00-732163-6

Typeset in Sabon by G&M Designs Limited,
Raunds, Northamptonshire
Printed and bound in Great Britain by
Clays Ltd, St Ives plc

MIX
Paper from
responsible sources
FSC® C007454

FSC™ is a non-profit international organisation established to promote
the responsible management of the world's forests. Products carrying the
FSC label are independently certified to assure consumers that they come
from forests that are managed to meet the social, economic and
ecological needs of present and future generations,
and other controlled sources.

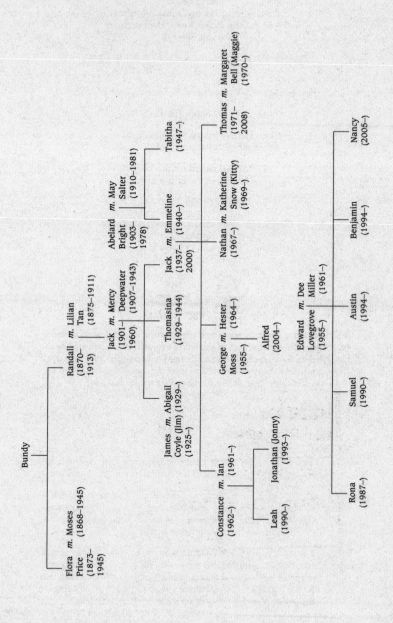

The Fishman of Sye

Once, there was a man. He was bearded and kind. He lived on an island in a stone-walled house with a tap that dripped, and a small peat fire. He had no friends to speak of. All his family were gone.

In his youth, he had been strong. He'd carried hay bales in one hand and lifted bags of grain up into the highest rafters. His farm had been neat and his pigs were fat; his shoulders browned in good weather. A handsome man, also. He loved a girl with sun-coloured hair and sometimes she'd smile as she passed him, so that his heart fluttered and his mouth ached. But above all else, he was shy. He'd blush when he heard her name; he'd stumble and not speak for days. *She is too pretty*, he thought to himself. And in time the sun-haired girl went away. She married another and the seasons blew on. Time passed. His beard greyed.

In the evenings he'd think of her. He'd sit by the fire and say *I am old, now. How did it happen?* The years had gone too quickly. His life had flown by, leaf-dry.

No children, no wife.

What a small life …

One night he was so sad he could not sleep. The loss kept him wide-eyed. He lay on his back, stared at the

1

ceiling; the sea unfolded in the dark. And the day that followed, he left his home. He walked to the north of the island where the grass was wind-bent, where the skies were fast and the sea thundered. Why was he here? He didn't know. But the wind tugged at his coat and foam skittered across the cold sand and the gulls above him called out *no! No!* He found himself on a stony shore.

I am so tired, he thought. *I am so tired of being me. I am tired of being alone.*

He thought of all the wasted years. Why had he never spoken of love? *Why didn't I tell her? Or see the wide world?* He hadn't stepped off the island, not once. It all seemed too late, now – too late.

He cried. He wept like a child.

But then he opened his eyes.

He opened them and saw a curious thing.

There was a man in the water. Not driftwood? Or weed? No – it was certainly a man. He bobbed, on the waves. He had black hair – wet, bluish-black – and a beard, and very pale skin. His eyes were round like a seal's were. He did not blink or turn away.

Who is …?

Who might swim, in such waters? With these waves that were crashing like glass? And with a north wind blowing as strongly as this? Yet this sleek-haired man did not struggle. He was not drowning or asking for help. He simply floated. He seemed to smile, as he floated there. And then he raised his arms – he raised them above him, pressed his palms together as if he was in prayer – and he threw those arms forwards so that his fingertips broke the water and his head and body followed in an arc. He dived into the sea, and was gone.

Briefly, there was nothing.

Then, in his wake, there was a tail – a huge, silver-flashing tail. It raised itself up, like a mirror. And it sank down where the black-haired man had been.

The pig farmer stood very still.

He blinked, shook his head. *A fish? Or a man? Neither? Or both?* And at that moment, at that precise moment, as the sea rushed onto the stones at Sye and as a lone gull settled on the rocks nearby, he heard a voice very clearly. It was not a human's voice. It did not feel as if someone was standing next to him; it was a deep, soft voice that seemed to be all around him so that the farmer turned, and kept turning.

It said this: *there is hope.*

The voice came off the cliffs. It rose up from the stones. He looked, but there was only the foam, fizzing, and the white lace of broken water where the tail had been.

That night, the farmer sat by his peat fire with a rug wrapped around him. He knew what he had seen. He'd seen a kind, human face and then a fish's tail. He also knew what he had heard.

In the days that followed, he spoke of it. *Do you know what I saw? At the cove called Sye?* Some laughed at him, of course. But others listened with shining eyes for their own hearts were tired, or partly so, and they longed for this to be true. Hadn't there been a legend, once? In a leather-bound book? They thought so. There had been a story just like the pig farmer's story – of kind eyes and a raised silvery tail.

Oh, how they wanted to believe it. They longed for this half-man, half-fish.

They wanted to hear *there is hope* for themselves as they stood by an evening sea.

The storms, in time, passed away. Winter moved into a dappled spring. And one day, as the farmer rubbed the bristled backs of his pigs, he heard a voice behind him. A woman's voice – warm and shy. *Excuse me? Hello?*

Her hair was no longer sun-coloured for she was older, also. But he knew who she was.

They married. She mended the broken tap in his house so that it did not drip. She rubbed his joints with linseed oil in the evenings and he combed her long, snow-white hair. He told her about the Fishman of Sye. *I saw him – with my own eyes* ... And she nodded, believing him. For what wasn't possible? What could not come to be? She had spent her whole life missing him – and she was with him, now.

They lived long lives together. Happy ones, too – they would sit outside his house as the sun lowered and whisper of their happiness. *My darling wife ... My love.* They are buried in the churchyard, side by side. They are in the furthest corner, near the blackthorn trees, and if you are ever on that island you can see them if you wish to, lay some flowers down.

* * *

There is hope.

It's strange, as all myths are. It is a familiar story, too, for many parents have whispered the tale of the Fishman to their children at night, or at bath-time, or on car journeys to pass the hours. He is ageless, they say, and cannot die. He lives as the fish do, in the quiet, thick-green depths, but sometimes he will surface and look over to the land. Even now, there is an islander who says he's seen the Fishman – his loving smile, his scales that catch the light as he dives. Others say, too, that if you ever feel comforted, or if you ever hear *there is hope* or words like it – *all will be well* or *you are not alone* – as you walk by the sea or as you lower one foot down into a boat, or as you watch the tarpaulin on the log-pile shake in the wind, or as you go to draw the curtains in the evening and pause because the last light on the water is beautiful, like gold, or as you find your boots reflected in the wet, firm, low-tide sand it means the Fishman is passing. He is offshore, watching the island. It means he knows you are hurting – and he does not wish you to be.

It was hard to have faith in that part. When I heard *there is hope* on a coastline, it was my own self, speaking – me, as my own comfort, trying to keep myself afloat. But what harm does it do, to believe in such stories? Mostly I think that it is better to.

One

There are stories that come from the sea and those are good stories. They are the best I have heard, by far. I know stories, but none are better than those I was told in coastal homes, with sour-smelling oilskins drying by the fire or the pale chalk of whale-bones standing on their ends. I smiled into my hands, as I listened. A brown-eyed man would ask *have I told you about ...?* I'd reply *no – tell me ...* And we'd lean forward towards each other so that our chairs creaked. Salt on the windowpanes.

Stories of loss, mostly. Of the love that came before that loss.

I crawled inside them, cave-like, and held my breath as I looked up.

There were too many stories to count. The sea brought them in, daily. Like the wide, glassy straps of weed that came ashore on the highest tides, they caught the light and beckoned me. A story? I'd come closer and kneel. I'd stare, as they were told. And they were always more beautiful than I thought they'd be when I first heard them, or found them in the sand.

That's how I imagine it. It's the best explanation I can give. There were so many stories on that island that it felt like they came in on the tide. Every day, there was something. On every pebbled cove or beach there were gifts left by the sea – plastic bottles, nylon ropes, shoes, a tyre, cottonbuds, the spokes of an umbrella, a sodden child's toy. Worthless? To some, maybe. But they were treasures, to others. A parched curve of driftwood could be dragged home and kept; a message in a cola bottle might change a life. At the beach called Lock-and-Key, there were lone wellington boots set upside down on its fence-posts – boots that had been washed up on that beach and were useless without their other, missing halves – and I've heard them called *unsightly*, this row of coloured boots. But I came to like them. I ran my hand across them when I walked on Lock-and-Key. I felt like I was one of them – weathered, and waiting. Fading and softening and watching the sea.

That's me, perhaps: the forager. I'd be drawn to the shards, to what life leaves behind. As if I had nothing, I gathered what other people would pass by or step over – a mussel shell, still hinged, or a length of sky-blue rope. I trod along the line of weed and plucked, bird-like, at the shinier things. And in that same way I hoarded all the stories that reflected the light and dazzled me – like the whale that answered the foghorn, or the phosphorescent night. There was a tale of grief I heard – with puffins in it, of all things – and I fell upon that tale as if it were unsalted water, water I could drink. It nourished me, somehow. A tale, too, about a single lantern that bobbed on the horizon every Christmas Night.

So yes – it was like beachcombing. It was all treasure to me. In my kitchen, I kept shells; I stuck briny feathers in vases. And in my head I laid out the stories the islanders told me – the caves, the Fishman, the flakes of silver, the seals who are wiser than humans, the girl who floated like a patchwork star.

I was born inland. I grew up where the wildest water was a puddle, or a filmy pond in a park. Stories were harder to come by there. Trees bowed with the rain, and I found sparks of beauty in a flowerbed or a pigeon's trembling, iridescent neck but it was not enough. I hungered for *more* – I sensed, always, that there was something more than this life that I was living. And then I fell in love when I thought I never would, and I came to live on an island so that the lines by my eyes deepened and my hair thickened with salt and ghostly-white crabs flitted over my feet and buried themselves in the damp sand, and every sea was different from the sea that had come before it – pummelling, or silent, or brown-coloured and flat. And the man I loved would tell me his stories. In time, others did. They poured whisky into my glass and settled beside me. They opened old books, said *look* ... I have known people who believed absolutely that a gull could talk our language, and that the souls of their drowned friends could be found in the rattle and foam.

I heard her voice in the water. I did.

And I've felt his hand on my hand, on that boat. You have my word.

I do have their words – I do. I swagger with the weight of my wordy, priceless stash. And when I re-tell their stories now, I know that some people mock me or mock the island, and they shake their heads at the impossibilities – *a Fishman? OK, right* ... I understand that – for I was, briefly, like them; I too have had my private doubts. But so much has been lost and found. So many things have come to pass that have no explanation and I half-wonder if you cannot believe in such stories unless you have lived or stayed in a house by the sea – until you have lost washing to a sea breeze or been bruised by the rain drumming on your anorak hood whilst trying to guide a dinghy in, in the blackest night. Until you have waited for a boat that does not come. Or until that boat is found but its crew is not. It is another way of living and not all can stand it. There is the word *salt-bitten*; it comes when hope is lost.

No, you cannot trust the sea – even now. Even with our satellites that tell us where we are. Even with our sonars, radars and computerised charts. Even with our space travel and vaccinations and our atom bombs and cloned sheep, and even though we can make a new human life in a Petri dish, we still cannot reach the furthest sea floor. We cannot breathe underwater or decode whale song. We cannot find a body, when it goes overboard. We may know that a human heart has ventricles and can be shocked into beating again, but we do not have the words for what immense and extraordinary emotions it can feel – what heights and depths, together. *Love* is too small a word – too small.

Abigail Coyle used to tell me, *we only know the foam* … A sweep of her arm, over the sea. And I'd walk home understanding her.

We do not know it all. That's what I'd tell myself, when standing waist-deep in water. When I sat on a boat I'd think of what was beneath me – the deep, deep chasms, the secrets and the dark.

This island is small, neatly shaped. Its cliffs are high as towers and streaked with white from the roosting birds. These cliffs echo with bird calls and to look up at them from a rocking boat is to feel tiny, and cold. Feathers come down and settle by your feet. They drift on the water like dreams.

There aren't many trees, on this island. Nor are there many houses, but there are some; they all have missing tiles, damp window frames and peeling paint. Their names are blunt: *Wind Rising*, or *Crest*. Calor gas bottles stand by back doors.

There is litter on the beaches. The wheel-arches of cars are brown with rust.

Strands of grey fleece shake on wire.

There is a lighthouse, too. It stands at the north end of the island and swings its slow, pale beam over the fields, the bedroom walls and the night-time sea.

Let us call it Parla. Names do not matter, as they never truly do in the tales I know. What matters are the people themselves – the souls who have lived on this island and how they have felt on its sand and rocks. Many generations of firm, resolute people have mended their nets here, or pressed their knees onto sheep as they've sheared them. The men have caught gannets for eating; women have gathered seaweed at low tide, with baskets strapped to their backs and their skirts hitched up. They have fed their children kale and sour milk, sang their sea songs, and they've lived in fear of God and the waves. That was years ago. But there are still photos – blurred, soft-edged.

Now, the Parlans live by other means – sheep, tourists, sponge cakes, crafts that they sell on the internet and send to the mainland in protective wrap. One woman knits tea-cosies and baby clothes; another paints in an attic room with skylights that close themselves suddenly in the gusty, north-westerly winds. No-one eats gannets these days. But they still have their own vegetable patches, and still reach for eggs under downy behinds. They still stand on the headland from time to time with their arms held out, and let their coats fill up with the wind. They still drink too much, or some do. They know the moon's cycle as their forefathers did.

And the sea. They still know the sea or as much as any human can. It is part of them, in their blood; it shapes their lives as the sea shapes a stone over the months and years. Some cannot sleep inland. They cannot be where there aren't sea sounds – for Parla is never, ever quiet. Even in calm weather there is the *lap lap lap* against the quayside or the *clack* of mussel shells as the water rises over them. At Tap Hole, when the tide is rough or at its highest, the sea sprays through the single hole in its roof – a puff and a splattering, like a whale's breath. Near the harbour, there are cliffs which are curved to make a bowl of water so that the sea is trapped, or nearly; it says *stash, stash*, as it tries to get out. The water here is weedy. There is an oily shine to the sea, at The Stash – and rubbish. Once, a rubber duck – and no-one knew why. *A well-travelled duck*, they called it. George Moss took it back for his son and it sits by their bath, even now.

The youngest Bright daughter – in her mid-sixties – remembers the single wave that rose up against the lighthouse one winter, when she was a girl. It smacked against the lantern's glass. It struck the tower with such a deep, thundering boom that she had felt it inside her – under her ribs. She'd held the wall, in fear. It woke something in her, that shuddering wave – a womanly knowledge that she both wanted and was scared of, but had no name for. She knows it all much better, now.

Maybe that's the sea telling stories of its own. Like me it has a lust for them; it cannot stop saying *listen to this …* *Listen to me …* After all, think of the tales it has – the deaths, the near-deaths, the curious lives. Even now, as I am telling this, there is the handclap of a wave that falls back into itself and the gentle hiss that follows. Soon, a sprawled, moon-blue jellyfish will rise to the surface and give two slow clenches. Against the black water, it will glow.

Before he died, Tom Bundy said *I have never known silence. Never.* He had been born in the fields at Wind Rising. Each hour of his life had had the sea in it. His early death did, too.

*   *   *

Can you hear it? The water? It breathes, as you breathe.

I want you to hear the whole island – as it is now, at this very moment. There is the sea's stirring, always. But also, there are many sounds on Parla which are more than the waves, more than stones being moved by them. The sheep bleat, throatily. A wooden gate squeaks open. There are tiny bells on a piece of string which dance, and call out *sing-sing-sing*. In a house with herbs on its windowsill a kettle is boiling – its metal lid is starting to rattle, and there are footsteps coming to it and a woman is saying *I'm here, I'm here* ... to the kettle, as if the kettle understands her. She lifts it up with a tea-towel; there is the sound of a mug filling up. Elsewhere, a dog scratches its ear. On the quayside, a child crouches; she watches a crab creep in a red plastic bucket, tapping the sides with its claws. The old pig farm, empty now, creaks in the late afternoon sun. There is also washing on a clothesline – four pillowcases which snap at themselves, and a pair of striped socks. The line itself bounces in the breeze – up and down.

There is the *tick-tick* of computer keys.

A mobile phone lights up and thrums across a table, before dropping to the floor.

There is a man in his bathroom, cleaning his ears of sand with a flannel's tip. He hums, as he does so – *dum-di-dum* ...

And there is a mother telling a story. She has her child in front of her, in his dinosaur pyjamas. He sucks the end of a white cloth, holding the cloth with both hands and he listens to her with eyes like the world. *Have I told you the story of the silver in the fields?* She is Hester – a true Bundy, with the dark Bundy eyes – and she knows her stories. She has the voice for telling them. She is Parlan, after all.

Can you hear these things? Each of them?

A gull is calling out – *ark ark ark!* It stands on the chimney of a cream-walled house.

And can you hear this: the brush of legs through long grass? At this moment, a young man is walking. He wears jeans which are damp and frayed at the hem. The lace on his left boot is undone, and its plastic ends tap against rocks as he goes. There is sheep dung pressed underneath this same boot; he feels it with each footstep so when he comes to a stile he puts this boot on the step and scrapes his sole against it. He twists his leg, checks. Then he climbs over the stile and briefly, as he climbs, he looks over to the house with the washing line. He narrows his eyes to see it – the striped socks, the yellow front door. He sniffs, steps down.

Brush brush. Through the grass.

It is early evening. This young man is fair-haired, freckled. He has caught the sun today – his cheekbones are pink, and his scalp feels sore. It has been the first day of sun in a long, long time and he'd not expected it. None of them had. He knows, in time, his skin will peel.

He is Sam Lovegrove, and he is twenty-two, and when he reaches the coast path he heads west.

The sea glints. In the distance, he sees Bundy Head.

To his right, the cove called Sye appears. It starts to show itself. As he walks, the cove widens and he looks

14

down into it. It is a fleeting glance, nothing more, for he does not expect to see anything. Nobody goes to Sye – it is a small beach, with no sand to speak of; its high cliffs make it shaded and cool. Who might go there, and so late in the day? *No-one.* And so he glances, that's all. A sweep of the eyes. But there is something down there today.

He stops. He stops so sharply that his right foot slips.

Sam takes two small steps towards the edge. *What is ...?*

Then he says *oh shit. Oh God. Oh my God ...*

* * *

Me, the forager. Or the salvager, perhaps – crouching in the wet sand to gather what is left. Is that what stories are? The debris of a life? The remains that can be dried, passed on so that a little of that life is passed on too, in its way? I have lost so much. So much I have never had, and so much of Parla I have looked for meaning in. And I miss it – I miss the island. I miss its pebbled strands, its button-eyed voles, and the weightless bones of cuttlefish that fitted the palms of my hands. I miss the people who I called *family*, or tried to; I miss how magical a winter's night sky could be for I'd never seen a falling star until I stood on that island, and I've not seen one since. And I miss him above all others – how I miss that one man. But at least I have my stories, sand-covered. A well-told story takes me back to Lock-and-Key.

Oh, the stories. So many.

A thousand strange things have been washed up on Parla's shores – loo seats, dolphins, a list of dreams in a sealed plastic bag. But it has never had a story which begins with Sam Lovegrove saying *oh shit, oh God* on a Wednesday evening as he runs down to the beach with his sunburnt shoulders and his left bootlace slapping back and forth, back and forth.

And it's never had this: a man, half-naked. He is lying on his front, his face against the shingle. He is dead-looking – still, white-skinned.

I know some wonderful stories – but this is the beginning of the best of all.

Two

He stumbles down to the beach. A steep path through gorse leads him there. He jumps onto the stones and the noise is sudden – the crunch of his heels, the clatter of rock against rock. He staggers, and then falls. Sam lands on all fours. The stones are powdery and the dark cracks between them are darker with old weed. He stares for a moment. Then he rights himself.

On, towards the shoreline. Over brownish wrack.

Oh God, he says. *Oh …*

It is not plastic, or sacking.

It is a human body. It lies at the water's edge. Its upper half is out of the water; its legs are still being lapped at by the tide. It lies on its front and the head is turned so that the man's right cheek (it is definitely a man) is pressed into the stones, and his right arm is raised above his head. He wears a white vest, or part of one. Sodden, dark-grey shorts.

Black hair. A black beard.

Shit …

Sam looks away. He breathes heavily through pursed lips. He tries to steady himself, puts his hand on his chest. Could he turn, go? No-one need know. *No-one has seen me coming here.* And wouldn't the sea come back and take it? Carry it out? Sam shakes. His hands are shaking and he thinks, *a dead body* ... He has not seen one before.

But he cannot turn and go. He must stay; he knows he must.

He looks back. The man's skin is white. It is perfectly white, like fish meat. The arms are thick, muscled. His back, too, is strong-looking – there is a deep groove where his spine is.

He is tall. Was. Was tall.

Oh ... His stomach clenches. He half-bends, as if he will vomit, and he expects this – he braces, locks his jaw. But nothing comes.

The body lies ahead of Sam. He tries to calm himself for he knows what he must do. He knows what needs to be done, right now, and so he lifts his left foot and steps towards it. He brings his right foot to join his left.

No smell. Would there not be a smell?

And flies, he thinks. *There are no flies.*

Carefully, Sam comes in. He draws level with the body and starts to lower down. He is tentative, scared of falling or getting too close. The stones shift, as his weight does, and he thinks *and what about the eyes?* He has found dead sheep before. They lose their eyes to gulls – the soft, jellied flesh is the first part to be eaten – and Sam feels nauseous again. His tongue tightens. But he has no choice: he has to see the face. He knows this but he does not want to and he is shaking as he crouches down. His breath is fast and his heart is thumping against his ribs so that they hurt and he does not want the eyes to have been pecked away or sucked out by fish. He does not want the mouth to be open, as if still fighting for breath.

Oh God oh God ...

Sam puts his palms down on the stones. He brings his face alongside the dead man's face. Nose to nose.

18

The man opens his eyes. Not fully, not wide – but his eyelids flicker and there are two black crescent moons of eye.

Sam yells. Falls.

He scrambles backwards, crab-like, shouting *holy fuck oh my God*, and as he tries to stand his left foot slips and the stones give way so he turns onto his front and crawls frantically on his hands and knees, and then he finally clambers up the beach and turns around.

There is the sea, and a gull's screaming, and there is a sound which is coming from Sam – a whimpering, a half-sob. His grips his hair with both his hands. *Not dead* is what he thinks. *Not dead not dead, oh Jesus*. He looks at the skin, the beard, the mouth which is moving now as if trying to speak or trying to clear itself of salt or sand or pebbles and the eyelids still flicker, and the right hand flinches. The fingers find a stone and try to close upon it.

Shit. Listen. I'm going to get help, Sam tells him. *I am. I'll come back*.

He sees a whorl in the man's beard, as if a thumb has been pressed there – familiar, in its way. A shell, or a rose.

Sam stumbles through the grass. His feet snag on roots and old wire; the sheep lift up from their resting places and bleat at him, and move. His breathing is loud as he runs towards the lane. He knows the house with the striped socks on the line is to his left and that a woman will be inside it, but he cannot go to her. Not her, of all people. He does not look across.

Down the hill. Past the ragwort, and the rusting tractor.

Past the sheet of corrugated iron that is half-lost in grass.

He turns right at the sign that says *Wind Rising*. He runs up the drive and the dog barks as she sees him, and the rooster stretches up and flaps his wings. Sam bangs on the back door which swings open on its own so he hurries inside saying *Ian? Ian?* The kitchen smells of casserole and coffee and dog hair and Ian is standing there, very still, with the kettle in his hand.

* * *

A man?

A man.

Dead?

No. I thought he was, but he's alive. He opened his eyes.

Washed up? Are you sure he's not just … Ian shrugs. *I don't know … Lying there? Sunbathing, or …*

No, he's washed up. Sam's hands grip the back of a chair.

Is he hurt?

Don't know. Probably. He is pale, Ian – properly white. I really thought he was dead. Oh God …

Ian sighs, holds up a hand to stop the boy talking. *OK. Fine. I'll get Jonny. And Nathan's in the barn. He's big, you say?*

Looks it. And heavy. Arms like … He holds his hands apart, showing him.

Ian takes a sip of coffee. He holds it in his mouth for a moment before swallowing. He takes a second sip, puts the mug down. Then he pulls on a jumper and walks towards the door, talking under his breath, but as he reaches it he turns to see Sam's still standing there, holding the chair. *Coming?*

Ian, listen …

The older man pauses.

20

He's dark-haired. There's a mark in his beard – like a whorl. I didn't look too closely –

Ian's eyes are hard. *Let's just get there. OK?*

*　　*　　*

Four men make their way across the fields as the sun starts to dip. They move quickly, without talking. The sheep move away from them, find a safe place and then glance back.

The Lovegrove boy leads the way. His shirt is darker under the arms; his forehead is lined for his age. He looks over his shoulder once or twice to check he is still being followed. The farmer from Wind Rising is next – greying at the temples, breathing through his mouth. He is Ian Bundy and he has the family build – stocky, short-legged. His son, too, has it. And they both have the family colouring – brown eyes, sallow skin, hair that is almost black. Jonny chews as he jogs – gum, which he snaps in his mouth with his tongue until his father says *get rid of that.* The younger man scowls, throws the gum into grass. The fourth man sees him do it. He is Nathan Bundy. He, too, is dark-eyed, but the summer has lightened his hair and it is long so that it brushes his collar and curls by his ears. He's the tallest of them. He has marks on his arms from barbed wire; he hasn't shaven for days. Nathan says nothing as they make their way to the cove called Sye.

Brush-brush – their legs through the grass.

They all have their thoughts, their worries.

A ewe watches them. The men crest the hill so that they are, briefly, four dark shapes against the sky, four silhouettes – and the ewe sees this. She shakes her ears, lowers her head. She tears, steadily, at the grass.

There, says Sam. He does not need to point.

Ian squints.

The man is still lying there. His right arm is still raised and his legs are parted. *Christ. He's big.*

Told you.

The tide is lower now. There is a metre or more of shingle between the sea and the man's bare feet. Ian makes his way down through the gorse, onto the stones which are dry, chalky to touch. He says, *steady* – talking to himself as if he were a horse or a dog. He holds his arms out for balance; his feet slip between the stones as he goes. He wonders when he was last at Sye and doesn't know. He is never on beaches. He hates finding sand between his toes or in his mouth.

Ian sees the black hair. The beard.

He kneels, presses his thumb against the man's cold neck. *Can you hear me? Hey?*

Is there a pulse? Jonny stands over him.

A moment. Then, *yep.*

Sure?

Yes – got one. Let's roll him over.

All four of them crouch, put their hands on his body. *After three?*

Ian counts.

As they roll the man over he makes a sound – a groan, as if in pain. There is a creak, too, as if his ribs are being released or a bone which was pressed upon can return to its right place. Grit sticks to his cheek. There is weed splayed on his chest, like a hand.

Ian stares for a moment. Then he reaches, takes the weed away. *We need to get him to Tabitha's. We'll carry him.*

Can we? I mean – Sam shrugs – *he's huge.*

He is, but there are four of us. We'll manage – have to. Ian taps the man's face twice, calls *hey! Hello?* As he does this he sees the twirl of hair in his beard, the rosette, and he rests back on his heels, wipes his nose with the back of his hand so that Nathan puts his hand on his brother's arm. *Ian?*

Let's get going.

They take hold of the stranger and lift him into the air.

It is as if they carry an upturned boat. The man is on his back, being moved head-first, with Ian and Sam beneath his shoulders. Their hands take care of his head, arms and neck. Behind them, his right thigh is resting on Jonny's shoulder and his left thigh is pressed against Nathan's ear. The men all move slowly, saying *careful* and *easy, now.*

When they reach the coastal path they move faster.

Nathan thinks, *I was in the barn ...* An hour ago, he'd been sitting on the spare tractor wheel in the barn at Wind Rising, filling the last few sacks with fleece. He'd been on his own, thinking of his wife. The farm cat had padded by, and the beams had creaked, and he'd been inhaling the smells he had known all his life – wood-dust, hay, diesel, sweat – when his brother had marched in saying *a man's been found. Washed up. At Sye.* Ian said it as if it happened all the time – like the ferry arriving or fences blowing down. An hour ago Nathan had been alone in the barn and now he is carrying a half-dead man who's barely dressed, cold-skinned and fish-smelling.

Things change quickly. But he has known that for years. Four years, or nearly.

He can hear the man's breath, as they carry him. His thigh is heavy, and his lower leg hangs from the knee and swings. His heel knocks gently against Nathan's back.

*   *   *

In the garden at Crest, a woman stands. She is blonde, wearing denim shorts, and she has a clothes peg in her mouth. One by one she takes her washing down. She lifts off tea-towels, a bra, two striped socks. The sun is lowering, and it glints off the windows. She pauses, looks. *There is still beauty*, she thinks – the light on the water.

Another woman – grey-haired, not blonde – makes her way past the island's church, poking at the weeds with her walking stick. She glances to her left. There are the Bundy men and the boy from the harbour carrying something high in the air. What? A boat? Part of a machine? The sun is in her eyes so she cannot tell.

The church glints, also. From inside, its windows are jewel-coloured – ruby, emerald, a deep royal blue. These colours lie down on the tiled floor.

On the west coast, the sinking sun catches the row of single, rubber boots that stand upside down on fence-posts. None match; none are the same size. They shine in a line, looking wistful. They cast their strange shadows on the scrubby grass behind.

And at the same time – at this exact, same moment as the stained-glass windows glow, unseen, and as the widow from Crest takes her washing inside – the men come to a stile. They stumble, hiss *watch it!* The man they carry hears this. His head lolls. He feels the rock of his body and the fingers pressing into him, and there is the *brush* of legs through the grass. He smells sweat, sheep, salty air.

He says a word. It is *sea*, or a word like it.

When he opens his eyes, all he can see is sky.

Tabitha looks at the clock on her kitchen wall. It is past eight. This means, to her, that she can pour herself a small glass of sweet, pink wine so she goes to her fridge and opens it. She loves the sound of a cork coming out. She likes the cool bottle, and choosing the glass from her shelf – for none of her glasses are the same. Small rituals.

Everybody has them. Her mother always tapped a wooden spoon twice against a saucepan, having stirred it; her father had names for the weight that would lower itself down the stairwell, and in doing so, turn the lamp.

She sips.

Berries. Vanilla, maybe.

Her home is Lowfield. It is small, cream-walled and south-facing – and it's a house with no logic, for the kitchen leads into the bedroom and the bath is in a room of its own, far away from the loo. Things creak. Floors slope. She says *it has character*, as most Parlan houses have – and why would she want a bland home? With paper lampshades and plastic chairs? She has furniture from her childhood here – a linen chest, a grandfather clock. Tabitha touches the clock as she passes it, her wine in her other hand.

There is logic in its name, at least. *Lowfield* – for it sits in a hollow, a nest of grassy mounds. Three sides of the house look out onto banks of gorse, bramble and grazing sheep; on those three sides, it is fully sheltered from the wind. When Tabitha moved here in her early thirties she had lain in her bed and thought *where is the noise? The rumbling? The spray on the windowpanes?* For these were the things she was used to. Her childhood had been in the lighthouse-keeper's quarters and so any inland sleeping place seemed eerie to her, and still. Surely an island home should rattle in the wind? When she came to Lowfield, a storm passed over-head one night and she knew nothing of it. She only learnt of the storm the next morning: as she stood in the garden in her dressing gown and looked at the fallen fence-post – upended, with black earth at the base of it – she told herself *this will make a good home. A safe place.* It also makes a good place for the tired and sick to come.

That was thirty years ago. Now, her waist has thick-ened. She has pouches of skin beneath her eyes and when she walks in her slippers she hears herself – the padding on the wooden floors, the slow pace. *I walk as if I'm old.* It has happened so quickly, or seems to have done. It seems like a day or two ago that she'd worn a red bikini, jumped from the sea wall.

Briefly, Tabitha feels sad. She has her regrets – but Lowfield is not one of them. It is hers; she has spent half of her lifetime here. It feels nurturing, as a home should. Cupped by the Parlan land.

The only room with a view of the sea is what she calls the *mending room*. She's always called it this. *Surgery* feels too grand for it: a white-painted room, linoleum floor, a small cabinet of pills and liquids that islanders have prescriptions for and others which she keeps *just in case*. A table and chair face the door. Behind them, she has a poster of the musculature of the human body – reddish and gruesome, which the children love. On the table, Tabitha keeps an African violet; she likes its dark, furred leaves.

This room has seen plenty, that's for sure. It holds its secrets – small ones, and ones that have changed a life and other lives. She, Tabitha, knows all of them. Lorcan, also, must have heard some strange confessions over the years – he walks with the weight of what he's been told, or so it looks, for he has lumbar pain that she gives him codeine for and a stern telling-off when he carries too many hymn books. They go to him for their souls; for their bodies they come to Lowfield, and so here it is that Tabitha listens to hearts and takes temperatures and tends to the wounds that come from a life of farming, or the sea – a half-severed thumb from the shearing blades, or rope-burn that has broken the skin. She knows who has high blood pressure, who does not sleep, and who is on the contraceptive pill. She knows who drinks too much, whose skin flakes under their clothes, who takes pills to thin their blood, who has athlete's foot, cold sores, piles. She knows of Sam's migraines, of her own sister's painful joints. And Tabitha has brought babies into the world, in her time – all five of the Lovegrove children and three of her own family have slid like eels into her waiting hands.

Tabitha sips. She thinks *all those secrets* ... Once, newly qualified, she'd believed that everything was curable – every human pain. But she was wrong to think it. Guilt, heartbreak – what cures them? Or simply makes them bearable? Nothing on her shelves.

Still – she views this room as safety. She wants each person who steps into it to feel cared for. With the pot-plant and the pressed bed linen, she has always tried for that.

In the far corner, there is an iron-framed single bed. Tabitha goes to it, sits down. She pushes her slippers off with her toes, swings her legs up and nestles back. From here, she can see the finger of land called Litty, the nettle patch which no-one has ever mowed or dug up because of the voles that live there. The tiny, tufty-eared Parlan vole – it is its own species, and rare, and she has seen one or two in her time or at least the nettles swaying where a vole has darted from. Beyond Litty, there is the water. The sea – scattered with light. What view was ever better than this?

She wiggles her toes in their polka-dot socks.

Tabitha drinks her pink wine.

*   *   *

You knock.

No, you. I can't take my hand away, it's under his head – see?

Ian curses. He is aching. He has carried a thousand sheep in his life, slung round his neck like a collar and he's carried boat engines and tractor wheels and his own kids when they were young – but not this weight, and not so far. *I'm too old for this*, he thinks.

He kicks at Tabitha's door. Three kicks, low down near the doorframe – all too hard.

The men shift. They are steaming like horses, sweat on their top lips and brows. The man they carry groans overhead so that Ian says, *hurry up …*

The kicking must have startled her for when Tabitha unlocks the door, she peers around it as if unsure of what she might find. But then she sees Ian. She sees all of them, widens her eyes. *Looks like you'd better come in*, she says.

She leans against the wall to let them pass.

The room smells of disinfectant and a false, lavender scent which comes from a bottle plugged into the wall. *Put him on the bed.*

He goes down heavily.

All four men exhale. Then they stretch, step away. Nathan straightens and his back clicks. Jonny rotates his right shoulder and says *Jesus. What do you think he weighs?*

Tabitha is by the bed. Foremost, she is the nurse – not the aunt, not the great-aunt or the friend – and she busies herself with what a nurse must do, lifting the man's head and arranging the pillow beneath it. She takes his wrist, watches the wall clock as she does so. With her eyes still on the clock she asks *who is he? Do we know him?*

Ian says *no.*

What happened?

Sam found him.

Where?

At Sye.

On the stones?

Just lying there, says Sam. *I thought he was dead.*

28

She nods; the man's pulse is good. Tabitha can feel the warm bloom of his breath against her arm. She feels the edge of the vest he wears, finds it is cold and hardening with salt – so she opens a nearby drawer, lifts scissors out. When had she last used them? For what? On whom?

She cuts away his clothing. The chest that appears is dark with hair. *Has he spoken?*

Jonny shrugs. *He's muttered a bit –*

He tried to say something, Nathan tells her.

So he's been conscious?

Yes.

He didn't lose it at any point?

Not since we've been with him.

Any wounds?

His hands – Ian points.

She looks. Ian's right – the fingernails are torn, and three of his knuckles are bruised. When she turns the hands over, she finds his palms are dirtied, rough and red-coloured. Pinheads of blood. Grains of sand. *Grazes.*

From what?

Rope, maybe? Hard to say. And here ...

There is more, too. On his left hand, in the soft web of flesh between the thumb and forefinger, there is a very different wound. It is neither fresh nor old. It is reddish-brown. Perfectly round, like an eye.

Tabitha cannot know what caused such marks. But hands mend and mend quickly; hands do not worry her too much. It is his head that Tabitha turns to now: the head, which she always thought of as a world in its own right – with its seas and land and weather, its mysteries that, in fact, no human brain can fathom. She snaps on latex gloves. Slowly, she starts to feel through his hair. She searches for cuts, or swellings, or a tender part that will make him wince. His hair is so thick she must move it aside, in sections. Where there is scalp, she presses it; like this she makes her way round his head – from ear to ear, from brow to nape. His eyes half-open. His lips move, as if he dreams.

No sign of swelling, she says.

That's good. Right? Sam is anxious.

Yes, Sam – it's good.

She peels off the gloves. There is a woollen blanket at the foot of the bed and she pulls it up over her patient, over his long, muscular legs. It does not reach beyond his chest so she tucks it round him, brings his arms to his sides. There is, Tabitha thinks, a strong smell in the room – of sweat, from the men, and cigarette smoke, but also fish and brine and an earthiness. Sheep.

She turns to them. *You needn't stay. It's late.*

He's OK? He's not dying?

No, he's not dying. A childish question from Sam. He stands there – awkward, thin, with sunburn and his unbrushed hair. Tabitha had delivered this boy. That day feels like yesterday. She remembers his mother in this room, refusing to lie down or to sit – she'd paced the room as an animal might. And then Samuel came out as she'd crouched on the floor, gripping the table legs, with Tabitha saying *one more! That's it!* How long ago was that? Two decades and more. She feels sorry for him, suddenly. He is both so old and so young.

He's dehydrated, and he's exhausted. And I'll give him a tetanus jab for the sake of it. But other than that, he seems alright. She shrugs. *We'll see what happens when he wakes. It's sleep he needs, now.*

They look at each other, briefly.

Ian moves first. He slaps his thighs once, rises up from the chair saying *right. That'll do me. Come on, Jonny.*

Jonny follows his father, walking in the low, rhythmic way that young men seem to – nonchalant, easy. He says *see you, Uncle Nathan.* He does not speak to Sam as he passes him. He brushes the leaves of the African violet; his draught moves the unpinned corner of a poster on mental health.

The two men walk out into the garden and are gone.

Sam waits for a moment further. Then, *will you be alright?*

Alright?

I mean, here – on your own. With this man who ...

Tabitha smiles. *I'll be fine, Sam. I've dealt with far worse than a sleeping man, I can promise you that. Will you tell your father what happened? I'll call him in the morning.* When he was born, Sam Lovegrove had been jaundiced. His skin had the hue of iodine, or old tea, and he had been so small. Now he is – what? Six foot?

Are you sure?

Honestly. Go.

So he, too, goes. He steps into the fading light.

It means that Nathan is left. He stands against the wall by the door, hands in his pockets, one ankle crossed over the other. His head is down as if looking at the floor, but his eyes are looking through his hair at the stranger who lies asleep on the bed beneath a blue blanket. It is a gaze of intent – a hunter's look, or a detective's.

I thought you'd linger, the nurse says.

*   *   *

He can smell the latex gloves and the glass of pink wine, and Nathan can smell fish in this room. The tang of it.

His aunt moves carefully. Plump Aunt Tab, with her pearl earrings and cotton-pale hair. She clicks her tongue, as she works – half-humming – and this is a sound that is hers, entirely. She seems to half-hum all the time. When he was a boy, Nathan would hear his aunt before he saw her because of this sound or her bicycle bell. She still has that bicycle. It has a wicker basket, a slight squeak, and he feels like a boy when he sees his aunt on it – leaning forwards with the effort. Tabitha, who warms a room by entering it with her cheery *only me!*

What do you think? he asks her.

She has her back to him. She is standing on her tiptoes, reaching up to the top shelf of a cabinet. With her fingertips she coaxes down a plastic tub that has envelopes in. These envelopes have transparent windows through which he can see needles.

What do I think? Well … She considers it. *It's strange, that's for sure. Where has he come from?*

A swimmer, maybe. Got tired.

Maybe. I'll call Rona – see if a guest is missing.

Tabitha places a needle in a metal dish. It chimes like a bell. Then Nathan watches as she moves to a second cabinet, takes a small key from her pocket and unlocks it. Inside, there are vials.

Tab? Don't you think …? But he can't say it. Nathan isn't even sure what he is trying to say except that he is shaken, confused, and that he does not like what's happened and does not want to be here but nor can he take his eyes off the iron-framed bed in the corner of the room, or leave. His aunt tilts her head. She is waiting for more words from him, and he has seen his mother stand like this. He has looked for his mother in a crowd and found her because of the way she has tilted her head, as a bird might listen for worms. They have the same nose, too. They aren't close and never have been. But they are sisters in how they speak, and move.

Don't I think … what?

Doesn't matter.

But it does – it does. And Tabitha knows this for she puts the vial down and comes towards him. She puts her hand on the back of his hand and says *I know what you're*

32

thinking. I thought it too. When I opened the door and saw the four of you holding this man in the air, I saw his hair and his beard, and I thought ... She pauses, smiles. *But –*

He nods.

We'll find out who he is. When he wakes up, we'll ask him.

Nathan knows there are many words that were never said, and must be said one day – but he cannot say them now. Not late in the evening and not in this room.

He feels tired, suddenly – bone-tired, heavy.

Go, says Tabitha. She squeezes his upper arm.

*   *   *

Nathan walks back through the fields. It is past nine. The sky is eerie – not light, not dark. At the north of the island the lighthouse is awake and it finds him – five half-seconds every minute of being dazzled, white. He climbs over fences, ducks under wires.

Last night there had been a northerly wind and last night he had not slept. All night, he had lain awake. *I should have known,* he thinks.

He thinks, too, how sore his back is from the man's weight. He thinks of the words he'd been trying to say, as they carried him – *sea?* It had sounded like *sea,* which isn't so odd since he must have been in it for a long time, at least. Whoever he is, he has swum – lungfuls of salt, salty-eyed. And as Nathan walks up the driveway to his home he thinks, suddenly, of the time when he and his younger brother had caught a crab off Litty's pier with a piece of string and a chicken bone – the biggest crab they'd ever seen. It was huge, orange-mottled. They'd wanted to keep it as a pet – and so they'd charged home, put it in the bathroom sink and hidden side by side in the airing

33

cupboard, waiting for Hester to come to clean her teeth. Two screams from their sister – one at the crab, and one as they burst out at her with a shouted *boo!* He hears it now – her screaming. And he can hear his brother's laughter – bright, like piano scales. He can see that crab.

He sniffs. Nathan looks up at the house in the distance. There is a light on at Crest. It is the kitchen light, he can tell, and he pictures Maggie at that moment – cracking an egg against a glass bowl or rinsing vegetables. She holds her hair back with a pencil, sometimes. Perhaps she is doing that now.

And Nathan thinks, too, of his wife.

When was the last time a person was washed ashore? A living person? It's not happened in his lifetime. The sea takes lives; it doesn't give them. There are no stories of a sea-given life.

I will wake up tomorrow. I will have dreamt this.

As Nathan reaches High Haven, he slows. The wind-chimes stir. Its lights are on and the windows are open and the curtains drift in and out, in and out, like ghosts.

*   *   *

By the harbour wall, Sam vomits. He has both hands against the stones, his legs apart. Afterwards, he spits. He wipes his mouth with his sleeve, steps away from it. Above him, a waning moon.

At Wind Rising, Ian goes to the fridge. He finds a bottle of beer and pulls it out by the neck. He shuts the fridge with his foot, twists the cap and drinks with his eyes closed.

When it is nearly midnight, Tabitha leaves the mending room. She has given a tetanus injection, and she's rubbed antiseptic cream on his hands. She's filled a glass of water and in his half-sleep, the man has drunk it – spilling some so that Tabitha had to wipe his chin, mother-like. She leaves him sleeping on his side.

In her bedroom, she takes off her wristwatch and lays it on the chest of drawers. She unpins her earrings, one at a time. When she goes to draw the curtains, she sees the grass blowing and she narrows her eyes when she sees it – is the wind northerly? It seems to be. She will know by morning.

By morning everyone will know. Within hours, there will be talking. The whole island will be whispering – *have you heard …? A bearded man was found at Sye*. Yes, there was; he sleeps in her mending room.

Once she is in her dressing gown, Tabitha goes back there. His breathing is steady, and deep. Parla, she thinks, is known for its lighthouse. It's known for the puffins which nest on its north coast, its tea room and its tender lamb. It's known for the wreck of the *Anne-Rosa* which divers come for, or used to. And it's known for the accident nearly four years ago which no-one has recovered from, as far as she can tell – certainly not Nathan, and not Ian and not Sam.

She settles next to the wrought-iron bed.

Her own life changed nearly four years ago. *Everyone's life changed three years, ten months, three weeks and four days ago, and we do not speak of it – we never speak of what we lost*. As if the loss would be greater if it was named and talked over. But it could not be greater.

He sleeps. This man who looks like Tom but is not Tom. She knows that he is someone else.

Tabitha stays with him all night. Sometimes he whispers; sometimes his lips move soundlessly and his hands seem to take hold of the air. He is handsome – incredibly so.

He is a gift. His face ... She cannot stop looking at this person lying here.

She is a sensible woman. Tabitha is the woman of swabs and antiseptic washes. She has seen sights that no-one on this island has seen or ever will and she likes to think she can keep her feelings packed away – popped on ice, perhaps. She has secrets that no-one knows of, certainly. But this is different. This man is not like anyone else who has lain on this bed, and it is late, and the sea is loud, and her feelings are not packed away or kept on ice tonight.

Please, she whispers. She does not often pray.

Let this be the start of ... Of what? What is she wanting? What does she hope for, as she's sitting here? The only words that she can find are *something special. Something lovely. New, and lovely, and good.*

There are moments that come to matter in our lives – defining, powerful moments. Sometimes they happen so quietly that they slip by unmarked so that only later do we look back and realise that they changed everything; sometimes, they are known for exactly what they are. Tabitha knows that this matters. Tonight is a night she will not forget. It is a curious, extraordinary beginning. This will not happen twice – not in her lifetime. And it is the start of something that she knows – as a nurse knows, instinctively – will change them all. She isn't sure how, but it will.

Let him stay, she whispers this. He is better than a bottle top, or a lone boot. He is better than any broken shell could be.

And the man stirs at the moment. He takes hold of the blanket, turns onto his back. *Sea ...* he says, as if missing it.

Sea ... as if that is where he longs to be.

36

The North Wind

Many years ago, there was a man with a bristled moustache who said *mark the air* ... He'd wander the fields, calling it; he'd take hold of wrists, at the harbour. In his last years of life, it was all he ever said. *Mark the air, do you hear me?*

He was one of the Tans. There are stories of the Tans that I do not love too much – a taste for whale blubber and for marrying too close. It was the Tans who'd see a distant ship and wish for it to founder – so they'd swing false lights at night, to lure it onto rocks. They knew (it was said) how to break knuckles with one swift blow, or how to grip a man's gold tooth and pull. Those were the Tans or most of them. Or so the stories go.

Lucas Tan was the last of his line. He'd lost his only son at sea. And it had not been the sea's fault, for the waves had been calm enough that day; a strong north wind had caught the boy, blown him overboard. *That north wind ...* Afterwards, Lucas swore. He stayed away from church. He eyed the clouds, clutched the bottle by its neck and said *mark the air ... You listen to me.* And those are the words he's remembered for – those, and those only. Slurred, pained, whisky-warm.

Was he right? Perhaps. For there are many winds. And there are so many stories of wind on Parla that if you ask to hear them, if you were to go to Abigail Coyle and say *what do you know about the different winds?* a new wind would appear, as she answered. A fast, unending rush of air would come from between her gums: *the different winds? Oh! So many ... Where do I start?* The wind that brings in fitful sleep? The first gale of the autumn? With the east wind, her husband swears that he can smell the mainland – heat, diesel, milk, spices, perfume, human breath.

But it's the north wind that she'll speak of, above all other winds.

The changing wind, Abigail told me. *It never blows without changing the island in some way ...* For better, or worse? Who knows. It can do either, and that's the truth. For the north wind has both mended hearts and broken them. It has brought both beauty and misfortune, restlessness and sleep. It has carried in babies but it has also taken lives and so the islanders worry when they hear the north wind blowing. They fear death – actual, physical, permanent death, but also the non-literal, where the heart has kept beating but its wish to keep doing so is small, very small if there at all.

*   *   *

It is past midnight.

In the house called Wind Rising, Leah is awake. She lies in bed and looks at the ceiling she has known all her life. The same paint on the same walls.

Leah is thinking of men. She thinks of Sam Lovegrove who ran into their kitchen five hours ago, saying *Ian? Ian?* She'd heard him. She'd put down her book, padded out onto the landing and looked down through the banisters.

Ian? Listen – a man's come ashore ... She'd seen his blond head.

Then they had left, gone outside. And Leah had stayed on the landing. She'd listened to the sounds of a house quietening – the fading of footsteps, the *slop* inside the kettle, having been poured.

And she'd heard a *tut-tut*. A pause; then a rapid *tut-tut-tut-tut-tut*.

Leah had known what it was. She'd turned, walked into the bathroom where the sound was louder, looked up. *Tut.* The air vent – white, with the strands of cobwebs on it. It only ever rattles when the north wind blows.

A man's come ashore ...

Leah sits up now. She kneels by the window, pushes the window up so that air pours in like water. Her hair stirs; her nightdress does.

I could be nowhere else. This is a Parlan night. It is a night in her Parlan bedroom – with the pink walls of her childhood and the known, old sound of a book's pages being turned by the breeze, one by one. It is a night like a thousand other Parlan nights in which she has listened to the sea's constant sound – not a breathing back and forth as might be imagined but a low roar that does not change pitch or volume. Tonight could be like all the other nights.

But it isn't quite.

She'd loved that *tut-tut-tut*. She'd smiled at it, in the bathroom – and she is smiling now. *A change* ... How Leah has longed for a change. For years, she has watched the same sights, on Parla – how the lighthouse turns, how sheep kneel to graze, how the *Star*'s gangplank drops onto the quayside at the precise time it's meant to. The mainland's shape does not alter; the rising damp in the downstairs loo does not fade. And for years she has heard the same conversations – about ferries, wool, if the hens are laying, if Milton has fresh milk in stock, whether she's had breakfast yet, so that Leah has rolled her eyes, thought *it is always the same, always the same. Why is it always the same?* Or at least, she used to think it. In time, the island made her heavier. It made her lie in her bedroom and think of nothing – nothing at all.

This slow, salty *sameness* – day in, day out.

But now? *Tut-tut.* And a man has come. The sea and the north wind left a man at Sye for Sam, of all people, to find. And as Leah had stood on the landing and looked down onto his red-blond hair she'd felt … what? *Hope.* That's what. She'd barely recognised it. She has not been hopeful – for what good could it ever have done? How might hope have helped her? And so to have it now, in a dark bedroom, feels tender and lovely and absurd. It is a green shoot amongst the snow.

A man's come ashore …

There will be an explanation, no doubt, and it will be plain and disappointing when it comes: he is a drunk or a lost guest or a man who fell off a passing ship or a swimmer who grew tired. It will be dull, and the green shoot will be lost, trodden on. *I'll go back to the old feelings –* the old weighing down. But tonight, for now, Leah hopes that he is something better; she hopes that he is not merely a man who fell overboard, or a prankster.

Hope. It is the frailest of words.

Others are awake, too.

There is a man in the island's Old Fish Store who lies, far from sleep. He also knows the wind is northerly. He knows this because of the sounds he can hear – the clear *ting* of halyards and the wire fences' song. He can hear the sea saying *stash … stash …* He is Jim Coyle and he knows his winds.

In a farmhouse with rusting cars outside, Nathan sits in the dark. He has a glass in his hand; he waits for the lighthouse's beam to whiten the curtains, lighten the room.

The widow at Crest is also awake. She squeezes a camomile tea bag against the side of a mug with a spoon, carries that tea bag to her compost bin. The kitchen light illuminates the night-time grass by her window and she watches it, spoon in hand. The grass flurries. She notes the wind's direction – *northerly?* She stands in her pyjamas with her unbrushed hair.

After this, she climbs the stairs. And she sleeps; she sleeps under a white cotton sheet, and what she does not know – how could she possibly? – is that when she next sees that camomile tea bag, dried out and paler in her compost bin, everything will be different. She will look at it and think *when I last saw that, I didn't know …* This is Maggie, and she knows how the smallest of things can take on new meanings, how a lifetime can change in a second or less. That used tea bag which is settling on the bottom of a plastic tub will, within a few hours, remind her of *before* – of a time when she knew less, felt less, and when Sye was a cove and nothing more. It will come to have a thousand meanings. In the hours ahead, Maggie will stare at that tea bag as if it can solve it all. But for now, it is only a tea bag. It sits in its own damp dark.

The lighthouse turns, as always.

Far out, a whale surfaces. Nobody sees it, but it does.

Three

The sky begins to lighten a little after four. In the east, there is a feathered grey, the softest of yellows. The daylight moves across the sea.

At nearly five, it comes to the eastern cliffs – the half-moon harbour, the towers of rock. The seabirds that roost here – fulmars, herring gulls – blink as the sunlight finds them. They bring their beaks down to their chests, and preen.

At the island's south-eastern point is the main harbour. Slowly, its water turns from black to blue. Light moves along the old sea wall, the railings of the *Morning Star* and the smaller boats that are moored there – *Calypso, Sea Fairy, Lady Caroline*. Their ropes shine with hanging weed. The windows of the harbourmaster's house glint, so that the child who sleeps behind them sniffs and turns onto her side, away from the light. There is a young man in this house who has not slept. He lies on his back, stares.

Above the harbour, on its south side, lies the Old Fish Store. It has a black slate roof – the sunlight strikes the nearest side of it. This is a squat, rectangular house. It is cold, too, as it needed to be in the days when the fish were kept here, laid out in a line. No fish in it now. Instead, two people lie in their bed with two blankets on. She sleeps, but he is stirring. He can hear the house creak, as it warms.

On with the sunlight.

A lane heads west, inland. It leaves the quayside and climbs past the ragwort, past the stones walls that have fallen, mostly, so that sheep step across them or nestle in their hollowed parts. These stones have lichen on them – as yellow as yolk, and lace-like – and they grow more yellow as the sunlight comes. The lane passes a picnic table and a phone box. There is a viewpoint here, with a large wooden board that names the other islands that can be seen from this spot – Utta, Cantalay, far-off Merme. By day, there are always tourists here, hands on their hips as they read it. But not now – not at this moment. It is too early. There are only sparrows and their short, burred flight.

The ground begins to flatten out. The island stretches ahead. The lane runs past more ragwort and a few small, blackened circles of earth where campfires have been, for this is the island's wild camping ground. The isle's airstrip is here too. It is rarely used: it exists for emergencies or when the sea is so rough that the *Morning Star* cannot sail and supplies on the island run low. A wooden hut says *Welcome to Parla* but salt has blistered its paint.

After this, there is the crossroads. It's small – a place where four dusty tracks meet each other, where most of the island's homes cluster like barnacles. Here, too, is the tiny primary school with its chalked snake drawn in the playground. It has hopscotch squares and a single swing; its roof is cherry-red. The school has five windows and in each one there is a letter, cut from coloured card. PARLA. The sunshine lights these letters up. It lights, also, the metal boot scraper outside the house next door. This house is the schoolteacher's; the only Bundy daughter lives here with her husband and son. Also, it is one of the few homes with trees: there are birches and an apple tree which no longer bears fruit. Bird feeders hang from them, for George loves his birds. They are what brought him here, to this island; they are also what led him to Hester – which makes him love his birds even more. At this moment, they are both sleeping. But the birds are awake and they squabble on the feeders, spill seed onto the ground.

The church is also here. It is wooden, white-painted, with a cross on its roof. The minister's house is wooden also but it remains wood-coloured and its wood is splintery. It has a trellis with ivy growing on it so that its door is half-hidden by its bottle-coloured leaves. They brush the minister's bald head when he goes in or out. He – Lorcan – has counted the steps it takes him to get from his bed to the altar and it is thirty-seven. He can hear the latch on the church door being opened, as he lies in his bath.

Parla Stores sits by a rhododendron bush. The shop is cave-like, inside – its shelves brim with tins, jars, bottles. There are also picnic tables outside, and an awning. There is no pub on Parla but this is the nearest thing to it. Milton sells beer, wine and spirits and turns a blind eye to locals sitting under his awning with aluminium cans. He likes hearing their laughter, coming through the door; he feels proud, somehow, to hear it – as if they have come here to see *him*. And Milton is proud of his noticeboard for amongst the ferry times and useful phone numbers he has pinned a plastic folder with leaflets inside – a map of Parla, self-guided tours, a little natural history, *Things to See and Do*. He is proud because he wrote them. They are all his work – typed out, and folded.

The crossroads is the heart of the island. The school, the shop, the half-pub and the church, all side by side. It is where the news is, where the stories are passed on.

South of here, the lane grasses over. It winds down past the island's graveyard and its long blackthorn hedge to

Lowfield. The sun barely finds this house for it is hidden by grass and gorse. The banks of earth beside it are so high that sheep have stepped onto its roof, or so the nurse tells it. But the sun finds her bicycle and its bell. Beyond Lowfield, there is Tavey – the pig farm where no-one lives now. The pigs are gone and its people too. For years it has been empty yet its furniture stands under dust-sheets, as if expecting to be used any day now. Nettles grow freely in these parts. In the nettle patch near Litty there are voles – anxious, with eyes like polished pins. They dart into undergrowth like gunshots. The lane ends on a shingle beach.

North of the crossroads, the island rises up. It gathers height quickly. After the school, the grass becomes sharper and thistles grow by the roadside. Here, the sheep are more plentiful. They lift up from the lane with their swinging, clotted tails. The first house is High Haven – a small farmhouse down a single track. It has a wood-pile under tarpaulin and four cars in its driveway, all without tyres, or engines, or doors, but Nathan keeps them all the same. It is in his nature, perhaps – to keep, to store. He hates loss; he has lost enough things. He looks at these old cars, now. Nathan is awake – he has barely slept – and he stands in the kitchen with a mug of tea and an aspirin on his tongue. He swallows the pill with a toss of his head, and stares at the empty wheel-arches. Beyond, he can see Wind Rising. It's the biggest farmhouse, and the oldest. Nathan grew up there. Now, his brother's family live in it – he sees the open-sided barn, the row of Calor gas bottles, the silage in black bales. Their dog is scratching her ear with her hind leg and Nathan can hear her chain ringing, or he thinks he can. He looks at his wristwatch; not yet six.

The woman at Easterly is also awake. Her cottage is beyond High Haven, along the same track so she must pass those cars propped up on bricks whenever she leaves her home. She does not like those cars, and she's told Nathan this. But why would he listen? At this precise moment, she stands in her dressing gown. She rubs rose-scented hand cream into her hands as she waits for the toast to pop up, and she thinks of her children, or those that are left. Emmeline lists them – *Ian, Hester, Nathan.* Her hands tell the story of a life on a farm – age spots, scars, papery skin on the backs of them – and she turns them over, studying.

The lane keeps rising. The north is the wildest part of the isle – the gorse is wind-bent, and the ditches are deep. In winter it is a harsh place, not made for life. But in the summer, the skylarks sing down upon it and to kneel and touch the earth is to feel its warmth. It is sunlit here, now. Here, at the island's highest point, all the coasts can be seen. A house with a yellow door perches in the north-east corner, near the cliff edge. It has gulls on its roof and tomato plants in its porch and its name is carved into drift-wood – *Crest*, propped by the door. The woman who lives here is brushing her teeth. She is in her early forties but looks older somehow. She bends down to the sink, spits.

After this, there is only the lighthouse. Its lantern is, now, sleeping. So, too, is the girl who lives at its base, who has turned the old lighthouse-keepers' quarters into a tea room and a few hostel rooms. She has worked hard for it. She sleeps on her front, in a floral vest and knickers that match. As the sunlight finds the back wall of her room, her alarm clock goes off and she stretches, rubs her eyes. Six fifteen. Rona could do with more sleep but she has plenty to do – breakfast, linen, fresh scones, her accounts. She tells herself this, as she turns off the alarm: *get up. A new day.* In theory anything could happen but Rona is pretty sure it won't.

*   *   *

47

Parla wakes slowly. It stretches, lowers a foot from its bed.

In Wind Rising, the top of an orange juice carton is pulled apart. Constance wears an oversized man's pyjama shirt that reaches her knees and a pair of walking socks. Her hair was black, once – raven-black, almost blue; now she has streaks of grey in it. Like a misty night, she tells herself. It is her reassurance.

She pours the juice. *A man?*

At Sye.

Dead?

Nope, he's alive. Or he was last night.

Who is he?

No idea. Without taking his eyes off the paper, Ian bites into his toast.

None?

He was barely conscious – he says this with his mouth full. *We couldn't ask him much.*

She looks out of the window, drinks. Constance was almost asleep when her husband returned last night. He'd climbed in beside her, beer-smelling, and she'd thought to ask *what happened tonight? Where?* But he'd been snoring promptly. He'd lain on his back, slept deeply, and so Constance could only imagine.

She'd not imagined this. *A man washing ashore ...* Incredulous. *Have you spoken to Ed about it?*

Sam was there. He'll have told him.

He should be told, Ian. A fishing boat or something might have gone down. There might be others out there who need saving. Shouldn't you phone him?

Sam, he repeats, *will do it. Or Tab will. Leave it.*

Constance watches him. And as always, when she watches him, she thinks *he is my children's father.* She thinks, too, *he's my husband* and that amazes her – that she is old enough to be married or that she was ever bold enough. But her first thoughts are of the children, always, who are not so childlike these days. Will Jonny have the same wide neck, when he's older? Will Leah's skin also wrinkle by her mouth, in time? They take after their father, she knows that – in their looks, and quiet ways.

She sips. *Ian?*

He makes a sound – annoyed. He wants to read the paper.

What does he look like? This man?

What?

This man from Sye. What does he look like?

She waits. Constance waits for the answer, and the longer she waits, the more she thinks *I know what he looks like.* She can guess.

Dark, he says, casually.

Skinned?

No – dark-haired. His skin's pale.

Not old, then?

Late thirties, maybe. Early forties. Hard to tell.

Beard?

He looks up. *Constance.* It is his warning voice.

She meets his stare. She holds her gaze until he looks away. Perhaps what surprises her is not that she was bold enough to marry, but bold enough to marry *him* – Ian, whose temper was as known as the *Anne-Rosa* is. And like the *Anne-Rosa*, it was mistrusted and whispered of and could rise out of the darkness, slick with hanging weed. She'd been told of it. But Constance was never afraid. Once, just once, in their early days of marriage they had argued about the farm – what had it been? A broken machine? A sheepdog that was not learning? She cannot recall it now and perhaps it does not matter. But Ian had struck the wall. He'd given a single roar and slammed his fist against it so that the wall shook. That had silenced them both – from loud voices to a sudden, incredible hush in which Constance could hear the dust settling onto the floor. Hands on her knees, she examined the plasterwork – broken, powdering. Then she pulled on her shoes and, without a word, she walked down the lane towards the harbour – meaning, absolutely, to catch the ferry and make her way back to the mainland, to the town she grew up in and still missed sometimes. Ian followed, pleading. *I'm so sorry ... Stay.* It never happened twice. On that quayside, Constance turned to her husband and vowed – swore with gritted teeth and her hand to her chest – that she would leave him for good if he ever struck another thing. *Anything, Ian* – the wall, the dog, a pillow, her. *I promise. Do you understand me?* Yes, he understood her; Constance always keeps her word. And he has shouted since, and he's slammed doors, and once, having argued with Nathan, he kicked the rainwater barrel with such power that it ruptured and the rush of water sent the chickens running in the way that chickens do – as if the world is ending. Ian can curse like no-one else she knows. And it is blunt, unimaginative swearing so that she winces. But that's all he's done, in twenty-four years. It is all he'll ever do.

Constance drinks her orange juice.

There is the *drip* of the kitchen tap.

Someone needs to tell Emmeline, she says, and pads out of the room.

It is the peonies she loves. She has always been told that the island's weather and its salt and thin soil would not suit them, that peonies could not grow on Parla. But she has grown them. She has tended them, and hoped, and here they are now. They grow in a cluster, facing south. Their pinkness makes her heart fill up, each time. When she walks back along the lane towards Easterly she sees them, and smiles – and it is like coming home to a person, she thinks. It is like being greeted. It is like a *hello*.

Emmeline kneels beside them. She holds a watering can and wears her sheepskin slippers. *Beautiful*, she tells them. *You are doing very well*.

It is one of the small benefits of living on her own: she can grow the flowers she has always longed to. Thirty years ago, any flowers she tried for were crushed by footballs and children's feet; fifteen years ago, she would have looked out of the window on a Sunday as she cooked the roast dinner for Jack and wished that she could be out in the flowerbeds with a trowel and a bag of manure, rather than sieving the gravy. She called it *a woman's lot*, back then. People matter more than flowers, of course. But now she has the time – at last. Foxgloves and hydrangeas. And she loves her peonies.

Emmeline stands, looks out to sea. *The unending sea.* She grew up in the lighthouse. Her, her parents and Tabitha had lived in one of the three houses at the lighthouse's base, so that the sea was so close and so loud that it felt like a fifth person – a family member who was never far away. Her earliest memory is being shown the pots of paraffin whilst licking the butter off a currant bun; her second earliest is polishing the lens. And she had loved her lighthouse life. She'd loved winding the weights back up to the top of the stairs, and learning Morse code, and she had loved the view so much that she'd dreamed of keeping the light herself one day. Emmeline Bright – with her own jacket and hat. But lighthouse-keeping was never seen as woman's work. When she married Jack Bundy at eighteen, she left the lantern behind her. She moved south and inland, into the farm called Wind Rising. From light and high seas to a dark-roomed house; from saltwater to sheep. Only half a mile from one life to the other, but those had been such different lives. And how many years had she walked through the creaking rooms of Wind Rising, with its missing roof tiles and open fire which threw smoke into the sitting room when the wind shifted itself? Long enough. Those years of smelling of sheep, of wedging paper under the uneven legs of chairs. All four children were born in that house, or near it. All of them were late to show their faces except Tom – of course. Tom leapt out early, as if too excited to wait.

She pushes fertiliser into the earth. *Easterly* – like all names on Parla, its name is forthright, brusque. It is simple – *as if we are all fools and need to be told plainly*. She, Jack and their youngest child moved here when it became free. A man called Strutt – a mainlander, sullen, bad teeth and bad manners – had died during those wild winter storms of nearly thirty years ago, and Emmeline had carried cardboard boxes of toys, books, bed linen, clothes and kitchen utensils over to Easterly in the following spring. Ian, as the eldest son, stayed at Wind Rising. He had been twenty-three that March. He took on the farm, with Nathan to help him – as boys were meant to, back then. They had no choice in it, really, for their father had started his heart trouble in the autumn before and could no longer farm. It had changed Jack – that shock, the air ambulance and the diet that was forced upon him left him a weaker man who could no longer haul sheep onto their rumps to shear them, or change tractor tyres. And Hester had already met George Moss. So Ian and Nathan became real farmers; and Emmeline, Jack and young Tom moved over the fields to this easterly place.

She counts on her fingers. Tom had been thirteen years old.

Those were my best years. Perhaps she should say that her best years were the first few of her marriage, or when all her children were young – but that's not the truth. She loved the days when her eldest boys were farmers, men in their twenties who were strong and well-made and living their own lives, men who'd kiss their mother's hair when they came in to see her but who went into her fridge without asking as if they were still small boys. She'd smiled, at that. Hester was in love – blooming with it. And Tom had spent his days running through fields or on beaches, coming back in the evenings with his pockets filled with shells or feathers or mussels for eating and with a head filled with stories. *Mum, guess what I heard?* She loved how he smelled. She loved how her youngest boy filled the house with his own sounds – his voice as he talked to the cat, his music, his bedsprings, the scuffing of his socked feet on the kitchen's flagstone floor.

Those were Jack's best years too, in some ways. He had nearly died, and survived it. A quietness came to him that he had never had before – gratitude, perhaps, or an awareness for the first time that he would be gone one day. He was a better husband, after his heart attack. He became the man she'd hoped for, all along. She remembers holding his hand in this garden, on a summer's morning like this.

Her peonies nod in the breeze.

How does a person ever speak of their loss? How do they find the right words for it? Emmeline has never really been the talking kind.

She looks down at her hands. The hand cream has served no purpose. She has soil beneath her fingernails, again – brown crescent moons. Only a farmer or his wife would have hands like this, day in and day out. She had made her wedding vows with neat, square nails, and the following evening she'd glanced down at her hands – dirtied from the chicken shed, and from picking blackberries from the patch by the back door – and had thought *this is how it will be, now. These are my married hands.* She nearly lost her wedding ring, once, during the lambing season. A farmer's wife's hands, even now.

Briefly, there is resentment. It rises a little, like a far-out wave.

Emmeline looks up. A man is coming to her. He is a man, but he is also one of her sons, and so despite his age she still sees the child who had knocked his front milk teeth out when he fell on the quayside, the boy who believed, solemnly, that he'd heard sleigh bells on the roof one Christmas Eve. Nathan wears a white shirt. He walks with his hands in his pockets and when he sees her, he frees one hand and holds it up at her. He bends his fingers in a small, boyish wave.

Hello, she says. She hugs him by the peonies, and she can smell the sea in his hair. She does not hug for long, but when Emmeline goes to pull away from him she finds that Nathan is still holding her. He holds her very tightly, too tightly. She waits. She stays as she is, being held, and it is only when his arms start, at last, to soften, that she leans back from him and looks at his face – at the straight nose, the shining eyes – and she breathes, *what is it? What's wrong?*

*   *   *

Nathan knew it had to be him who told her. Ian wouldn't think of it. He'd call it *unimportant* or *nothing to do with me*. He probably slept well last night, snoring in Wind Rising as if nothing had changed, as if no man had been found at Sye.

Nathan has not slept at all. He knows it shows. Kitty said as much when she crept downstairs to find him still sitting in the armchair, an empty glass tilted in his lap. She'd said, *you look like crap, Mr Bundy*, smiling and stroking his knee.

As he'd walked along the lane to Easterly he'd tried out the different words in his head, whispered them under his breath, and he'd hoped that perhaps his mother would be out – that he'd find a note on the doormat saying *gone to shop* or elsewhere. But he'd looked up and seen her. She'd been tending to those pink flowers of hers, and he'd thought *she looks old.* The hunched back, the iron-grey hair.

When they'd hugged, Nathan had felt small again.

Now, they stand inside. She is looking at him, waiting. She licks her lips as she always does when she is nervous, and she says *is it Kitty?*

No.

Hester, then? Ian? The grandchildren?

No, Mum. Everyone's fine.

You? Are you fine?

Been better …

Are you ill?

Mum … He's forgotten the words. He tries to think of them but cannot so he puts his hands on top of her hands and says *listen. Some stuff happened last night. At Sye.*

Sye? She is frowning. *The cove?*

Sam Lovegrove was walking up there –

What happened? Did he fall, or …?

Sam's OK, too. Mum, listen – he found a man. Washed up on the beach.

Emmeline is still.

Sam thought he was dead, but he wasn't. He was lying on his front … Sam ran to the farm and got us – me, Ian, Jonny. We all went to Sye, and we carried him back. Took him to Aunt Tabitha's.

Nathan pauses, breathes. He watches his mother's face, and waits until her eyes show what he knows she will, shortly, be thinking. He waits. He waits. And then he sees her eyes change.

She says, *Oh God …*

Mum, it isn't Tom.

How do you know? It might be.

He takes her wrists. *No. It's not. That's what I'm here to tell you. It is not Tom.*

Does he look like him?

Nathan winces. *In part, I guess. Yes. But he is too tall. He is too tall, and he is wider than Tom ever was. The teeth are wrong, and –*

It's been four years. People change in four years. They grow.

Mum –

He's at Tabitha's? She breaks frees of him, hauls her jacket off the hook behind the door. *I've got to go there.*

Mum, he's not Tom –

She shakes her head, she can't hear him. She is fumbling in the pocket of her jacket, finds the car keys, and she trips out of the house into the sunlight and gets into the car.

Nathan calls, *Mum!* But he only calls it once. He is too tired to stop her, and knows she cannot be stopped. He stands on the grass and watches her go – over the potholes, past the log-pile. Once her car is gone he shuts his eyes.

The wind pushes at him. He can feel it, buffeting.

When he looks again he sees a plastic toy windmill on a stick, beside the fence. It turns, in the breeze. It is red, or it was – years of sun have faded it. He watches it turn. A northerly breeze.

What now? He knows.

Somebody else needs to be told – about this washed-up man.

*   *   *

The plastic windmill turns, and catches the light.

In the mending room at Lowfield, the stranger still sleeps. Tabitha watches his chest rise and fall.

In the harbour, a gull stands on a boat's tarpaulin cover. It drinks from a pool of rainwater that has gathered there.

To swallow, the gull lifts his beak to the sky, straightens its neck and gulps twice. Afterwards, it shakes its tail.

Sam sees this gull. He is at the top of the harbourmaster's house – a double-fronted, red-bricked building that sits on the quayside. From his attic room, he can see everything – the harbour, the sea wall, the open water beyond it. He can see the mainland too – dipped and bluish, like a sleeper's back. It is a good room. The eaves mean that Sam must stoop in places but he likes being here at the top of the house. His bedroom is untidy, boyish – a music system, a games console, a dartboard, crumbs on the carpet, mugs of cold tea, a row of free weights that he lifts in the evenings as he looks at the view. A single bed which is never made.

He sits on this bed now. He sits with his hands underneath him, looking out to sea. Sam did not sleep last night, or barely. When he closed his eyes he was there again – standing on the coastal path and looking down at Sye. He could see the man exactly. He can see him now.

Dark hair.

The fingers that tried to close around a stone.

Last night, Sam had thrown up by the sea wall. When he'd returned home, wiping his mouth, he'd found his father watching the news and whispered *Dad? Something's happened.* He'd sounded young, afraid.

Things are passed on here. Houses, jobs, names – they are handed down to the next generation because that is the island's way. This has always been a Lovegrove house. Sam's great-great-grandfather had been the captain of the first *Morning Star* and he'd built this house himself with a clear sense of the Lovegroves yet to come. He'd captained the boat for fifty-six years. When he died, his son took over; then his son did. And a century later, the captain and harbourmaster of Parla is Edward Lovegrove, with his receding hairline and chapped hands, and last night this man had been watching the television with his feet on the coffee table. He'd lowered his feet when he saw Sam's face.

What is it, son?

Ed is the law on Parla, if there is such a thing. *Ed will know* – a common phrase. It's only based on his first aid certificates, his knowledge of the water and the radio in his study which he can talk to the coastguard on. It isn't much, but it's enough. *A man's come ashore.*

What? Dead?

Alive.

Do we know him?

No. But for a moment, I …

Sam shifts now, stretches. He can feel the weight of a sleepless night on his shoulders. A night of hearing the curtains stir, of watching the hours tick across the neon face of his clock. In the last few minutes before daybreak, he'd been nearing sleep – drifting, growing heavier. But then the phone had rung. It had bubbled up the stairs, rousing him. His father had answered it. He'd said, *hello Tabitha. Yes. Yes – Sam told me …*

Everyone will know by now, Sam thinks. *Or most of them, at least.*

This is a fact that he is sure of: it is hard to have secrets here. Something happens and the island feels it. If a cat kills a bird in the morning, the feathers will have blown into each house by nightfall; if there is a quarrel on the quayside, the account of it will be unloaded with the rest of the boat, and carried inland. *Guess what I saw …* And taps will be turned off by women who think they have misheard their children or their friends, and say *what? Really?* Elbows will be taken hold of in the lanes. When he was a boy, there was a fire at the school one night and the red-edged curls of paper floated over the island, settled on the outboard motors, roofs and bonnets of cars – and

Sam thinks news is like that. It gets everywhere. Never any secrets, never any surprises and he has wondered if that's what has buckled Leah in the past – the lack of privacy, the way that all things are known.

Phones will be ringing. Hands will reach for other hands. *Emmeline* ... Will she rage? Grapple? Most likely.

And Sam thinks of Maggie. Who will tell her? And how will she be, when she's told? He imagines her face. He sees the lines by her eyes, how she holds her fingers up to her mouth as she listens. How broken she can look.

Nearly four years.

He glances down at *Sea Fairy*. Her green tarpaulin is streaked with gull droppings. She bobs in the corner – old, unloved.

*   *   *

The sun is high and white. The grass is shining. Laundry is pegged on washing lines.

All the colours seem bright, as Nathan drives. He squints at the school's roof, at the glossy tail of the rooster at Wind Rising, at the ragwort sprouting in the lane. Even the lighthouse's paintwork seems brighter to him so that he reaches up for the car's visor and tilts it down. Has there been a hotter day than this, this year? He doesn't think so. He drives slowly, with his window down. His right forearm rests on the door and he can hear the long grass brushing the underside of his car. Once he'd have loved this weather. He'd have taken beers into the fields or left them in a rock-pool to cool, as he swam. Or he'd have taken a rug up to the lighthouse and the northern coast and spent the afternoon there – him, and Kitty.

A ewe treads in front of him.

One of mine. Nathan knows this. He knows his own, amongst Ian's; they are Texel, firm-bodied with blue tags in their ears. They are trickier to shear in that they're strong beasts, and two weeks ago he'd had to kneel hard on their ribs and tie their hind legs as he'd sheared them. *Shearing* ... It's in the Bundy blood. Ian, Hester and Nathan could all handle shears before they learnt to ride bikes or to add and subtract. They knew how to catch a sheep, drag it back and grip it tightly between their thighs before they knew how to spell *Cantalay* or *Merme*. Tom was the exception. He'd shear, but he'd have one eye on the water. Nathan grew strong from hauling sheep and mending fences; Tom's arms thickened from lobstering, from pulling on the cord to start the outboard motor, from rowing into hidden coves.

Are you sure he's one of ours? Their father said this, once. *We're land folk, not sea.*

Nathan glances to his right.

Crest is coming into view. He sees its yellow guttering, its matching yellow door. This is the island's highest point – the whole coastline can be seen from its driveway, from Litty in the south, round to Bundy Head. The house had been derelict, once. Once, it had been four stone walls with a leaking roof and the brown streaks of sheep urine on the skirting boards. But it was always the best position to live – the height, the views. Nathan remembers ducking through it as a child and feeling how a king in his castle must have felt – alive, amazed, buffeted by wind. Tom, also, felt that. When he was twenty-four he'd said, *do you know what I'm going to do?* For six summers he worked on that house. He'd hammered, hauled and rung friends on the mainland; he'd buy beers for his brothers before saying, *you couldn't help me with ...?* He made Crest a home again. And what a home – with bookshelves made of driftwood, curtains hung on lengths of rope, a septic tank, a compost heap, a chair forged out of wooden crates, a single solar panel as dark as a burnished eye. There was the chalky knot of whalebone Tom used to prop open the door. And the kitchen table had been part of a fishing boat, once; her name, *Coralee*, still hangs on the staircase. Nathan has seen it.

Tomato plants, too. Those were Maggie's addition. The porch is south-facing and she's filled it with them so that Nathan knows how the porch will smell today, when he enters it – the sharp fruit, the trapped heat.

He turns right, along its driveway.

Crest. He loves it and it saddens him – both.

He turns off the engine. There is a sudden hush, and he wonders what he will tell her, what words he will use and if they will be the right ones.

She appears. She steps out of an outbuilding, into the light. She holds a tin of yellow paint which is dripping down its side. Yellow paint on her arms and hands. Maggie looks up.

She smiles: *hey*.

Nathan shuts the car door. He comes so close that he can see she has yellow paint everywhere – on her cheeks, her nose, her collarbone. Her hair is tied back but one strand is loose and is blowing across her face so that it makes her blink, and the tip of it is yellow. There is the smell of sheep and fresh paint and Maggie's washing powder and as a cloud's shadow passes over them he thinks, briefly, how beautiful it is – to be standing here.

Nathan?

He doesn't want to tell her. *Just passing*.

She eyes him. *Liar*, she says.

Maggie feels afraid. No-one is ever *just passing* – and not Nathan, of all people. Nathan, who tends to leave her be.

A strand of hair is fluttering, but she does not reach for it. *Tell me*.

A man's been found. Washed up.

Washed up? From the sea?
He nods.
Alive?
Yes. He's at Tabitha's.
Is it –?
No. No, *it's not.*
She tries to put the paint tin down, but it tilts, and spills, and he comes forward saying *careful. I've got it. Here – give it to me.*

*   *   *

Nathan leads her inside. He knows her house, and he knows to duck slightly as he steps into the kitchen, under the doorframe and the hanging copper pans. She walks with her hands held in front of her, as if walking in the dark.

Sit down.
It's not Tom?
No.
Maggie hears the small hesitation, looks up.
For one small moment, I … Nathan shrugs. *He looks a bit like him.*
Dark?
Yes. *And the beard. And he's big – tall, broad …*
But not Tom?
Not Tom.
You're sure? Her eyes are round. They are like the stones that come ashore, the stones that have been rolled and rolled through the years, thrown against other stones. They are grey, with a navy edge.
Mags, I promise. This man is not him.

They sit side by side, at the table that used to be *Coralee.* Maggie runs her fingers over her lips. *Who is he, then?*

We don't know yet. He's still sleeping.

Where was he found?

Sye. He was lying on the stones. Sam found him. He came to Wind Rising for help and we carried him.

To –?

Lowfield.

She considers this. She takes a deep breath, releases it slowly. *OK. Well ... Tom never liked it – Sye. Said it was dank, hard to walk on. If he was going to wash up, he wouldn't wash up there.*

It is a half-joke; they are nervous words.

Is he hurt?

No. Doesn't seem it.

Does Emmeline know?

Yes.

He watches Maggie. She says nothing for a while. There is a single crumb on the table, and Nathan watches her as she places her forefinger on it, rolls the crumb from side to side. Left and right. *You came here because you knew people would talk.* It is not a question.

You know how it is here.

She says *yes I know.*

He cannot think of anything to say. There is nothing to say to her that he has not said before, or tried to say, and so he sits, scans the room that they are sitting in – the spotted oven gloves, the chopping board with an apple core on it, the ferry times on the noticeboard. There are shells everywhere – cockles, whelks, a purple-tipped sea urchin on the windowsill. Beside it there is a vase of feathers with sand still on them, feathers whose blades have torn or split. Maggie the forager. She is always looking – but aren't they all? His eyes settle on a photograph. It is held to the fridge with magnets and it is of Nathan's younger brother and Maggie; they are wearing anoraks, with their faces pressed together, cheek to cheek. Tom's arm is in the foreground, leading to the camera – he was taking the photo himself. A bright, blustery day.

Where was that taken?

She follows his gaze. *Bundy Head.* Then she lifts her finger off the table, brushes the crumb away with the thumb of the same hand – a short, rough sound. *Nathan, are you still hopeful?*

Maggie is like no-one else. Tom had said so, too. Nathan remembers the moment when Tom stepped down from the *Morning Star* six years ago, walked up to his brother and said, *I've found her.* Just three words, but Nathan knew what he'd meant. He himself had found Kitty not too long before, or she had found him, and he and Tom had gone back to Wind Rising that night and opened the rum, toasted these women who weren't like the rest. Tom described Maggie to him – a wary, slender, blonde-haired woman collecting pint glasses outside The Bounty Inn, a tea-towel stuck through her apron which was longer than her black skirt.

Hopeful? He thinks *the years* … The years which have been split into months and the months which have been split into weeks and the weeks into days and the days into hours and hours have been split into a breath in and a breath out, and Tom has been missing from all of them. Hope becomes tired. It fades, regardless of how much you wish it not to.

That he's still alive somewhere? Didn't drown?

I imagine it, Nathan says. *Sometimes.*

She nods. *Yes. I imagine it. I still imagine him walking up the drive. But is that the same as being hopeful? I don't think so.*

This man isn't Tom.

I know.

No, she's like no-one else. She's smart, and hard, and vulnerable, and she still uses Tom's boat, still lifts and lowers his lobster pots when most other widows would have left the island entirely perhaps or at least left the sea well alone. She wears his oilskins even though they're too big. Only once has Nathan seen her cry. *Can I do anything?* He knows there is nothing that anyone can do.

And for a moment Maggie is silent. She looks at the table as if she has not heard him, as if there is something on the table that Nathan cannot see. Then she flinches, turns to him. *Help me with the doorframe? I've got more paint on myself than* ... She turns her wrists over, showing him. A small, sad smile.

She was Tom's. He will always help her if he can.

* * *

The red car skids on gravel. Its door is thrown open. Emmeline appears, hurries to the front door of Lowfield and she bangs – twice, *bang-bang* – on its glass. *Tabitha!*

She waits, briefly. Bangs again.

Her sister's face appears behind the glass and then the door opens. She glares, her forefinger raised to her lips. *Hush! He's sleeping!*

So it's true? There's a man?

Keep your voice down.

Is there?

She nods. *Ian told you?*

Nathan. Weren't you going to?

Tabitha flinches. *Don't be snapping at me, Emmeline.*

They study each other, shifting their jaws.

I suppose you'd better come in.

Tabitha leads her sister into the kitchen, shuts the door. She sees her cereal bowl in the sink, waiting to be washed; a used tea bag sits on the draining board with the teaspoon still attached to it. The floor needs mopping – Tabitha can hear the soles of her slippers sticking to it as she walks and she hopes Emmeline can't hear that. She notices these things, when Emmeline's here.

He came ashore at Sye. Sam found him.

I heard that.

He went to Wind Rising, got your boys. Jonny, too.

Is it Tom?

The nurse expected this – but not so soon, or so bluntly. *No, it's not. Did Nathan say he was?*

He said he looks like him.

He does – a little. Same colouring.

So it could be. And he came out of the water, so –

I know he did. And yes, he has dark hair, and a beard, and there's a likeness of sorts. But Em, it's not him. Do you hear?

How do you know?

Because there are differences! Big ones! He's too tall to be Tom. Too broad. The nose isn't right and the teeth aren't the same, and those aren't his hands, and ...

Teeth change! He could have changed them. He could have grown ...

Em ...

I want to see him. A statement, of course.

He's sleeping. No.

I won't leave till I see him.

That stubborn streak. Tabitha narrows her eyes, thinks *that's Emmeline*. The petulant child who grew into a fierce, resolute grown-up who rarely laughs or takes no for an answer. But then, so much has happened. And Emmeline's had to be tough, she supposes: Jack as a husband, that farm and four children. Four to begin with.

The grandfather clock ticks.

Fine, Tabitha says. *You can see him. But –* she holds up a finger – *no waking him, Em – whoever he is, he needs to rest.* And she leads her sister down the hallway to a door with frosted glass.

*   *   *

He sleeps, this sea creature. This man from the waves. This tired Poseidon.

Firstly, Emmeline sees his size. He is as broad as a boat, and as long as one. Then she sees the long lashes, the tiny lines by his eyes. His nose is perfectly straight. The beard is black – not a deep brown with a reddish hue, and with no grey flecked in it: it is as black as night is. His eyebrows are of the same blackness. The tip of his left ear is creased. The backs of his hands are veined and sore-looking – huge, capable hands.

Has he spoken?

Not much.

The man breathes like the sea.

Emmeline is in the mending room for a minute, no longer. It is enough.

She walks out into the sunlight. She cannot name it, or describe it – what she is feeling now. *Disappointment* is not enough of a word – not nearly. She had known, deep down, it wasn't him. In her heart she'd known that he could not be Tom – *it can't be, it can't be, not after so long* – but she had hoped, all the same; she had snatched at the faintest of chances because she is his mother, and she must, and so she had stumbled and demanded and banged on her sister's door and now Emmeline feels unsteady, foolish. Unspeakably sad.

Tom had a scar on his nose from a childhood fall; his lips were thinner, equal-sized. She'd know her boy in the dark, even now. She'd know him in a crowded room or by smell alone or handwriting.

Tabitha comes by her. *I'm sorry.*

Oh, I'm sure you are.

Emmeline leaves, and as she goes she feels, too, the swell of anger – as if someone, somewhere, is laughing. As if a trick has been played.

*   *   *

Who else? Who else cannot know what to think or say? They are all like fish on land now – blank-eyed, open-mouthed.

What a day ... Ed Lovegrove stands with his hands in his pockets; he looks out to sea. *Boy oh boy, what a day* ... Eighteen years as a harbourmaster, thirty-nine years as a harbourmaster's son before that, and Edward can't remember a man being washed ashore like this. Bodies, yes. He's had his deaths to deal with – Jack's, a birdspotter's, that man from Utta who caught his foot in the line as he was throwing out pots so that they found his boat going round and round and when they hauled in the line he was already half-plucked at by fish. Ed fears the watery deaths. It is the watery deaths that he feels he can prevent by watching the weather, noting down each boat that docks here, keeping an eye on the weather station that lives at the back of his house. He has a rain gauge; there is a small anemometer to measure wind speed and wind direction. He tends to it, like a man at prayer.

But a person who has appeared? That the sea has given?

Tabitha rang earlier. She'd given the details – the beard, the injured hands – and Ed had not known the words or the way forwards. He'd said *it isn't a death, is it? So ...?* A man washed ashore is the stuff of books; it is not what happens in the twenty-first century to an island that relies on tourism and migrant birds and the sinking price of lamb. An island with a coloured line of jetsam – plastics, netting, nylon rope – on every beach like a scar.

We wait until he wakes. We do nothing till he's woken. I should call the coastguard in case …

OK, said Tabitha. *But not the police. Not yet.*

Fine. Not yet, Ed agreed. The police, he knows, would bring trouble of their own.

So Ed had settled in the office of the harbourmaster's house and made the call. Mac had answered. He was eating something. With a half-full mouth he'd said, *really? Jesus. Need an air ambulance?*

Tab says not. Any boats down?

There had been the distant click of computer keys, and when the clicking stopped he'd heard Mac swallow, clear his throat. *Nope, no boats, Ed. Well, there was a dinghy capsized about twenty miles north of you, but both men were picked up. He's not one of yours? A guest, or some such?*

I'm sure he is. Just checking, you know.

Or some half-fish creature? A part-whale? Haven't you guys got a tale about that sort of thing? A hard, single laugh.

Mac – who Ed has never warmed to. *Thanks*, he'd said, hung up.

*   *   *

The day fades. The sky pinkens.

It is low tide. The beaches are glassy. The wading birds are reflected in the sand and sometimes they make their short, skimming flight to a different stretch of sand and land with their legs stretched out.

Curlews. Nathan hears them.

He turns off the engine but he sits, for a while. He stares at the steering wheel. Nathan has no thoughts at this moment: he is empty, worn-out.

Kitty watches him. She wears a floral apron, and as she'd been picking bits of eggshell out of a bowl of yolks she'd heard his car, looked up.

Her husband is staring at something – the dashboard?

Then he climbs out. The car door shuts and there is the crunch of the gravel, and from an upstairs bed the cat jumps down with a muffled thud as Nathan comes into the hallway, kicks off his boots.

She wipes her hands, goes to him. He tastes of salt. *So?*

They sit at the kitchen table, facing each other. His wife has a sweep of navy-blue powder on her eyelids, and Nathan sees that some of this powder is also on her cheek-bones as if it has dusted down through the course of the day. She smells as she always does – lotion, Miss Dior, a touch of turpentine. *Kitty Bundy.* At first, she'd called it a dancing name.

Mum went straight to Lowfield. I told her it wasn't Tom but she still went.

Of course she did – softly said.

Seven years of marriage but the word *wife* can still feel new to him. This woman – rich-haired, curved, slow in her movements – leans forwards, over her glass. She looks down into it, holds it by the stem and swirls the wine very carefully. Her hair comes down as she does this. She has not aged – not even slightly. She looks as she did when he first met her, when she turned around in a scarlet dress.

And Maggie? Did you go to see her?

I did. He sighs, rubs his eyes.

How did she take it?

It's been a long day, Kit – which is his way of asking for silence, now.

She leans back. She takes her hair and gathers it, holding it on the top of her head with both hands, and for a moment Nathan can see her white neck, the tiny tattoo of a bird at the nape. *Well. Mine was long too. I've worked all day – ten hours of it. Do you want to hear about it?* She waits.

Nathan says nothing.

Kitty lets go of her hair, pushes her chair back. The bird on her neck goes away.

Maggie was calm – Kitty is certain of this. Maggie, who is too neat and reserved and dignified to wail in company, or throw things at the wall. Small-boned and gentle. And she is contained, in the way cupped water is – full of reflections and moments but they pass too quickly for Kitty to read them clearly. As Kitty rinses the plates of omelette, she can see Maggie perfectly – how she'd waded out from Lock-and-Key beach on the night that Tom died. Her pink shirt had darkened as the water reached her waist, and she'd called out *Tom? Tom?*

Vulnerable, and lonely. Kind. Old-souled.

And she is on her own, of course. No family in the world. Having Sam Lovegrove watching your house at night is not proper company. They all try to see more of her, but she hides herself away.

It is not how Kitty would grieve. She, if she had to, would grieve wildly – with noise, mucus, paint on the canvas, blustery walks on beaches, curse words and exhausted sleep. But everyone grieves differently just as everyone loves in different ways. Emmeline is resentful; Nathan has retreated or almost, and he still drinks on his own at night. The crate that she leaves in the lane for recycling is always clinking, and full.

Their cat – tabby, overweight – butts her head against her shins.

Kitty leans down to stroke her, and as she does this she wonders how you can grieve a death if you have no bones, if you have nothing to bury or go back to. Poor Maggie. *Poor thing.*

When she turns to speak to her husband again, she finds his chair is empty. He's gone away soundlessly, so that Kitty drops the tea-towel onto the worktop and stares where he had been.

*   *   *

And so the bedside lights go on, one by one.

The television's bluish glow flits in island sitting rooms. Curtains are pulled into the middle, and closed. In a bedroom of Wind Rising, a girl with bitten fingernails holds her mobile phone. She sits cross-legged on her bed, and types *sounds like a hard day. Hope you are OK.* Does she put one *x*, after this, or several? Leah chooses one, and presses *send*. The words fly. *Sending.* Then, *Sent*.

Beneath the lighthouse, in the old lighthouse-keepers' quarters, Rona Lovegrove bends down. She peers through the glass door of her oven, watches her sponge cake rise. She has heard this man looks like Tom. She thinks of the Bundys, and thinks of love.

Jim Coyle lies in bed. He lies in his own darkness. He tries to imagine the lighthouse's slow flash. Jim – like the Brights – was born in the lighthouse-keepers' quarters; unlike the Brights, he became the lighthouse-keeper himself, in time – and he misses so much about it. The drowsy tick of cogs in the lantern room. The sweet smell of paraffin. Sticky, blackish knuckles from polishing the brass.

He is blind now. But Jim still knows each crack in the plaster, each decorative curl on the wrought-iron fireplace where he used to toast crumpets, each speckle of paint that made it onto windowpanes. There was a loose brick in the boiler room which he kept his penny whistle behind. Is it still there? Might it still play the same tune, if he blew?

Beside him, his wife reads. He can hear the pages as she turns them, how their bottom edges catch the bedspread to make a dragging sound. He asks *what book is it?*

He asks, but Jim knows. The book has a leather smell. He'd heard its spine crack as she'd opened it.

Abigail says *Folklore and Myth. You know the one.*

Yes he does. And as soon as Jim had heard that a man – bearded, very handsome – had been washed up at the cove called Sye, he'd known that this was the book that his wife would turn to. She'd take it from its shelf, and find its fourteenth page. She'd smooth that page with her palm.

Dearest, she says – *do you know what this reminds me of?*

Abigail of the stories. Abigail who is eighty-three years old and yet whose love of this one book is absolute, childlike.

The Fishman. Your Fishman. The one you saw off Sye.

And there it is – the word he knew was coming. Like so many other words, it is uttered and the breeze catches it and it is carried out of the Old Fish Store over the island. It blows against the rusting cars at High Haven; it scuds on the beaches with the night-time spume. It has been down on the sea bed, perhaps; for years, it has been half-forgotten, tapped at by passing claws. But Abigail has hauled up *Fishman* now. The word surfaces – beautiful, glass-bright.

*   *   *

This word will make its way to all of us, in time. It will knock against our doors and we will all be saying it. Even I will talk of the *Fishman* – but not yet.

Night. People turn to sleep. They close the back door, or rub cream on their feet. They finish their chapters or lie in deep baths with tea lights next to the taps and think about the day's events. In the cottage by the school a couple are making love. The brown dog at the foot of their bed yawns with a whine, flaps his ears, and they break away from their kissing and smile at the sound in the dark.

One by one, eyes close.

But also, two eyes open. In a room that smells of lavender, two black eyes open, blink twice. Three times.

He lies very still, listening.

After a while, he lifts the blankets, looks down at his long, white legs.

As for Maggie, she climbs out of the bath. She wraps a towel about her. Four years have passed, or nearly four. Who told her the grief would lessen? Grief does not lessen; it changes, and perhaps she has changed so that she can endure it better. But the grief does not grow less.

She misses him beyond words. She will never have the words for how much she misses him.

The Seals with Human Hearts

Of all the sea creatures – whales, turtles, lobsters with their intricate, grooved tails that can slide into themselves like a fan, the jellyfish, the squid, the octopus that I reckon knows far more than I can ever know – it is the seal I love the most. I always have. And it's hard to be sure if I love the seals for the stories I have heard of them or for their expressions – quizzical, trusting. Both maybe. Both is most likely.

The first seal I ever saw was near Tap Hole. It was winter or late autumn, at least, for I wore woollen gloves with a matching hat. I had the hat pulled down very low. It covered my ears and brushed my eyelashes.

The seal looked human at first. I thought someone was swimming. But then I stood on the edge, squinted and thought *I know what that is* ... Its head was glossy, its eyes were round. Its body was freckled, slick.

Sea-hounds, Emmeline called them. For how they barked at night.

Or *they are the souls of the drowned men* ... So Nathan said. He knew his stories and told them, from time to time.

Me? I liked Abigail's version most of all. In her well-worn armchair and with her Earl Grey tea she unfolded her book called *Folklore and Myth* and said, *in the beginning, when the world was made, the seals were given human hearts* ... I asked why – and she'd looked up, surprised. *I don't know why! It doesn't matter why ... What matters is that it says so.* She tapped the page – *see?* I like this because it is fitting; it seems a tale that's *right*. For seals are drawn to human voices, after all; they bask on rocks, human-like, and they have eyes that are expressive as human eyes can be and I might easily believe that seals speak our language and feel our private human pains. That they grieve as we do at the world's sorrows – at its wars, famines, its loneliness and bombs.

Also, they can fall in love. There are tales of seals loving a person so much and so deeply that they wish for that human to join them, at sea. They wait, offshore. They sniff the salty air, and call. And so it has been a form of consolation, in the past: *she didn't drown, not really. Her soul lives with the seals, now* ... Where she is loved, and well-cared for. Where they dart, dapple-bodied, through shafts of light.

*   *   *

Abigail Coyle believes this. For her, it is the truth.

Her sister was loved by the seals. Thomasina was loved for she looked like them – with eyes so black that Abigail could see her own face looking back at her. She has a faded photograph that she keeps by her bed – both of them, in matching pinafores. They do not look like twins. They never did. Abigail is the shorter, plumper girl – her dress is straining at the buttons, and one sock is rolled down. Thomasina is taller, with her hair untied so that half of it covers those seal-eyes. But it does not hide the look of suspicion, the narrowed stare as if she does not trust this moment or the person who is saying *good ... Hold it ... On the count of three ...*

Abigail turns in bed. She looks at this photograph now. Thomasina. Who was openly called *the beautiful one*.

She drowned at fifteen. She floated in that pinafore – a damp, patchwork star. And she is buried in the ground but Abigail believes – *knows* – that her sister's soul is not in Parla's graveyard, in a wooden box. Instead, her soul – *her*, Thomasina's true self – rolls with the seals that loved her, and which she loved in return. In that cave, they found her. *Join us*, they said, gentle-eyed. *Come and swim at our side*. So her twin sister – the elder by nine minutes, the taller by three inches and who could do backbends and walk on her hands – lowered her nose and mouth under-water, closed her eyes, and did.

Abigail pats the pillow. She sorts out the blankets, tucks them round her.

When she heard of this strange, bearded man, her first thought was of her twin. The sea is Thomasina's. All things that come from it belong to her – the pearled insides of mussel shells, or a squid's dark ink. And her second thought? It had been of a story she knew. Kept in a leather-bound book.

It has been a long time since she took *Folklore and Myth of Parla, Merme and the Lesser Isles* off the sitting-room shelf. But this evening she bent down to it, blew off its dust.

It was her mother's book. In Abigail's childhood, it was hauled off the shelf in Wind Rising after stormy days or days of such hardship that her mother cried. They read it at bedtime. Its pages were turned very slowly, and they sounded like a person saying *hush, now* ... So many stories. Their mother read them over and over: the whale that answered the foghorn, the gannets which gave their fish to good people, the changing wind of the north. They became friends and they became the truth, for Mercy believed them absolutely. *We only know the foam*, she'd say – meaning this human world is merely the very surface of it, and there is more, so much more, that we lack the vision for.

Abigail's mother was from Merme which is an isle known for its strangeness. They ate many things but not seals, never seals – for seals have human hearts.

It is a well-thumbed tale. The seal that has been drawn here lies on its side, one flipper raised as if in greeting. But Abigail keeps turning ...

She goes to the fourteenth page.

The Fishman of Sye. It is barely a story – merely a description of this part-man, part-fish. *He is tall and strong*, it says. *He is dark-haired and does not age*. There are two drawings of him. In the first, he is in the water: his shoulders are grooved and muscular, and the tip of his tail can be seen. In the second he is on land. He walks on white, capable legs and he is watched by others who are amazed and smiling. Beneath this, it says *he comes ashore to restore hope and wonder!* He is bearded, and black-eyed.

Hope and wonder. Abigail smiles. She can hear her mother saying it. She can see her mother's long, straight hair falling down onto the page as she followed the words with her finger. *Once, long ago ...*

The northerly window frame rattles to itself. Jim lies beside her, breathing through his mouth so that he makes a soft, popping sound.

Abigail has not always believed. She did in the beginning. She believed absolutely just as her mother did, and so did Thomasina who claimed she'd seen his tail. They believed all the stories entirely – why should they not be true? *If we exist, why shouldn't they?* And it made Abigail feel safe, somehow – to know that seals understood her and a shell that knocks against your foot as you walk is *your* shell, meant for you, and that nobody actually ever really dies. She'd smile in her bed, to think of this. But then Mercy did die. And a little after, Thomasina died too, and Abigail's faith was swept out of Wind Rising and lost like autumn leaves are lost – scattered and not coming back. *Where is the Fishman, with his bright eyes? Where are the whales that speak of love?* How she wanted to see them. How she wanted proof. She'd cry so that her tears dampened her bed-sheets; she'd wear her twin's coat to bed and snuffle into its sleeves. And one night, Abigail looked at the pictures in her mother's book and thought *please ... Send me a sign.* Something to prove that the people she loved were not truly gone; something to show her that yes, there are souls, and yes, there is magic, and there are reasons behind everything so that nothing is ever over, or lost. *Please ...* And as if the Fishman heard her or as if the seals heard and passed the message on, there was a new sighting of him. Not by Abigail; Abigail didn't see him. But the lighthouse-keeper's son did. The awkward, slightly spotty boy called Jim confessed that yes, he had seen him – a bearded man and a mirrored tail, near the cove called Sye.

Over six decades have passed since then. Six decades, and Abigail can't climb over stiles any more. Her feet tend to be blue-coloured so she has to prop them on a stool, when she sits. So much has been and gone. And for six decades she has believed in something she herself has never seen but has longed to. *And he is here now.*

I have been waiting. That is how it feels – as if the Fishman has always meant to come to her and this – *now* – is his chosen time.

Abigail settles back, closes her eyes.

Hope and wonder. There has never been more need for a touch of that. These are not good days – with all the world's troubles that she hears on the radio; war in dusty countries, abductions that chill her to the bones. Who is making money on this island, now? No-one is making money. They count coins like beans. Fleece and meat make so little; lobsters do not always come and tourists are the same. No-one seems to have *plans* as such – no little dreams that may one day be made tangible – and when did that happen? When did the dream-making end? The ambitions, however small? Hers had been small, but she'd had them: a husband, a safe place, a solid Parlan life. Good health for the ones she loves.

And there is so much sadness too. It is a sad isle, for certain. Abigail sees it, and feels it: it is on everything and left there, like salt.

He will come ashore for one or for many.
He will only stay until the next full moon.

She turns out the light. *Folklore and Myth* lies on the floor beside her; twice in the night she will visit the bathroom, and both times she will bend down to feel its leather edges. It is more than a book to her, as this man is far more – far more – than just a man.

Four

Can you see him now? Legs that seem to have no end? The dark matting of his hair that, if a hand was laid there, would cover that hand? His body was hard, too – harder than other bodies, as if he was not only skin and bones. Was he even human? He felt stronger than all the humans I'd known and it made me ache – this strength under my palms, this anchor.

But I do not touch him yet.

I have not even met him – but I will.

He is looking at the ceiling of the mending room. He looks without blinking – the white paint, the single hair-thin crack.

He can smell the sea. Also he can hear it, and he lifts his head. He tries to sit up, and in doing this there is the bed's creak, and the dragging sound of his dry heels against the cotton sheets.

Curtains move; the window is open.

He can also hear footsteps. They grow louder. *Pat, pat.*

* * *

Tabitha knows he is awake before she comes into the room. A nurse's intuition, perhaps, or a woman's. She pushes the door and she is right – he is there, trying to sit up. His arms are bent and he is wincing. She puts down the water she is carrying and says *careful! Careful! Here – let me help ...*

He has been sleeping for over thirty-six hours. In that time she has watched him turn, heard him murmur; she has held glasses of water to his lips, whispered *drink* – and he has drunk. So she knows that he is real enough. But seeing him now – awake, moving ... He is even larger as he moves. His chest is defined as chests, on Parla, don't tend to be so that a deep cleft runs down from his throat to his waist.

He exhales, as if pained.

Are you OK?

A thick, even beard. Hair like a thatch. There is sand, also. Last night, she'd cleaned sand from his skin, ears and nostrils but not from his hair – and it is on the pillow, in the crook of his elbow and in the creases of the sheets.

Do you understand me?

He gives a single nod.

Good. Tabitha blushes. The question seems childish. She hands him the glass of water. *You need to keep drinking.*

He takes the glass.

Where does she start? What can she say? *Do you know where you are?*

A flinch, which is *no*.

On an island called Parla. You were found on a beach the night before last. Do you remember the beach?

She watches him drink – the long draws of water and the movement of his throat. He drains the glass, lowers it. *A beach?*

Yes. A stony one. She takes the glass from him.

The man shakes his head.

I'm the nurse. Tabitha. Bright. My father kept a lighthouse so it's a fitting surname. Her smile is quick. *Your name?*

For a moment he looks at her. Then he turns his stare away and looks out of the window, at the dark-green nettle patch and the sea beyond. He is thinking. He thinks for a long time and in that time Tabitha looks at his profile, the lines on his forehead. She hears the grandfather clock in the hall. *I don't know –*

You don't know your name? Really?

I'm sorry ...

It's alright. It will come, I'm sure. No headaches?

No. And he looks troubled, then. He looks lost, so that Tabitha lays her hand on his forearm. It is all she can think of doing. He has come from the sea like driftwood. He has no memory and marks on his hand that she cannot fathom, and this is like an old, old tale that is hard to have faith in, in modern times. She is sixty-five, and it's the twenty-first century, and surely there are no mysteries left? Falling in love is serotonin. Phosphorescent water is not God's light.

Yet here he is. Sea-smelling.

Do you remember anything?

Being in the water.

Good. That's something. She pats his arm. *How about food? You must be hungry.*

No answer.

A drink, then? Tea?

He says *tea ...* And he says it as if he does not know what *tea* could be, or perhaps he is agreeing to it – Tabitha can't tell which. But he says *tea ...* again, and he looks grateful, very tired.

Tea for two. She smiles. *I'll be back in a minute. You stay put.*

She goes to the kitchen, feeling happy. She puts the kettle on.

The wind lifts a flake of rust from a car, at High Haven. The ivy that grows on the minister's house taps against the wood.

Alfie Moss is by the primary school. It is closed for the summer but he stands in its playground all the same. He does a clumsy somersault on the fence and when he lands he wipes his nose on his bare arm.

The primary school is three rooms in a grey stone building. It has a single classroom with its desk, globe, and its stack of plastic drawers with the children's names taped on them. It has a whiteboard at one end that squeaks when his mother writes on it. There is also a tiny kitchen and beside it there are two toilet cubicles – one with a pink door, and one with blue. Alfie uses the blue one, as do the three other boys that catch the boat from Utta. He doesn't live on Utta; Alfie lives next door.

Alfie steps back from the fence. He is checking his palms for splinters when he hears footsteps, looks up. His mother is coming down the path; her hair is a cloud and the gold cross around her neck catches the light as she comes. She shouts *Alfie! We're late – into the car.*

They drive down towards the harbour – past the viewpoint, and the airstrip. Alfie presses his nose to the glass. He squints at each person who passes. He has heard there is a new man on the island – he came from the sea and he has no name. He has heard, too, that he looks a bit like Uncle Tom. But Alfie is too young to really remember his uncle Tom.

* * *

Three times a week the ferry comes and goes. For nearly a century, a boat called the *Morning Star* has made its way across the sea, tilting left to right and followed by gulls. This ferry – the vessel that sits in the harbour now – is the third to be called this, so it has *Morning Star III* painted on its prow and perhaps it is larger than the *Stars* that came before. But it has the same blue bottom. The same white railings with lifebelts on.

On two days – Monday and Wednesday – it leaves Parla and sails directly to the mainland and back. It is nearly a two-hour journey in each direction when the weather is kind, or when Ed does not peel away from the usual route to follow a dolphin pod or a whale's spray. In the summer, he often does this – for the passengers are mostly holiday-makers who live in cities, far from the coast. For them, a flash of back in the water is a gift, and he loves how they point, say *look! There!* In choppy sea the journey may take over three hours. In high winds or high water, the *Star* does not run at all.

On Fridays, it makes its way over via the other isles. For these other, smaller islands this is the only ferry service that they have – one boat every seven days. Parla is busy and easy to reach compared to these strangely shaped rocks: Utta, with its standing stones and cluster of salt-walled homes; Say, with the many sea stacks that gannets whiten; and Cantalay, where there is a single sheep farm and a ruined fort that the wind whistles through in winter. Merme is uninhabited, now. No boats go to it. Nothing does, except the puffins and they do not stay long.

Today it's Friday. Today, the *Star* will go out to these islands. It will creep in and out of their harbours, carry lives and luggage elsewhere. The ferry is fuelled and ready. Its white railings are shining in the morning light. The metal gangplank which the passengers must walk upon is also white and when it is lowered down onto the quayside there is a sudden, hard chime which sends up the gulls, makes a black cat flinch down against the ground.

It is nine twenty in the morning. There is a slight glint of dew on the fields and there is already heat in the sun. Most of the islanders are at the harbour. The grass verge that leads down to it has their cars parked upon it – cars with no wing mirrors or hubcaps, and most have dents in their sides. Hester steps out of a hatchback, pulls open the door behind her seat saying *out out out* to Alfie.

As they walk down, they pass a purple car. Its passenger door is open and a small, denim-covered bottom is beside it; its owner's head and body are still inside the car. There is the smell of baking, and ginger. Hester glances inside as she passes – she sees the dark butter icing of a chocolate cake. Alfie does too – *Mum, look ...* They hurry down to the *Morning Star*.

Rona straightens herself, sees them go. In her arms she carries six plastic, airtight boxes. They are transparent – they hold scones, chocolate cake, iced gingerbread, a cheesecake with grated limes, flapjack with apricots, and a huge, powdered Victoria sponge that's filled with home-made jam. She rests her chin on the uppermost box, shuts the car door with her foot.

On the quayside itself are the island's men. Edward Lovegrove, of course. He wears a luminous jacket with matching trousers and a baseball cap with *Skipper* on it. He takes the cargo – suitcases, bicycles, cardboard boxes – and puts it in a crate that rests next to the boat. *Anything else?* He calls this out and Rona quickens her step. *Yep, Dad!* Her car keys are hanging from the back pocket of her jeans and they jangle as she hurries.

There are other men in bright-yellow clothing – the crew, the men who have worked on *Morning Star* for years, or all their adult lives in some cases. George Moss

– late fifties and not yet greying – stands at the end of the gangway, a rolled cigarette between his thumb and fore-finger as if throwing a dart. He sees his wife and son coming. Alfie waves cheerily. *On you hop*, George tells him. Hester's hair is wild-looking, today – the curls are tight like springs and he loves it like this, wants to push his hands into it and grip those curls at their roots. He winks at his wife as she passes.

Sam Lovegrove and Jonny Bundy are also in fluorescent yellow. They are both on board, making the ferry's final checks – securing lines, checking lists on clipboards, hand-ing out brown paper bags just in case the water gets rough. Sam has not slept properly for two nights now and it shows in his face. There are shadows under his eyes; the sunburn has lessened against his pale skin. Jonny is by the winch. He leans over the side of the boat, watching Ed pack up the crate. Rona, he thinks, is looking good today. She always looks good – but those jeans are tight and when she peers over the side of the crate to make sure her cakes are packed well, and safely, he can see down her top for a moment. White lace – *very nice*. She has sunglasses pushed up into her hair.

Nine twenty-five. Ed shouts, *last call!* Kitty hears this and kisses Nathan. She carries an overnight bag, steps onto the gangplank. She pauses to say something to the skipper who laughs, touches her shoulder. Two tourists are the last ones on – clanking with binoculars, sour-breathed from the seasickness pills they have taken, sad to be leav-ing Parla for city life.

Sam lets them pass. Then, at that moment, puts a hand on either side of the gangplank and leans down from the deck. *George?*

The older man treads out his cigarette, looks up.

Has Maggie been? Haven't seen her yet.

He nods. *On the far side. Under the tarpaulin.*

She must have come early.

She was waiting for us. Maybe seven thirty? She's done herself proud, though. One of them is a monster.

Sam steps back. He goes to the far side of the ferry. Sure enough, he finds the black plastic crate with tarpaulin on it, and he crouches down beside it. Slowly, he peels the covering aside. The lobsters shift as he does this. Their smell is fishy and cold. They are midnight-coloured, their claws tied with elastic bands, and he wonders what time Maggie went out to get them this morning – first light? Maybe it was still dark when she went. *Maybe*, he thinks, *she's not sleeping either*, and he imagines her, in that little boat – hat and gloves, setting out at dawn. The birds would still have been roosting. Perhaps the first sign of daylight was a pink glow in the east and she would have seen it – on her own, in that boat.

Everything about Maggie makes him sorry.

He covers the lobsters back over, secures the tarpaulin to keep them safe.

*　　*　　*

On Fridays, the boat doesn't come back. It takes nearly three hours to dock at the three smaller islands, making the journey to the mainland nearly five hours long, in the end. It's too much to return the same day. So tonight, the *Morning Star* and its crew will stay overnight in the mainland's harbour with the stacked lobster pots and fishing fleet. That's a pungent harbour, ten times bigger than Parla's. It has the ferry office, a youth hostel, a small museum of fishing life, The Bounty Inn with its picnic tables and a trailer which sells cockles in paper cones. The gulls are bold, beady-eyed. Some will take a chip right out of your hand, and laugh as they eat it – *ark-ark!*

Nancy knows all this.

She sits cross-legged on the sea wall. She looks at the quayside, the dark sand and the *Star*.

Ferry day, in Nan's head, is *her* day – or her family's. Her father runs the boat. He runs the whole harbour and has to write down which boats come in and out, and he has to listen to the radio each night to hear what the weather will do. If it's too rough to sail, he runs a red flag up a pole. Nan likes that flag. It is the same height as her bedroom window, and it goes *snap* in the gales as if it's talking to her. He marks down sightings of whales, too, and rare birds. But Nan's father spends most of his time caring for the ferry. He polishes the brass bits, scrubs down the deck, sponges the green mould from the life-rings that hang on her sides. Sometimes, the ferry is hauled out of the water and run up onto rails as if she were a train. This is the boat's dry dock. Nan has stood beneath her as the *Star*'s rested there, and looked up. It feels like looking up a fat lady's skirt.

The ferry will leave any minute.

She squints. The winch lifts the crate from the quayside. It swings a little so that her father puts his hands up against it, guides it across. Jonny operates the winch from the boat. Nan isn't too keen on Jonny. He once called her a *rat*, as if she couldn't hear, and Rona doesn't like him much either. *Creepy Jonny Bundy* which sounds like a nursery rhyme.

Rona. Nan studies her. She can see a beaded chain on her sister's left ankle and her toenails are painted bright pink. Rona is watching the crate because her cakes are in it. She makes cakes for her tea room at the lighthouse, but she also makes them for a café on the mainland – a café with dried starfish in its window and deckchairs outside. Nan has been there, with their mother. Last summer they went. They had banana bread and a coconut slice, both made by Rona two days before. In loud voices they said how good the cakes were, how they were the best they'd ever had in all their living days and everyone should try some so that the café would order more.

Nan's favourite cake in the world is a chocolate brownie. Definitely. For her sixth birthday she had a plate of brownies, with actual cherries in. That was her best birthday yet.

Her father and brother are on the *Morning Star*.

Her mother and sister are on the quayside, watching it.

Ferry day is our day. The gangplank is pulled up, on board. The ferry begins to shudder, the water behind it starts to churn and very slowly the *Star* turns from the quay. She can see Alfie Moss, waving. She can see her brother Sam, too – his yellow hair which she is sometimes jealous of. Kitty is also on board – her skirt is blowing and she wears sunglasses so that Nan can't tell what she is looking at. Perhaps she is looking at Nathan, but he is not looking at her. His hands are in his pockets, and he's looking at the ground. Maybe there's a shell, there? Or a beetle? He looks at the ground for a very long time.

*   *   *

There is a track which leads from Crest towards the most northerly part of the coast. At the cliff edge, there's a fence – wire that sags, rotting posts. There is a sign by a break in this fence which reads *Do Not Use In Wet Weather* – but Maggie has often used these steps when the rain has been so heavy that it has bruised her. She's used them in a thunderstorm. She's used them at night.

They are slick, black steps cut into the rocks and which lead down to a small harbour. Uneven steps, and steep. Once, perhaps, they'd been used for smuggling since the lighthouse's beam never reaches them and they can't be seen from the sea; but they are not used for that now. They wind down into darkness and end, abruptly, on a slab of rock. This slab is the quayside. It is lost entirely at high tide and so it is both rough with barnacles and velvety with weed, and Maggie is careful when treading on it. She comes here three times a week, or more: *Pigeon* is kept here.

Pigeon. Named by Maggie herself, long ago.

So she can always find her way home.

Maggie started early today. She dressed in the half-dark, made a flask of tea, put a head-torch on and made her way down those steps. She looked east, as she readied the boat. She looked through the harbour's narrow opening and saw the dawn – pink, grey, the last blue of night.

And she'd hauled on the cord to start the outboard motor, thrummed across the water, past Sye and Bundy Head. A cool, early morning. The smell, always, of fish and diesel fumes. She'd felt the motor's vibration, heard the quiet slosh at her feet of water that had come aboard in various ways – off the pots, or rainwater – and it is the same every time. It does not change – how *Pigeon* smells, how the silence rushes in when she turns the engine off. There are the same rituals as there always were, and she finds a comfort in them. *Pigeon* is familiar. So are the orange fibreglass buoys, the sound of the sea against the boat's sides, the gulls that follow hopefully, the ghostly loom of the lobster pots as she pulls them up from the dark.

Nothing changes on Parla. That's what she was told, when she first came. *It stays the same – just so you know ...* And Maggie had loved that. She'd loved the idea of a safe, strong, unchanging life. Just Tom, and her, and the water.

But then he died. And everything changed. *Nothing changes here* proved, in fact, to be the greatest of all lies. He died and so much died with him; countless more things were lost. She learnt this: that grief changes more than you ever thought it could. All certainty goes away. All strong things stop being strong. Tom was there and then he was not: and so what could be relied upon? Nothing felt safe any more: a lone sock felt symbolic; an embrace from a friend seemed like a trap; letters had no meaning or too many meanings so that *sorry for your loss* felt coded, impenetrable, too hard to understand. Maggie believed, for a time, that she was being lied to. She'd eyed others, looking for that lie. *Nothing can be trusted* – to be kind, or safe, or to stay with her.

I will not feel or care for anything. I will rely on nothing.

But no-one can live like that. Maggie tried to be self-reliant, and hard – but she could not fully. She had to give shape to her days. She had to hold her hand out or she'd sink, she knew that. And it was routines that Maggie turned to. Tentatively, she sought comfort in small, necessary, practical things – so she'd make proper coffee in a cafetiere, clean the bath, pluck tomatoes from her plants and inhale their bitter smell. She'd pull the cord on *Pigeon* as she used to when Tom was still living. She'd bind the claws of lobster with coloured elastic bands.

And this place. Coming here.

Maggie is walking, now. She has left the half-moon harbour; she is walking down the island's western coast. *The wild west*, Tom called it: bare, fully exposed. No other islands lie to the west of Parla; from here, there is only the open sea. And centuries of storms and thundering water have battered it – picked off rocks, and scooped out caves so that this coastline echoes. The sea booms; the birds wail. She hears them now, as she walks.

This was her routine, too: she'd walk on this coast at every low tide. For two years Maggie would come, twice daily – so she has come to know each stile, each thistle patch, each rabbit hole. She knows each track through the gorse, how the word *Tom!* bounces back to her from every dank cave wall. And in the early days, before she believed that he was truly gone, and not returning, she'd step down the wooden staircase onto Lock-and-Key and tread across its sand. For it is on this beach that a whale stranded itself, where the best shells have come, where there has been driftwood so smooth and bleached by the waves that they looked like bones and it's here that Maggie has found pottery shards and a piece of glass that had been so worn, so turned over and over by the sea that it had been rolled into a ball. A marble as green as an eye. There is a fence, too, on which those lost rubber boots have been hung – boots that have been washed ashore without their other, matching halves – so they look out to sea forlornly. And if something of worth – something she'd loved, and still loved – was to wash ashore, she has always believed it would be here. *This beach*.

Lock-and-Key. Named because the headland to its south is shaped, or partly, as the beach is. It has the same outline, but inverted. *One might fit the other ... If you squint*. So she was told.

Maggie steps down the staircase now.

The row of rubber boots is still here – still waiting.

Tom. Who knew all the beaches. He knew each cave, each promontory. Tom was Parlan entirely, and so he knew the history of houses, the names in the graveyard, how puffins fly, how to coax the lugworm out, how to read the weather by clouds or a sheep's positioning, how to cook mussels in garlic and white wine. So many stories in his head – of love and loss, of the old pig farm. Maggie had been in awe of this.

You're lucky, she'd told him.

I feel it. Kissing her.

She was told time would help. People said it to her, meaning well: *give it time ...* But time does not help. All that happens with time is that you grow tired – so hugely, indescribably tired. He was everywhere and nowhere. He was in the gold band on her finger but he was not in the house, not in their bed. And she began to grow tired of walking on this beach: walking on this beach meant she was looking at each sodden piece of cloth, each inch of rope, each footprint in the sand thinking *is that his ...?* She would hurry towards new driftwood. She'd make her way to each line of faded plastic in case it held a clue. And one dusk – one awful, half-lit, winter dusk – she'd thought she'd seen a person lying on Lock-and-Key. In the gloom, she saw it: a dark and indefinable shape at the water's edge. So she ran. She dropped to her knees as she reached it. She plunged her hands into the shape, gasping, swearing, saying *Tom* with sand in her mouth and tears in her eyes – and it was weed. Just weed. Two metres or more of tangled wrack which had fooled her, briefly, in the evening light. And she knelt by that weed, and sobbed. *He is not coming back to me. He is not coming back to me.* She knew, she knew. She knew he was not. She had to admit this, kneeling there.

Maggie never wants another moment like that moment – no more crouching next to weed. No more *Tom!* – sand-tasting. And so for four years she has tried to live a small life. A safe life. No changes.

No hope, and no loss.

But now this ... A man. A man has come ashore. Nathan says *just passing* and she spills her yellow paint, and for one tiny, impossible moment ...

Maggie closes her eyes. The wind finds her hair and it tugs, tugs.

I have to see this man. She must. He is not Tom; she knows he is not. But he is a new, rolled mass of weed; he is a new indefinable shape that she must kick at, at least, to make sure of. For otherwise, she will always be thinking *what if ...?*

She will see him tomorrow.

This human driftwood. This jetsam that washed up with more unwanted things.

*   *   *

He is sleeping again. He is upright but his eyes are closed. Tabitha smiles, and takes the empty mug from his hand.

People are children again, when they sleep. Their frown lines go and their worries do, so that they lie as they would have lain in their childhood beds. She's seen it enough. Her brother-in-law, Jack Bundy, was a fierce, bad-tempered piece by day but she found him sleeping in the armchair once, and his left hand was near his face as if trying to hide himself or, even, suck his thumb. He'd looked like a boy, not a middle-aged man. *And if Jack Bundy could look sweet-natured ...*

She brings the blankets around her patient. She wonders, briefly, who else has done this for him – for whoever he is, he'll have had a mother. Does he have a wife? There is no ring. No white mark where a ring has been.

Amnesia. It's a new one for her. Nearly half a century since she became a nurse, and how many amnesiacs has she met? She will have to research it – books, online.

Tabitha pads through to her kitchen.

It is small, square. It is dark, too, for its single window looks out onto a bank of grass. A sheep has been here this morning – she can see its fresh droppings, berry-bright. Tabitha exhales, picks up the phone. The task she must do is motherly.

Hello? It is answered after two rings.

Em, it's me.

What do you want?

I have a request ...

There is silence from her sister.
Well – it's this …

*　　*　　*

The quayside is empty, and still. Nancy cannot see anyone now – just their black cat and a gull that walks like a man in a waistcoat, his hands behind his back. The gull has eyed the cat; the cat, in turn, is treading in the shadows, keeping her distance. As a kitten, she got pecked at; her ear is split at its tip.

Nancy shuffles forwards, drops down onto the sand. There is a shell here – blue, and chalky inside. She brings it right up to her eye and looks at it. It is joined, with two halves and when she presses those halves together the shell clacks, like a mouth.

She makes the shell say *hello* to the cat. *Hello* to the mean-looking gull.

What have you there, little Nancy?

The voice makes her jump. She turns. It is old Mrs Coyle with her walking stick and her butterscotch breath. She has made her way down from the white house, near the sea wall. There is a line of sweat between her nose and mouth. Mrs Coyle dabs at it.

Another lovely morning. All this lovely weather!

She tucks the tissue up her sleeve.

May I join you?

They sit side by side on the harbour's bench. Nan swings her legs. *It's a shell.*

And a fine one, too. A mussel shell. Look at that blue …

I found it down there.

Well, they're common enough. Have you eaten mussels?

Nan shakes her head. She likes doing this, as she has glass bobbles at the end of her plaits which knock against each other. She shakes her head more than she needs to.

Your brother could find you some, I'm sure. Whilst he's out walking.

Nan picks at some grit she finds in the shell. She is not sure what to say to Mrs Coyle, or what to say about mussels, so she says *Sam found a person on Wednesday night. He was washed up at Sye.*

So I heard.

Daddy says he probably fell off a boat.

Does he? Perhaps.

Nan looks up. *Do you think he did?*

Fell overboard?

She nods.

Well, perhaps. It's nine miles to the mainland, which would be a very long swim.

She squints at the ferry. *Is he a ghost, maybe?*

Oh I think he's real enough. Your brother carried him! So did the Bundy men. If he was a ghost how could they carry him?

A pirate?

No pirates.

Nan studies the shell. *I think he's a pirate.*

No, no. I don't think so.

Who do you think he is, Mrs Coyle?

Abigail smiles. *Me?* She stays quiet for a moment. She takes the tissue out, dabs her nose and pops it back again. Then she leans towards Nancy and says *do you like stories?*

Stories?

Yes. I thought most children liked stories.

Only good ones.

Ah! Very wise. Have you heard of the Fishman?

She looks up from her shell. *A Fishman?*

The Fishman. A man who has the tail of a fish, but he can also grow legs and come ashore?

Nan stares. *He's a fish? A fish who grew legs?* She looks down at the shell, wide-eyed. Maybe she has heard the story. Maybe Alfie told her in the playground once. And there is a book on her shelf – a pink spine, with thick cardboard pages – which has a mermaid in it, and so she turns and says *like a mermaid?*

Abigail considers this. *Yes, in a way. But it's always a man in the stories – a strong, bearded, good-looking man.*

The mussel shell goes *clack.*

My husband saw him, once. At Sye.

Nan's eyes grow like moons.

Jim was young, but he remembers it. Says he looked up from the beach and saw a man swimming – a man with dark hair, and a very solemn face. Then he went under, and where he had been swimming there rose a huge, silvery tail …

Mr Coyle saw him? Properly?

He did.

And this is him? This man is the Fishman he saw? But he's got legs now?

Abigail smiles. *Why not? Humans think they know everything but there is so much more.*

They are watched, as they talk. One of the oldest and the youngest inhabitants of Parla, side by side on the wrought-iron bench.

Dee Lovegrove stands in her bedroom. She has taken a pillowcase off the radiator, and she folds it by the window. Outside, she can see them. Nancy is wearing her denim dungarees with the heart-shaped buttons. She insisted on plaits this morning but one is already escaping its band and there's mud, Dee notes, on her knees. Never, ever tidy. Nan discards clothing like petals, sticks her fingers into all manner of dirt. It was sheep dung last week, and diesel the week before. Little Nancy Lovegrove. Dee feels a pang of love. It is the sudden punch of it that she always feels with her children – Nan's reddened knees, or how Sam puts his sunglasses on, patting the sides to make sure they're in place. Today, Rona had looked so beautiful, standing on the quayside with her arms full of cakes and Dee had watched her step back from the crate, shield her eyes against the sun. Dee had thought, *she's mine*. All grown up.

And her other boys, too. After Sam, there came the twins – as alike as shoes are. In the first few years of their life, it was Dee and Dee alone who knew who was who, and it was their ways that told her, not how they looked. Ben would gaze past her, as he lay on the changing mat; he'd watch a bee or a bird's shadow on the bedroom wall – whilst Austin's eyes would be on her, and her alone. Austin spoke first by three weeks. Yes, Dee knew who was who.

A pang, too, for those boys. Where are they now? Backpacking. Sticky with mosquito repellent, drinking beer with foreign names. Meeting girls, no doubt. Austin claimed he would not shave again till he was home, and Dee tries to imagine it – that wriggling tot on the flowery changing mat being able to grow facial hair at all. Ben wants to get his eyebrow pierced. How did it happen? *Be safe, boys. Drop me a postcard, sometime.*

But they fly. It is what the fledged birds must do, and she's always known that. The nest can't always be full.

She looks at Nan. Nancy aged six and three-quarters, who is far from fledged, thank God. There are the great surprises in life, and then there is Nan who was conceived after half a bottle of sweet sherry and a fumble on the sofa when Dee was nearly forty-four. She'd thought it was her menopause until she was sick in the footwell of the car. *The risks* ... Ed had been nervous. But a life had been made so the life must be born. And now that life is swinging her legs on the bench outside.

Above them, and above the stone wall, is the sea. Wide, wide water. In the far distance is the white dot of the *Morning Star* and the trail of white water she leaves in her wake. It will be a house of girls tonight – just Dee and her youngest daughter. She wraps her arms around herself. Her other son, too, is on the *Star* – her second oldest child, with his stoop and silences, with his migraines which make him whimper with the pain. Sam, who loiters near Crest, runs along the coastal path or stays in his room, lifting weights. He does not do much more than this. No speaking, no letting go of the old ghosts. He trawls his self-blame as boats trawl their nets; it gathers everything, and slows him down, and one day she fears he'll go under.

*   *   *

At Lowfield, the nurse is outside. She stands in her garden and watches the wind, as it blows through the grass. The nettle patch at Litty whitens, for the undersides of the leaves are paler than their tops. She loves these small moments.

In comes a car with a broken exhaust.

Emmeline parks, and climbs out. She leans into the back of the car and lifts out a large black plastic bag; the plastic has stretched and greyed in places where Emmeline's fingers have been. *Here.*

Perfect. Tabitha goes to it. The bag is passed over as a child might be – with the nurse's hand going underneath it, bringing the bag to her chest. *I'm sorry I had to ask, but it's all I could think of.*

I'll want them back.

You'll get them back. Of course you will.

And I don't want them torn. Or damaged.

They're already torn and damaged – aren't they?

Emmeline sniffs, ignores her. *Has he said anything yet?*

Not much.
His name?
No. Thank you for these. And Tabitha goes inside.

In the kitchen, she unties the bag and reaches in. There is a cream shirt, a blue jumper with a hood. Socks. T-shirts. They are clothes that Tabitha partly remembers. They were Tom's – fraying, stained or worn-out clothes that he'd kept at his mother's house. For once he'd met Maggie, he'd wanted to make room for her clothes – in his wardrobe, up at Crest.

Tabitha makes a sound – a sigh, perhaps.

She knows the human body is muscles and veins. She studied it for years, and has learnt how blood is pumped, the names of bones, where the organs are, which diseases and afflictions can damage the body itself – but there will always be things she cannot know. Is there a soul? She is undecided. Easy to say there is not. But at this moment, Tom is with her. Tom, or a part of him, fills the room entirely: it is as if he's sitting with her, or leaning over her shoulder as she breathes these clothes in. For she is sure she can smell the soap, breath, hair and lemony aftershave of the man, her nephew, who's been dead for four years. She finds him – or an essence of him – on these folded clothes.

The sun lowers. The grass darkens, and cools.

In Wind Rising, Constance is knitting. This is how she earns a little income – making mittens, hats and blankets and selling them online. She listens to the radio, as she knits. The news is as it always is – weighted, sad.

At Lowfield, there is *tick-tick-tick*. Tabitha types *am--nesia* into the computer, and scrolls down.

A mouse waits, waits, and then runs the length of a wall.

And this: *Have you seen him yet?*

Leah reads this on the screen of her mobile phone.

She replies: *Not yet. Soon.*

It is how they are – Sam and her. Once they had been more than this. Once, they were playmates in the simplest form of the word – pushing each other on swings, lying in the long grass, fishing for crabs with nylon wire. They'd sit side by side on the *Star*, as it took them to secondary school. But that changed. After Tom's accident, Sam was blamed; Leah's father said *don't talk of that boy in this house – do you hear?* She could neither speak of him, nor see him; and Sam had no real wish to be seen. So their friendship became distant; it chose to exist as words on a screen. Now, it is formed of secret, night-time messages that no-one else will ever see. That, and not much else.

The blame is less, these days. Sam's name is mentioned in Wind Rising again; he is not called *that boy* ... But nearly four years later and this is still how Sam and Leah speak – with their thumbs and silently, alone in their bedrooms. An odd form of friendship but it suits them. Odd – yet no less real or tender as it had been when they were younger, peering into puffin holes. More tender, even. Certainly more wise.

*   *   *

Midnight. Past midnight.

Three people are still awake.

Maggie lies in the dark. She imagines her husband sitting down on the bed. He used to take her fingers and kiss them one by one, and that's how she knew what he was hoping for. It would be the start of it – one kiss, then two …

And beyond Crest, beyond the footpath that leads to Sye, a bedroom light is on. Downstairs, in the old lighthouse-keepers' quarters, Rona stands by her sink. She smiles. She counts under her breath, knowing exactly how many seconds lie between each flash of the light. *Nearly, nearly* … And so the room lights up.

She is lit up, also. Briefly, her skin is white.

It also lights up the man who is with her. He is untying her apron, feeling the back of her neck with his thumb. She feels his hands upon her. She turns.

I made your favourites, today.

Did you, now?

Fruit scones, and …

Stop talking, Nathan whispers. The light turns, so that the room is in darkness. He fills up her mouth with his mouth.

The Giants and what became of them

On the tenth page of Abigail's book called *Folklore and Myth* there is a drawing of four columns of rock. Sea stacks. *Sea towers*, some call them. For long ago, Parla's wild, western sea carved four pillars out from the coast, and left them standing awkwardly. They make a strange picture and they make a strange sight, from Lock-and-Key. And like all strange things or all things of beauty, they have a story to them. I knew they would have. As soon as I saw them I stopped, said *what are they? Over there? What's their story?*

He told me. In turn, I gave him a soft, teasing push. *Giants? Tom! There were never giants …*

Don't laugh – even though he was laughing, too. *You wanted a story, did you not, Maggie-May?*

*   *   *

It was many years ago. On each of these islands there lived a giant and each giant was feared, in its own way. On Merme, there was one who breathed a black fire and these flames burnt the mountains away; it is why Merme is flat, even now. Cantalay's giant groaned, thunder-like. The giant on Say had a murderous heart and he spent his days making weapons out of the broken rocks. He stored these weapons in a cave. There are stalactites in that cave, even now – moon-white, and dripping. The Sayans say they are the giant's swords and that one day he'll come back for them and that will be a dark day.

Utta had a giantess, or so it goes. She had long, swinging breasts and a heavy gait that cracked the earth so that rivers were made – and it's true that Utta has plenty of rivers whilst the other isles do not. It sings with streams, on rainy days. They all find their way to the sea.

And Parla? What of the Parlan giant? How vast and terrible was he?

He was not vast and he was not terrible. He was small, shy, ashamed of his kind. The Parlans did not fear him and they did not fear the tall dune grass that he lived amongst, near Store Bay. They fed him, sometimes. In turn, he might lift their boats from the water or plough a furrow with his hand. The giant made hollows in the sand at Store which have not gone away.

The other giants mocked him. Too quiet. Too kind.

One day they called across the water. They claimed he had no strength at all. What giant was he? Who was not very tall and had no powers? Who brought shame upon them all, or so they said? They dared him to prove his strength.

Throw rocks, they chanted. *Lift the houses!*

No, said the Parlan giant.

Tear up the trees and toss them high!

No, he replied. *I will not.*

Scoop up the sea and fling it wide, so that boats may go under!

Never.

And they were so angered at his calmness, at his soft voice and softer soul, that the giants laid a curse upon the islanders – that all Parlans might be turned to stone. For what better way to punish him than to damage the ones that he loved? They flung the curse across the sea, like spray. But the giant's eyes were so mournful at the thought of this that they glinted, mirror-like, and they reflected the curse so that it returned to them. So the four sea stacks near Tap Hole are the four giants of Utta, Merme, Say and Cantalay – turned to stone by their own foul curse. One stack has a heavy upper half, with a cleft at its centre. They say that this stack is the giant-ess – that she has retained, in rock, her swaying female form.

*　　*　　*

Rona thinks of this. She thinks of the womanly sea stack – its curved parts, its higher weight. It makes her smile. A man, surely, dreamt of such a tale. A lonesome fisherman, perhaps, looked up at the stacks as he went by them and saw, on that third stack, two rounded rocks and the groove that runs between them and the slight hunch as if those breasts are too much to bear. At sea, so much is womanly. Boats are female. The winds are calmed by a bare female chest. Surely the work of lovesick sailors? Men with phys-ical love on their mind? Maybe a sailor, a long way from shore, might see his wife's body in the white surf or her long hair in the fronds of weed? He might hear her breath in the sea's sighing breath.

Sea shanties. All the best ones are about missing a girl.
Nathan sleeps beside her.

He lies on his front, his head turned away from her. Rona thinks of pushing her fingers into his hair; she wants to nuzzle him, move her left hand down. But these things will wake him. He sleeps lightly and she knows he needs his sleep.

I am a woman now. Once she'd been as dormant as the sea stacks are, but now Rona is awake – capable, assured. And she is in love with a married man. She is in love with this man, this farmer who rubs his chin as he's thinking, who presses his face into his upper arm when he sneezes – a neat, boyish sneeze. Has she always loved him? For a long time, at least. For a long time, each passing thing has made her think *Nathan* ... This man, sleeping here.

She does not believe in ownership. Rona rejects – or tries to – the idea that a vow and a handful of confetti means he can't be loved by, or be in love with, anybody else. Nobody is owned. He is, she tells herself, choosing this; he is lying in her bed because he chooses to. He could be elsewhere but he is not. *And I love him*. Rona has the fervent hard belief that all young lovers have – which is *no-one has loved like this before. Our love is stronger than all the other kinds.*

There is nothing she would not do for Nathan Bundy.

The lighthouse swings in, swings out.

Five

Leah wakes. She lies on her side, her legs tucked up. The curtains stir beside her, and she can smell the sea.

She stays as she is – no yawning, or stretching out. *If I stay perfectly still, it will be like I am still sleeping* – and the world will not know she has woken up. As a child, she'd play such games. She took to hiding in the coal bunker, or under the bed, and once she hid in the barn behind the tractor's back wheel so that her parents grew cross, and later, concerned. *What are you always hiding from?* Leah never quite knew.

She is nearly twenty-two and still pretending to sleep. On her last birthday, she had asked for nothing more than a sandwich lunch and a walk with her mother. Her gift had been a necklace which she had known was beautiful – her head had said, *this is beautiful. Look how it shines* – but her heart had felt nothing, as she'd looked at it. She saw how delicate it was. It was a pearl on the thinnest of gold chains and as her mother had stood behind her, fastening it, she'd said *there you are, my baby girl …*

Baby girl. That had been her name for the first ten days of life. *Baby Girl*, for they'd believed she was going to be a boy and so had no name prepared for her – no better, proper name. For those ten days, she could have had any name. And if they'd called her something else, not *Leah* but a different name, would she be like this now? Would she have a different nature? Different hopes, and fears? *Baby Girl* – like a blank page. Like a low-tide beach that had not yet been walked upon so that it seemed to be waiting for her and her alone.

Leah Grace Bundy. In it came. And she was happy, wasn't she? She has clear childhood memories – climbing the metal bars of the sheep pens, pushing chocolate buttons onto a birthday cake or hugging the pet rabbit, finding a coin where a milk tooth had been left. Yes, she was happy. Shy, watchful, self-contained – but happy, in her way.

Slowly, Leah sits up. She looks to her right, out of the window. Her bedroom is above the porch, so that when she was smaller she'd lean out of the window and see her father's bald spot, or the flowered hair grips that Aunt Kitty still likes to wear. There is a view of the driveway, too. The rooster who is threatened daily with the casserole dish is treading by the wire fence. His ladies – plump, gingery – peck at seed, or the flying ants which nest in the hardcore that is piled on one side. That hardcore was left there, after the laundry room was built. No-one's ever moved it, and ragwort sprouts there now. Driftwood is pinned to the gatepost; *Wind Rising*, it says.

This is the view she has had all her life. There was the secondary school on the mainland and, later, six weeks of university – but otherwise it has always been this.

The lane, running north to south. Beyond it, the roof of High Haven.

She gets out of bed. She takes down her dressing gown and fastens it. She's always been quiet, she knows that. But Leah wasn't always this heavy-hearted. This weight (*It*, as if it does not have a proper name) only came to her four years ago. She'd been on the mainland, at the time. She'd always longed to get there – to have a life of music, neon, buses, cinemas and adventure in a place with people she was not related to. No gulls, no lighthouses. Leah had been inland, walking the wood-panelled corridors of a university that smelt of books, aftershave, chalk dust. And she had liked it at first – she'd liked to pull back her curtains in the morning to a new view entirely; a cathedral spire over the rooftops, an office block that looked like a hundred eyes at night. But slowly, Leah altered. Or rather, everything altered except her. There were lectures, parties, libraries, alcohol, boys with friendly hands and girls with glittered make-up, and so much that was new – and yet Leah was still *Leah*. Still nervous. Still quieter than most. She'd look at the name she wrote on her essays – a first name too small to matter, a surname which dragged its anchor through the mud. *I am Parlan. I have a Parlan accent. I come from a line of surly farming men.* And so what was the point? What exactly was she trying for? All she saw were the painted words *Wind Rising*, the way a sheep would gallop frantically with its dragging fleece when they tried to catch it at shearing time. *Stupid*, she thought – to be studying textbooks or discussing poetry when she was rooted to Parla by name and birth. *I am out of my depth. I don't belong here.* In bars, they told jokes she didn't laugh at. They talked of bands she hadn't heard, of films she hadn't seen. They took drugs she didn't want so whilst they danced and sang and found dark corners, Leah sat on her own and looked at her trainers, at their sheep-dung and saltwater stains, and she knew that she was lost. Unmooring herself, day by day.

Uncle Tom helped. She'd call him, whisper *I'm not coping very well …* And he listened. He told her that she was bright, deserving, funny, remarkable – and loved. *So very loved, Leah. Remember that. Promise me?*

I promise.

Then he died. He went overboard in the autumn. Her mother had rung with the news so that Leah had heard about her uncle's vanishing whilst standing outside the Students' Union, with a low battery so that her mobile phone beeped like a hospital heart. A warm, gritty wind had blown around her. She'd said *gone? Uncle Tom? I don't understand* ... And if Leah had been struggling before, this buckled her; if she'd felt heavy up till then, this dragged her to the ground and kept her there. That was the start of her depression. What Leah refers to as *It*.

Leah walks across the landing, locks the bathroom door.

They say there is a family curse. Her great-great-grandfather Randall put his shotgun in his mouth one New Year's Eve. His son, her great-grandfather, had broken the bones in his wife and children, or so she'd heard behind closed doors. What had been the tale of Thomasina? And why are Leah's own family so mute, so reluctant to talk or smile or embrace? When her father stands in a room with Nathan or Hester, they do not say much and nothing that matters. They stand, arms folded.

But she will not think of the curse – not today.

The word *Fishman* has come.

Leah heard the word last night. Her mother said it over a saucepan, having passed Dee in the lane. *Abigail thinks he's the Fishman* ... and Leah had stared, put down her fork.

Fishman ...?

She turns on the taps. As the sink fills, she looks up at the air vent – hears its *tut-tut-tut*.

*　　*　　*

He sits on the edge of the wrought-iron bed. The blankets are around him, tucked up under his armpits. He rubs his right hand across his beard.

Tabitha says, *here you are. Some clothes.*

She lays them on the bed. There is a shirt, trousers, a grey jumper. Smaller items. He looks down, feels the edges of them and whilst he does this Tabitha leaves the room and then returns with a pair of boots hooked over her fingers. *I'm not sure what size these are, but try them on. They might do.*

Thank you.

The bathroom is down the hallway – last door on the right. There's a towel in there, and a toothbrush. Use whatever you need to.

Tabitha? It is the first time he has said her name. He has pushed himself off the bed, so that he is standing tentatively. His left hand still touches the mattress, but he stands straight, and keeps his balance. *Doesn't someone need these clothes?*

A fly is knocking against the windowpane. They both hear it. The nurse's eyes go to it, briefly; when she glances back she is resigned, half-smiling. *No* – a whisper. And then *no* a second time.

The bathroom, when he finds it, is small – the frosted sash window is propped open with a block of wood; ivy curls under the window, into the room. He touches its leaves. They feel waxy, and thick. The mirror is flecked with water marks – and it is low for him so he must stoop to see himself.

My face. My beard. His black eyes.

In time he washes. He turns on the showerhead over the bath. When the water has warmed, he lifts one leg over the side of the bath, hauls the rest of himself into it. It hurts to do this as if his body does not know these movements.

Once in, he tends to himself. He lathers up a soap and washes his hair, his torso and down to his thighs. Sand crunches under his heel. When he looks down he can see grains of it in the white enamel tub. It collects by the plug-hole, the colour of rust.

And his hands. He sees their grazed palms. On the looser skin of his left hand he sees the scar – round, reddish-brown.

It is all new, he thinks. *The ivy. This island.*

Parla. He says the word. He looks in the mirror, as he says it.

In his mind, there is a flickering. There is another word he wants to say. He wants to breathe it, as he has breathed it, lovingly, before. But he shakes the word away.

He towels himself. And then this man puts on a red-and-black checked shirt whose top three buttons he can't do up and a pair of jeans that are too short in the leg, too tight when fully buttoned so that he will, later, use Tabitha's safety pins – and the man they found at Sye unlocks the bathroom door.

* * *

To the north of the island, a ewe scratches her shoulder against the step of a stile. Back and forth. Her eyes are closed, feeling it.

And Rona opens the tumble-drier door. From its scented cave she hauls an armful of bed-sheets. They are warm as toast, and she carries them to the sitting room where she shakes them out and folds them. Today, five more guests will come. Here at the Lighthouse Hostel and Tea Room she has three white-walled dormitories – rooms which were once for the lighthouse-keepers and their families but which are now filled with bunk beds and lockers and *No Smoking* signs. This had been a sad place, for a time.

When the lighthouse was automated, the rooms were locked up. But six years ago Rona had pressed her face against the window of these buildings and imagined what she might do with them – a hostel, a café, a place of her own. *All things are possible* – so her mother always said. *If you want something enough, it can be.*

Rona knows about wanting.

She counts five pillow cases, five duvet covers. Five single sheets.

Upstairs, the dormitories have all been emptied for the day. Her guests will be walking the coastal path or heading down to Store Bay with their hats and windbreakers. Binoculars and picnic rugs. Why not? She'd be down there, too, if she could be. Rona was born on Parla, but she cannot remember such a row of cloudless days.

She had asked Nathan, *what will you do today?*

Repairs. Whilst the weather's good. It wasn't a good answer but she took it, heard its tone.

Nathan. There are things imprinted in her that she has carried since she was small – her love of baking, her birthmark like a star, how she can hold her breath underwater for longer than anyone she knows. Once, she swam Parla harbour without breaking the surface. She has carried her will which is stronger than most.

And *him.* She reckons he is part of her, now – like air in her lungs, or water. Him with the scar like a comma under his eye, and the skin on his waist that she has closed her teeth upon so that he flinched, said *ow …*

Rona throws a white sheet open, lays it across the bed. She tucks the corners down and as she straightens back up, she glances out of the window. The sea is at its bluest. She can see gannets, far out. Nearer to her, beneath the lighthouse, she sees the highest stones of Sye where no-one ever goes. She's heard about the man they found. Her father rang her on Thursday morning to ask if any of her guests had disappeared, so that she'd thought *there's been a suicide, or a fall from a cliff*, and she'd had to lean against the wall for reassurance. But all her guests had been accounted for. And she's not had any bearded men in their early forties stay at the lighthouse for a long time, if at all.

Who do you think he is? This man?

But Nathan had shrugged, turned away from her. And perhaps other people would have lain in the dark and thought about this stranger, but Rona thought, instead, of Nathan Bundy. Of what they'd been doing an hour before – her to him, and him to her.

Outside there are tables to be laid. Rona carries nine white tablecloths into the sunlight, and returns for the salt and pepper pots. Also she has stones – heavy, rounded stones – with numbers painted on them. They are cool in her hands. Five springs ago she'd gone down to Sye with a bucket and lifted the smoothest stones she could find – nine of them, all dry and pale-grey. Kitty had suggested it – *bring them to me, and I'll paint the numbers on, if you like.* Kitty the artist, with her silver rings – and how could Rona have refused it? Rona looks at the one she is holding. It is 8, and an orange-shelled crab is painted by it. 5 has a lobster. 1 and 3 have black-backed gulls. Customers have liked these table numbers. They have asked where they might buy them from – paperweights, for their inland homes. And Rona has said, *do you know the smaller farmhouse? With the cars outside? It is called High Haven ...*

4 is a whale, blowing its spout.

And there is more, of course. There are canvases on the café walls, inside – romantic landscapes called *Parla at Dawn*, or *Litty* or *View from Bundy Head*. *West-Facing* is the largest of Kitty's paintings – wide, red-coloured, the lighthouse silhouetted against a setting sun. It is the most expensive, too. Who would pay so much for them? Rona shakes her head, not understanding it.

There is, sometimes, guilt. She wants what she wants but Rona is, also, human. She thinks of how Kitty looks, when she paints – rimless glasses on the tip of her nose, her hair held back with a tortoiseshell clip or a fabric flower or, once, two wooden clothes pegs – and it hurts her. Kitty is so kind – and it makes this hard to do. But also, Kitty is different – bare-footed, with a wind-chime in the garden and a curious tattoo and she's talked about star signs before which no-one is sure of. She's *alternative*, perhaps – and surely that doesn't suit Nathan? Surely he needs a traditional wife, who understands the farm and island life? The weather, the sheep? How lonely the winter months can be?

This is what she tells herself. *I would be the better wife.*

The hems of the tablecloths shimmy like chorus girls.

When Rona licks her lips, she can taste his aftershave.

* * *

At this precise moment, the dog from School Cottage squats in the lane, and urinates. She leaves a dark patch behind her. A small snake of it creeps around pebbles, down into a ditch.

The rhododendrons rustle their leaves.

I am walking down to Lowfield. My thumbs are hooked into the pockets of my linen trousers and I wear a silver necklace with a tiny silver *M*.

The *Morning Star* has returned.

Ed stands on deck. He holds the hand-rails, looks down as the space between the *Star* and the quayside grows smaller and smaller; then he feels the gentle knock. Jonny jumps down from the boat. He lifts lines, and throws them back up to George. And soon, George whistles. *All done.*

Ed crouches. He and Sam lower the gangway so that it hits the quayside with that high, strong chime that the skipper loves. It means *safe*. It means *home*.

It feels as if he has been away from home for a while – not one night, but longer. He does not like it, but he has grown used to it – the four crewmen staying the night in the hostel off Front Street on a Friday night, the threadbare pool table in the hostel's bar, the fruit machine that Jonny puts his wages in. The warm beer. The sticky floor and the broken locks on the toilet doors. The only benefit – the single one – is that he spends a little time with his eldest son. He can eat a meal with Sam, or walk across to The Bounty Inn and have a pint or two in there. But it is hard to talk to him, like trying to prise a lid off a jar that has, perhaps, been dented.

Daddy!

He turns. And there is his surprise – the child who is yet to keep him awake at night with worries, and regrets, for she is only six years old, and for Nan the world is bright and safe. She still believes – adamantly – in Father Christmas. In Parla's church, she treads very carefully down the aisle, for she claims that it is bad luck to step on the line between tiles and that if you do, the brass eagle who holds the Bible on his back might come to life, and swoop down.

She says *do you want to hear a story that Mrs Coyle told …?* And he picks Nan up, carries her as she breathes *Fishman* in his ear.

The crate comes to rest and its tarpaulin is peeled off. Milton reaches in, clamps his pale hands into the cut-out handles of cardboard boxes, and pulls. Here are his grocery orders – the kidney beans, the tuna fish, the yeast, the cat food, the intensive conditioner that Hester needs, the blank CDs, the notepaper, the oatcakes, the rosehip oil, the candles, the sliced ham, Lorcan's piano music, the cartons of fresh milk. He hauls them up, and as he does this he smells perfume – something sweet, expensive. Kitty is beside him. She beams. *Milton, guess what?* She has her fabric flowers in her hair and rings on her thumbs, and she tells him she is going to have her work exhibited – in a proper art gallery, on the mainland. *An exhibition! Which means I will be a real artist!*

Milton thinks – not for the first time – how lucky her husband is.

As for George, he is scanning the quayside. He has a brown envelope in his hand. It has money inside it – a pad of folded notes. It's Maggie's payment, for her lobsters – and yet where is she? She should be here to collect it. But he cannot see her car or her white-blonde hair.

He'll take it to Crest later.

And George hopes, as he stands there, that she is not hurting. This stranger is hard news for them – but surely for Maggie most of all.

*   *   *

She walks past the red telephone box, the old tractor which rusts in the ditch. There are sparrows in the hawthorn bush by the churchyard; they chirp, as she passes.

Maggie sees Lowfield's roof. She sees the grassy banks that surround it. As the lane winds down, its garden comes into view.

There ... It stops her. She shields her eyes: a tall, dark-haired man is standing in the garden. Broad. Bearded. And she is calm, at first. But then Maggie's eyes widen and she says *oh my God* ...

His shirt. I know that shirt ... It is red and black – and Maggie knows there is a hole in it, a hole made by a spark from a bonfire five autumns ago, so that she had yelped to see that spark and she'd patted it out with her mittened hand and she knows there will be burn marks on the cloth – brownish, gold. There will be a missing button, too, and the left cuff will be frayed because Tom caught it on the wire fence above Store Bay as he climbed over it on a rainy day – they'd both heard the cloth tear and he'd said *uh-oh* as children do – and Maggie starts to run down the lane. She runs, and the man turns at the sound of someone running and he is tall, so tall, and he does not step back or lift up his arms as Maggie comes through the gate shouting *you! You! You're in my husband's shirt. Why are you in my husband's shirt?*

He does not look startled; he does not look afraid.

She reaches for the frayed cuff and pulls. All she can think of is *this is Tom's shirt* – so why is he wearing it? She takes hold of the collar, too. She can feel his beard's roughness on the back of her hands and she is saying *take ... it ... off* in the same rhythm that she's pulling in. The collar does not move so she grapples with the buttons now. She tries to undo them. She pulls one off entirely so that there is skin, suddenly; it shows between the shirt's two sides. White skin, black hair. She swallows, lets go. And then Maggie knows: she sees the truth as she had seen it whilst she'd knelt in winter sand with her wrists plunged into bladderwrack. She knows it is not Tom.

Of course it is not him.

A sound from her, now. It is high, like a whimper. A small, injured noise.

Then *thump*. She strikes him. Without knowing it or meaning to, Maggie strikes his chest with her half-opened hand – weakly, far too weakly for harm – but she strikes him once, and then a second time. Three, four, five strikes against his chest and the red and black shirt whilst saying, *take it off* but in a quieter voice, now – quiet, as if pleading.

Maggie feels afraid. She did not expect it, but she does. And she knows that she is getting closer to him – and yet he does not take her wrists, say *stop* or back away. He allows this striking, somehow. He stays where he is as a rock would, but he is warmer than a rock. She can feel the warmth against her hands and forearms; it rises, with his body's scent. And Maggie stops. She turns her fists back into hands, lays their palms upon him. *Firm. Broad-chested.* She keeps her hands upon him – and at that precise moment, Maggie wants to rest. She has a yearning to be still, to lay her head against him as she has laid her hands. It is overwhelming – this sudden wish for silence, for a resting place. Like a harbour or a cave or, strangely, she thinks of woods – a place of green, with shade and no sounds but the wind in the branches; grass so thick and lush that she may lie in it and not be found. And she wants this: *peace*. To sleep – and to feel safe, as she's sleeping. She looks at her hands. She moves her thumbs gently, feels the strength that is beneath them. He has a warm, clean, salted, unknown smell.

Maggie rests. She has to. She feels she has no choice in it. She sighs, as she finds him – her right cheek on his chest, on the red and black shirt.

Stillness.

The wind cannot find her for she is sheltered.

His chest moves, as he breathes – a rise, and a slow fall ...

Margaret!

She jumps. Maggie makes a sound, falls back.

Tabitha is standing by the front door. She is holding a tea-tray, and her hair is pinned back in two brown grips, showing a line of scalp. She looks shocked. She must have seen the fighting, or heard it, for she says *enough! Do you hear?*

Maggie stumbles. *I …*

What are you doing? Were you hitting him?

He's – she is breathless – *he is in Tom's clothes.*

He is.

Why?

Because the man had none of his own. What were we supposed to do?

Nathan has clothes. Ian. George.

Maggie … She exhales. *Look at the height of him.*

And Maggie does. She turns back towards this stranger. She sees the shirt but now, for the first time, she moves her eyes upwards – up, past his collarbone, up over his beard. He is looking at her with eyes that are black. Black eyes.

The nurse's voice is much softer. *I was going to tell you. I'm sorry, Maggie. Tea?*

The cup is pressed into her hand. *Emmeline doesn't mind?*

Probably. But he needed clothes – and these are old, worn-out. Tom was done with them. They would never have been worn again, anyway.

His hands are huge. The skin between the thumb and forefinger is red; on one hand, there is a scar like a hole that has sealed.

He needed something, Maggie.

Yes.

She can feel the shame, now – she, Maggie, who tries to be composed. Maggie, who cannot remember the last person she touched and yet she'd fought him, scratched him. There is a mark on his neck which is now starting to show.

He has amnesia. Temporary, I'm sure. Tabitha holds the lid of the teapot as she pours. *The mind can choose to shut down, sometimes – with traumas and hardships.*

Amnesia?

It happens.

I'm sorry, he says. His voice.

Maggie looks up. How can his eyes be black? And how can they shine, all the same? And how could she have struck him and then brought herself against him and rested there when she doesn't know him at all? When he is a stranger? He looks back at her. He looks without blinking, tilts his head – as if he is astonished, as if she is brand-new.

Later, Maggie takes the tray inside. She rinses the teacups at the kitchen sink, places them upside down to drain. She dries her hands on the tea-towel and sees that she is shaking.

I do not understand. I do not understand.

How can he have no name? How could I have –?

He is in the doorway. The sun is behind him so he is almost silhouetted and she wonders if he has been watching her – how she rinsed the cups and then looked down at her hands.

I'm sorry. I won't wear this again. I didn't know ... I don't want to upset the people who are being so good to me.

Tom would often dress whilst doing something else, like talking on the phone or cleaning his teeth or reading the paper, and so he'd find odd socks on his feet that night. A vest, back to front. His pants, inside out. *You don't remember anything? At all?*

I remember being in the water. Kicking.

What else? What about before?

No. Not yet.

It is late afternoon. The light is beautiful. It makes the grassy banks at Lowfield gold, or nearly gold. She glances down, sees how the backs of her plimsolls have been flattened by her heels and how old the laces are, and she knows that Tom would have kicked, also. He'd have wanted to stay living.

Just not that shirt?

Not this *shirt. I promise.*

And please don't – she looks away, trying to find the word. What is the word? The expression for what she fears and could not survive? And what did she feel as she fought him, or as she rested? Nothing makes sense, at this moment. He is not Tom and yet she is feeling … She can't find the words. She sighs, stops trying: *don't fuck us over. This island is* … Broken? Tender? Tiredness floods in. She regrets how she has spoken, she is ashamed by the language but she is so tired, so very tired. All the small struggles. All the trying she has done and she shrugs, gives up. She leaves the sentence as it is.

A feeling. It flutters, as if waking.

And with that, Maggie moves past him. She steps into the light.

Kitty walks barefoot; she can feel the three days of sun in the tarmac, and she swings her sandals in her left hand.

High Haven. She passes the rusting car parts, the log-pile, the dog cage where no dog has been kept for years. Old wooden crates are piled on it now and a metal bucket is green with rainwater. So it is – living here. Living with a farmer. She didn't expect it but she hasn't minded so much.

Kitty pushes the door, walks in.

Nathan?

There is no answer. She did not expect there to be one – not late in the afternoon when the sun is still warm and there are sheep to count, fences to mend, thistles to tug up and burn. Once, he would have been waiting for her – standing on the quay with a clean shirt on and his easy smile. Or he may have been here with the kettle singing, wet-haired from a shower. But these days, the wind has blown at their marriage so that it has changed shape and he is not making tea for her or towelling his hair.

It happens to all marriages, of course. In time. She tells herself this: *it is normal.*

And it could be worse ... She has seen Maggie on *Pigeon.* She's watched her sit, and stare at the water.

Kitty puts her keys on the table, pads upstairs.

She wants to tell him, *I am an artist.* She wants to tell him about the gallery on the outskirts of the town, about the owner who said *I think your work is ... bold, inventive, appealing.* She wants to tell her husband that there will be an opening night, and reviews, and she wants Nathan to be proud of her. To hold her, to whisper *well done* in her ear.

But where is he, to tell? Not in the house. Not in the shed outside.

She goes to the bathroom, turns on the taps. The water thunders into the tub.

Kitty walks into the bedroom, undresses. She hums softly as she does so, lifting the necklace over her head and unhooking her bra which she hangs on the end of their pristine, uncreased, perfectly made double bed.

*   *   *

Can you hear the bath running? Kitty humming?

Can you hear a string of bells tinkling in the northerly wind?

Jim can. Jim Coyle stands with his hands on the gate, and hears them. These bells mark the cliff edges so that he does not fall. His wife's idea – bells that are meant for a cat's collar strung up on baling twine. They bounce, and say *sing-sing*.

He hears more, besides. A lamb calls for its mother somewhere near The Stash; also, there is a skylark. It peeps, high up.

Jim's hearing is the gift that a thief handed to him. It is what he was offered when his sight was hauled away. He's always known he'd go blind, in the end. His father had begun to knock his shoulders on doorframes or drop cups when he was middle-aged; by his seventies he'd walked like a man in the dark. Jim can sense light and shadow but little else. *Retinitis pigmentosa*. He'd rather he didn't have it, but as his eyes grew worse his hearing grew better. His sense of smell did. His taste and touch. When he kisses his wife he can taste tea, medicated lip salve, denture fixative cream. He can smell her lily-scented moisturiser. To kiss her is more of a treat than it ever was with his working eyes – that's what he thinks, or tells himself.

At this moment, his wife is walking along the earthy path through waist-high grass that leads from the cross-roads to the Old Fish Store. He knows this because he can hear her. Her stick brushes the grass, taps the brambles back towards the church wall; sometimes she pauses and flattens a nettle's branch by standing on it, breaking its stem. And he can hear Abigail's breathing – steady, and low.

It grows louder. He turns. There is the shuffle of her feet, the smell of dust and lotion and she says *you'll never guess, Jim. You won't guess what I saw.*

They sit in deckchairs, side by side. Abigail smoothes her skirts, readies herself.

She says, *it's definitely him.*

You saw him?

*I did – at Lowfield. And the size of him! And the beard!
Oh, he is as handsome as he is in my book ... But do you
know who else? I saw Maggie.*

Oh?

And do you know what she did? She hit him, Jim.

Hit?

*She struck him on the chest. And he just ... allowed it.
He didn't try to stop her. He looked so calm, and ...* She
takes another sip. The bells sing. *He's the Fishman.
Definitely.*

Jim thinks, *my wife* – who has more faith in a leather-
bound book and its stories than she has in medicine, or the
local news. Who seeks out stories – fairy tales, the impossible – because she prefers them to what the truth, most
likely, is. She thinks that he has not lost his sight from a
genetic disorder but from a lifetime of lighthouse-keeping
– the flashes, the polished brass, the long nights peering
into the dark. Legends are her meat and drink. They
sustain her old body, lighten her voice. In the past few
days she has been stronger, more talkative – like the girl he
remembers with the hay-seeds in her hair.

Abigail. Who has weathered more storms than he ever
saw from his lighthouse. She is a boat that has knocked
against rocks but made it. *I love you, Mrs Coyle.* How he
does.

She lifts his hand, kisses it.

*　　*　　*

The Fishman ... Is this him? With the wound on his hand
as if someone had tried to hook him out of the sea? With
his briny smell and mirrored eyes? Some say *yes*, already.
Some yearn for him to be.

Ed, of course, does not believe it. He of the weather station, the shipping forecast and the radio. He who, as a boy, loved his metal detector because it showed what was actually there – what he could hold in his hand and keep safe.

There's no such thing as a Fishman, he says.

Nan, with a mouth full of mashed potato, does not agree. *There is, too. Mrs Coyle told me.*

She's just telling stories, Dee tells her softly.

She says Mr Coyle saw one.

Jim Coyle is blind ... Sam shakes his head.

Before he went blind!

Enough, Ed says.

Silence, for a time. Then Nancy spikes a pea with her fork and says *he's still the Fishman.*

And so they eat, at a table with spotted cloth napkins, and Ed wonders how it happened – that he's the captain of a ferry on a little island where a man with no memory has come ashore as the odd rubber boot comes in on Lock-and-Key. What can Ed do next? He has talked to the coastguard. He feels he ought to call the police but Tabitha's words – her precise words – had been *let's wait a bit longer ... I see no need, just yet.* And he is inclined to agree. He does not want to call the police; the more he thinks of calling them, the more he fears what would follow if he did. And there is Tabitha, too. She has been good to his family; she has delivered each of his children, helped with broken bones and chickenpox and migraines and Ed will never forget the time he saw her arguing with Emmeline outside the island's shop. She'd said *it was not Sam's fault! Don't you see that?* So he is grateful – indebted, even – to Tabitha Bright.

No police would be his preference, and hers. But he is also aware that this island is not his island. Perhaps this is not fully Ed's decision to make.

Later, as he stacks the dishwasher, he says *do you think I should hold a meeting?*

A meeting?

A vote of some kind. He's amnesiac, he could be anyone … Ian isn't pleased. And as for Emmeline …

Dee lowers the tea-towel. She smiles, kisses him. *Sounds like a good idea.*

Sam's mobile phone flashes blue. He reaches for it.

The message says *sleep well. L x*

It is not much, but Sam is glad of it.

He replies *you too x*

The island at night. I can see it. Sometimes I would wake, put a coat over my pyjamas and walk out into the dark. I'd see the small nocturnal moments that no human was meant to.

They are happening now. There is the blackish glint of bladderwrack at Sye; down in the ditches, a creature moves across dead leaves. In the church porch, a spider plucks its web and the lighthouse finds it – a silver web with its little rounded maker who tucks up its legs at this sudden light. I've seen bedside lamps come on. Once I saw two silhouettes against a bedroom curtain – two people who became, as I watched, one person – and I looked away embarrassed. Is this happening, now? At School Cottage, maybe.

A curlew calls – bubbling, sad.

The minister sits at his piano. Lorcan tries his new music – the first four bars. He cracks his knuckles, tries again.

In the nettle patch there is a vole. It chews a stalk – up and down. It stops, waits. A shadow? It passes. And so the vole resumes its chewing – up and down, up and down.

Midnight passes.

Clocks flash their green neon numbers: 12.03. Then, 12.04.

At High Haven, the bed is no longer neatly made. Kitty lies on her left side, propped up on her left elbow. Her right hand is on her husband's stomach and she is saying *it doesn't matter, it's fine. Maybe we try again in a while?* But Nathan knows it's not fine. Tom. This washed-up man. Rona in her knickers and nothing else saying *do you love me? Say you love me* ... He is rum-breathed and red-eyed, and nothing is fine at all.

*　　*　　*

The lighthouse turns.

The hours pass.

One in the morning, then two.

At Lowfield two lights are on. In the mending room, the stranger lies on the iron-framed bed. He stares at the ceiling but he does not see its paint: he sees, instead, a woman. She is the blonde, hurting woman who had struck him saying *no* ... He'd wanted to hold her. He is only thinking of her.

As for the nurse, she reads. At this moment, she is sitting in the middle of her double bed with all her nursing books on either side of her, open and facing down. She has typed the word *amnesia* into the internet.

There are no marks on his head. None. No bruises, or swellings.

He was not drunk, when they found him, and he does not shake – so the amnesia cannot come from alcohol dependency.

It leaves two options. Just two.

She takes off her glasses.

The first option is that his amnesia comes from a trauma of some kind – not physical, but emotional. Something has happened to this man that his heart and mind cannot cope with, so that his brain has chosen to forget it all. Wipe away the trouble, as a high tide does. What has he seen, or felt? An event too hard to bear, it seems. It makes her sorry to think it. But that is the option she'd prefer – because the second is that he is lying. That he has not forgotten anything, and is just pretending he has.

She puts the books on the floor, one by one. Then she reaches across to her bedside lamp and switches it off. The darkness is sudden, welcome.

In this darkness, she smiles. *There is a third option, of course.*

He could be Abigail's Fishman. A Fishman, with brand-new legs and lungs. He feigns amnesia for what else can he do? Humans would not truly believe him. So he cannot speak of what he knows – of shipwrecks, and whale song, and shafts of filtered light.

The Loss of the Anne-Rosa

Once I asked Tom this: *why do you love the sea so much?*

We had been on Store Bay. It was an autumn afternoon. Spume was flying, skittering over the sand and against our boots and my hands were so cold that I blew on them. Tom was wide-eyed, amazed. He smiled. *You're asking me why?*

All night, he talked – of storms, of tides, of incredible fish that could not have been imagined by any human brain. *Some produce their own light*, he said. *Some, far down, carry their own lanterns* ... Octopus can change colour; whales can recognise their pod, their friends. Once, a turtle passed him and lifted its nose, gave a tiny puff of breath as if in greeting. And he told me the story of a silent, mist-grey sea, not long after sunrise – how, as Tom had sat in *Pigeon*, he'd thought, *I am not alone.* He'd known it: *there is something in the water. Something behind me* ... He'd stayed as he was, held his breath. He waited. Waited ... And very, very slowly, two black orca fins passed by on either side. They were knife-straight and shining. *I looked up at their tips.*

Orca? I gasped, clamped my hands over my mouth.

Orca. I could have reached out and ...

He had a thousand stories. Sometimes he'd say, *I wish you could have seen that too* – and I'd nod, take his hand; I wished I'd seen it too. But if a story's well-told it places you there. I saw those orca passing by.

*   *   *

The *Anne-Rosa* was no ghostly galleon with a pirate flag. She was not lured onto rocks by wrecking lights and there were no smugglers hiding liquor or rubies in her hold. It would make a better story, I know. But she was a tanker, in the end.

She was empty, having unloaded on the mainland hours before. But it was wartime: fires made the mainland's cities glow at night, and submarines stalked the deeper waters, and as the *Anne-Rosa* made her way past Parla her left side was blown away. The noise shook the island. Water churned and whitened; it belched as it closed around her portholes and decks. The Parlans ran to the north coast – but what could they do? The sea was too stormy for their small fishing boats. They could only clutch their coats to their throats and pray. *Lord, in their hour of need …*

You could say God heard – or you could say that the *Anne-Rosa*'s crew were hardier than most or that it was luck entirely. In any case, their lone lifeboat made it onto Lock-and-Key and some men reached the shore on their own by clinging to driftwood or just swimming for their lives. They were ushered into Parlan homes, given blankets and broth and a whisky or three. All of the men survived.

So the *Anne-Rosa* is not a grave. But it carries a sadness all the same. At the lowest tide, the hull will partly show itself and to see its dark, dripping metal is to be reminded of all lost things. I have seen it twice. Both times I mourned what I'd had for a time, but no longer.

Visitors often ask if someone died, in that wreck. They take a leaflet from Milton's shop and go to each place that is marked on it – Tap Hole, Sye, the nettle patch where the voles live – and when they come to Bundy Head they ask, *did they die? The crew?* Some islanders say *yes* to that. It's a lie, but it's the answer the tourists want. They want a wooden wreck like a pirate ship with mossy candlesticks and coins still down there, held by skeletal hands. *On wild nights, the ship rises up ... They say there was gold on board ...* although there is certainly no treasure in the *Anne-Rosa* now. The Lovegrove twins told me this. They used to dive her rusty shell, inch through her half-open doors. They parted the weed and only found eels there – blank-eyed and toothy, mouthing *oh, oh, oh ...*

*　　*　　*

Maggie dreams of the tanker tonight. She dreams of how it must have swayed, back and forth. Did the men shout? They must have shouted. In her dream they are shouting the names of those they love.

She has dreamt this before: that a skeleton lies in the *Anne-Rosa*'s walls. All the men survived except for this one man. Against the iron hull are the bones she knows – the collarbone she traced with her thumb, the spine she heard crack as he stretched. Flakes of rust float through the darkness. There is a jawbone whose teeth she has seen before – counted, touched with the tip of her tongue – and eye sockets that have no sight, now. There are no brown eyes. Tom does not lie in the *Anne-Rosa*, she knows that – for divers would have found him, if he was lying there. But she dreams he reclines gracefully. He turns his head towards her. She sees his wedding ring.

Maggie ... Sighed out.

She wakes. Her name echoes; her body feels damp. She gasps as the eels do – *oh, oh*.

Later, she sits on the loo seat, her arms wrapped around her waist. Sometimes, when he bent down, she would see the knots of vertebrae beneath his skin, like a row of knuckles. The skin whitened against them. She can see this so clearly. She can see his mouth. How can it now be a jawbone with teeth and nothing more? She knew it when it was warm, flesh-coloured. She knew how he'd bite his bottom lip when thinking, or when she'd ...

Maggie blinks it away.

She tears the paper, dabs at herself.

The lighthouse turns, and as she flushes the loo and washes her hands she thinks of the man at Lowfield. *I don't want this; I did not ask for this.* What had she felt when she saw him? What had she felt when she'd struck him and what is she feeling now? He had said *shh*, very gently. As she'd rested, he'd put his hand on her shoulder – lightly, as if she might break.

She treads back to bed, ashamed.

He had also whispered, *I know* ... Or at least she thinks he said it. He'd said *I know*, as if he knew Maggie, as if he'd felt her sadness or met her before. But how could he have done? *I have never met him.* She'd remember, surely, if she had.

No memory. It is not easy to believe it. But perhaps it is not easy to believe any of it – the size of him, his face, how he was found at Sye. Hard to believe this life at all, and hard to believe that someone could make love to you, press a kiss into the space behind your ear and say your name and smile at you and then, within two hours, be gone. Dead. How can she believe that? Even now, she can't.

So maybe he has no memory.

Or maybe he is a Fishman, as she has heard. Maybe there is silver in the fields and an underwater world. Maybe seals do, in fact, have human hearts and know what love feels like, or being in love – and maybe she'll believe every story ever told. Why not? The only thing Maggie won't believe, what she refuses to believe is what others may, in time, choose to: that this huge, nameless black-eyed man is the sea's replacement for the loving man it took.

Six

Hours pass. The tide comes in and out.

At daybreak, I go down to *Pigeon* and I find a feather there. It is a gull's feather and so I see it long before I come to it – it glows, in the half-light. It is beautiful, far from perfect. Its comb is splayed, broken; its downy lower parts are matted with salt and it could not beat air now. It could not offer flight. But I take it, pocket it.

*   *   *

And at the house called Easterly, a kettle is newly boiled. It sits, steaming. Emmeline lifts it, pours it into a mug.

She has not really slept. Sleep has been hard to come by for the past few nights and so she has found herself doing crosswords in bed at two in the morning, or sewing on buttons, or reading her book on gardening – dog-eared, tea-coloured.

Last night she went to Easterly's spare room. It has been *the spare room* for years – fifteen years or more – but in her mind it still belongs to her youngest son. It had been his bedroom when they first came to Easterly. They had painted the walls a fine sea-blue, and the curtains were navy with cushions to match. A boy's room, Tom's room. And she may call it *the spare room* to her other children, or Tabitha, but in her head it remains *Tom's room* even now, and it remains Tom's bed, and it remains Tom's sheepskin rug at the side of his bed which she'd put there so that when he woke up each morning the first thing he felt was soft, soft. And last night Emmeline had sat here. She'd looked at the shelves. The empty cardboard box that she had lifted his old clothes from – grey jumpers, old socks.

I doubt I'll ever need them, he'd told her, long ago. But this is an island. It costs, always, to take unwanted things away – and so a broken fridge sits near Wind Rising, and an old sink has been filled with soil and plants, and Nathan has rows of wheel-less cars that merely *sit* and will never be mended. And so Emmeline stored her youngest son's holey, worn-out clothes.

She sniffs. This man – washed up like wood is.

She'd had no wish to lend anything to him. But how would it look, if she had kept those clothes? Held onto them? Bitter, she supposes – resentful. Tabitha might have called her *unkind* – but what does it matter, what Tabitha thinks? She made up her mind long ago.

Hester rang. Hester is a Bundy in how she looks – the thick hair, the deep-set eyes – but she does not have the temper, not at all. On the phone, she'd used a gentle voice: *Mum, are you alright?*

Why wouldn't I be?

I hear he's wearing Tom's clothes, and ...

Hester wore her brothers' clothes too when she was young. It was cheaper that way, and practical; there are photographs in which Emmeline's children look like four dark-eyed boys. Hester had worked just as well as them. She'd wanted to match their shearing times or running speed, and *perhaps she got that stubbornness from me ...*

That tight little stare that Hester had which meant she was thinking *yes I can, yes I can …*

I know what I am doing. Emmeline said it on the phone. That's a phrase she's heard over and over, in her life – the truculent, close-minded retort of a farming man who needed no help or would not admit to it. She knew such a man for over four decades: she married Jack when she was eighteen. It had rained on their wedding day.

Jack. She leans back against the sink, and the draining board. They were married forty-two years and three months before a heart attack took him. Forty-two years – an adult lifetime, for some people. She tells herself that she chose this life – the sour-smelling sheep, boots in the hall, dog hair on the armchairs and bathroom towels – but did she? Truly? She married when she was a child, still. Her mind and heart had yet to reach their adult size, or strength. What she had seen in Jack was adventure, a taste of real, grown-up life – glamour, even, although it's impossible to think that now. Her naïve eyes had seen him handle a ewe, as she birthed, and Emmeline had wondered how those hands might feel between her own legs. He'd been good-looking and strong. He'd often wandered up to the lighthouse at strange hours and sat, mute or nearly, in the corner of their sitting room which Emmeline had thought to be romantic in its way. At twenty, Jack wanted a wife. He announced it, as one might announce one's plans for the day. Emmeline had been smitten and he'd liked her capability – her size, and her hefty child-bearing hips. And so the eldest Bright child married the youngest Bundy one on such a blustery day that the church door shook during their vows.

Forty-two years. So much became normal – his waterproofs hanging in the porch, the creak of the wooden stairs. How he sucked his tea through his teeth, as if sifting it.

For over four decades Emmeline did the same things, over, and over: shampooed her children's heads on a Sunday, mopped the kitchen floor on the Friday, and every autumn she'd pick the disc of greaseproof paper off the top of the blackberry jam she'd made the autumn before, when everything had been exactly the same, but she'd made that jam thinking *maybe things will be different when I make more jam next year.* But things never were – except for a few more grey hairs. The children would be taller but they'd still leave muddied boot-prints on the floor. And she'd still buy aspirin or antiseptic cream or plasters as often as others bought yeast for bread – mouthing *it's not for me* to Milton and trying to smile. A bag of peas lived in the freezer that she'd press onto herself in the bathroom, when the rest of the house was asleep.

Year after year. Forty-two of them.

She puts bread in the toaster, presses it down.

When she is asked how many children she has, she still says *four.* Once, she said *three, but one is missing at sea*, and the face of the girl who'd asked it grew flushed, and she'd stepped away, embarrassed. *Four* is the better answer. And it's the true one – for until she has Tom's bones to bury in the Parlan earth, Emmeline will keep hoping – as if her hope is something tangible that might help him, like rope or a torch's light. She cannot retract it. She cannot say *he is dead* in case it might, somehow, make him so – and she doesn't understand how others can say it as firmly as they do. She is his mother, still – and so she tells them, *yes, four children. Three grandchildren.*

Ian, Hester, Nathan and Thomas. Her best words are these names.

She sips her tea.

A man with no name. What might Jack have said, to it all? *Bloody nonsense*, most likely. *Let him sort himself out.*

Emmeline holds her mug and looks out across the flowerbed. At that moment, she thinks of three things: that the peonies are beautiful, at their best, maybe – not fully unfurled but nearly, and should she cut some for her bedroom or leave them where they are? She also thinks of this man at Lowfield with his black, black beard and the whorl in it. Again, there is the wave of resentment: she resents him (or hates? Is it hatred she feels?) for not being who she longs for him to be, who he *should* be if there was fairness which there has never been. And thirdly, Emmeline remembers how Tom would take her hands without warning and dance with her round the kitchen to no music at all except for the sea and the calling sheep, and as they danced he would ask *how was your day?* Past the fridge, down the hall.

*   *   *

Her second son walks across the fields.

Nathan wears a quilted jacket. It is sleeveless, navy-blue. In its pockets there are fence staples – sharp, so that they pierce the lining and scratch against his waist – and Nathan holds a hammer in his left hand. His feet snag on grass, the stems of buttercups.

Ian had rung as Nathan was cleaning his teeth. He'd answered the phone with a frothing mouth, and heard *there's a gap in the fence above Tap Hole. Think we've lost one.*

You on it?

No – I'm off to church.

He'd spat his toothpaste in the sink. *Church? Seriously?*

Yeah. Ed wants to talk to us afterwards.

Ed?

About this man. Just see to the fence, will you?

Nathan has not had breakfast – coffee, but no more. There is a slight wetness to the grass, as he walks, so that the toes of his boots are darker than the rest. He looks up. Swifts are darting.

He'd left Kitty sleeping. He'd glanced at her, as he'd dressed. She looked beautiful. She always does – but maybe a husband sees his wife as an islander sees water, in that he sees it so often he stops seeing its shine. He hardly ever watches the sea any more. The tourists stare for hours, but Nathan has no time to, and does not feel the need. But then, once in a while, he will glance out and see its bright water. Once in a while, she will throw back her hair.

Last night she'd worn cream lace, and there was a deep, fruit scent on her belly and the insides of her wrists – plum, or fig. Her hair had parted on either side of him.

Shit. He winces.

She'd said *these things happen* ... No, they don't. Or they do, but they should not. Perhaps he deserves the embarrassment of it but she doesn't. Not Kitty, who talks to plants as she waters them. Whose fingertips smell of turpentine.

On their wedding night she'd asked *so am I now a farmer's wife?* Kitty's never looked like one – not as his mother did, or as Constance can do. Kitty, who has no broken veins from bad weather and no jumpers that fray at the neck. She shakes the earth from vegetables, but she also paints a rich, regal purple onto her toes.

What had Tom said, when he'd met her? *Brother, you don't do things by halves* ...

He can see the broken fence. Above Tap Hole, part of the wire has come away from its post and has curled up to leave a gap that a sheep could easily get through. The post itself is crooked – from years of wind, and of being scratched against. Nathan comes to it, pushes it back and forwards in the earth. It's been here a long, long time. Nathan's father would have put it here, or his grandfather. Even his great-grandfather farmed on Parla, although it isn't farming he's known for. He put a shotgun in his mouth and pulled the trigger with his toe. That dark Bundy cloud that no-one speaks of. He wonders if this fence-post had been Randall Bundy's work.

Randall. Nathan's father had wanted to call him that. Emmeline refused. She'd called it a cursed name, chosen another and no doubt Jack resented her for that. But who can argue with the person who carried the child, pushed the child out? Bled?

There are strong women in Nathan's life. Kitty is strong, in her way. If she found out about two nights ago, or the other nights, she would rage – she'd flame, and fight. But inside, he knows she'd be breaking.

He doesn't want her breaking. Not Kit.

The grass is damp. He kneels down upon it, feels in his pocket. The post is rotten, or as good as. It will need replacing but he can't do that just now. He can only knock a few staples into the post, enough to close up the hole until he can return to do a proper job.

He hammers them in, straightens up.

When was the last time he was happy?

Nathan turns to go. But as he does, he glances down towards Tap Hole. There is a sheep down there. One of this year's lambs. *Ach* ... It is rare, for a sheep to fall – they are sure-footed beasts, meant for sloped land – but this side of the isle has loose soil and breaking cliffs. Grass grows over edges so that you could step too far.

I should have checked the fences.

Did it die as it landed, or after?

He thinks *I let it down.*

And Nathan thinks, too, *I love her. I love my wife.* He had shared a bath with her one New Year's Eve. They'd drunk red wine and counted the old year out through the scented foam. *Ten ... nine ... eight ...* And he had felt happy, then. But that was seven years ago.

Tap Hole booms near him. It is where his Aunt Thomasina lost her life. She hid in the cave as the tide came in. And perhaps that would have been fine, on other nights. But that night there was the *sly tide*, the highest tide so that the cave filled up entirely. Had nobody told her? About the sly tide?

Her brother – Nathan's father, Jack – had found her. Floating on her front. Her head, being the heaviest part, was hanging underwater and her arms were bent at the elbows, so it was her torso that Jack saw, and the legs which trailed as herons' do. They were straight and pale behind her, as she drifted out with the tide.

*　　*　　*

At Crest, Maggie is painting. She returns to the gutters with her brush and yellow paint. She tries not to think of the tall, nameless man.

The black cat from the harbour is rolling in the dust – left to right, right to left. She shows her underbelly where there is a patch of white.

And a gull stands on Jack Bundy's gravestone. It marks it sloppily; there is a greenish tinge to the dropping, and it coats the *J* of his name.

There is talk that parts of Parla's church are made from the timbers of a ship that sank off Utta, and that Parlans had scavenged and claimed what they could. Most say that isn't true. All the same, the roof does creak like a boat. Lorcan has always thought this. He came to this island two decades ago and it was the noise he noticed first – the slow, hushed stutter that a boat gives when it strains on its lines. *It wants to be free. To sail away ...*

It creaks like that today. Perhaps it is the northerly wind or some other reason entirely. But he talks of *God's mysteries*, he talks of *the faith we must have in the unknown and how God will never leave us without comfort, or alone*, and the eaves shift above their heads so everyone looks heavenwards when Lorcan says *amen*.

Two hymns, and a blessing. Lorcan states, kindly, as he always does, that the church is never locked; *it is always open for prayer and reflection* – and then he mentions a red umbrella that was left behind last Sunday. *Anyone's?* No-one says so. Perhaps it was a tourist's – he will leave it by the door, just in case.

Now Lorcan clears his throat. *And Edward? I think Ed would like to take a moment to ...?*

The captain stands, moves out of his pew. He wears a shirt that is ironed and buttoned up to the neck, and his hair has been combed back. He tells them what they all know about the bearded man, which is very little: where he was found, by whom and when; of his minor injuries; of his height and breadth and quiet voice. How he is at Tabitha's. How he can give no reason as to how he came to Sye.

Amnesia ... Ian scoffs to himself, but they all hear.

I know, Ed says, palms raised. *I know. It sounds impossible. But here he is ...*

Does he have an accent? Constance.

No. Nothing. No clues at all.

What now? What of him? What do they do?

No-one mentions the police. Not a single person in this place of worship suggests that Ed calls the station on the mainland and asks them to come out. He is not surprised. They have their reasons – unsafe cars, tax evasion, the tiny abattoir at the back of Wind Rising which is *only a rumour* if anyone asks. And aren't there curious plants in Milton's airing cupboard which he dries, bags and sells to Jonny Bundy? Oh, Ed knows it all.

So are we agreed? We let him stay?

Send him back. Emmeline's voice. *Just put him on the ferry and send him back.*

A murmur swells up, now. Dee turns in her pew and reasons with her; Tabitha states very firmly that she is not prepared to do that – *I am*, she declares, *a nurse and he is my patient* – and she stamps her foot as she says this, as if underlining her words. Ian calls to his aunt: *what if he's a thief, Tab? A murderer or rapist? We know nothing …* And this makes Tabitha stand, flushed, and Emmeline stands also and so they become the two sisters that the island has always known them to be – standing on either side of a space and pointing, raising their voices, not hearing the other in any proper way – and they are so loud in their quarrelling that nobody hears Lorcan at first. He is banging a hymn book against the lectern. *Enough!*

They keep going.

Enough! Emmeline!

Now they stop. There is a sudden hush. The women lower themselves. Lorcan is a measured man and they have not heard him shout before.

I think, he says, *it would be ungodly to send an injured man away.*

Who could argue with that? Or with Lorcan?

The roof creaks as if it agrees.

So it is decided. So it will be: the nameless bearded man will stay until he is mended. He will stay until he remembers, or until he chooses to go.

Emmeline can barely contain her fury. Nor can her eldest son, who mutters as he walks away – *this will not end well …*

But as for the rest of the congregation, they do not mind too much. He is different, after all. He is handsome and curious. And they cannot perhaps name the feeling that they have had since he came ashore but it is a feeling they do not want to be rid of, quite yet. Leah does not; Abigail does not.

Nor does Tabitha, who smiles as she cycles downhill.

Such sunshine, she thinks. *There has never been so much sun.*

*　　＊　　＊　　＊*

I was not at church. I did not see or hear the Bright sisters, as they fought and jabbed the air. All day, I was running the yellow fan of a paintbrush over wood, trying to think of nothing. But no-one can think of nothing – *nothing* itself is *something*. And I was thinking of eyes as black as the space inside my cupped hands.

It was Constance who told me. She saw me, walked across the fields.

Do you object? To this Fishman staying here?

Fishman?

She'd smiled, dismissed the word. *Whoever he is. Tell Ed, if you want him gone. Ed would listen to you.*

I wonder what my life would be like if I'd said *yes. Yes, I do object. Yes, I want him gone.*

I didn't say that, of course. I wiped the paintbrush on a cloth tied to my belt-loop and said that it didn't matter to me, either way. I squinted at Constance, smiled, shrugged. *He can stay, if he wants. Or go.*

Leah. She of the bitten fingernails and small, neatly made words. She is walking, and that in itself is a newness; she has found even walking hard, in the past. Sat herself down on the ground.

There is an old towel wrapped around a piece of their electric fence to make a safe crossing place, and so here she climbs over. The rabbits do not run from her. Gulls hop a little, and then look back.

She is aiming for Lowfield. She is making her way south, across the fields of Wind Rising and towards its grassy banks. Tabitha's old bicycle is propped against the wall. As she comes closer, Leah sees the window of the mending room is open and its curtains are stirring.

He is there. He is sitting on the bed, looking down.

Leah stands by the window. She angles her head, looks through its curtains. *He is handsome. Sad-looking.*

Excuse me? she says.

Leah, she tells him. *From the farm there? The big one? My father and brother helped to carry you from Sye.*

I don't –

Know your name? I know. Doesn't matter.

They go slowly; they walk at her pace which is a careful one. He walks beside Leah where he can; where there are stiles or gorse to pass through, the stranger drops back and follows her. She is thin-boned and pale – paler than him, even – but she climbs over wire fences without touching them as if stronger than she looks.

He sees the small things. She bites her bottom lip. Her nails are torn, picked at; the skin beside them is dry.

See those? Sea stacks. They were giants once, or that's the story …

Leah Bundy. Had the nurse mentioned her? The nurse has mentioned many people. Last night, he had sat in the kitchen at Lowfield and listened as she spoke of what she thought he should know: *now that you're staying for a while …* Tabitha talked of tides, homes, the shop's opening hours, the chestnut mare, the family names, where the puffins nest. She talked, too, of herself – of her sister, of her own nursing days in foreign lands where she found a mosquito bite as big as her thumb, where she fainted through heat – and he'd thought *she wants to talk. She wants to be listened to.*

Perhaps this girl is like that. Leah, whose face had appeared at his window; whose hair seems to twist in this wind so that, as she walks, she holds most of it down. One hand on the nape of her neck, one pointing. *It is Bundy Head, in the distance. And that's Wind Rising – where we live.*

He looks. A broad, stone house. There is a dog chained outside it, a barn with a small concrete room at its rear. A single towel flaps on the line.

You remember nothing? At all?

I remember being in the sea.

Sye?

No.

They talked of you in church. There was an argument. Emmeline's my grandmother – did you know that?

No, he hadn't known that.

Most people are related, she tells him – *in some way.*

They pass to the south of Wind Rising, towards the east and the single lane. Leah walks by his side, but slightly ahead. She tugs at the taller grass as she goes, and when she has a long stem of grass in her hand she holds it up in front of her, tries to divide it lengthways with her thumbs. Her eyes are on this piece of grass.

Have you heard of the Fishman?

Fishman?

There's a story of him. An old story – older than anyone here. He's a man with a tail, lives at sea. He grows legs and comes ashore when people need him to.

He has nothing to say. What can he say?

But Leah keeps talking. She throws the stalk away, tells him that her great-grandfather used to be the lighthouse-keeper, and there is a café at the base of it now, that there used to be a pig farm but the pigs are gone, and as Leah steps over a stile into the lane she says *and that house? With the yellow door? Maggie lives there. You've met her – haven't you?*

He nods. He thinks *she knows* ... They must all know how he met her.

Yellow. He wonders when he last saw yellow – for what was yellow in the night-time sea? In his former life?

Leah takes him back, towards Lowfield. She shows him the school and its playground; they pass the shop and its wall of rhododendrons which are no longer flowering, but their leaves are glossed – and he listens to Leah, as she talks.

But in her silences, he glances back. A yellow door. *Maggie.* He wants to say her name.

He wants to ask about her but does not.

Leah decides this: *he is kind.* He is handsome and very tall and yes, he is kind. He'd held back a branch as they'd passed the rhododendrons so that it would not catch against her skin or clothes.

Not a conman. Not a thief, like her father said.

And he *listens.* She has talked and talked – of shearing, haymaking, vegetable patches, the church, the chickens that they keep; and he has *listened* to her, without inter-rupting. Without yawning or saying *come on* ...

She looks across. *He is meant to make things better – the Fishman. That's how the story goes. Abigail Coyle has the story in a book – if you want to know more about yourself. She lives by the harbour. The house of bells?*

He slows, shakes his head. *You think I'm a Fishman? Half-fish?*

Maybe. Aren't you?

Leah can imagine it – his hair, underwater. Light reflecting off his swimming back.

*   *   *

She is right. The house of bells is the place. When I was needing answers or comfort or a little rest, or to be told the best of stories, I made my way there. I followed the *sing-sing-sing*. I'd tread up the path and they would be waiting – always, as if they knew.

Maggie is walking there now.

The sun sets, as she goes. The sky is every colour as she makes her way down – navy, silver, orange, red – so that if it was ever painted or written of, it would not be believed. *No sky*, they'd say, *could look like that* ... But it could; this sky does. She is walking underneath it and she knows that there is beauty, still; it does not stop existing.

She comes to the Old Fish Store. An evening breeze on its bells.

When Abigail opens the door she gives a small, bright *ah!*

I wondered, she tells her, *when you'd come to me. It's been a while.*

I know.

This is a room that Maggie knows. She knows the Earl Grey tea and the framed, embroidered map of Merme that hangs by the door. She knows this flowered armchair, for she'd come here in her early island days – to hear of whales that spoke, of night-time seas that glowed. That was a different time. A better time.

You look so tired. Sit ...

Maggie sits. *Have you seen –?*

Him? The man they found? I have. You have, too.

You know?

The older woman smiles. *I saw you strike him, darling.*

Maggie flushes. *You did? Oh, I don't know why I did that. I just –*

Hush, now.

I scratched him, and –

Margaret. She takes Maggie's hands down from her face. *I have something to show you.*

Abigail carries *Folklore and Myth* from the bookshelf and lays it on Maggie's lap. And Maggie looks down, touches it. She remembers this book. It has been years since she last opened it but it feels as it used to – parched and rough, under her palms.

Open it.

The drawings have not faded; the stories are, of course, the same. Maggie turns the pages, and it is like seeing half-forgotten friends: the seal, and the foolhardy man who was turned into a black-coloured stone. There is the tale from Merme that she always loved – of a whale that fell in love with a girl's singing voice and stayed near her, could never leave. Maggie finds this story, smiles; the whale's round, dolorous eye peers up through the waves.

It's beautiful ... I'd forgotten.

The fourteenth page. Keep going.

She turns a page, two pages ... And Maggie catches her breath. She stops, stares. For he is there: he is drawn on the page as clearly and precisely as he has stood in front of Maggie in a red and black shirt. *It is him ...* It is exactly like him. If he were to swim and look back at the land, he would look as the Fishman does in this drawing; if he were to walk, half-bare, on the damp sand he'd look like this Fishman does in the next. Maggie swallows. She looks up.

I know, says Abigail.

How –?

See what it says? Hope and wonder ...

He looks like this. Exactly like this.
I know, dearest. I know.

*   *   *

Fishman ... I spoke it out loud. I walked back through the dark and I said it over and over, feeling the shape of the word. Perhaps the sheep heard me. Perhaps the moon – a crescent, yellow-coloured – watched my lips as I spoke.

I cannot talk of the power of want, of how much desire can do. I don't think it can be measured. I think *want* is forgotten too quickly or dismissed as being worth far less than the other feelings – love, hate, envy. But to *want* something ... To wish for it so much that you think you cannot last, your heart and body cannot continue to hunger for something as much as this. It comes from loss. We want what we do not have. We want what we had, but don't now.

I did not know why I'd struck him outside Lowfield like that. Nor did I know – or I was not ready, maybe, to acknowledge – why I had laid my head on his chest, or why I had tried so hard to forget the white patch of skin in the space where a shirt's button should be. But I knew I wanted safety: a simple, painless life.

Abigail had said *see? He is the Fishman. And others might think I am a mad old woman but ...* She'd shrugged. *Here he is. Here, on this page.*

I walked past the church, past the fields. The lighthouse found the sheep, as it turned; five seconds a minute they glowed on the dark-grey grass.

I decided this, as I walked: that yes, he was this creature. *He is half-man, half-fish.* I would believe it. I would tell myself that he could live underwater, that he had had scales and a bright tail. For this made him non-human.

This made him impossible to have feelings for. Who could want a fish? No sane person would. Despite his face, and black-mirror eyes.

Not human. I repeated it.

Not human. Not at all.

And so.

It is night. I run my bath and climb in.

In High Haven, Kitty can't sleep. She goes downstairs to find her husband sleeping on the sofa, a bottle in his hand. It saddens her so much that she lowers herself down, sits beside him for a while. The white light moves across the walls.

Lorcan is also awake. He sits on his piano stool, peers at the music – a nocturne – on its stand. He hums the tune to himself – *tum-ti-tum-tum* … It is trickier than he thought, this piece, but one day he will manage it. One day he will play it without all his mistakes. He lifts his fingers and puts them on the ivory. He exhales slowly. Then he presses down.

And Sam is almost sleeping. He lies in his attic bedroom, one foot still on the floor. He is nearing sleep when he is woken: there is a thrum against his mattress. The springs vibrate beneath him, so that he jumps. He gropes for his phone. It flashes blue, with this: *1 message received.*

I've met him. He's wonderful.

Sam wonders what to reply. He stares at her words.

A rock pool reflects the crescent moon and stars.

The Message in a Bottle

On a low-cloud day, many months and years ago, a bottle was found on a beach. A glass bottle, with no label – a bottle like so many other ones.

This bottle was wedged between rocks on the beach called Lock-and-Key, at its southern end. And it caught the eye of a man who rarely walked on beaches. For him, they were unstable places – windy, too cold. Sand in the eyes.

It was late and he did not wish to be there, but his daughter – five or six years old – had asked to come. She was crouching by a rock pool, a bucket by her side. The highest tide – the tide they called *sly*, sometimes – had passed through that morning and left its gifts behind. Shells, pebbles, wood as smooth as bones.

They meant nothing to him. No shells in his pockets as he went; no interest in the rounded stones.

Daddy! And he looked down. He looked down to find his daughter squinting, holding up a glass bottle and in that glass bottle there was a piece of paper – folded, written on.

He tipped the note out, opened it.

Please let this get better. Five words and five only.

Black ink, neatly done.

*　　*　　*

He hadn't kept it, of course. Ian is not the keeping kind. He had put the note back in the bottle, popped the bottle in his pocket and binned it, later, as they walked home. Leah had been dragging a strand of egg-wrack behind her. She'd been chirping as she used to. She talked to the things she passed – litter, old deckchairs.

Please let this get better.

He'd mocked it. He'd dismissed it as foolish, sentimental. *A message in a bottle? Please ...* The stuff of romance novels or films he'd never choose to see. It had annoyed him, somehow, and he'd walked too fast for Leah so that she'd called after him – plaintive, shrill. He carried her in the end. He made her leave the seaweed behind so that she'd called out *bye, weed* – mournfully. And later in the evening, as she slept with a cockle-shell in her hand, Ian had sat down at the kitchen table and said to Constance, *we found a note today.*

A note?

He told her. He recited it, rolled his eyes and Constance put down her knife and fork and said *you didn't keep it? You didn't bring it home?* She was angry for a while. She did not understand why he'd chosen to throw something away that had (he can still see her, pushing back her plate) *meant so much to someone ... Ian, it's like a prayer! A wish! And you put it in a bin?* All night she had brooded. In bed, she had radiated a dark, unreadable heat. He'd thought of touching her, sensing he had made a mistake that had hurt his wife far beyond his own understanding. Was this Constance's anger? Or a

158

woman's? When he dared to place his hand on her back she raised herself up off the mattress with her forearms and said *no*. Clear.

By morning, the anger was gone. She shrugged at the memory of a sea-travelled note, hummed as she ate. Constance forgot it, and Ian forgot, and he hasn't thought of it since then. Not once. Fifteen years have passed in which he has not looked back at that lemonade bottle with the curious wording that it held – why would he? He doesn't like beaches and he doesn't find wonder or beauty in a scrawled note in a bottle that he can only view as littering the sea.

And yet ... Here he is. The words that meant nothing fifteen years ago are in his head.

He exhales. He swears to himself.

Ian stands on the edge of Bundy Head. It is early morning, and the day's already warm. Beneath him he can see the body of a ewe. He'd found it by chance and brought it here – he always does with the dead ones. In comes a wave. It peels across the rocks, breaks around the sheep and covers it. The sea will take away all things you leave.

Tom. Always Tom, in some way.

He is in evening skies, and in lobster pots. In this man that's come ashore.

And is Tom in the message, now? Did the words mean nothing to Ian fifteen years ago because at that time he had not known loss? Now, he is a different man. He still farms, he still sleeps on the same side of the bed in the same room and Constance still sleeps on her front, arms bent. But he himself has changed because Tom went. They all did. They all turned to something in the aftermath of it. No-one stayed the same: Leah came back from the mainland like a ghost; Constance tucked herself away with her knitting needles late into the night, dropped stitch after stitch and fretted about money; Jonny said nothing.

Of course he did; it is what Bundys do. *We shear and we plough and say nothing.*

Did it get passed on in the genes or in other ways? Other ways, surely. Emmeline is not Bundy by blood and yet she is the one with the fewest words of all. She would place words out at breakfast as she handed out the butter or a boiled egg. She had certain phrases – *how nice*, or *not now*, or *never mind* – which she'd hold out in the same manner that Leah had held out that glass bottle, and they all accepted it because she was their mother. What else is there?

Ian knows he is the same as her. Or rather, he is not like Jack: he makes sure of that.

He walks back across the fields. And as he goes, he sees the eastern side of everything on Parla is gold-coloured; the sun finds the eastern edge of each fence-post, each car and chicken shed. Their western sides are in shadow. *It is*, he thinks, *beautiful*. And if someone was with him would he say it? Or would he let this beauty go unmarked? And does he ever really talk of anything at all?

The barn. He thinks of the barn at Wind Rising. It comes in a rush: Hester and him. How old? It doesn't matter. They had run there because of what they had heard – the single sound of a breaking glass. That was all. But they had run to the barn in case that broken glass signified the start of something that they, as children, did not want to hear – more glass, raised voices. The sun had been low. The barn had been striped with shadows, and Hester and Ian had said nothing at all to each other. They'd run for the same reason; they both knew what happened in that house from time to time – and yet they said nothing. They sat on a bale and let the minutes pass. Swung their legs. Twisted hay.

Hester is, maybe, the only one that speaks. She has found God whereas Ian remains hard and Nathan is no better – a drunk, or nearly one. They have faith in nothing – whilst Hester tends to the church's flowers and wears that cross around her neck and she chooses to believe things happen for a reason. *Tom's death was* ... What had she called it? *Part of His plan* – as if she didn't mind it when she did. Oh, she minded. They all minded, and still mind. Ian has heard her crying – in the school once the children had gone, in the church, the fields.

This man. This bearded amnesiac who they talked about in church as if he is of significance; a miracle of some kind. He is not a miracle. He will have a story; he will have a lie.

The house called Wind Rising gets closer. He imagines the breakfast that will be waiting, the steam from the kettle that clouds the windowpane. He has lived nowhere else. All his life – half a century of life – has been spent in its rooms, scuffing over its flagstone floors.

Please let this get better.

Why now? Why these words now? He can't be sure. He pushes down the uppermost strand of a wire fence, climbs over it, lets the wire spring back up and he has so many questions. They come to him for the first time: who wrote this plea? This message? And who, precisely, was the writer hoping to reach? A deity? Someone who could, in fact, help them in some way? And why? Why would he (Ian assumes, strangely, the writer was a *he*) choose to write a request on a square of paper and give it to the tides instead of saying it to someone who could, perhaps, help? Maybe he wasn't a talker either. Maybe he wasn't a believer, and this act was the closest he could bring himself to prayer.

It makes him a little sad. Compassionate even.

Ian also sees the irony as he enters the house. If it was a wish, it's not been granted. If someone fifteen years ago had hoped for some divinity – for the note to be found by someone of worth or purpose or a little magic dust – it could not have gone more wrong. That bottle washed up by the feet of a man who believes in nothing – nothing whatsoever. *Me*. Just a man, a farmer. How could he make something better?

There is no magic in him. There is nothing divine about a man whose boots are grooved with sheep dung and who can never find the words.

He washes his hands.

There is no God, no Fishman, and no point in stories. There is no life other than the one we see and so who would write a note, send that note to sea?

Ian cannot remember believing. When he was very small he may, for a year or so, have believed in Father Christmas; but it didn't last. He learnt the lie before his siblings did – but he kept his new, adult truth (*it's Mum and Dad, stupid ...*) to himself as they crowed on Christmas morning. What has he believed in since?

He dropped his dreams like marbles and they scattered and ran so he can never get them back, now. Surely, at his age, it is too late to try.

Seven

A week, by now, of sunshine. These were *offered days* – an old Parlan saying for days of such sunshine and calm, blue sea that they felt like a gift. Rare days.

Towels were laid out on Store Bay. Milton sold ice creams in little paper tubs. And I found a cormorant standing on a buoy that marked my lobster pots – blue-black in the sunshine, with its wings held out. It stayed as it was, very still. Only when *Pigeon*'s prow bumped against the buoy itself did the cormorant dive into the water – as deftly and soundlessly as oil.

My laundry dried within an hour.

The earth in the horse's field grew powdery.

The rock pool near Litty that was deep enough to swim in grew as warm as a bath. I saw Kitty floating in it – a dark-red swimsuit with a purple trim.

I could not remember better weather. There had been hand-fuls of days – two, three or four in a row – during my first Parlan summer in which there had been beach cricket, dancing and late-night beers outside Milton's shop; I remember looking up at the clearest of night skies. But this had been a week, now, of heat. *And it's lasting a while yet*, Ed said.

Of course, it was rumoured it was the Fishman's doing.

Maybe my patient brought it with him, said Tabitha, as she cycled past me in the lane.

And it was good lobstering weather. Hard to check – or to want to check – the pots in high swells or driving rain, and a lobster is less willing to clamber into rope and wood when the tides are running at their strongest. But these were flat waters. They shone with the sun. Each pot that I lifted had a life in it. I wondered how it was for them – to be taken from the sea's dark chamber into this dazzling light.

Emmeline passes Crest in her car. She glances over, sees Maggie tucking tarpaulin over a black plastic crate and she knows what is in there. She never liked lobsters herself. She does not like the meat nor does she care for having to crack into their bones – and the cost? Too much for too little. She won't be fooled.

She drives past the old tractor wheel, parks beside the lighthouse.

It is another day of sunshine and as she stood in her kitchen, rubbing cream into her hands, she thought *I will go to the café. Order a coffee – foam and steamed milk.*

She will drink it in the courtyard where she used to play.

It was a good child's place. A lighthouse. How many others in this world can say that they grew up in a world of mirrors, bulbs, brass and talk of shipwrecks? Not many, but Emmeline can. There were three lighthouse-keepers. The job was always too crucial, too lonesome, too demanding of wakefulness to be left to one man alone and two was not much better. So at the foot of Parla's lighthouse there were three lodgings for three men and their families – identical, cream-coloured buildings which formed three sides of a courtyard, and they had three back gardens, three washing lines ... The Brights, the Coyles and the Hallidays. Everything was *three*.

She'd liked it. As with so many things, she only knew how much she liked it when she had let it go. When she went to draw the curtains at Wind Rising, she would see the light turning and she'd feel a punch of regret, or home-sickness. The day that the lighthouse was automated was the second-worst day of her life. But how could Jack have understood it?

It's only a building, he said.

All earth, those men. They were sheep farmers and left the sea to others. *Land is our business* – Emmeline remembers her father-in-law wheezing this, when he first heard that his only son was marrying that homely Bright girl who was all brine and tides. *You're a farmer, now. And that light won't last ... Men won't need a lighthouse in the future, Emma.*

It's Emmeline.

Emma. Mark my words.

She did mark them, sourly – but he was wrong for the lighthouse might be automated now but doesn't it still swing its light each night? It does. It was Old Man Bundy who did not last – for his lungs gave up on Christmas Eve the following year, and Emmeline had toasted the news with cooking brandy in the kitchen when the rest of them were in the sitting room, in black.

She parks the car. The lighthouse's buildings are all painted a pristine white now, with pale-brown doors and window frames. They shine. She smiles: *Bright*.

Rona looks up, slows. She tidies herself and then she finds her best, wide smile and says *hello, Emmeline! Which table?* Smoothing out the tablecloths as if talking to a queen.

Emmeline selects one and settles.

The courtyard is swept; the paint is unblistered.

Is this Emmeline's home? In her bones? Or did home become the stone walls of Wind Rising? Or has her true home become Easterly, with its peonies and garden chairs? *Home is where the heart is* but Emmeline can't be sure where her heart is any more. Her husband died twelve years ago. He died when he still had four children – one curly-haired daughter, three warm-bodied sons. And so her heart is not with him. Perhaps her heart is quartered and a part of it is with each child – three Parlan houses, and the deep blue sea.

She closes her eyes.

Tom had not been planned. She had borne three healthy, vigorous children and had not wanted a fourth. There weren't enough bedrooms, for one thing. And not enough money, if truth be told – for when did sheep bring in fortunes? Not in her lifetime. Three children were plenty. But men can be insistent on a winter's night when there's beer in their bellies and women can unlock themselves from their bodies and go elsewhere, when they must – so nine months later Tom slipped out. His head was perfectly round – she remembers that. And she swears he was smiling. A joy – when joy was so hard to find.

The coffee is brought. Emmeline sips it, licks her lips.

She knows she ought to hold a hatred for Jack, of some kind. There were moments of such darkness in her marriage that she was shocked into a numbness when they happened – a cool, empty otherness in which she felt no pain. When she fell, she would stare at the skirting board; she'd press her lips together, shut her eyes. The shock itself crept in later – in the shower, or out in the fields.

She hates those moments, now. Emmeline can see herself against the oven, both her hands up by her face so that it might not be marked for a bruised face needs answers from children, whereas a bruised body does not. She was always so calm when it happened. She'd accept it and not cry. Afterwards, she would lock herself in the bathroom and tend to the new shapes of her, the colours, as if it was not her body. Sometimes she'd sing under her breath.

It is how it is. I have no choice. Where does one go, on an island?

Yes, perhaps Emmeline should hate her husband. But nothing – nothing – is as simple as that. Jack was also the man who spoke to his lambs when they came into the world – *welcome, little one* – and who dressed up as a pirate on the school's last day of term. He knew the constellations. He would rub Emmeline's feet as they watched the evening news, tending gently to each pink toe. And he gave her the four best things in the world, her four strong hearts, her daughter and sons. How could she hate him? She loved him sometimes.

And she knows about his childhood, too. She knows what Jack endured. What Abigail and Thomasina went through.

Emmeline sips her coffee. No, she does not hate him. She hates what he did and she hates plenty more besides, including the concern that came from others who may, perhaps, have wondered about a certain bruise or an odd-shaped cut. How Emmeline hated that. What business was it of theirs? Even now she narrows her eyes, and even now she hates Old Man Bundy who might have kicked the dog but he did far worse to his children. Jack never did that. He never turned to his children except to teach them how to tie knots or castrate the rams. To lift them onto bales of hay.

And the truth – Emmeline's truth which she has never spoken of – is that after each time that her husband had struck her, as she sat on the edge of that bath and dabbed at her bloodied places, she felt relief. She was relieved –

more than anything else. Like a cloudburst, it cleared the air for a week or so. But also, she was relieved because as she bled, she would hear her children out in the fields, trying to catch a sheep to ride or blowing grass between their thumbs. She'd hear their laughter or how they'd call each other's names – *Nay-thaan* ... And yes, she felt relief. She felt gratitude that it was her, not them. And she felt sorry for her husband, who had spent his own childhood hiding in strange places with his frightened sisters. Who had found one of those sisters, floating like a glove – four limbs, and one long twist of hair.

Be strong is what she told herself. *Be the warrior.* And if it meant she was quiet or stern, then that's what it meant. If it meant being sharp-tongued then that's what she became. *We all have our forms of survival.* She never thought of her own sake. Perhaps she did a little – she had her secret drawer of flesh-coloured creams and powders that she'd pat on with her fingertips and so much could be hidden by good woollen tights. But she was fifth on her list of concerns. She was fifth – for when you bring a life into the world it is that life that matters far more than your own. When you have four precious lives, you would endure far more than the odd thrown saucepan or having your hair grasped so tightly that you find a bald patch there, later. You endure *bitch*, and far worse. These things are easy. These things are light as air and barely a trouble if you can then walk downstairs and see Hester licking the jam spoon, or Ian lying on his front by the fire with his football sticker album or Nathan using a ruler as a sword saying *take that! And that!* Or Tom in his red swimming trunks when it was too late to swim, or too cold.

She became wise on the day she gave birth for the first time. She thought then, at that moment, what she thinks now. *I would endure every pain, every fist, every slung word, and I would be pummelled into the sand or held*

*underwater or thrown on the fire or be torn apart or all
these things if it meant my child was safe and well.* She'd
give her own life – unquestionably – if she had to. If it
would do any good.

Those red swimming trunks.

She remembers how he dived off the jetty once, at high
tide, and those trunks had somehow freed themselves,
surfaced before him. He'd spouted like a whale, widened
his eyes. *My shorts! Mum!* Laughing and laughing.

Emmeline sniffs.

She knows the islanders think she is cold. They think
she is bitter, as tight as an oyster and perhaps she is. How
she spoke in church hardly helped, in that. But how could
she be any other way? She had no choice. A boat can only
float for so long unless it's well-sealed, and she's known
some stormy weather. She's known the pitch and toss, how
you hold on for your life and pray for dawn to come. She
stayed afloat but not without its costs.

*   *   *

At Wind Rising, an orange Calor gas bottle tilts to its left.
Softly, it clunks against the bottle next to it. The dog sees
this. Her ears prick.

Nan, in turn, sees the dog. She also sees sheep mess and
bugs because she is in the long grass, but she does not
mind these things. She lies on her front. There is a big blue
sky, and skylarks are singing, and she can see the crossroads beneath her.

These grasses are Wind Rising's grasses. When an ant
hurries over her hand, she knows the ant belongs to Wind
Rising. She also knows the story of silver in these fields
and she wonders if this ant has seen any on his walks – a
flake of it, like a moth's wing.

She waits.

169

I am an explorer, she tells herself. With her chin on the soil, the grass is like trees. *I am in the jungle ...*

Then she sees him. The Fishman is walking up the lane.

Nancy was two and a half when Maggie's husband dived off his boat to help someone from drowning, and then drowned himself. She does not remember him at all. So as she watches this tall, bearded man walking past the rusting tractor with his eyes on the blue sky and the birds that sing down to him, she does not think of anybody else. She does not think of Maggie, or the three other Bundy children who are grown-ups now.

She thinks, *it must be hard – to walk. When all you've known is a fish's tail.*

The tabby cat emerges from her sunny spot, tail up. Nan hears her mewing – a noisy, broken, demanding sound – and the man bends down to speak to her. How he touches the cat is nervous, at first; he holds his fingers above her head, not sure how to stroke her. But the cat pushes herself up onto her back legs to reach his hand, and she drops back down into the dust with a thud. *Mew!*

He is very tall. His legs are long, so his tail would have been.

And now the man who was found at Sye begins to walk to the north. He puts his hands in his pockets as he does so, and twice he turns round to glance behind him for the cat from High Haven is following him, trotting beside the stone wall, and it is only after he has spoken to her again – bending down, hands still in pockets – that she stops, and lowers her tail.

He leaves.

The cat watches for a moment, as if forlorn. Then she settles and begins to clean herself; she investigates her lower half, one leg stretched up in the air.

*　　*　　*

Maggie puts the car into second gear, rises away from the harbour. She passes the picnic table, where two tourists are sitting. They do not notice Maggie, or her car. The view is too good, here. The sunshine.

She bears right at the crossroads, heads for home.

The car smells of seawater – cold, fishy. She wonders how much those lobsters will fetch her and she imagines the restaurant with white cloths, the long forks for spearing the deepest meat in their claws. Neat italic script on a stiff menu that reads *Parlan lobster*.

And she sees him.

It is the man from Sye. He is walking ahead of her, along the lane. He hears the car and steps to the side, into the verge, to let her pass.

Briefly, she thinks *keep driving*; briefly, she is afraid and thinks *carry on, don't stop*. But part of her, too – the stronger, hidden part – says *it's him: stop* ... as she approaches him. And this is the part she listens to.

Thank you.

I was passing. Seems wrong not to offer a lift, at least. Where to?

She is aware of his size, of the space he is taking up in the car. She wonders, also, if he is noticing the empty cola can at his feet, or the blankets and rope on the back seat.

The cove called Sye.

Sye? Really?

I've not seen it yet. Or at least, not since I was found. I thought if I went and sat there a while ...

Maggie says nothing.

She grinds the gears as they climb higher. The harbour, the old pig farm, the crossroads and most of the homes are behind them. Ahead, it's wilder country. More sheep and fewer people. She can see Crest on the hill. It looks so small from here. She can see her jacket on the washing line, and the wheelbarrow resting by the gate.

There's no road to Sye, she says. *It's a footpath. I'll drop you there.*

It's not out of your way?

No. I live near it. See that house? The washing? That's Crest.

He leans forwards. *Good spot.*

It is.

The car windows are down. The sound of the sheep comes in. She sees how they hurry away from them – a fast, clumsy walk, with their swinging tails. Or they stand as they are, and stare.

Here. She slows the car in a gateway. *Cross the stile. Keep walking.*

Thank you. He climbs out, shuts it. And before Maggie drives off she leans across to the open window and says *listen, if you want a glass of water, or a cup of tea ... There's nowhere else but the lighthouse up here, and Rona will charge you for them.*

Your water is free? A smile.

Maggie pushes the car into gear, drives up the lane.

*   *   *

She had the same scent as before – salt, lotion, fabric conditioner, something almost floral which he can still smell, now. The backs of her hands, as she'd driven, had looked older than the rest of her. He knows that will be the life she lives – outdoors, seafaring, cold water and soil. He looks at his own hands. The round, brown scar.

He walks along the sheep track until he finds the coast. The path drops through gorse. On Sye, the Fishman finds a dry place amongst the larger stones and lowers himself down. He brings his knees towards his chest, loops his arms around them. And like this, he looks out. He looks out and sees far more than sea – more than waves and a gull, flying.

I did not expect this. Want this.

He thinks of her tiny, sideways smile. Her hair, by her temples, is almost feather-like.

*   *   *

Tabitha is fastening three bamboo canes. She has twine in her mouth, pliers in one hand. It is the season for runner beans and so she needs a frame for them – a tall, bamboo pyramid that they can climb upon. Her vegetable garden is untidy, she thinks. Ragwort and dandelions.

He has gone walking. Her guest, her patient. Her imaginary son.

The house is different in ways she can't define. There are the obvious signs of his presence: the boots in the porch, the new toothbrush that she bought from the shop beside her own. But there is also a feeling to Lowfield – she *feels* he is there, or has been. She can't describe it further, and can only add that she likes it: this extra, passing life.

She is thinking of him – the man they're calling the *Fishman*, now.

And so when she hears the steady footsteps of a man on her gravel path, she expects to see him there. But it is not him.

Ed sees the nurse before she sees him. Tab – who is kneeling in her vegetable patch, frowning over the top of her spectacles at a knot that she's just tied. Her hair is white, now; her figure has thickened as Ed's own has – but she is still the Tabitha Bright he knew, as a boy. Long ago.

She sees him, rises. *Hello, Eddie.*

Inside, as she cuts a slice of cake for him, Tabitha says *he's out walking. If you wanted to see him.*

Our mystery man? Not as such. Wanted to know how he was, I suppose.

The grazes on his hands are much better.

Memory?

Haven't asked. But it will come back, in time.

How much time?

Could be anything … Have patience. Tabitha smiles.

He takes the slice of cake. *Your sister wasn't too pleased.*

In church? Ha! A quick, dismissive laugh. *When is she ever?*

It must be tricky for her, when this man looks –

I know. I know, Ed. But this man can't help being who he is.

Or who he isn't.

She nods. *Quite.*

There are eight years between them, in age. It hardly matters, now; now, Tabitha is a close friend, a fellow islander, the first person to hold all of Ed's five children as they slipped into her arms. She is sixty-five and Ed is fifty-seven and it makes no difference – age is nothing, these days. But it mattered when he was eleven years old. Oh, it had mattered then.

No more from the coastguards?

Mac? No. He said he'd let me know if he heard of missing boats, or crew.

Her hair had been so blonde that summer. It had been like no other hair he'd seen – in colour, or thickness. He'd wanted to touch it – to feel the downy whiteness at the nape of her neck or the down on her arms that matched it. His friends would whisper they'd seen her undress, once, or touched her bra on the washing line, and her name was *the* name to Parlan boys – the shiniest coin, the starriest night. The beautiful girl from the lighthouse: *Tabitha Bright.*

And Sam?

Ed chews, swallows. *He seems to be coping. He walks a lot. Works on the ferry, still. I think he thought this man was Tom, at first. Just for a second or two.*

He is sleeping?

Not sure. He says so.

And she'd had a scarlet bikini. He'd watched her swim, once, and afterwards she'd walked over to him whilst towelling her hair and said *not coming in, Eddie?* She'd paused, brushed a pebble from the sole of her foot; she'd untwisted the side of her bikini top. She'd had no idea – and that, perhaps, had been Tabitha's real beauty; the fact she'd never known, for a second, that she was beautiful at all.

They go outside, into the light. They talk of the weather, of Rona's café, how Nan is spending her time at the Old Fish Store, asking for stories about this half-fish. The nurse asks his advice on her strawberry plants which haven't done well this year.

Tabitha?

She looks up.

Have we done the right thing? About the police?

She was off the island for nearly fourteen years. When she'd returned – browned from a fierce, African sun, thinner and with wiser eyes – Ed had been in his twenties and *perhaps, perhaps* ... But it was gone. Done. That deep boyhood love for her had faded. And maybe it hadn't been love at all but an adoration – lust, but nothing more. Love is what he has, now.

Love, he thinks, *is Dee.*

Yes. We have done. And she has more lines by her eyes when she smiles, but it is still the same smile.

* * *

Nathan and Ian move a length of electric fence, widening a field. They look alike in how they move, in how they call to each other. The dog from Wind Rising is with them; she crouches, tongue lolling.

It is the dog that sees the Fishman first. Her ears prick, and she whines. It is enough for Ian to straighten up so that he, too, sees the Fishman walking through the longer grass.

Nathe. Look.

They stand side by side.

The Fishman crosses the stile. He is a shape, for a moment – a dark shape against the sky. Then he steps down, makes his way up the lane to the house with the shed, a porch filled with tomato plants. The house with the yellow front door.

Maggie has washed plates; she's cleared the kitchen table of newspapers and envelopes; she's raked her fingers through her hair.

He is a fish. He is not human.

She stares at the bathroom mirror. Turns her head from side to side.

Three knocks. *Tap tap tap.*

Maggie walks along the hallway, opens the door.

Are you sure you don't mind? he says.

In the kitchen she makes a pot of coffee. He is warm, from his walk – she can feel his warmth, as she moves behind him to take the mugs from their hooks. She puts sugar on the table, and milk. *So – how was Sye?*

I remember it, I think. The stones.

You like it?

He shifts, not knowing. *It felt cold, almost.*

I know. Those high cliffs. The lighthouse doesn't find it. They say smugglers used it – a long time ago. His hair is incredibly thick. It could be gathered between two hands as her own hair can be.

There are stories here, he says. Not a question.

Of course. It's an island. It's how they spent the evenings before the radio, the TV ... Maggie moves, opens a drawer. *And who are we to say they aren't true? We weren't there.*

The Fishman?

You've heard? I know how it sounds. But there's a man on Parla who swears he saw him, as a boy. A shrug. *And I'm not going to doubt him. Jim and Abigail have been good to me.*

She knows he is watching her. She feels his eyes on her back.

See anything? At Sye?

I tried to find exactly where I came ashore, but ...

How about memories? Find any of them?

It is a sharp tone. She hears it and regrets it.

He likes her kitchen. He likes the wood – driftwood, he assumes – and the fact that the table seems to be part of a boat. He likes the light which comes through the south-east-facing window; he has noticed how much he is craving the light.

It brims, this room. There are notes and timetables pinned to the fridge. Dried flowers hang from the ceiling amongst the ladles and copper pans. On the wall beside him there is a line of knives held on a magnet, and a small chalkboard on which she has written *milk* and *stamps*; a third word has been crossed out. There is wine, unopened. An apron hangs on the back of a chair. The oven gloves have polka dots and there's a bowl filled with tomatoes and he thinks *these things are hers. She owns them.*

Also, there are shells. The Fishman sees one at first, and then he sees many – on shelves, on the draining board and the windowsill. Periwinkles, cockles, a huge conch shell that could not have come from these waters. And there is a glass vase in which she has put feathers – dozens of feathers that are split, sandy, damaged. Mostly grey or white.

You like feathers?

She follows his gaze. *Yes. Shells. Stones that have been rolled into balls.*

Does much come ashore?

Depends on the weather, and tides. But yes. There are always whelks, mussels ... Bottle tops. Hubcaps, some-times. A typewriter, once ... She hands him a coffee, picks up her own. *Ian found a message in a bottle, years ago. Before I came.*

No men?

Bearded? Tall? Memory loss? She brings her mug up to her lips. *No, we've had none of those.*

Perhaps it is the feathers in the vase. But she makes him think of birds. She is wearing a white shirt with long, linen trousers – too long, so that the hem is dark – and yet there is a grace to her, a movement to her arms as a bird may tuck its wings.

You're not an islander?

A shake of her head. *No. I came on the boat. I was born inland, lived there. I'd never heard of Parla till I was thirty-four. Maybe that's why I have these shells ...*

And feathers?

Maggie shrugs. *They aren't from pigeons. That makes them new to me.*

Do you miss it?

The mainland? She considers this. *Some things. Not enough to go back there – or not yet. I know people who can't spend one night inland. They can't sleep where there is no sea, no sea's sound.* She does not look up. *What about you?*

Me?

Yes, you. The fabled Fishman, the fish that grew legs and walked onto Sye. Do you miss the water? The whale song and shoals of fish?

He opens his mouth to speak, but does not.

He comes here to restore hope and wonder. The Fishman. Are you going to do that for us? She doesn't know why she speaks like this – sourly, as if testing him.

Hope and wonder?

You look exactly like him. I have seen the drawings and they could be drawings of you.

*　　*　　*

A woman with a small tattoo stands in the empty house. She has moved from room to room. She has called his name, as if coaxing.

Nathan is rarely here – he tends, by day, to be digging or building, or out in the fields with Ian. Burning ragwort. A few months ago he was lambing and he'd come indoors to eat or to rinse strings of blood off his hands in the sink. Even when he is here – on a chair, or watching the television, or upstairs on their computer – he is not *here*, not with her.

Kitty can feel nothing so easily – numb, in every sense. Once, she was fire and appetite, and she'd run up to the attic to fling down new colours or sketch wild lines of charcoal on white. Now? She wants things back that may never come back. She wishes she was younger; she wishes her husband was in this bedroom and not wherever he is – which is drunk at Milton's, most likely, or lying in a field. Trawling the beaches, bottle in hand.

It is not what she wants – this absence. How long can a person live with what they do not want? Or live with what

makes them unhappy? Once this island had meant everything that was honest, loving and good.

* * *

Late, now. The lighthouse opens its white eye.

Jim Coyle thinks he can hear piano music.

The chestnut mare blows through her nostrils and it
flattens the grass into stars.

Those moments that we remember. The tiniest moments,
or parts of a moment – a *tap* of a nail against a mug or the
sound of a man swallowing, or how the sweeping beam
finds the kitchen walls and then leaves them. We count the
seconds, he and I.

At Crest we are sitting in darkness. I have not stood,
turned on a lamp. All we have is the glow of a waning
moon, and the lighthouse when it comes.

He has been here for six hours. We have talked a little,
and sat without talking. I have given us a small meal –
cheese, fruit, bread.

All the while, the sea has spoken. And all the while I
have known what he has been wanting – longing – to ask,
but has not.

In the end, he does not have to ask.

I tell him. I say *I want to tell you how my husband died.*

And he replies *yes* – as if grateful. *Yes – OK.*

*There's a boy on the island called Sam Lovegrove. He's
fair-haired, tall. He found you, on Sye – remember? He
has a boat called* Sea Fairy *– it's still in the harbour, with*

a green tarpaulin. He doesn't use it now but he used to. He used to take tourists round the island in it – the caves, the beaches that are hard to reach on foot. Bit of money in it. Nearly four years ago he took two boys out. It was a warm day, the sea was calm ... But off a beach called Lock-and-Key one of the boys went overboard. I still don't know how and Sam doesn't know how but over he went. And he'd had a lifejacket on but it can't have been fastened properly or perhaps it was too big for him because it came off in the water. He lost it, and there are currents off that beach if the tide's on the turn, and the lifejacket was gone and this boy began to struggle. They were trying to reach him, and I guess they were shouting because Tom was out in Pigeon *and he heard them. He was baiting the pots near Bundy Head but he heard them and so ran the boat down to Lock-and-Key. He turned off the engine. Dived in. Saved him.*

Saved the boy?

Saved the boy. Tom was a strong swimmer. He was the best swimmer on the island and he got this boy, pushed him up into the air so that they could grab him and haul him back onto the boat, and I don't know if they were slow to turn back for Tom or if the current had picked up or if he was just too tired from the swim or if he got cramp or something else we'll never know of but when they turned round there was just sea. Empty sea. He was ... gone. Her eyes are huge. She stares at nothing. *There were boats and helicopters for three days. We searched every beach, every cave.*

The kitchen is in darkness now; they can only see each other's eyes.

He was declared dead two weeks later. But I kept looking. We all kept looking. And four years later, here we are ...

Somewhere, a clock ticks.

I loved him. I love him still.

He says *I am so sorry.*

I don't blame anyone. So many people blame Sam, or did. But I never have.

I swallow – a single, soft sound. And in the hush that follows it, we look at each other.

There are things we know and cannot be sure how we know them, but we know them all the same. And I know what he's thinking. I am also thinking it.

* * *

Even now, I can see us perfectly. I can see how we were, how we sat without moving for a very long time.

When it was too dark to see him, I rose and turned on a lamp which half-lit the kitchen – a glow that caught the sides of things. The side of the fridge, the side of shells. The left side of his face.

I did not wish to be still. I was tired but I could not be still. I feared stillness and I feared how he was looking at me so I moved through the room doing small things that did not matter – moving a spoon, touching the feathers in their glass vase.

He stood. He came behind me. He did not touch me but he was close, very close, and I felt as I had felt in the garden at Lowfield – old, in need. *Turn around*, he said.

No.

Maggie ...

I couldn't turn. I knew what would happen if I turned – that I would weaken again, lean gently against him so that I would hear his heart and he would touch my shoulder or more than my shoulder. I wanted it and feared it – both. And so I stepped away. I walked into the hallway and opened the front door and stood beside it, looking down. The evening air filled the house.

The Fishman watched me do this. He nodded, as if he understood.

He came towards me and the open door.

I can't, I said. *Not yet.*

His was the face of a saint, or the face of someone who knew what the truth was when others did not. Yes, he understood it. He understood it all – loss, want, how things end and how they begin. He did not say any more. He only smiled very sadly as he passed me, and walked out into the night.

I watched him go. He went as the pots did, when I lowered them into the water – fading, fading so that you think, briefly, *don't go, stay* … But then the darkness has them. It takes them entirely and they are gone from sight, and it seems they were never here with you at all. Were they ever real? Did you ever touch them? You stare at the water where, once, they had been.

The Wild Sheep and
the Stormy Night

This was always an island of sheep. Sheep are well-suited to rough land and thin grass – and so it was always sheep that the Parlans raised, sold and ate. I have seen the photographs. I have seen an old, whisky-coloured reel of film in which the sheep may be brainless but they're still quick-footed. Still outwitting the men.

Stupid beasts. Nathan said this. One afternoon when Tom was still alive, we had helped to shear them – we'd wrestled the sheep down and kept them there. Nathan never drank in those days, or rarely. The three of us were sitting on a stone wall, sticky with fleece. Damp from kneeling in sheep dung that had been loosely, frantically made.

Stupid. You know the story of how they charged?
Charged?

Tom smiled. With a mouth full of sandwich he said, *this is a good one – tell her, Nathe.*

Tell me, I nodded. *I love stories.*

*   *   *

Hester is combing her hair. She is picking through it – grass-seeds and old leaves can lose themselves in her curls. She used to hate them. There are no grips or bands that last; there is no spray that holds her hair for more than a minute or two. It is thick, bush-like, so that when George first took her to bed he spent half the time stroking her dense, wilful locks, amazed by them. *Look how they spring back up when I pull ...* In time, he'd stroked the rest of her. But it all began with her hair.

Like fleece.

She hates it less, now. It is her – part of her. And if George loves it, then it helps. But in the early days, her father would call her a *scruff* or a *gypsy* – although he'd never hiss these words to her directly. Always to her mother, or someone passing by. *Look at the state of that one ...* as if Hester's hair was her doing, and she chose those curls.

I never chose the curls.

She never chose anything except her husband, her motherhood and her trust in God. The rest of it was put upon her and she bears it and does her best. But even at forty-eight she has small dreams of straight blonde hair – Maggie's hair, or how Nancy's will be when she's older. Hair that doesn't snag on branches or barbed wire so that you are left there, calling out for help, which happened several times when she was younger. Hanging and holler-ing next to tufts of fleece.

She has always known the tale of how the sheep charged. Nathan was the one for telling stories, and he told this tale one evening as they sucked lollipops in the barn. All four of them – Ian, Nathan, Tom and herself. The lollipops were cherry-flavoured.

A roll of thunder. It shook the metal arms of the barn.

Ages ago, there was a really wild storm ...

So it began. Nathan spoke of a parched summer that led to a night of such thunder and shaken sky that the lanes became rivers and the smell in the air was of wet earth and wet stones, and there were no stars or moon to see by for the rain was blinding, too strong. The islanders listened to the drumming on their roofs. The Parlan voles tucked up into balls. Boats rocked, and hens curled their toes.

A flock of sheep went mad. That is the story – that the flashing light and the banging sky and the gusting wind that seemed to have no direction at all in how it raced through the grass and tore through the nettles were all too much for a flock of two dozen sheep or so. Where to turn? They did not know. They bleated, circled in the dark. Their ears were flat and their eyes rolled and their nostrils clenched and unclenched, and there was one sudden, low slap of thunder at the back of the flock so that they started to run. They charged blindly and unwaveringly towards the west coast; they fell off the cliff and into the sea. They died on the rocks or drowned very promptly, for the sea had been huge, shattering, monstrous. Nothing could float, or survive it.

So they died.

In the morning, when the storm had passed, there was no sign of the two dozen sheep save for a line of trampled grass. The farmer could not understand it.

And this is what Hester knows, as I know it, and as Abigail knows it from her leather-bound book – that if you walk on the beach when a storm has passed by, so that the air is clean and the sand is strewn with driftwood and plastic and lengths of rope, look at the foam that's been left there. Often, there'll be a line of foam – brown-coloured, thicker than foam tends to be. The wind may catch it and blow it, as it blows all sea foam – but this is fibrous, heavier. It rolls, turns itself over. It does not skitter, or fly.

This is not foam, is what they say. It is fleece from the long-drowned sheep. And it is sent ashore to remind the one who finds it – you, me, the person walking on that beach – how lucky they've been to survive the bad weather. *See? Others did not.*

Others did not. Hester lowers the comb.

They had all listened in that barn. Cherry-breathed. Tom had said, *poor sheep.*

And Nathan had shaken his head and said *but we're alive, aren't we? That's the point of the foam when we see it. It's to tell us we're still here. See?*

Like everyone on Parla, she has her share of guilt. She has her guilt because she thinks she could have saved him, somehow – a sisterly warning, a tale of some kind – and she has her guilt because she is here when he is not. But also, she got out of there. That's the expression she's used herself, over and over: *I got myself out of there* ... Or rather, George got her out, by marrying her. By coming to Parla on a birdwatching trip and not watching any birds whatsoever; he'd watched Hester, instead. What if she'd not married him? Stayed at Wind Rising with the boys?

I survived and he did not. The brown foam that the sea leaves behind is pollution, most likely, and the two dozen sheep will have made a good meal for crabs and fish and diving birds. But when she sees fleece on wire, or the scudding froth of beaches, it is Tom she thinks of. Tom who, like the sheep, made the wrong choice that day.

Part of everything is missing. Nothing is quite as it was before.

He was the most loved, without question – so radiant and eager that it felt like he had been born for a reason, or that he knew something the rest of them did not. He was precious – they all knew it. Like the few rare shells that come ashore after a storm and are not broken.

I was his big sister. Proud, and sad.

Where has he gone? Sometimes it is like he was never here – she has merely imagined the embraces he gave her in which he lifted her off the floor. There is not even trampled grass to show where he has been.

Eight

I have never – not once – asked for love. I was not born with it; I'd had no family and no sense of home, and so I never missed it. I never sought it out or prayed for it to come.

And so Tom had been unexpected. I had not woken that morning and thought *I will meet him today*. I had only ever gone to that harbour town because I was tired of my impermanent, shifting life – the rented homes, the jobs I grew bored in, the men I did not feel enough for and so had to leave without warning. I thought a harbour would suit me. A place of safety and rest.

But it proved to be a place of love. *Love* – after all this time. And love proved to be a smiling, dark-haired lobster-man called Thomas Bundy – how could I have guessed that? But life, I've learnt, has its surprises. And I would say that most of the things that I have asked for over the months and years have, in fact, not happened. I used to ask for Tom's safe return; later, I prayed to find his bones. After that, I feared losing his face, or my memory of it – his pores, say, or the shape of his lips – and I could never remember them when I longed to, when I thought *please don't let me forget* … Only later did they come back: a clear, perfect vision of his teeth, as I was standing in a shop queue or trimming the fat off bacon so that I'd pause, amazed, grateful, teary-eyed.

For me, it is the unasked things that seem to come.

And I did not ask for the Fishman. I had not hoped for love a second time. Why would I have hoped for love? I did not want to replace the husband whose ring I still wore, whose surname I still signed cheques with, whose handwriting was still in our shared address book so that sometimes I would touch where his hand may have rested as he wrote a postcode or a name. I formed a wall around me; a wall of protection. I feared that wall breaking. Fear had made me fight him outside Lowfield, saying *no!*

All I wanted was an existence where I could put one foot before the other, and then the other foot in front of that, and lift feathers from the beach which were remnants of a passing life. The salty shards of a greater thing.

I would tell him this, in time. *I didn't want you to come. I didn't ask.*

And his answer? He touched me, said *and I didn't ask for you. But look …*

*   *   *

In the days after we'd talked at Crest, I stayed away. I thought of him constantly. I said *he is a fish* over and over; I tried to keep to the north of the isle.

All the same, I heard him spoken of. Over glasses of wine or rich, black slices of Rona's chocolate cake I started to hear stories about this nameless man – how he changed the lightbulb in the school's porch, or helped Lorcan move his piano against a different wall. Milton told me how the Fishman had stood in the mare's field and shown Leah how to blow a blade of grass and it was this shrill, sudden sound that had made Milton walk to his window and see him, for the first time. *Big fellow, isn't he?* I stood in his shop, listened. And then I shrugged, cleared my throat, pretended that I had no wish to know.

I asked my lobsters if they'd seen him. *Have you? Passing by?*

I pulled up my vegetables and thought *how about you?*

As for Nan, she sprang out of a ditch near the Old Fish Store, rapped her knuckles against his knees and yelled, *just checking!* Laughed until she had to sit down.

Not all spoke highly of him, of course. Some sucked their gums at the mention of him, and gave a hard *ha!* I went to Easterly, and Emmeline hissed *he is up to no good. I'm telling you, Maggie. Do you know what he did? This morning?* She'd opened her curtains to find him in her driveway. He'd been crouching by her single rose bush as if entranced. The flowers had been browning; they were past their best, dropping petals like pink rain and yet he'd leant down towards them, touched them tenderly. *I mean – what on earth …?* Such a thing enraged her. Emmeline had thrown open her window, called out *can I help you?* She'd said it in a tone that implied she intended to give no help at all.

Nor were the Bundy brothers keen. They were kicking at the rotten fence-post above Tap Hole when they looked up and saw him at Tavey – the old pig farm. *What the hell's he doing?* For the Fishman had been walking round it – feeling the planks that were nailed to its windows, pressing his shoulder against its softened door.

* * *

Late afternoon. It is late afternoon and I do not want him and yet I think of him. I have no answers.

The north wind gives white tips to the waves.

I am sitting in *Pigeon* as if *Pigeon* can help.

Abigail Coyle sits in the graveyard. She sits on the bench with the south-facing view. It is where she always sits, when she comes here. The brambles and blackthorns hide her from the lane, and she can see all across the southern coast – Lowfield, Tavey, the little shingle beach. The mare swings her tail as she grazes. The sea is glittered and bright.

I am the only one left.

She comes here to rest, and be still. But she also comes here to be close to the family she no longer has – the ones who have all passed on ahead of her, into the earth and sky. Once, long ago, Abigail had siblings. There had been her breathless twin, with crooked front teeth and a slight yeasty smell, and their brother Jack – Jack Junior – who had ears like spoons and a hiccupping laugh. Abigail remembers running after them. She couldn't keep up, but she tried. She can see it, even now – the blackened soles of Thomasina's feet and the *punch punch* of Jack's skinny elbows as they ran ahead of her, shouting *slow coach! Come on!*

I was always the slowest. In running. In living her life.

Abigail, being the eldest, should have died first – but she did not.

She shifts her weight on the bench.

I am the last. Not of the Bundys – that was her maiden name and there are plenty of other Bundys in this part of the world, that's for sure. But she is the last of those three children who had their cheeks scrubbed with a wire brush before church, every Sunday, so that they might be clean for the all-seeing Lord. The last of that generation.

The last of the Deepwaters, too.

Mercy Deepwater ... A good name. Dependable.

A magical name too, in its way, and Abigail knows very well that she is as much Deepwater as she is Bundy, that she might have been born with her father's surname but the other half of her came from a strong-boned, raven-haired woman who was bestowed with a name – as many islanders were – that might protect her from her watery life. Mercy from the water. Mercy from the winter gales.

Her mother, who had a taste for puffin meat.

Who sucked on old crab shells.

Oh, it is like no other island; Mercy used to whisper this to her daughters and son. Little Merme. So far out to sea that it could only be glimpsed on the clearest of days. Once, it was known for its seaweed and the fearless birds that would dive at your head if you walked near their nests; also for being so small and remote and so *traditional*, which could be both an insult or praise. But now? Merme is forgotten now. The last few people who lived there were lifted off and taken away half a century ago – for what kind of life had theirs been? All gales and bad nutrition. A six-hour boat ride to the mainland, on the best of days. And it was such a flat, treeless island that on stormy nights a wave might throw itself over a house or two and wash people out of their beds onto their stony floors. Mercy had told them.

We picked a herring out of the chimney, and ate it. And the widower Cooley saw a boat move through his house and out again. These are true stories.

Abigail sniffs.

Mercy Deepwater. Who lost three siblings to the sea, or disease. Who had spent her childhood prising barnacles off rocks and sewing gannet feathers into clothes to make them warmer so that *I thought I might fly, if the wind caught me right, like the Meddle girl who was blown away* ... Behind their black-walled house they'd grown potatoes and kale. Kept a few hens. It was a blunt, relentless way of living – and so when a farmer from Parla took a fancy to Mercy's shining hair, it felt like a chance for a better one.

A better life? Ha. Abigail tuts.

She tells herself this, as she sits here on this bench: that if Mercy hadn't wrapped herself in a rug and rowed across to Parla to marry a farmer called Jack, then Abigail herself would not exist. Nor would Jack Junior, or Thomasina. Nor would the four Bundy children that Jack went on to make, or their three children, or *their* children which are yet to be made. It fans out – the lives. And all because Jack Senior looked up one day and saw a woman that he wanted in the same way he might want a bottle of rum or a hearty meal.

Abigail tries to think this way – of the positives. The happy things.

So did Mercy. She smiled, all the same. She pressed cold stones against swellings, saved the teeth that Jack knocked out and she stitched her own head one night with a darning needle, her reflection in a polished spoon. She hummed and shrugged and kissed her children, and she found her solace in a leather-bound book called *Folklore and Myth*. It held the stories she'd grown up with, which she had been told in her own mother's voice – the Fishman, the speaking birds, the sea stacks off Parla that had been giants once. There was no pain that could not be lessened by turning the pages of it. Mercy's husband blackened her eyes, or he dragged her over the flagstones by her waist-length hair – but she'd patch herself up, usher her children to bed saying *ssh, it doesn't matter, I'm right as rain* and she'd return with the book and unfold it.

The world is full of magic. You must remember that.

Abigail does. She does remember it.

There are fists and sorrow, but there are also seals with human hearts and a Fishman who said *there is hope, there is hope*. And at the one time when she doubted it – when she felt that there was no magic at all – Jim Coyle came along and saved her. Casually, he'd told her *and he had a fish's tail* ...

A sparrow pecks near her feet. It tilts its head, says *tink!*

Abigail looks down. She knows how she is talked of, here. *Crazy old woman*. Maybe, once or twice, *a witch* ... No-one else believes in what Abigail believes in, but these people didn't have a mother who'd grown up on black beaches, shinned up rocks to steal a fulmar's egg, tugged teats every morning, watched her friends get buried at sea or who'd sworn she'd seen a sea snake with her own blue eyes. Live far out, and you believe strange things. Live a hard life and you believe in things that make it better. You'll see these things whereas most people will not – an evening star, a phosphorous sea. Abigail thinks that perhaps most folk are too busy with their jobs and houses and huge televisions to look out of the window and see what's *there*. To listen. To breathe sea air.

Mercy lies here, now. Her bones are under her husband's, since she died before Jack Senior did. She fell asleep and did not wake up. There was blood on the pillow when Abigail found her. She tugged her mother's finger, whispered *Mummy, wake up*.

Mercy from the water, and Mercy from the winds. But not from a brain haemorrhage when she was still so young. And two years later Thomasina died. On a sly tide – the highest tide of all – she'd run down to Tap Hole in her patchwork pinafore. *Why?* Everyone asked it. *No-one goes into Tap Hole* ... But Abigail knew why, as they watched her coffin be lowered down.

If Abigail had managed children, she'd have named them after her lost twin – all of them. Every living thing which she passes is called *Thomasina*, in her eyes. A bird. A single bud.

Sixty-eight years since Thomasina died. And yet she does not grow old. She is still firm-bodied, dark-haired. Can still do handstands. She has no age spots, no spaces where teeth had been which she can push her tongue into. No arthritic knees, or varicose veins.

Abigail is sad, of course. Her sadness is a real, touchable thing and it sits inside her as her organs do. But just as she knows she is sad, she knows this: *they are not gone.* How could they be? Their spirits swim through the water; their souls flash in the sunlit spray. Abigail has felt them – as she's pruned her flowers, or sat on the bench by the harbour wall; she has turned, as if expecting to find them standing there.

No, they are not fully gone. Abigail believes this absolutely. She believes it to the point where she can say she *knows.*

There is more to this world than the life we are living. There's a whole other world, under the waves.

Carefully, she stands. And she runs her hand across the top of Thomasina's gravestone as she leaves, like how, as girls, they would let go of hands – gradually, moving their fingertips over each other's palms, as gently as raindrops. She has done this for sixty-eight years and there is a dip on the stone from this. She has worn the stone down with her loving goodbyes.

*   *   *

Kitty is in the shop. She is buying bleach, loo roll, tins of beans, wine and a packet of biscuits; with her armful of groceries, Kitty opens the shop door with her foot and slips outside. As she passes the noticeboard, with its ferry schedule and tide times, she pauses. She glimpses a new note pinned there. It's handwritten, on pink paper. It is Tabitha's writing – elegant, curled – and it reads, *If anyone has information they think might help the man who came ashore, please call Tabitha – Tel: 159.* She has described him as *six foot five, early forties, dark-haired.*

Kitty presses her lips together.

She starts to walk, but for the first few steps she is still looking at the noticeboard, still holding the shopping in her arms so that when she steps into the lane she walks straight into a woman who yelps, surprised.

Sorry! Excuse me. I wasn't ... Did I step on you?

Rona shakes her head. *No. I'm fine.*

Sure?

Fine. Really.

Kitty smiles. She shifts her groceries. *How's the lighthouse? I hear you're busy up there.*

I'm baking now. Need more flour, so ... She tries to pass by.

How are my paintings? Any sales?

Not for a while.

Ah well ... Kitty thinks the girl looks tired. She has shadows under her eyes and her arms are thin. All that baking and not enough flesh on her bones. What is she, now? Twenty-four? Twenty-five? *Have you seen him?*

No. Who?

This man. The one they found on the stones at Sye.

Yes. Briefly. You?

From a distance. Not to talk to. It sounds all so impossible, doesn't it? An amnesiac washed up like that ...

Silence from Rona.

Anyway. I'll let you get on. Good luck with the baking.

Yes.

Kitty climbs into the car, passes her groceries onto the passenger seat. Perhaps it's genes. After all, Sam is just as difficult to talk to, just as reluctant to be looked in the eye.

But then there is Nancy, little Nancy Lovegrove who talks more than all of them put together, who envies Kitty's amber ring and who has told Kitty that she looks like gypsies do in her picture books – black-haired, skirted, with hoops in her ears.

Rona steps into the shop. She walks with her hands out, as if she might fall. When she comes to the chest freezer, she takes hold of it. *Shit …*

Nausea. Guilt. Her breathing is irregular and she tries to slow it. She stares at the tensed backs of her hands.

This can't go on, Rona whispers.

He needs to tell her. He needs to tell Kitty about us, now.

* * *

None of the fences are strong. Sheep rub against them and storms tilt them over. Sometimes they are taken by campers for firewood; this infuriates Ian. It is theft, and he says so. *Our livelihood*, he snaps – *pulled up to toast marshmallows on …*

He and Nathan are at Tavey, on the southern coast. The pigs are long gone – but the old metal shelters for the pigs are still here; rainwater sits in the trough. Ian has not been here for years. Why would he come here? But they needed more than pig shelters for their pigs, long ago: they needed strong fences, too, to stop the pigs from wandering – thick wire and firm stakes, driven deep into the ground. And aren't they wasted, where they are? There are no pigs to keep any more, no vegetable patch to protect. No-one lives at Tavey, now.

Ian surveys the posts. *They'll do. How many?*

A few. Six? Maybe more.

You do it. He passes the sledge hammer over.

Nathan takes it, finds a decent grip. He takes three big swings, catches the nearest fence-post with two of them. The post shifts to its left. The hole it sits in widens, so that the men can see dark earth.

See if that's done it.

Ian pulls the fence-post clear of the earth, drops it to the floor and he says, *talked to this man yet?*

Nope.

Going to?

Nathan exhales. *Don't plan to. Reckon I'll just leave him be.*

Let him find his memory ... He hears his own sarcasm. *You think he's lying?*

Ian looks up. He has been clipping the wire from the wooden post, and he says *come on, Nathe. An amnesiac gets washed ashore? I don't think so.*

Then what? He's nothing to gain by lying.

Hasn't he? How about a free home, free food? Hiding from the police? Who knows what he was prowling round this place for the other day ... Maybe he's going to win our trust and then rob us blind. Give it time ...

The post is thrown behind them, onto the grass. Nathan swings the sledgehammer at a second post which leaves the earth more easily and as they both kneel down to pull it free, the younger brother says *Tab says it can happen. She's looked online, read her books. Trauma can do it.*

Ian does not reply.

He is thinking, at that moment, of their mother. He wonders how she feels, kneeling in her flowerbed, knowing a man wears her dead son's clothes. He knows that if he asked her, she'd say *I'm fine.* But he doubts she is.

They haul the posts to the Land Rover, heave the sledgehammer into the back.

You been drinking today, Nathe? He expects to be sworn at for that.

What?

You smell of it.

No I bloody haven't. His brother is incredulous.

Last night?

Yes, last night – at Milton's. I had a beer with Milton. What's wrong with that?

There are conversations that are too known and tiring to have. This is one of them. This, Ian thinks, is all too heavy to be brought out again, as a chest might be hauled out from under a bed, the dust blown off. He hasn't the energy to talk of this now, or to remember.

Just get in the car. Let's mend this fence.

The car rolls over the grass. The windows are down, so that the breeze moves through it and flutters the litter on the car floor – receipts, newspapers, crisp packets, a plastic bag.

Silence, between them. The sheep bleat.

Maybe he's the Fishman, Nathan says. *Heard that?*

Yep.

Aunt Abigail's certain.

Ian smiles – a quick, wry smile. *Aunt Abigail's fucking nuts.*

And briefly it is like they're not middle-aged men, but boys – talking like they used to, laughing behind their hands or sharing out toffees as they sat on hay bales. *One for you, one for me, one for you …* The years vanish, briefly. Ian looks across at Nathan and sees the boy who lost his two front milk teeth by tripping on the quayside, and whose dream was to fly to the moon.

We spoke of him. And when we weren't speaking of him, we were thinking of him. We were all thinking *what does he know? Why is he here?*

And *who* ...?
Who could he be?

The stranger himself is asking *who* ...? He wants to know more of the Fishman. It is how he is known on Parla, now; it is the name he answers to, or lifts his head at. It is what Maggie calls him – for she has no other name.

If you want to know more about yourself ...

He wears a dark-red shirt. The skin on his forearms is already darkening from his days here; his hair shines in the afternoon sun. The Fishman passes the viewpoint, the telephone box. And as the path starts to lead down towards the boats – the *Morning Star*, *Sea Fairy*, *Lady Caroline* – he hears what he's been listening for: a dainty call of bells.

He has to duck, to enter the house.

Abigail is radiant. *I've been waiting for you.*

The Old Fish Store is a dark house. It has thick walls and small, square windows – and so it is also cool. He steps into a room with a table lamp. There is a small fire, despite the days of sun.

Jim Coyle is sitting in the corner. He tries to stand as the Fishman enters but the Fishman says *please – there's no need*. He goes to him, bends and puts his hand into Jim's hand. It is their first meeting – or their first proper one.

Ah, says Jim. *Hello.*

His wife says *look who's here.*

I've been told I am ... half-fish?

Abigail smiles. *The Fishman of Sye*. She takes the heavy, leather-bound book, shows him the fourteenth page.

And there he is – there is his own face, his own body. There is his height and breadth; even the dark hair on his chest is *his* hair. The stance of the Fishman as he walks onto land is how he himself walks and stands, and all he can do is stare at this. He has few words. *This book ...*

It was my mother's. All the island stories ...

The man in the drawing has black eyes. His tail, when he has it, is as silvery as stars.

Surely you remember? That you came from the water?

I can't ...

But he can still taste salt. If he licks his lips, he is sure he can taste it; his lips are still dry from his time at sea. And his hands; he looks down at these two hands of his which are no longer grazed or rough or red but that old wound remains – the circular wound like a dark-orange eye. A hook, perhaps. Or a place of broken skin, made by a lobster's grip. How is he here? How did it happen?

Jim has seen you before. Haven't you, Jim?

The milky-eyed man has heard every word. He sits very still, hands in his lap, and without moving he says *yes, I saw you. A long time ago. I saw your face and your raised tail.*

At this moment, the Fishman feels their goodness. He feels it as he feels the pages of *Folklore and Myth* – clear, and real. And this story, he knows, is old; this story – *his* story – is as worn and warm as a blanket might be, a blanket that so many children or adults have wrapped themselves up in on stormy nights or when feeling lonely or afraid. When he looks across to Abigail her eyes are shining. She, too, has been warmed by this tale.

How long can I stay for?

Not long. Until the next full moon.

What if I like it? Have reason to stay?

She shakes her head kindly. *The Fishman needs water; he is half-fish. In the story he must always go away.*

Jim listens. He listens, and he breathes the man's smell – grass, soap, the slight fish tang that Maggie can have when she's been on her boat. There is something else, too – what else does he smell of? He hears the book's pages creak as they are turned.

Jim cannot see. But he has learnt that sight does not merely come from the optic nerve and retina, and cones within the eye. He can see a sausage grilling merely from its sound and he can see the Lovegroves' cat from how she feels under his hands. And he can see this man, now – for he remembers the bearded face, the huge, raised tail off Sye. And Jim wants, at that moment, for Abigail to go – for her to pop into the kitchen or pad upstairs to the bathroom for a minute or two, no longer. He wants to reach for this man. He wants to take his hand again, to feel his hand with both of his own, and he wants to talk as two men with secrets will always talk – sparsely, low-voiced. But Abigail does not go. Instead she says *Maggie loves this book, you know. She has sat where you are sitting too many times to count. She was here the other night, talking of you.*

The moment, for Jim, comes later. He finds his walking stick, follows them into the garden. He hears Abigail talk of the old pig farmer, how he found true love so very late in life, and *isn't the weather glorious? It is rare to have sun like this.* She shows him her geraniums; she touches the string of bells.

And Jim lets go of his stick. He opens his palm, so that it falls. It clatters onto the path – and he hears the Fishman come nearer, crouch down saying *I've got it – don't worry. Here …*

Thank you. The stick is held against his hand – but Jim does not take it. Instead, he grasps the Fishman's wrist, leans forwards.

He says, *do not tell the truth*. Jim Coyle spills these five words into the space between them – the salty space, the space that is cool with an evening breeze. Jim tightens his grip. He moves his eyes as if trying to see the man he is holding. *Do you hear me? Understand me?*

Yes. Yes, I do.

As for Abigail, she has not heard. She is minding her geraniums. She is noting that they are being blown from north to south, so that the north wind is still blowing. Still – how long for, now?

These are strange times and the Fishman is the proof of it: him, with her husband. Pressing his walking stick back into Jim's hand.

*   *   *

You could ask *how do I know this?* How do I know this happened, when I wasn't there? But the fact is, both men told me. I would hear this from both of them in time and both their stories would be the same. The Fishman did hear – he heard Jim very clearly. *Do not tell the truth. Stay the Fishman. It is what they want – do you hear?*

Jim told me this, too: *I knew he loved you. As I sat in that chair.*

I doubted it, of course – who can smell love or the feeling alone? But he'd not meant love exactly. Jim said *there was a scent to him … For a while I could not place it*. But Jim Coyle knows the sea's sounds, and he can tell the wind's direction from other, smaller sounds and he knew when the tide was out simply from the stronger, acrid seaweed smell as wrack dried in the midday sun and so it did not take long for Jim to say *gardenia! That's what it is*. The Fishman had smelt of gardenia – a sweet, white, feminine flower which does not grow on the isle.

Me. I wore it. I had not worn it for years, but as I had waited for him to walk back from Sye and knock on my door, I'd found my bottle of gardenia scent. A dab on my throat, and one by each ear. Jim had smelt it on me, in the past; later, he smelt it on the beard of the man who, they say, walked out of the sea.

Sam writes to Leah tonight. Or rather, he is not writing – he is sending a message on his phone which reads *thinking of you*.

At the lighthouse itself, Rona is also typing. She sits at her computer and has written: *I ran into Kitty today, at the shop. Did she tell you? It was dreadful. I know she is a good person – sometimes I try to tell myself she is not, that she's a bad wife and deserves all of this – but I know that's not true. She's kind. She's very beautiful.*

It gets harder the longer we wait. There will never be a good time to tell her, Nathan – you know that, don't you? It's better for Kitty that she knows soon. If you don't tell her, I will.

I could make you happy. I'd spend my life making you happy. Lots of fruit scones.

As for her brother he has been sitting on the stile that leads to Sye. Sam smokes, and thinks *the last time I walked here, I was carrying the Fishman. We held him in the air, like a boat.* And it feels like it just happened, but also it feels like months ago – months or years.

At Crest, Maggie's bathroom light is on. He looks up at the house – its shape is darker than the night-time sky. He would not knock; he never would. Instead, Sam walks along its driveway and places a single plastic bag on her doorstep. It is not much. It is a few eggs, tea bags, a single candle, a note that says *let me know if I can help*.

* * *

She does not hear him. All she can hear is *stash* ...

Maggie lies in the bath. Her eyes are closed and she thinks of the sea. Tom would talk of *sea music*. He knew the shanties, the old sailors' songs and he'd sing them to her, as she bathed. He'd sit in this room, beside her.

When will I see my true love again?

Soon, says the water; soon, says the wind ...

Sometimes he would take his hand and lower it, into the foam.

The Man of Sea Shanties

It has been a long time since Parla but I still hum its sea
shanties. I still sing its saltwater songs.

I was told this, and learnt it: that from the stubbled
mouths of fishermen straining their eyes for herring shoals,
or perhaps from the round, plump, wanting mouths of
wives who were left by the fireside with their teats stopping their babies' own pink mouths, there have been
songs. Incantations. Prayers with a tune.

I love their names alone, which are songs in
themselves:

'Five Ladies' Lament'.

'When Will You Come?'

'And Will She Wait For Me?'

'For Agnes-May'.

And they are love songs, I learnt that too. They might
have been sung to haul nets in to or to row in time or to
shorten the hours but they have love in their words more
than anything else. For the sea may take lives away, but it
can't touch the love. Love cannot be splintered or drowned.
It lasts, and so there are songs.

It feels like a lifetime ago, when I first heard them.
Which it was, I suppose.

But enough. This is about Maggie, mouthing the words in her night-time bath. It is about the man from Sye who she will love. And it is about Nathan who knows the songs – all of the songs.

*　　*　　*

He knows this one, from Cantalay. Like the isle it comes from, it is simply done.

> *When will I see my one true love again?*
> *Soon, says the water; soon, says the wind.*
> *When might I see her brown eyes again?*
> *Soon, says the water – soon.*
>
> *When will I breathe in her sweet breath again?*
> *Soon, says the water; soon, says the wind.*
> *When might I feel her warm skin again?*
> *Soon, says the water – soon.*
>
> *When will I watch my love sleeping again?*
> *Soon, says the water; soon, says the wind.*
> *And when must I leave her behind me again?*
> *Soon, soon, soon ...*

Nathan whispers it, now – or rather, he hums the tune very softly and the words are half-mouthed. *Soon ...*

He knows them all – all the old sea songs. His grandfather knew them. Granddad Bright, with his jar of peanuts, his Bible, the crackle of his pipe as he smoked it. Missing front teeth. *Come and sit by me, boy.* He'd called Nathan *boy.* Not the others – just Nathan.

When will I breathe in her sweet ...

He pauses, drinks. It is past midnight, and the house is silent. Upstairs, the cat sleeps where Nathan knows he should be.

I'll teach you a song, boy ... He taught them all. Abelard Bright polished the brass but he also polished the old, old songs. As the weight in the stairwell lowered itself down so that the cogs turned and the lantern did, he found the words and handed them over. He sat in a wing-backed armchair. Nathan sat on a cushion at his grandfather's feet. Tweed slippers. Dog hair on his trouser legs.

Only ever him. Only the one grandchild there. Why never Ian? Or Hester? They had no interest in it, perhaps. They never sang.

Just him and his Granddad Bright.

Soon, says the water ...

And then Tom. Tom came along, and he sang. Tom had his own songs – wordless, but with a tune of sorts so that one night in Wind Rising, when Nathan and Tom shared a room with bunk beds, the elder brother had pushed his toes up through the slats of the bunk above him and said *do you want to know a song?* And Tom's head had appeared upside down, saying *a song? Is it good?*

That's how it started. The boys' bedroom, in the empty hours. Noises downstairs – a breaking of glass or a single bad word – and Nathan's eyes would open and say *do you want to know another song? Or story?* Other things, too. He showed Tom that if you pressed two shells over your ears you might hear the sea's secrets.

I can't hear anything.

Here, like this ...

He drinks. The song is in his head. Peanuts are.

My wife. Kitty who I love.

He looks into the glass, at the last of the whisky. Rona comes to him, too. She rolls into his mind, the birthmark on her hipbone, the vertical line she gets between her eyes when she implores him – *stay* ... She is all hands. She has no shyness to her when she asks for what she wants. Their first kiss had been ambush; she'd clambered across to the driver's seat of his Land Rover, pressed her mouth against his. Sometimes he thinks he hates her, but he doesn't. He doesn't hate *her*. It's what he does with her that he hates; he hates that she thinks he is worth loving perhaps because look, look how he sits here, drunk again, with Kitty upstairs and the ghosts, and where is Tom now? Not singing.

Not singing. Nathan says this, raises a finger. *He is not singing.*

He drains the glass, puts it on the table.

His grandfather, if he'd still been alive, would talk of God. He'd say, *Thomas is with God, now* – because the Brights had their faith as all lighthouse-keepers did. A framed square of embroidery in their hall had said *Have no fear, for the Lord is with you*, and it looked like a promise, hanging on their wall. A promise made to Nathan. He believed it for a time and then he did not believe it, because as a boy he'd knelt and prayed, but no help had come.

He is not singing ... Nathan exhales. He runs his palm over his hair. Drunk, but not so drunk that he can't see Tom's worth against Nathan's own. *If someone had to die, why was it him? Not me?* There wasn't a single thing that Tom did to hurt a person, or sadden them, and yet he was taken and is dead whilst Nathan got all of it wrong but is still here on Parla, whisky-mouthed and failing too many people to count. Why wasn't it him? Who is worth far less than Tom was? There is never fairness.

When will I hold ...

He sniffs. Curses, under his breath.

He has been told that all the best sea songs are about loss – what people yearn for. What people miss. Nathan misses his grandfather and he misses his own wife but it is his little brother he is seeing now, at half past midnight –

that upside-down head of his as he said *a song? Really?* His hair hanging down.

Tom, who deserved better. He should not have died young.

It is only in these moments, these lonely hours, when Nathan truly feels it or allows himself to – the absence, the size and the permanence of it. By day, he tries to hide it; sober, he tries to box the loss away. Don't people drink to forget? Not him. Not this man. He drinks to feel the hurt in all its force – for the grief to crash and swell. It is how he opens the sadness that comes with knowing that the boy who drew crayon pictures of them both on the bedroom wall, with smiles and sheep, is bones, now – *bones* – and not singing. *I want him back* – his brother. But don't the singers of songs all want something? Doesn't everyone on this island? Don't they all miss Tom Bundy? But Tom is not coming back.

Nine

She has a dream, and it is this: that he is with her again. That he is not wrapped up in weeds, with fish swimming through his ribs: he is fleshed, and warm, and with her. He kisses her neck. He lifts her hair to one side and kisses the skin behind her ears. Then he moves down, touches the skin across her collarbone and then he kisses that, too, and in the dream Maggie gasps so that he draws back, anxious. Suddenly he is not Tom. He is the Fishman and he is saying *am I moving too quickly? Are you OK?*

She wakes. She wants to say *no, keep going*; she wants him to be there beside her, propped up on one arm.

The Fishman has a dream also. It is a dream of water, but also a dream in which there is a kiss – a small kiss in a green-walled room. He wakes, and the dream stays with him. It takes a few minutes for the dream to fall away.

*　　*　　*

Tavey is the most southerly building on the isle. It sits in the south-west corner, in the fields beyond Lowfield; its windows mostly face onto a shingle beach. The gorse bushes and nettles in its garden are so high that they brush against the wooden boards that have been nailed across the glass – chest-high, or higher. The grass, too, is overgrown. Half-lost amongst it are the last, rusting signs that it had been a pig farm, once: troughs and three shelters of hooped, corrugated iron. Flowers bloom, here: decades of fresh pig manure have led to honeysuckle, foxgloves, ox-eye daisies.

The Fishman is here again. He pushes at the door with his shoulder; then he puts his knee against it, and his hands. Slowly, the door gives way. Inside it is small – two rooms, only. But there is furniture here, and no smell of damp. And as he stands amongst its dust and its faint scent of sheep and trapped air, he sees that if a person can have a second form of life – if a man who has swum through night-time seas can grow legs, and *kick*, and come ashore to a place of kind people and to a woman whose small, coy smile makes his heart stir when he sees it – then why shouldn't a building? Have a second life, too?

When he asks Tabitha, she looks surprised. *That place? It's been empty for ...* She blows air through pursed lips, thinking. *Ten years? Maybe not quite ten.*

Who lived there?

Moses Bundy. The pigs were his. After him? A shrug. *Just ... tourists. Birdwatchers. It was rented on and off for years. And then people just stopped coming.* She looks up, enquiringly. *What are you thinking?*

I could work on it ... Try to.

Work? Fix it?

It wouldn't take much. A few nails, some paint. I could make it a good place again.

You could do that?

With tools. I think so. Do you know who owns it?

She shakes her head. *The rent went to Jack Bundy and he's a long time dead.*

So now?

Emmeline's? Abigail's? Ian, maybe. God knows. I don't think it matters. If you want to fix it, fix it. Who can object? It's just – she waves her hand – *sitting there …*

Thank you.

Tabitha eyes him. *Can I ask why? It's a strange thing to do.*

He smiles. He thinks to himself before he answers. And he says *because I want to be helpful. I want to make a difference. And I'd like to say thank you in a better way than words.*

* * *

In a cool, airy attic a woman with the tattoo of a bird on her neck is drying a paintbrush, her weight resting on one hip. Before her she has a view and, before that, an interpretation of it – the red tiles of Easterly, a textured sea of many different colours. Black, green, navy, white, yellow, electric-blue.

Kitty muses. She rubs her left calf with the sole of her right foot so briefly she is balanced, stork-like.

She's yet to meet an islander who fully understands what she does. Nathan tries to, or did. They met here, on Parla, one midsummer's eve. Kitty – freshly single, heavily laced with both the zest and heat of freedom and the weight of such a drawn-out separation – came to the island for the longest day of the year, to feel as much light as she could after too long in darkness. She was half-drunk. Cider? Cider, which she doesn't drink and yet somehow she was drinking it. A backless red dress. No shoes.

Nathan asked her to dance; that's how it started. When she'd told him *I'm an artist – oils, mostly*, he'd looked

concerned, afraid even. *Artist?* He was a farmer. *Sheep ...*
– as if regretful. But there were worse things. And his
hands felt gentle against her back, and he'd been drinking
cider too so that when they kissed it was fruit-juicy,
apple-sweet.

Kitty puts the paintbrush down.

She can hear the wind-chime in the porch. The dog
from Wind Rising is barking in the lane.

So far, Kitty has made her work into greetings cards and
framed prints and she has sold a few originals through the
lighthouse café. Rona has been generous to let her hang
her artwork there; the percentage that Rona takes is small.
But now, I will be exhibited ...

That word. *Exhibited.* It thrills her, but to Nathan it
had meant nothing; he'd said *that's nice* as if he'd barely
heard her.

There is someone at the door – three raps.

He stands before her in a dark-red cotton shirt and grey
tracksuit bottoms. He does not lean against the doorframe
nonchalantly, or have his hands in his pockets; he does not
look annoyed at how slowly she's answered the door. He
only stands.

Kitty?

Yes.

I'm ... He points his thumb over his shoulder, back
towards Lowfield.

She tilts her head. *I can guess who you are ... I think
I'm the last to meet you.* They shake hands, business-like,
and she blushes.

She has seen him from a distance but nothing more than
that.

Kitty is not what he expected. There is an old, broken
fridge propped up against the porch, a crate of empty

bottles beside it and the boots that stand in a row are all muddied and sheep-smelling – yet the woman who stands on the doormat is fragrant, barefoot, moving languidly. She has an emerald-green line around her eyes; earrings brush her jaw. *Tools? Oh, we have heaps of tools ... What do you need?*

Not too sure yet. Hammers and nails, certainly. A crowbar. If you have a saw, and any spare wood, or ...

He follows her to the shed. She talks, as she goes – apologising, mostly, for the shed's disarray, the cobwebs and the smell of turpentine. She opens the shed door. Inside, blackness. Then Kitty finds a switch – *click* – and the illumination is sudden, flickering and huge. He stares. There are workbenches, car parts, an upended boat, shelves that spill with old paint tins. Tubs of screws, bolts, nails. *Help yourself. Take anything.*

Really?

They're here to be used.

He watches how she presses her lips together, how she flexes her toes as she looks down at them. *She is sad*, he thinks. It is clear. *Is Kitty your real name?*

Katherine. But I've always been called Kitty. She looks up. *You? Still nothing?*

I think I am the Fishman ...

She smiles. *Of course.*

Kitty stays. Together, they move through the shelves. She finds him gloves – canvas ones, hard-wearing – and screwdrivers, sandpaper, a claw-hammer and nails. As she does this Kitty asks *how long will you be here for? On Parla?*

A while.

She does not press for more than that. She accepts it, moves her hair to one side. Then *you probably know that we're a quiet place. Not much happens – or nothing good. Any –* she pauses, thinks for the word – *excitement or adventure is rare and I think we feel it all the more because of that. Do you know what I'm saying? What I'm trying to say?* She turns the silver ring on her thumb with the forefinger of the same hand, waits. Then, *I like Maggie. Maggie has been through so much. We all have, I guess.*

Maggie?

Come on ... It's a small island. We talk. She teases: *we have eyes ...*

What can he say? He can think of no reply to her.

Kitty does not wait for one. She only nods as if she is happy now and goes back into the house. And later, when the man from Sye is pulling his bag onto his shoulder to make his way to Tavey, he glances up at the house and sees her. Kitty, the artist. She stands by her easel but she is not looking at it. She is looking at him.

He thinks, *she looks like she is underwater*. Or he is underwater, looking back at her – her mermaid's hair, her sorrow and her mouth which moves a little as she watches him, as if singing or reciting, or as if in prayer.

*   *   *

In the day that follows, new sounds come. There is still the sea, of course; still the soft squeak of Ed's anemometer, as it turns in the wind. And there are all the brief, passing sounds that a person's day may have in it – the rattle of a saucepan as it comes to the boil, the *clack-clack-clack* of cream being rubbed into hands. The staccato slurp from Nan as she drinks milk through a straw.

The damp hiss of a candle being lit from another. I do this, in the hush of Parla's church.

But there are, too, new noises. And they come, it seems, from Tavey: the slow squeak of boards being prised off windows, the *bang* as they're thrown onto the ground.

Emmeline looks up from her flowers, listens.

Leah pauses as she carries a bin-bag to the dustbin. She wrinkles her nose, thinks *what is …?*

And George Moss, too – he hears the sounds from Tavey. He is filling up his bird feeders with peanuts and sunflower seeds, and he stops, calls out. *What's that? Can you hear that?* His wife comes to the doorway. She tucks her hair behind her ear, as if to listen better.

It's coming from the pig farm, Hester says, unsure.

*   *   *

Tabitha had said *who can object?* But afterwards she knew very well who could object to these hammering sounds. She knew who could glower, stamp her foot. *It's only a matter of time …*

It is mid-morning. Tabitha is readying to make her way to Lorcan, packing her nurse's bag. Stethoscope, bandages, lint, an eye-bath – all the items that she carries with her on her rounds, *just in case*. She shuts the bag, lifts it. Then the telephone rings.

Tabitha? What's he doing?

Good morning to you, too.

Your man. What the hell is he doing at Tavey? I can see him right now, and I can hear him. You know that's Bundy property?

Is it? Casually.

You know it is! What is he doing there? If he damages a single –

Damage? Oh for God's sake, Em – of course he's not damaging it. And frankly, if it's Bundy land, it's Abigail who owns it, not you, and I happen to think she'd be delighted to know he was doing something useful with the place. It's been an eyesore for a decade.

With that, she hangs up.

That's the advantage of telephones; Tabitha can escape her sister's anger in one swift move.

Emmeline stares at the receiver she's still holding. Tavey? Isn't it hers? It was Jack's, and she was Jack's wife. But then, what of bloodlines? Maybe it *is* Abigail's. *Well, she is welcome to it: a rundown shack with pig shit on its stones.*

Emmeline sniffs.

Rage. It is always in her. Sometimes, fire-like, it is merely the glow of warm ashes that, if blown, could redden and grow; other times she cannot contain it. Now? Her anger simmers. Emmeline hates it, of course – the sound of work. But is it because it is Tavey? Or because it is *him* – this man who should be Tom, but is not? Or are there other reasons? Perhaps this is the sound of progress – of *betterment* – which feels wrong and unacceptable when Tom is not here; how can there be progress until her boy is found? Or it is Tabitha. Or the north wind. Maybe all these things.

Emmeline listens: the sea, and hammering.

She puts the receiver back down.

*   *   *

The two rooms now are flooded with light. Sunlight streams in through the windows; on floors and far walls, it makes window shapes in white.

He walks towards a window, stares. He can see the islands; Leah has whispered their names to him and he says *Cantalay* ... The sea glitters. It is nothing like the sea he knew and swam through. The sea he knew was black-ish; it seemed to push him down. Is this the same water?

So much has changed, since Sye. Since folding up his tail.

Maggie brushes through the grass. She wears jeans with a hole in one knee and a white blouse that is thinning from years of wear. She, too, has heard. As she'd dug in her garden, she'd paused at the sound of planks being prised off, flung.

I have never been to Tavey. Not inside it.

That is why she is walking there. It is why she's treading through the fields, ducking under wire, moving past the waist-high gorse and pausing in the doorway of the old pig farm. *To see Tavey.* No other reason.

The room is filled with daylight. It makes his black hair bright.

So much light. I had no idea …

He smiles. *Come here. Look at the view.*

She joins him. She looks across the shingle beach, out towards the isles. *That one? It is Utta. They say it had a giantess whose weight and bad temper cracked the land, gave it streams. It is the only isle to have them.*

She is the woman he can't stop thinking of. She smells of flowers, and earth.

Without turning from the view she says *I think I was rude. The other night. I was rude in how I asked you to leave.*

No. You weren't rude.

I was. I wanted you to go because –

It's OK.

Let me tell you. I want to tell you. I was afraid – that's why. I don't let many people stay for as long as you stayed. People drop in, but … She drops her gaze. *I don't know who you are. I don't know your name or why you are here. All I have in my head is that you're a fish – a fish! There is nothing else. No boats have gone down. I've listened to the news every day and there's nobody missing from any of the crews, and who could have swum here? From the mainland? All I have is that you're a bloody fish …*

Maggie turns. She drifts back, through the room. Slowly, she moves past the hearth, its wrought-iron grate, past a wooden table and a single chair. She moves towards the far end where there is a stove and a metal kitchen sink and, as he watches her, the Fishman wants to speak to her – to speak plainly, to fill the room with all the truths that he has. His wound; his name. The constant taste of brine. But he does not tell her.

I hate being afraid. She says it very quietly.

Of what?

Of you. I don't know you. You could be anyone. Am I meant to just believe that you're just a decent man?

Is that so hard to do?

A sigh. She rubs her eyes. *I thought I had found a … Peace. A lonely sort of peace, perhaps, but still peace. A form of it. And then you turn up …*

Maggie has stopped walking. And so, very carefully, he starts to make his way through the room, as she has done. He treads through the dusty shafts of light. Maggie is still rubbing her eyes, and yet she knows that he has come to her, that he is standing before her now.

Don't. Please …

He touches her. Her shirt is as thin as air.

I don't know what this is. I think of you and I don't want to think of you.

I think of you too.

Maggie drops her hand. *Everything is so hard …*

And she cries. She tries not to, briefly – but the tears come. Her forehead wrinkles; the skin by her eyes becomes starry with lines. Her mouth opens, chick-like.

The Fishman puts his hands on her waist. He lifts her.

She allows it. Instinctively, Maggie lets him place her very gently onto the old metal draining board. Their faces are level now.

I am, she says, *so scared. I've not felt like this since ... And I don't know who you are. Do you know how that feels? I don't know who* – She hiccups.

I won't hurt you, Maggie.

How – a sob – *can you say that? You're a ... fish, or* –

Because I won't. Believe me.

How can I believe you?

Maggie ...

He moves in around her. His arms go around her shoulders and he brings her against him so that Maggie's chin rests on his own shoulder and he can hold her, he can hold her properly as he has thought of doing from the moment that she struck him. He says to her *shh* ... And she cries. He strokes her hair, as she does so. The minutes pass this way.

He has so much to tell her.

Maggie pulls back from him. Her eyelashes are damp, and have split as feathers do. He can smell gardenia.

Her mouth is near his mouth.

*   *   *

It takes so little. It takes so little time and so few words.

Kitty knows this. She knows how things can fall apart with the smallest breath of wind.

She is in her studio, at the top of High Haven. The sky is starting to darken when, at last, he comes back. The front door opens; she pauses with her brush in her hand. There is the sound of his boots dropping onto the floor and the banisters creak as he takes hold of them, and she knows he is angry. *Kitty?*

He has been in the shed, maybe. Or he has heard that this Fishman is hammering nails with Nathan's tools, or both. *Attic*, she calls out. Waits.

His anger is never the family anger that she has heard of: he never curls his fingers into his palm to make a fist; he never slams his knuckles against walls or furniture and she has never been afraid. *I have never been afraid of him.* But her heart is beating in time with his footsteps as Nathan comes up the stairs.

They are only tools ...

My tools! Mine! They're expensive. And –

I lent them! Lent – do you understand that word? It means you'll get them back.

And it didn't used to be this way. It didn't used to be a sour-smelling house with pillows and a blanket downstairs by the sofa and a cat that mostly keeps outside, and it didn't used to be that in order to be spoken to by him – looked in the eye and spoken to – she would have to irritate him so that he'd shake his head, disbelieving, and fit his lips around such words as *you had no right ...*

No right? Nathan, I am your wife!

He could be a thief, or –

They're tools – they aren't gold bullion! He wants to fix up Tavey – that's all ...

She flings down the paintbrush. One hand on her hip, the other pressed across her forehead and Kitty shuts her eyes. She wants to ask him *when did this happen? How have we let it?* She has not seen her husband for too long, too long: it is not the physical absence of him that hurts her but the other, dreadful way in which a person can be absent. It is like sleeping next to a shell. It's like how, as a child, she'd turn a boiled egg over in its cup so that it looked perfect and her parents might think it was still uneaten, still full and rich. It's not full; it's hollow and does nothing, and it will break when tapped. *This will break.* Kitty will break it.

They are just tools ...

She moves past him. She goes downstairs and does, swiftly, the things that Nathan probably does not know must be done or has not done for years – cleaning the worktops, clearing out the plughole in the kitchen sink. She does it briskly. She lifts things, slams them down. Once, Nathan would leave flowers in a jam-jar by her bed – cowslip, or campion; she'd wake to find primroses beside her glass of water. Now? She cannot reach him. He, in turn, could reach her so often – over and over – but he does not choose to. Arms by his side.

A thousand times over she has knelt beside him, said *what's the matter? Talk to me ...* And his one thousand replies were always *nothing. Leave it. I'm fine.*

Four years ...

She thinks of that boiled egg. She sees it turned over in its cup. She'd thought that no-one else knew of its emptiness – *they think it's still full of egg ...* But she had been a child. Now she is a woman and she thinks *of course they knew it was a trick.* They all did, and they still do. Even a man who has no name or memory can look at her and see that she is giving up. She tried to fool them all but she has failed.

And at that moment, she looks across the fields. Maggie is there. Maggie is walking through the sheep, so that the sheep part like water. It is a sight she's seen before, but also, it seems different. How is it different? Kitty asks herself *where has she been?*

But she knows. Kitty can tell. For when she looks to the south of the island, she can see a long, green river of grass between two banks of sheep to show where Maggie's come from. It leads down to Tavey. It ends beside its gorse.

The unhappiness rushes in. The quiet loss and envy.

Love feels like a dream she had; a dream, and nothing more.

An early moon-rise. It is a half-moon, or nearly – a pale slice against a navy evening sky.

Sam Lovegrove sees it. He is leaning out of his bedroom window, smoking. He inhales, exhales, and then stubs the cigarette out on the windowsill.

When will it be full? What of the tides? It matters to Sam; he likes to know, as his father does, what the water will be doing in the same way as a soldier might eye his enemy and make notes. *Always*, he thinks, *better to know* – and with that, he makes his way downstairs. He goes into his father's study, sits at the computer.

Tick-tick as he types.

Sixteen days until the moon is full again. A Friday. There are numbers and symbols by this date that he understands – tide times, the times of sunrise and sunset – but there is also one he does not see too often. He leans forwards in the chair.

Sam scrolls down.

Ah … He swears.

He, like all the Parlans, knows the stories. He knows the legends and fishermen's songs. This doesn't mean he believes in them: mostly, he does not. Sam knows that a phosphorescent sea is not a sign, merely a build-up of plankton, and seals cannot fall in love. But he has one belief. There is, Sam admits, one small superstition that he is wary of.

The sly tide. That's its Parlan name. On this computer screen it is called the *perigean spring tide*. Two names, but they mean the same thing: it is the highest tide of all. When it comes to Parla, it seeps into the dunes, partly submerges the wooden stairs that lead to Lock-and-Key. It leaves driftwood in fields and fills rabbit holes. It comes when the moon is closest to the earth and is, also, full – and so it does not come often; three or four times a year, at most. But no-one is too fond of it. No-one really trusts it. It is called the *sly tide* because of the trouble it brings.

Men drown in it, Sam – so he was told. *Hearts break with it. Whales beach themselves ...*

Oh, he'd mocked that. He'd half-scowled, half-smiled and said *yeah, right ...* But there had been a sly tide when he last sat in *Sea Fairy*; a sly tide when he last saw the soles of Tom Bundy's feet as he pushed off from *Pigeon* and dived overboard.

Sixteen nights.

Sam shuts down the computer. *I will tell Maggie*, he thinks. For she has her lobster pots; she thrums out in her little boat three times a week, on her own. And he will tell her because she is *Maggie*: she is who she is. She is *her*.

So yes, Sam will warn her; it is his duty to.

*   *   *

At Lowfield, the grandfather clock ticks.

Tabitha stands in the hall. He sleeps – she can hear him, in the mending room. She hears his breath; she hears him say *sea ...*

Why does he say that? What does he dream of? Or is it a memory that he cannot speak of yet? One day she'll ask him. Or perhaps one day he will tell her of his own accord; he will take her arm and say *Tabitha, I remember.* But it won't be tonight. Tonight, he sleeps.

She turns to go. And as she does, she hears this: *Maggie ...*

What? She pauses. And the word comes a second time, as if making sure.

Tabitha steps back. *Maggie?* Briefly, it surprises her. But then she thinks, *of course* ... And it does not surprise her at all. For she can see them, as they were – standing in her garden, nearly two weeks ago. Maggie had leant, gently, against him. He had touched her shoulder and looked down at her blonde hair.

She has a fleeting sadness, as she climbs into bed. Or perhaps it's not sadness, but a shallow, passing envy – at having one's name sighed out, like that. Tabitha would love to think that someone, somewhere had breathed a soft, desirous, nocturnal *Tabitha* ... or that she has simply been in someone's dream. *To have been longed for.* But she is pretty sure that she has never been that.

Never mind. So it goes. And she turns out the light, settles down.

Also, she thinks *I am glad.* She is truly happy for the widow and this man. She has seen Maggie's frail, stooped shape in the pews at church; once, she saw her kneeling in evening sand at Lock-and-Key – and the nurse cannot imagine how it felt, to have that loss. To have such love, and lose it.

For love, she knows, is rare. Deep, romantic love does not pass by often and for some people it may not come at all. And so how can Tabitha mind it, when it comes for someone else? She doesn't mind it. She can only help them. *I will help them* – so that their love can strengthen; so that Maggie's little heart will not break a second time.

Kitty and the Jellyfish

Dawn, eight years ago. On the dark, reflecting sand of Lock-and-Key there were wading birds and small, translucent crabs that skittered, and hid. The sea had left its marks – ridged, compacted sand. She felt it, in the arch of her foot. When she pushed down, the sand seemed to whiten with her sudden weight.

A woman with midnight hair. She had twists of scarlet in it, and her hair was long – down to her waist. She wore a long, red dress – last night's dress, for she had not slept or been to bed – and she had to lift her hem as she walked down the wooden steps. She knew nothing of beaches. She had never walked on a low-tide beach before and so she crouched at rock pools, bent down for shells. Her shoes were hooked on her fingers; she swung them as she trod over the mirrored sand.

Her name was Katherine, and the night before she had danced in the fields for midsummer's night. A local man asked her *why have you come here? To Parla?* He'd been handsome – tall, a shy smile. The cider had made her bold so that she'd looked him in the eyes and said *to meet you, perhaps.*

That was the start of a story. What a fine start, too – bold, so that the listener might widen their eyes and say *really? She said that?* And Kitty smiled, as she walked – at her boldness, at the Parlan man who'd thumbed the hem of her red dress as if red was not a colour he knew. She picked up a stone that was perfect, sea-round: *this will always remind me of now.*

And this: a jellyfish. Near the water's edge she found it – sitting fatly and symmetrically, as if it had been placed there. Blue – but not an earthly blue; it was milky, opaque, lunar in some way, and its skirts were lined with a darker shade. She trod around it. *Is it still alive? Can it survive, on sand?* If not, should Kitty lift it up and carry it out to the sea? She considered this, but did not. Instead she thought, wistfully, *it is just how things are ...* and she crouched beside this creature, gluey and round like an eye. *I've never seen such a life as this ...* And as Kitty crouched in her backless dress, she realised that she wasn't really meant to – no human eye was meant to see this jellied globe of life. It was designed for depths. It was meant to clench its way through a darkness that she would never know of, and perhaps only an hour ago it had been doing just that – rhythmic, beautiful. An hour ago, where had she been? In a hay barn with a man called Nathan Bundy – and no jellyfish was meant to see what they had done.

It amazed her, as the whole island had.

Kitty had come to Parla for a weekend, hoping for nothing but time on her own – peace, a place to recover from a failed relationship, to begin to mend from it. Just that. She hadn't predicted Nathan. She hadn't predicted a man looking at her as he had, or feeling what she now felt. She'd never imagined a jellyfish left on the sand.

Later Kitty learnt this: that the creature she saw that morning had had no heart of its own. No brain, no blood, no stomach, no bones, no eyes or ears. She frowned, at hearing this. Then how could it be a creature? When it lacked as much as it did? And Kitty liked it less, for a time. But then she quickly pitied it. She thought of how she had clung to Nathan, not caring that hay-seeds were in her hair or that twine was rubbing the back of her thigh or that someone might find them or that this act – this impulsiveness – was *not her sort of thing* ... She had grasped him, kissed him, and it was her heart that was making her feel like this – breathless, sore in the loveliest of ways. *Poor jellyfish*, then. To have no heart. To live a heartless life in a silent dark.

*　　*　　*

Kitty stands where she did, eight years ago. No red dress. There is grey in her hair, lines by her eyes.

And no jellyfish. The sand on which she'd found that bag of milky blue is bare – unmarked, save for twine and plastic bottle tops. It is a long time dead, of course. It had been dead, no doubt, as she'd bent over it and considered its firmness, its halo of skirts in their different shades of blue. Is anything left of it? Probably not. No bones to unlock as the flesh gives way: nothing to clink down to the floor.

No heart. No ache.

She wants to laugh. If she does not laugh she will cry, and so Kitty bunches her mouth into a smile and looks up. *I'd pitied it* ... She remembers that so clearly – pitying the jellyfish for it could never feel what she had been feeling at that moment; it would never know what she had known the night before and she'd said *goodbye* to the dead jellyfish as if she'd been the lucky one. She'd walked backwards, barefoot. *Goodbye* ... Swinging those high heels.

Fool. Things change. She should have guessed at it – that an adult life is not row upon row of sex on hay bales and it is not fireworks and it's hard to stay in love. How she'd been as she'd walked on a beach at dawn – flushed, newly opened, still smelling of him – had been exceptional, magical. How could it have lasted? That hope? Being so alive?

So yes, she pitied the jellyfish, then. But there have been moments since when in fact she's envied it. Who could not, sometimes, envy it? She longed to just *exist*. To move without thought, or feeling. Just to have a languid, rhythmical life where no-one else could find her, where her life was easy – where she could simply *be*.

*   *   *

Nathan has not forgotten. He remembers that night, too – the dust that came off the hay, the way she'd held his gaze and said *maybe to meet you*.

Eight years. And he knows nothing of the jellyfish. He has no idea that his wife ever saw it and hasn't quite forgotten it; he does not know how its meaning has changed for Kitty over time. Once, it was proof of what she had found; now, it's proof of what she doesn't have.

He sits at the back of High Haven. He turns his wedding ring over and over. This – his ring – is his version of it: it was love, at first. It was love without end. Now he feels broken to look at it. *She deserves better ... Always did.* Hasn't everyone he's loved deserved much better? He says *Kitty* and he closes his eyes. Eight years on, and his heart still gives its own clench in the darkness to hear her name – just to hear her name spoken or to see it written down.

Ten

The day after my tears, Hester came to me. The *Morning Star* had docked and she was dropping mail off, as she sometimes did – door to door. *So – have you heard?*

Heard what?

The pig farm? Our Fishman can use a hammer ... And I felt her eyes on me as I took my mail, smiled.

Yes, everyone knew. He'd taken Kitty's tools on a Wednesday afternoon; within twelve hours it was known as much as all truths are. And perhaps it was the newness of it, or the thought of seeing inside Tavey when it had been locked up for ten years or more, or maybe it was the fact that the Fishman would now be visible – no longer mostly at Lowfield but out in the sun, shirt off, working hard – or something else entirely: who knows? But people were intrigued. *What will he do with it? What state is it in?* As I passed the shop I heard Milton say *that place must have some view from it ...* I said nothing. I kept walking whilst thinking *yes. It does.*

I stayed away for two days. I lifted up lobster pots, lowered them back down; I looked at the gold ring on my left hand.

But others went. Tabitha, of course. She called out *knock-knock*, left her shoes by the door. She moved through its rooms, remembering – for she'd been in Tavey when she'd been younger; she'd played in its fields, when the pigs had gone. *This place*, the nurse said, *could be wonderful* ... She fingered its walls, sat on its bed. And later, she brought over candles, cushions and a rug for the floor. *A feminine touch ... That's all.*

Ian went. Him, of all people. I saw him walk with purpose; he carried a hand-saw – orange-handled, with a plastic guard that covered the saw's teeth – and he gave no greeting or polite exchange. He merely said *this is better. Nathan's saw is* ... A wave of the hand, dismissing it. *Blunt. Old. Useless, frankly. If you want to saw wood, saw it with that.* Ian who did not trust this man; Ian who had few words.

And Nan. I was walking near Litty when I heard her – a wild, shrill *yee-arr!* that sent up a herring gull, and pricked the sheepdog's ears. I shielded my eyes. *What is ...?* And I saw Nan swinging onto the Fishman's back. She yelled *stand up! I'll be so tall!* He rose very slowly. He grew, and grew, so that Nancy gripped his shirt, laughed a fast, delighted laugh and it was at that moment that I thought *I can trust him*. It came, as I watched them: *yes, I can.* For she laughed with joy – a laugh I had not heard on this island for far too long. And he was so gentle with her when he set her down. I was moved by it. I put my fingers to my mouth and kept them there. Had I seen this before? This moment? It felt tender, recognised. But I knew I had not seen this; it was the first time I had seen this happen, in my life.

Nan, in her blue dungarees. Bossy, radiant Nan.

Having dismounted, she took his arm and shook it. The air was filled with her happy chant of *again, again, again, again, again!*

* * *

Leah wears a flowered top and jeans that are rolled to the knee. Grasses brush her shins; she feels the wind against them. Still the north wind. Still the bathroom vent's *tut-tut*.

She takes the coastal path, and glances down. The sea is calm as it has been for over two weeks now; she has seen the sea far wilder than this. She's seen a wave so vast that when it came towards her she'd thought *it is alive* – a real, breathing, sentient thing that had its own intentions. She'd thought *it comes to take me* – and it had terrified her. Made her go indoors.

The sea scares her far less, now. She is proud of this, as she realises it. But she still is not ready to walk on Lock-and-Key.

The Fishman has dust in his hair and beard. He holds a nail in his mouth which he takes out as he straightens up. *Come in.*

Thought you might need some help.

He smiles. *You want to help? There are jobs if you want them ...*

She steps closer. *What are you doing to it?*

Not much – it does not need too much.

Finding its former glory?

Something like that. He glances around them. *I reckon it was lovely, once.*

Piggy. Pig-smelling.

Maybe. He smiles. *But the views ...*

There are cobwebs, bird droppings. In the corner there is dust that is blue-coloured, hairy, and it makes a rough, singular movement away from Leah as she passes by it. She can remember Tavey before it was boarded up. She remembers the tourists who came and went – binoculars knocking against their chests, or with wetsuits hanging out to dry. *Is it for you? Will you live here?*

No. I can't really stay.

No? Why not?

It's not where I come from. He smiles. *I know that much, at least.*

Leah says *can I say something? About you? I know your memory's gone. And I know that it'll come back. And I know there are people on Parla who want to know what your name is and how you came to be here. But I think, maybe, that I don't want to know. I don't want to hear you're a lawyer or a dentist who fell overboard or some guy who swam from Utta for a dare, or …* She shrugs. *My dad says you're just playing us. And I hate that. I hate that he says it. I want you to know that it wouldn't make me happy – to have that as the truth.*

She can't explain it better. Leah cannot put this into words. It would take too long and too much out of her to talk of her illness, the weight she bears, the way she misses her uncle even now. She does not try. Nor does Leah want an answer from this man; she had asked him no question so how could he answer? She wants no explanations. She has no wish to learn what caused the circular scar on his hand or why he says *sea* … She likes what she has chosen to believe: that he is the Fishman. She likes the wild, impossible, beautiful truth she has decided upon – that he says *sea* because he misses it; that the scar was caused by a squid's beak or a conger eel and that those huge, broad hands of his have spent years underwater, fingers fused together and pulling his body through the dark.

She starts to sweep. A small job but it helps. She pushes the blue-coloured dust into the light. Neither of them speak. What can he say? She'd said *be the Fishman. Stay the Fishman, please* – and he'd blinked at Leah, given a single nod.

* * *

Kitty stands at the quayside. Her eyes are rimmed in kohl. She is going to the mainland for two days and by her side she has three canvases that are padded and wrapped up. *Please*, she tells Ed, *be careful with them* ... She watches as he carries them into the wheelhouse. *Safe*, he assures her, *and sound*.

Rona, too, is there. She hands five airtight boxes to George, who carries them on board. Lemon sponge, apple tarts, a tiered chocolate cake.

They look sinful – gorgeous ... Kitty tells her.

Maggie has been on *Pigeon*. She leaves her lobsters on the quayside, in their plastic crate.

After this, she goes to Tavey. She steps in to find Leah, who has a broom in her hand and a cobweb in her hair.

Hi.

Hey, Leah. Is –?

Yes. He's outside. Leah tries to hide her smile – a tiny, understanding one.

Maggie and the Fishman do not go very far. They only walk to the small shingle beach, look out at the water.

Merme is out there, somewhere.

He tries the word, considers it. *Where Abigail is from.*

Her mother was. You know?

I've met her. Seen her book.

Ah ... Maggie smiles. *Of course you've seen the book.*

And he listens as she talks about the stories: not the ones in *Folklore and Myth*, but the others that she knows, the ones that have not been written down – of the whale that answered the foghorn, the gannets that give the fish they've caught to the people they like, as a gift. *On Say, there was a woman who cried so much that the gulls took pity on her, and cried on her behalf. It's why they sound as they do – the gulls.* She shrugs. *I like that tale.*

He wants her to say more than this. He wants to hear all her stories – hers. Of the child she was. Of the dreams she had. What she loves – he wants a list of them to keep. And in turn, the Fishman longs to sit Maggie down and tell his own stories – of brine, of pain, of a flashing light over a night-time sea.

He wants to lay his own gifts in her lap – not silver fish, but words. But what does she believe in? *She will not believe in my words.*

Maggie likes how he looks, today. He is browning with sun; the lines by his eyes look deeper, as if he's smiled more. When she shows him how to skim stones – bent knees, a fast wrist – she likes how his forefinger curls so neatly round that stone. Snug.

When you start to remember – your name, or your story – will you tell me?

The wind catches a strand of her hair. He takes it, smoothes it back and says *you will be the first person I tell.*

*   *   *

To the north, a girl with an ankle bracelet and a floured apron picks up her mobile phone. She leans back against the oven door, begins to write a message. She has the low, tight feeling in her belly that she has with eagerness or simply with the thought of him.

Saw K leaving. How long for? Can you stay tonight?

She pushes the phone across the worktop and looks out of the window. It had been hard to see her – hard to be standing next to her. When Rona had first seen Kitty this morning, in her long grey dress with a navy trim and a fabric lily pinned into her hair, her first thought had been *she knows; she is leaving because Nathan's told her.* But then she saw the small overnight bag, the three rectangular shapes wrapped up in brown paper and heard Kitty laughing, so that Rona thought *no, she isn't leaving. No, she still doesn't know.*

Guilt. Like a hole that she knows is there, always, and yet tries to tread round. *Don't think of it. Don't think of it.*

Think of him, not her.

* * *

Jim can hear a hundred things. He hears *stash … stash …* he hears the gull above him. He hears his own belly and it is asking him for food. Also, Jim can tell that the Lovegroves' cat is here, reaching up from the grass and padding at the bells. Jim can hear the new, uneven *sing-sing-sing* so that he knows exactly where she is. She will soon grow bored. She will start to groom herself, or lie down in the shade.

He can't remember the last time that Abigail mentioned the old pig farm. Years have gone by without its name being spoken. If Abigail has ever mentioned Tavey, it has only been in passing – as she gave directions to a tourist or talked about the voles which live near there. It has been lost to her, perhaps.

Jim knows why she does not discuss it. Tavey has its stories. It has seen things, as she has, that she has no wish to talk of. *Tavey.* Once, before they married, Abigail whispered into his ear what Tavey had been to her, as a child. *I used to hide there … We all did.* And it troubles Jim enough – the mere thought of his wife, aged eleven or twelve, choosing to hide inside those half-moon shelters with the pigs and their pig stench. It troubles him – so how must it have been for her? Her, who did the hiding?

He said *what were you hiding from?*

But he knew. Her father was Jack Bundy Senior who Jim knew – they all knew – treated his sheepdog better than his wife. Mercy lost a tooth for every year. She would cover her mouth when she spoke, in the end. And so when she died Jack Senior must have looked elsewhere.

No-one would think to look in a pig sty ... And so she told him how they'd charge over the fields – Jack, Thomasina, and the puffing Abigail – and clamber in amongst the pigs, amongst the mud, urine, kitchen scraps, bristled skin and excrement. They'd try to breathe quietly. They'd sit in a line with their knees to their chests and hear their names shouted over the fields. *Don't you try to hide from me!*

Afterwards, they always swam. They'd swim fully clothed to wash the dirt away and hang their clothes on the back of kitchen chairs at night so the fire might dry them as they slept. Jim hated this knowledge. He had always known that Abigail's scent was her own sweat and a little wood-smoke and now he knew why. *How often? How long? What happened if they did not run fast enough?* Too many questions which he never asked, and he has no wish to ask her now.

It was a good hiding place ... Always sadly said. But one summer's afternoon Thomasina didn't think so and she ran to Tap Hole instead. Her twin and her brother crouched amongst the pigs, wiping their noses, and thought *where is she? Why hasn't she followed us?*

He hears her behind him. She comes into the garden, and her pace is slow so that he knows she carries something – a tray, he thinks. There is the *chink* of cups.

He says *Abigail?*

I'm here. There is the sound of the tray being lowered.

Jim reaches. He finds her sleeve, and then travels down it until he finds her hand and squeezes it. *How are you?*

How am I?

About Tavey? The pig farm? About the Fishman mending it?

Oh! She settles down. *I don't mind it at all. He'll take those shelters away, I should think. The troughs, too. It'll be a better place for it* – and she pats the hand he holds her with.

Maggie sits, hunched. Her arms are rigid so that her shoulders are pressed against her ears, and she looks at the floor. Silence. Except for a distant bee that is knocking against the glass.

The smell of polish and candlewax. Dust.

She is not alone. There is this bee that flew into the church when its door was propped open by Hester, as she watered the flowers – but there is the minister, too. He carries an armful of hymn books. He sings, as he walks. *Dum-de-doo …*

Then he sees Maggie. *I'm so sorry …* He walks a little slower, treading quietly.

It's OK. I wasn't praying.

I didn't hear you come in.

It's fine. She puts her hands in her lap. *How are you?*

Me? Oh, I'm as well as I can be.

Back pain?

Always a little of that but there are worse things. He tilts his head, eyes her. *And Maggie, how are you?*

How is she? She gives a smile, shakes her head. *Confused. Scared, a bit.*

Can I help?

She's not sure if she should talk. But then she asks *Lorcan, do you think there is one great love?*

Human love?

Yes.

Romantic?

Yes.

He lowers the rest of his books. *I think love changes. I think how we love when we are young is different to how we love in our later years. But it does not grow less.*

He will know; she is sure that he knows. He has ears and eyes and a heart that has seen more of the world than she ever has. Tabitha comes to him with codeine for his back, and they will have talked of the Fishman and her. He must know who she's thinking of.

Maggie. Lorcan settles next to her. The pew creaks, and she feels it sink a little. *I don't know much. But I know that love is infinite. Love for one person does not lessen because you might start to love another, too. Look at families – do you think a parent's love gets watered down, the more children they have? It keeps on going. What a wonderful thing! It grows and grows ... I know you are not talking of children, Maggie. And I know the vows you took – I helped you to say them. after all. But ...*

The bee knocks, high up.

It is – he says this slowly – *a short life. A remarkable life, and rich – but our earthly life is not long. I think there should be as much honest love as possible.*

She sniffs. *And loyalty?*

Ah. Loyalty. I cannot tell you what to do, Maggie. But you are the living one – you are the one with the bodily life. What – he asks – *would you have hoped for Tom? What would Tom have hoped for you?*

She swallows and looks at her hand. There it is – smooth and gold. The hand itself has weathered – it is lined, thinner-skinned, and it has its marks from lobstering, from kitchen burns and barbed wire. But her wedding ring is just the same. It has not changed from the day he pushed it on her finger in this church, by this altar.

You will never stop loving Tom, I know.

I still miss him.

I know. And I can only advise. I can only tell you that nothing will change your love for him – not death, not another love …

She looks across. *Thank you.*

They never truly leave us. We carry them in us – you know that, don't you? And he stands, touches Maggie's shoulder – awkwardly but meaning it, as a father might.

We carry them in us and *nothing will change your love* – and I lit a candle in the church, afterwards. I stared at its little yellow flame. It was the only candle and yet it lit the walls and the umbrella stand.

You are the one with the bodily life and I knew he was right. I understood, now, that I was the one who was left behind and so it was me and me alone who could enjoy the things that Tom had loved – the house martins' nests at Wind Rising, the taste of our tomatoes. It was me who was still here, and so I looked – studied – all the things that he was no longer there to see. I spent a night by the nettles, listening to the voles rustle through the stalks. Once, when I dug for radishes I found an earthworm and held it in my palm, stared at its ribbed collar and its blind pink head, twisting for the dark, and I ran my hands along *Pigeon*'s sides because he used to do this before every voyage and he no longer could. *Live.* I saw the word in a newspaper six months after he died and I didn't understand it – how could I live? The word offended me. It seemed cheap and shallow, and I turned the page. But later I would sit by the fire with a glass of wine and wonder how I could describe its taste for him – smoke, plums, damp straw? I used my body for him. I did the things that he could not because his body was gone.

Live. I had to try. I knew I had to, and that he would want me to.

She makes up her mind as she steps out of the church.

At Crest, she runs a bath. In the wardrobe, Maggie finds a dress in peacock-blue.

*   *   *

The bee in the church grows tired. For nearly two days it had knocked, and knocked. It lies on the windowsill. It does not move.

An old, tired bee – its furry head lies down on the paint-work; if it was to be prodded it would give a single, weary buzz.

It nearly dies, on that sill.

But then, a piece of paper – an old till receipt – is pushed up against it, and a finger nudges it whilst a voice says *on you go*, and then the bee is lifted up on his white flying carpet, and it is carried outside – out into the late-evening air. It is popped onto a dandelion leaf.

Lorcan, of course. A life is a life, in his eyes. All have been made by the same kind hands – and if he can help a widow who is newly in love, and happy, then he can also help an elderly bee find its way outside.

Gardenia on her collarbone. Lotion on her shins and hands.

Her necklace that shines out – *M*.

She walks over the fields. She carries a blanket. She hears the wings of insects rising from the grass as she goes. The lighthouse finds her, passes on.

Candles at Tavey. The smell of sanded wood.
Two knocks.

He opens the door. It is Maggie, and she wears a dress of deepest blue – the shimmering blue of a dragonfly. She has caught the sun. A freckled nose, paler hair.
He does not smile. They look at each other.
She steps in. She swallows as if she is nervous and she looks at his mouth as if it's that, his mouth, that she is wanting. Maggie drops the blanket to the floor. And then she puts her hands on his chest and she pushes him back into the house so that he's walking backwards. She follows him in.
She closes the door behind her with her foot.

*   *   *

This is how he kisses her.
Firstly, he takes his hand and runs it into her hair. His fingers close upon her scalp – not too hard, but enough to show his purpose, what he also wants. His head is angled slightly, so that when his mouth comes down onto Maggie's mouth their lips are not perfectly matched, or even. He partly kisses the skin beyond her lips, the corners of them. The shadow where her chin begins.
A sound, as her mouth opens. There is the damp click of their tongues.

This is how she kisses him back: with her hands and forearms pressed against his body and pushing up onto her toes so that he needn't stoop so far. She pulls back for a moment, then re-enters. She opens her eyes as she is kissing and sees that he, also, is looking: she sees herself in his polished eyes.

Later she says *I will always love him. Always.*

I know.

She takes one strap of her dress, unties it. Then she unties the other one.

The Fishman stares. He touches what he sees with his fingertips. Then he turns his hands over, feels her body with the backs of them.

Maggie? Are you sure?

She smiles – a little sadly. She studies the top of his trousers – the silver button, the zip, the belt-loop that has broken. They both watch as, slowly, she takes the zip and pulls.

The Silvered Nights

The light caught us, I remember that. Every minute there were five half-second flashes, and so five times a minute I saw him – muscular, bare. In one flash, he was over me; in the next his face was coming down. We were in darkness, then we were lit. Then we were in darkness.

It must have seen so much – that lighthouse. Over the years of being here, it must have flooded so many tiny moments with its light: bodies moving together; boats being pulled up into a night-time cove; a ewe giving birth so that she blinked when the light passed over her. It finds the rooftops and the blackthorn trees and the stone walls which look, somehow, more textured by night, more shadowed and strange. It turns over the gravestones, one by one. For a second, it makes each bedroom white.

There are hundreds of stories about it: ghosts, shipwrecks, the dreams the light can bring when it sweeps a room, the moths that come to the lantern room's glass.

Tom told me about the silvered nights. He had learnt about them from Nathan, many years before. In winter, in the shortest days, the light would start turning whilst they were still awake; they'd put down their homework, go to their window and watch it glint off coils of wire, wing mirrors, the sleeping farm machines. And if the moon was full, then it, too, would glint off metal – the dog's chain, the gas canisters, pennies on their windowsill, tools left in the fields. It caught the backs of beetles as they crept up stalks of grass. So much light, flashing, that Nathan called them *silvery. Look – it's one of those nice silvery nights ...*

And the story is this: that these nights are magic. That on such nights – a full moon, a turning light, a sparkling sea that crashes – flakes of silver are made. Who knows how? They drift down, to the ground.

All those shiny things. The metal rim of spectacles, as they rest at a bedside. The crescent of light in the mare's brown eye.

The ring in the nose of Tavey's old boar – long ago.

You know these nights. You feel them, as you sleep. And when the morning comes, you must rise and dress and walk out to the fields at Wind Rising for it's said that these are where the flakes fall – here, in this grass alone. I don't know why. Why not in the graveyard, or on the tarpaulins of boats? No – it is always Wind Rising. And I have looked out of my window on a moon-white night, seen the lighthouse turning, and imagined those silver flakes, as they're falling. Settling like fish scales into its midnight grass.

*   *   *

Sam knows it. Like all children who grew up on the isle, he knows that story of silver in the fields. His mother whispered it. She tells it to Nan, now; he has heard her, through the bedroom wall. *When the moon is full and silvery ...*

He cannot remember if he ever believed in the story or not. Perhaps he did what most boys do – openly mock it, wrinkle his nose and say *that's rubbish* – whilst secretly glancing down in the grass as he passed by Wind Rising. He isn't sure. But he knows that Leah believed it, for a time. How old had they been? Ten, maybe. She'd been standing there, as if waiting for him – dungarees with one button missing so that the bib was half-unfolded. *Are you looking for silver?*

No.

It's here. If you look. I found some.

You did?

A flake of it. Hands behind her back.

That was Leah, before the fade came. Before the sea mist of depression rolled in without much warning and dampened her, softened her so that she had less strength. She had always been *sensitive* – that was the word he'd heard for her and it was the right word. She saddened at the lobsters that Tom hauled ashore; she bruised, as ripe fruits do. And one day, as Sam lay in the grass beside her, he glanced across and saw her pulse beneath her skin, as if her skin was so thin her heart might break it.

Still. There is something in Leah. A flash of metal. A piece of grit in the pearl.

When Tom died, she came to Sam. When everyone else was wandering beaches, scanning the water, calling out *Tom, Tom*, Leah came down to the harbourmaster's house, pushed the door open, walked up the stairs past Dee who was saying *Leah? What the …?* and she'd opened the hatch into his attic bedroom, throwing up dust and light and old cat hair and she'd sat down on the edge of his bed. No words. She'd just sat there beside him. In time, she took his hand.

Sam smokes, at this moment.

They used to do that, too, in the fields – share a cigarette. She'd return it to him with a moistened end, where her mouth and tongue had been.

Now she works at Tavey. Leah who has lived through books for so long – poetry, or romance fiction. Did she think she could never be happy? Or never be worth happiness? Yesterday Sam saw her pause from her sweeping and drink from a bottle of water, and some of that water ran down her chin and onto her collarbone and Sam could not imagine a book containing that sort of beauty, that brightness or that *life*. Could he ever tell her? Like the silvered nights, it has to be seen to be fully believed in. He watches the moon's cycles; Sam watches the tides and he knows when there might be the next night of silver – magic, milk-white.

Twelve days until the full moon.

Twelve days until the sly tide comes.

There is a flash of blue, not silver. Did Leah sense his thoughts, or share them?

He looks down at his phone, presses *read*.

A message from her: *goodnight xxx*

Eleven

Maggie wakes before he does. The room is barely light – grey, soft-coloured. It is cold, too, and so she takes hold of the blanket, pulls it up around her shoulders. Not yet five. She shivers once, turns.

He sleeps on his side, facing her.

Maggie looks. She looks at his sleeping face – the eyelids, the slightly parted lips. He is resting his left cheek against the back of his right hand.

Last night he'd asked her, *are you sure?*

And all she could know was that as she'd walked towards him, through the evening fields, she'd felt her heart beating. When she'd glanced up at the moon, she'd only thought of him. *I never asked for this …* And yet she'd smiled, as she was walking. She'd smiled, passing the gorse.

His face, Maggie thinks, is a beautiful face.

Yes. Yes, I am sure.

Tavey, where no human has slept for many months. Mice have, and spiders; rabbits; birds. But it has been years, even, since a single human life slept beneath those rafters and longer, far longer, since two humans – a man and a

253

woman – have shared a blanket in this house, or their breath, or their own heat.

He opens his eyes, now. He opens them onto her profile, the curved shell of her ears.

Hey.

She turns. She blinks, as if focusing. And he suddenly loves how she looks at this moment – her knotted hair, how she rubs her eyes with the backs of her hands, how she mouths *hey* ... back to him, as if scared of saying it. This coy, embarrassed, sideways smile.

Day. A day like every day before it and yet brand-new.

The bed in the mending room has not been slept in. It is white, smooth. There is no glass of water beside it, no sleeping body in its depths. Tabitha stands in the doorway: she knows exactly where he's slept.

And so she gives a soft nod, pads into the kitchen. She turns on the kettle and reaches for a mug. And Tabitha imagines how it must be for Maggie and him, at that moment – waking together for the first time. Are they looking at each other, with no need for words? Are they amazed, and grateful? Are they smiling nervous smiles?

They will remember it for always, Tabitha is certain – a room with no curtains, skin on skin, and a sea-cool dawn.

*   *   *

Sun climbs; the chestnut mare stamps a hind leg once to rid herself of a fly.

The man from Sye watches Maggie go. She looks young in that blue dress, and she walks through the fields with her arms by her sides. When she reaches the crossroads she pauses, looks back.

He is not the only one who sees Maggie, of course. It is a small island; most of the windows and doors look onto other windows and doors and Emmeline has woken to find that her runner beans have drooped down their frame, sunk to the ground, so she is in her vegetable patch with garden string and her reading glasses pushed up into her hair. She binds the plant back to its wooden frame, frowns.

And she looks up. Emmeline glances up at movement in the fields and thinks *Maggie? At this hour? And in a sundress when the sun is barely up?*

Then she knows. The thought settles like dust, covers everything.

Unlike her sister, it is not calmness that she feels.

*   *   *

I have slept with ... Maggie walks through the rooms of the house, turning her wedding ring. She is frantic, for a while – hauling out the box in which she keeps Tom's letters, his gifts, the order of service from their wedding and saying *sorry, sorry, sorry* ... and bringing old photographs of him to her chest. But this passes. This angst, this self-retribution leads to a deep sleep. Maggie sleeps on the sofa, the box by her feet, and the dream she has is of feathers, falling down around her. She dreams, too, of a beard, and a whorl in it. It looks like a star. It looks like the place where a thumb has been pressed and turned, as if to say *this is one of the good ones. This one. This one, here.*

In the afternoon, she goes to Sye. She remembers her husband on this beach – the slight grey at his temples, the groove beneath his nose where no beard could grow. The sea sucks the shingle. And Maggie thinks of the day she found a crab's claw here. She'd held it up. *Tom?*

I still don't know his story. Or his name.

Maggie can only call him *Fishman*. And perhaps he is, indeed, part-fish – and that somewhere on this beach he has hidden his rainbow tail. Between two rocks, or under weed.

She walks back to Crest in the evening. As she passes her shed, Maggie smells tobacco; it makes her look up. A man is at her door. He is kneeling, with his back to her. But then he hears her footsteps, or perhaps he merely senses that he is being watched for he rises, and turns.

Sam?

There are three hydrangea blooms on her doorstep. They are a deep lobster-blue, wrapped in tinfoil. He glances at them, blushes. *From our garden. I –*

Sam ...

I thought you might like –

You don't have to do this. You don't.

Want to.

He looks at the hydrangeas, sniffs – and Maggie feels that she could touch his unhappiness. She could grasp his guilt.

I thought you should know. The sly tide is coming. Eleven days.

Eleven?

A week on Friday. Just so you know. I know it's superstition, but ...

Sam, I have never blamed –

But he interrupts her, says *they need to go in water. They've not had any water for an hour or so.*

No-one blames him any more. Once, perhaps: Emmeline had hissed her curses, wrapped herself in bitterness instead of letting out her grief; Ian had had to be restrained by

Milton when, one day, he saw Sam passing by. But this did not last. Blame has no purpose here; it changes nothing. It does not lift Tom out of the water and pop him back on *Pigeon*; it does not bring his voice back to Maggie's ear. She knows she could say *we do not blame you* over and over, for always, but it would still mean nothing to Sam. He brings dark-blue flowers out of guilt; he mutters *your fault* as he stands on the deck of the *Morning Star.*

Maggie watches him go.

She knows that Tom would have never wanted him like this. He'd have never wanted Sam to grow so heavy, so old. Her husband would have sought Sam, sat next to him and said *stop this, now. Be kinder to yourself. Why feel guilt for what was not your fault? It was my choice – to dive in.*

He'd have winked. Nudged Sam's shoulder with his own.

I am fine – I am. Move on.

*   *   *

There are no secrets. All things are known – or if people do not *know*, they will suspect it. They use their eyes and ears: as fishermen are rumoured to have a natural sense about where the fish are passing or when the wind may turn, so Parlans have a natural sense for the feelings between people. If they have their suspicions, they tend to hand them on.

Hester has Emmeline with her tonight. Sometimes her mother comes to eat with them. She steps into their cottage with a casserole, or vegetables that she herself has grown. It tends to be the four of them – Hester, her mother, her husband and her son. But tonight, Alfie is in bed. Alfie, who refused to eat his potatoes, wailed, and so George is upstairs with him – she can hear his low, reprimanding voice. Hester would change nothing about her son except that stubbornness. In time, it might have benefits. It might make him successful, when he's grown. But for now, it frustrates her. Leads to wasted food.

Emmeline pouts. She pushes back her plate. *Well. I saw an interesting thing.*

Hester hopes this is not about Tabitha. So many of her mother's sour expressions are made when she's thinking of Aunt Tab. *Oh?*

This ... man. Who's got his hands on Tavey.

You make it sound like he's throttling someone ... Hester rises, walks to the sink.

Does he sleep there now?

Sleep there? I doubt it. She runs the tap. *Why?*

Maggie came from there. This morning. It wasn't yet seven and she was wearing this flimsy summer dress ...

Hester fills a glass, turns the tap off. She has no real wish to know what her neighbours feel or do. *So? It's not our business.*

Isn't it?

No. Not in any way.

Tom –

Was her husband. Was. Past tense.

That man –

Seems lovely, Mum! Have you talked to him? Spent time with him? He changed the school's lightbulb – did I tell you that? He's good for Leah, too. No memory doesn't make him a bad man.

Silence, from Emmeline. She runs her tongue over her gums, dissatisfied. *I don't like it.*

Doesn't matter. Mum, it's been four years – four. None of us could stay as we were ... Be fair.

Fair? Don't talk to me of fairness.

And anyway – all you saw was her walking. That doesn't mean anything; it doesn't mean a single thing except that Maggie can walk.

Later, Hester gets ready for bed. She looks in the bathroom mirror, runs cotton wool over her face. *Maggie had only been walking* ... But Hester is human, as they all are – and she wonders if there had, in fact, been more than that. *If there had been* ...

She looks down. Can she imagine it? The Fishman and Maggie? Yes – she finds she can. They are both mild-mannered, contained, softly spoken. They both gaze at the water. Have their own mysteries. Salt in their hair, on their skin.

Maggie. If Hester hears that name and closes her eyes, there is one specific moment that she sees. It is not when she first met her. It is not Maggie's wedding day.

It was Hester who heard the news. Hester, who Ed called before anybody else. He rang her and whispered *there's been an incident* – told her that search teams and helicopters were both on their way, that Tom was a strong swimmer and she should not fear the worst – not yet – and *will you tell Maggie? Could you?*

It is the hardest thing that Hester's ever done. She will never forget the expression – Maggie's stumble, the frail sound she made and how she ran out of the house without speaking and charged through the fields to Lock-and-Key. She'd leapt down the wooden stairs; she'd raced, fully clothed, into the sea. And she had waded, and waded. Called out – *Tom!*

It was Nathan who brought her back. He swam out after her, allowed Maggie to fight him – *no, no. Let me go* ... As the light faded, he walked up the beach. He carried her in his arms as he would carry a child.

And that's it. That's what Hester sees.

She sees it now, in this bathroom. She stares at the sink but it's Maggie that she sees – shouting out and tearful. Flailing in the dark.

Hester joins her husband. She lifts the duvet, crawls across to find him. George says *your feet are cold* and kisses her head without taking his eyes off his book.

The day after Tom's disappearance, Ian had come to her. He'd taken her wrist and said *you think there's a God? Ask Him for an answer. Ask Him to give Tom back.*

It doesn't work that way. But Hester asked, all the same. She lay down on a church pew as she used to as a little girl and whispered *why have you done this? To him? Please, don't …* She'd trawled through the Bible and found nothing; she cried until strings of saliva led from her mouth to her fists. She was exhausted, and when Lorcan found her sleeping there he placed a blanket over her; he left a small electric heater near her, so that Hester would not wake up cold in the night.

I think Maggie might be in love with the man from Sye. Or close to it.

George puts down his book. *What?*

I think. Not sure.

And is he in love with her? Hest?

I don't know.

He turns to her. He fingers her curls, pushes the curls aside so that he can see her eyes. *How would you feel? If they were in love?*

I'd be happy. And she finds that she means it.

*   *   *

The Fishman finds Tabitha. She is in her dressing gown, sipping a glass of pink wine.

I'm just going to Crest. I won't be long.

The nurse merely sips, smiles knowingly. She flexes her toes in their woollen socks.

All day he has thought of Maggie. He has watched the fields, thinking *come to me. Come.* But she did not come.

He walks up the lane, knocks twice on her door.

Maggie looks tired, pale-eyed. He says *do you regret it? All day I've thought you might be regretting it.*

No. Have you?

No ...

She is in her pyjamas. He sees this now, and she does. A grey-green tartan – and they both smile at this. Maggie blushes, reaches for a coat.

Together, they walk into Crest's garden. They settle on the bench, look south across the island at the bedroom lights, the church's roof. The sea is dark and silver – both.

He takes her hands, warms them. *In Abigail's book, it says the Fishman comes ashore for one person or many.*

I know.

Whoever I am, and whatever this is, I know I came here for you.

*   *   *

Near them, at High Haven, Kitty waits.

She sits in the chair she has been sitting in for hours, now. She has watched the kitchen clock. The cat, at times, has joined her – settled on her lap, purred so that she's felt the vibration through her knees. But the cat is outside now.

She turns on a light.

She waits, and waits.

When at last he comes, drink-smelling, he does not speak. He moves into the kitchen like a man who's been defeated – by life, or himself, or by her. Does he expect her rage? For the wild, stormy Kitty to fling her words and arms at him? For passion? That was how she was, once. But it is too late for that – for the fire and challenges. They have not worked. And as Kitty returned from the mainland she knew that she'd grown sour and disappointed with the life she lives with him.

Nathan rubs his eyes. He looks at her.

She still loves the man she married; Kitty knows she does. But she can scarcely find him in this man – this man, here.

In a simple voice she says *I can't do this any more.*

Nathan sits. He looks at the way her hair and her eyes are the same dark colour, how her silver earrings hide amongst that hair.

I'm dying on this island ... Dying in this house.

The house?

The house, the marriage ... You barely speak to me. We hardly see each other and when we do, we fight. I can't remember the last time you touched me willingly. Do you know that?

He blinks. He wants to disagree with her, to list the times that he has taken her hand or kissed her unexpectedly, but he knows she is right. He can't remember either. There are no times.

Do you think I can live on nothing? I can't live on nothing.

She is not angry. She is just tired. She looks away from her husband, out of the window to where the lighthouse swings and she can smell the island's smell – sheep, fish, salt, earth. *I'll catch tomorrow's ferry. Go to the mainland. Stay with friends to begin with. Paint.*

Nathan looks at the floor. *How long for?*

I don't know. I'll phone.

What do I tell people?

That we're taking a break, because that's the truth. And then Kitty smiles sadly, breathes out through her nose as she does so – a half-sigh, a wise sound. *Let's face it, Nathan. I don't think they'll be surprised.*

They make love that night for the first time in five months. He moves his hands over her, remembering her shapes and textures. She is responsive, and warm, and he hears her small, childish sounds. He likes them, remembers them.

But the next morning, she packs her clothes and paints, tells him not to forget to water the pot-plant on the landing and he drives her down to the harbour. He is aware of her two bare knees beside him, the bracelets that clink on her arm. When she boards the ferry, she stumbles, and a tourist that Nathan does not know takes her arm, says *steady …*

Kitty holds the railing, looks back. She gives a single, small wave to her husband, her fingers kept together.

Nathan goes home. He switches on the kettle, sits at the kitchen table. There is a newspaper beside him, and he sees she has finished a crossword. On the windowsill, there is a broken geranium stem in a sherry glass, and lip balm, and he thinks *she has held this spoon. Sat in this chair.*

In the bedroom, Kitty's perfume is on everything.

The Puffins and the Mother

Long ago, when horses still worked in the island's fields and when women still wore skirts to milk their cows, there was a war. The wireless told them so. A war that would be over by Christmas, they said, and several young Parlan boys went to the mainland to enlist for it. They waved from the *Star*, as it took them away. The islanders cheered, waved back.

It was not over by Christmas.

Two brothers – red-headed, thin-limbed, crooked smiles – died, in that long war. A letter came for their mother so that she buckled on the quayside. *Not both, not both …*

Yes, both. She trawled the isle. She sought them, as if they had never left – in caves, on boats that rocked on their moorings. Where had they gone? What had they loved? Her boys, her two dear boys.

In their short, teenage lives they had loved the puffins more than other Parlan things. When they were not carrying sheep on their backs, they would draw the puffins that nested on the north coast. They sketched them and coloured them – bill after cheerful bill. Her boys had loved those puffins, and so, in her grief, she began to hate them. She hated their waddle, their curious eyes. It hurt her to see them – for how could they be living when her boys were not, now? Where was the fairness? How could a puffin mean more than her sons?

She took her dead husband's air rifle and lay on her belly, above Bundy Head. She shot bird after bird through their feathery heart. Left their tiny bodies there.

After this, her grief moved on into the deep, slow sobs that feel so strong that they may break the ribs or stop the heart entirely. Every cell of her body ached for her boys. And in time, her grief moved on again – into quiet waters. She became regretful of the puffin deaths she'd caused; she saw the sadness of them, the waste and cruelty. Hadn't her sons loved them? And then, surely, shouldn't she? Slowly, she came to. She'd watch them, on her sons' behalf; she'd hear their throaty call. And the hurried, low-down flight of these birds, their waddling gait or their moustaches of sand eels brought her closer, much closer, to her two red-headed boys. It was a way of *feeling* them. She could not see them, but they were with her – sitting on Bundy Head.

It is not much of a bedtime tale, I know. Who wants war, death, and a grief that leads to other deaths? But like all stories, it has its worth. It means something to me.

I know this: there is no sense to grief. There is no pattern or shape or texture, and there are no books or stories which can lessen the pain at losing a person you have loved, and will always love. There are no rules, with loss.

Look at Parla. Look at how the grief rolled out, as gas does – darkly, and touching everything. Look how Nathan spun, drank, pressed his face into a duck-feather pillow and howled at long last so that no-one might hear him. Look how Emmeline took to brushing her hair very neatly before sitting on her dead son's childhood bed. Hester would write *be with us* in the church's prayer book – *be with us*, nothing more.

Sam lifted weights. Or he lingered by my house as if awaiting orders.

Leah refused to go to Lock-and-Key.

*   *   *

Maggie remembers hearing the tale of the puffins and the mother who was not a mother any more. She heard the story, and like most people on the island she did not understand it – *she shot them? Why?* It made no sense to her. She imagined it – this solid, dark-haired woman lying in the grass and muttering curses with one eye closed as she aimed. How could she have hated them? If her sons had loved them? *Don't we preserve what the ones we love have loved?*

That was then. That was before.

But hate is part of grief, Maggie knows that now. It is as strong and defined, in grief, as shock is or that deep, unbearable space which opens up inside us, a cave we walk into with our arms apart and we shout *where have you gone? Where have you gone?* They who were so real – who were warm-bodied, noisy, brimming with life and memory and future plans. How could they be over? We do not understand it, and then the understanding starts to take root and show itself and we realise that we will never see them again, never watch how they move or hear new words from their mouths. And then the anger comes in. *How dare he be dead? How could he have left me?*

Maggie has had her anger. One evening, not long after her husband had been lost to the sea, she had sat in *Pigeon* off the north coast. She had been checking her pots – wearing the thick, waterproof gloves that she always does, and hauling on the weedy ropes so that the pots rose up into view. There were several buoys, back then – orange, faded from salt and sunlight. They were fibreglass so that when Maggie rapped them with her knuckles, they made a hollow sound. But there was one buoy that was different from the rest. Before she'd met Tom, when *Tom Bundy* was not a name that existed for her, one buoy had broken when he'd dropped it onto rocks. In need of another, he had improvised – three empty, plastic containers lashed together with blue baling twine. Three plastic oil drums, bobbing on the water like transparent balloons.

That evening, Maggie came to this buoy.

And without reason or warning, she hated it. Suddenly, she brimmed with hatred for these containers. *This plastic shit* ... The buoy was garish and amateur to her. It seemed to have some joke in it which she did not want, or did not understand, and it shone with Tom's resourcefulness and thrifty ways and uniqueness, and humour, and his handwriting was on the side of these containers so that she hated – passionately – the mere existence of them. How could they be here when the person who made them was not? It felt obscene. It felt like mockery and she hated it, hated it.

She leant over the side, hauled the buoy in.

Maggie, with her penknife, cut at the baling twine. Five years or more of surviving the seas and stormy weather but the twine undid like butter against her angry blade. She hissed as she did this. She spat, *stupid things*.

She threw them – one by one – into the water.

Maggie sat there for hours. She felt the rage pass over, and move away. She watched the three plastic oil drums part from each other and drift off on the currents, one of them trailing a length of baling twine.

*   *   *

Later, in bed, I regretted it. Where would they go? Now that I had freed them? Would they float endlessly? Maybe they would travel the world, comet-like. They would bump against a surfacing whale or tap the snout of a turtle or be pummelled or cut by a tanker's propeller. Or maybe they'd come to rest beneath a palm tree, far away. When I considered this, I felt sad, somehow. As if plastic had feelings, too.

Also, I felt ashamed. I am so rarely angry; angry is not part of me and yet look at the rage I had felt and shown. Had I been seen? Slashing at them, swearing like that? Had someone on the coastal path looked down and seen me flinging the drums away? I'd thrown them like footballs, with both hands.

I regretted it but it was done. I could not undo it. I could only learn from it, and understand grief better – the different shades and shapes to sudden, immeasurable loss. And to see it as a story, albeit a strange one: three plastic containers, a boat, a penknife and the absence of the man I had adored.

Twelve

Kitty went as the summer grew old. She wore dark glasses on the *Morning Star* so that no-one could see her sorrow – but I think Sam did. He knew the signs; he saw how she leant on the railings, looked down at the sea as if the sea could help. Others did not see it. Wasn't she showing her work at a gallery? They assumed she was going there, for a day or so.

It was me they talked of. No-one had seen me with the Fishman – *with* him, in a sense beyond being merely in his presence; but they knew. Leah, cleaning the windows, saw my blanket on Tavey's bed; Milton glanced down to the pig farm one night, and saw me moving through it. Lorcan, too. He never mentioned it, not once, but I think he knew I lit candles in his church for other reasons now – for what had been, and what had been lost but also for what had been found.

And Tabitha, of course. I'd stayed a second night with him, and a third, and on the morning after that the nurse came over to Tavey, sang out *only me!* I was embarrassed, at first. I thought *she will judge* – and I pulled on my shoes, hurried out. But I should have known that she was not the judging kind. Her smile did not have shadows. Later, on the quayside, she whispered *I'm glad* as she passed by. She looked proud of me, almost – as if a prize had been won.

*   *   *

At the lighthouse, Rona foams milk. She cuts a slice of chocolate cake and carries a tray outside. And normally, she would talk to the guests as she places the tray down or say *here you are*, brightly, at least – but not today.

This morning, she heard from Nathan. It said two words: *she's gone.*

Rona had stared. She'd had to sit down. *Gone? Actually gone?*

This is a day she has imagined for years. It is a day she has dreamt of since she was seventeen, when she first started wanting him – of their marriage ending, of Nathan being free. In her dreams, it ended easily. She imagined them agreeing, smiling, and Kitty saying *go to her – to Rona. I know that you love her* ... And wishing him the best as he walked out the door. Foolish, of course. She doubts that it could ever happen that way. How had it happened? *Did he tell her that he loves me?* And did he watch as Kitty screeched, threw plates to the ground? Perhaps she fought. Perhaps she knelt, and begged for him to stay. Perhaps she threw back her hair, hardened her jaw and said *I have never loved you anyway.*

She swallows. *Which?*

Did he even tell her? Surely he told her.

She replies to him: *you told her about us, didn't you?* Puts the phone in her pocket, goes out into the sunshine with a plate of cherry scones.

*   *   *

Tabitha is in the mending room. It is cool, lavender-scented. Her cupboard doors are open and she counts out small white pills for Abigail. Blood pressure. *It comes to us all*, she thinks – old age. Or it does, if we are lucky. She tilts the pills into a brown bottle, labels it.

A bang on the door. *Where are you?* Barked out.

She finds her sister in the hallway. *Yes?*

I have a question.

Tabitha waits.

I saw something. In fact, I keep seeing the same thing – three times now. Emmeline nods, lowers her voice. *You know what I'm talking about.*

No I don't.

Oh, you do. Maggie. Leaving Tavey at first light. Is she staying the night with him, now? Your precious patient?

I am not talking about this.

No? A man who could be anyone at all? And Tom's wife?

She inhales, turns. *Maggie is not his wife.*

Don't you ... Emmeline reaches. She takes her sister's shoulder and pulls Tabitha around. Her face is red, puckered. There is a hardness in her eyes. *Trust you to be like this.*

Like what?

Not on my side! Never on my side ...

There aren't sides to be on! How are there sides? I just want everyone to be happy.

How noble. And Emmeline slams the door as she goes.

Jim hears that slammed door.

So does a rabbit. It darts into its burrow, its tail shouting *white!*

And we do – we hear it. I am at Tavey. I am looking at the lips of the man with no name; I am pressing the soft, full pads of his mouth with my fingertips. We sit, and do not speak. But soon, he starts to smile. He smiles and I, in turn, start smiling and he reaches for my hand, moves my hand away.

What? What is it?

Ticklish, he says.

Then the door slams. And when I step outside into the gorse and sun, I see her – Emmeline, walking away. She marches from Lowfield with her arms swinging.

The Fishman comes beside me. *Us?*

I think so.

We watch her make her way past the church, up the lane.

*   *   *

When we were not together – talking, kissing, leaving a line of crumbs in the garden and watching the sparrows come – he was working. Tavey was now taking shape.

Those boards which had been nailed over the windows meant that their frames were not too damp. A little, in places – but he shrugged, said *they'll be fine*. No boards, however, had ever been nailed over Tavey's front door: its wood was rotten, now. I could push my thumbs against its lower half and they would leave their thumb-shaped mark; its corners were blackened, and sponge-soft. It needed replacing. He also talked of shelves, skirting boards, a windowsill, a mantelpiece. I had never guessed a Fishman might know so much about wood.

George heard of this. He came, knelt by that door and picked at it; he tapped his jawbone as he thought. A week later, and secretly, George met a man on the mainland and returned with booty: a secondhand front door with a rose made out of coloured glass and two dozen lengths of pale, fragrant pine. *Called in a favour*, he winked. *Don't ask.* And I heard George spent a day at the pig farm, then –

measuring the wood and marking it with pencil. Smoking in the gorse with a mug of tea, the pencil still behind his ear.

Together, too, they hauled out the troughs. They dug into the ground and freed the old pigpens, making sure the honeysuckle stayed where it was. *Bloody hell*, said George, sweating. *They're heavier than they look* ... And as the light faded, the two men opened beer bottles and leant against the fence. It looked good – the garden, the second-hand front door.

Thank you for your help.

You're welcome.

But George was not the person who came to him the most.

It was Leah. Little Leah – who was not *little* as such, but she had spent so long trying to take up less space on earth or staying indoors that she seemed to be small some-how. In the past, she'd been a feather as I had been a feather – drifting, existing and not saying much. But then she came to Tavey. She sanded down the woodwork. She boiled the kettle on the rickety stove. She found a loose floorboard and called the Fishman through. *Here. Hear that?* Smiling. She shifted her weight back and forth, back and forth so that it squeaked.

*   *   *

Tabitha walks on Lock-and-Key. She wears green trousers that billow in the wind; they make a snapping sound, like flags. She hears them, and the Fishman does; the nurse does not walk alone.

She is not sure if she suggested a long beach walk or if he did; it seems like it just happened. Emmeline had left, stamping footprints into the turf; Lowfield had shuddered with the slammed door. And Tabitha had made her rounds, bought milk, emptied her washing machine and even then

– hours later – she still felt her home was shaking. Or maybe she was. *That sister of mine …*

She took off her glasses, cleaned them. And when she put them back on, the Fishman was with her – standing in the kitchen, tilting his head. *Tab? Are you … alright?*

So she knew he had heard the slammed door.

Now they are here, and the northerly wind is so strong that she wants to close her eyes and lift her arms from her sides and feel it. She did this as a child. She'd climb onto the foghorn, straddle it and imagine that she was not her, not Tabitha, but a bird in flight. There is something about winds. They clean her, strengthen her.

It was about me, wasn't it?

She nods. *The two of you. Everyone knows, of course.*

She's angry?

She looks out to sea. *Em is always angry.*

What I feel for Maggie –

Oh! Tabitha touches him. *Don't stop or change because of Emmeline! Gosh, no.* She shrugs. *I doubt her anger is about you anyway.*

The wide, dark flatness of Lock-and-Key when the tide is out. There are whelks, limpets, cockle-shells, the leather straps of kelp. Wading birds hurry, at the water's edge. Tabitha can see her reflection, in the sand – and she could live nowhere else, now. Not now.

You don't seem like sisters, he says. *If you don't mind me saying so.*

The nurse looks across at him, and up. *In how we look? Same nose.*

Same nose, maybe. But I don't mean that way.

We aren't close. Never were – not really. There's seven years between us and that's a big gap. She steps over channelled wrack, kicks through a length of blue nylon rope. It catches round her ankle and she leans down, pockets it.

But seven years feel less as you grow older, don't they?

She smiles. *You know a lot about the rest of us when you know nothing of yourself.*

But he is right. She knows he is right. Seven years was a lifetime, once. How do you play with a twelve-year-old girl when you are five? When you are finally twelve years old she is not twelve; she is nineteen and married and gone. There was barely the chance to be close to Emmeline. There were some moments but they were as brief and rare as a whale, cresting. And as lovely, too.

She remembers tennis with her. They fashioned two rackets from planks of wood and hit a ball against the lighthouse wall. There was sunlight so that they were squinting. Emmeline had laughed, said *good shot!* When had that been? Had it happened at all?

We fought. It is a confession. Tabitha leans in to him. *We had one huge fight. About a man.*

Jack. The boy from Wind Rising. Tabitha noticed his ears before she noticed any other thing – ears that stuck out a little too much. She saw, too, there was dirt there – a line of it, as if it had been drawn. He never said much. He'd appear in the courtyard of the lighthouse-keepers' cottages and squint, twist his toes into the dust. *Jack's here!* Tabitha would shout it without moving, narrowing her eyes at this sullen boy. Why did he always visit them? She'd ask but she was never told. Once, and once only, Abelard said this: *sometimes he needs a place to come. And so we'll let him. Understand?*

Emmeline married a man called Jack Bundy and I didn't like him. That's all.

Why not?

He was ... hard. A hard man. He threw stones at the gulls. The Bundy men had a reputation for being bad to their women and I worried for my sister.

He looks at the sand as he walks, but glances across. *You told her this?*

Not at first. She knew the rumours. And how do you reason with a woman who's in love?

She had literally bitten her tongue. As Emmeline walked down the aisle in a cream dress, Tabitha had taken her tongue and pressed her teeth down upon it to stop her saying what she felt in her bones which was *this man doesn't love you enough. Not as much as you love him.* In the wedding photos, Tabitha looks sad. She could never hide what she felt, or not well: when she looks at the photographs it is her own sadness she sees.

You were scared for her.

Yes.

And she missed her. There was that, too – that despite the seven years, the lighthouse was not the same with the empty single bed, the tea left in the teapot because it held enough for four mugs when there was only a need for three. *Jack is her husband. And she is my sister* – and so Tabitha would visit and make cakes for her, and when their first baby arrived – Ian, with his milky smell and squawking mouth – Tabitha had been so amazed, so filled with sudden, tender love that she embraced her sister, or tried to. An awkward, clumsy hug.

On my eighteenth birthday I went down to see her when she hadn't been expecting me. She was nursing Hester – Hester must have been a month or two months old – and I saw the bruising. She said she'd fallen after the birth – weak, tired ...

You argued then?

Not then. I took her word for it. But later – just a few weeks later – I went back round and she had a cut up in her hairline. An inch long. It had crusted, by that point – but it must have bled very badly ... That's when we argued.

I was leaving for the mainland a few days later and I was scared of leaving her. I said some things ...

How easily it happens. The words spill out and cannot be retracted. She speaks as freely now as she had shouted, all those years ago – words like *tyrant* and *bully*, and *you are blind! Blind!* Tabitha had raged so that Hester had wailed, and Ian had come downstairs with frightened eyes and a thumb in his mouth to see his aunt saying *what of the children! You think it will only be you? Are you mad?* And then it came – the slap from Emmeline. A slap that sounded like a gunshot.

I think I called him a bastard. Worse still, most likely. I told her that she would be a bad mother if she stayed and I had no right to say that. I was eighteen ...

Yes, how easily it happens. How easily, too, the years join up like daisy chains or beads of blood in water so that it looks like one long cloud of it. How easily one's own life takes over – Tabitha's studies, her friendships, her own beating heart and, later, her nursing in parched desert countries all swept the years away until it felt too late to sit down with Emmeline and talk about that slap of the hand and those hot words. By the time Tabitha came back to Parla for good she was thirty-two. The argument had been nearly half her lifetime ago, separated from her adult self by famine and disease and love that hadn't worked out, and many small tragedies – so that their fight had felt too distant to go back to. They were not the same people. Tabitha was jaded, trailing her loss; Emmeline was the mother of four and tougher than Jack, now. Sealed up like a clam.

But you still feel it.

She nods. *Hard not to. I have sat here for three decades and watched my sister try to hide what she was told was love when it was not love at all. How was that love? What a waste ...*

They come to the end of the beach. There is foam that the wind finds, and it skitters. To her right she can see their footprints; two of hers for each one of his. So tall. So good to walk beside.

It isn't too late. Nothing's too late.

She shakes her head. *Too much time has passed.*

I don't believe that.

She is angry with me. She's an angry person.

Not fully.

Tabitha looks up. *How can we still not know your name? You must know it. You must, by now.*

He says nothing, looks pained.

I know you have your reasons. I guess we all have our reasons. Emmeline made her choice and that's just how things are.

On the beach, they talk of other things. They crouch amongst the weed – the emerald sea lettuce, the bladder-wrack that shines like bottle-glass. *She is happy. It's good to see her happy* – and Tabitha means Maggie. He knows who she means.

Yet when the nurse goes to bed that night it isn't the weed she thinks of. She does not think of the shell that she saw him pick up, and keep.

It is of time passing. It is of the grandfather clock in the hallway that has counted every minute of every hour for the past two hundred years or more. It is of too much time slipping by to ever make a difference to how she and Emmeline speak to each other, or act. How many years? Half a century since Tabitha shouted *you're a bad mother* in front of young Ian, and far worse things – *if you don't leave him ...* Huge declarations from a child – a *child* – who knew nothing of love or how the heart works. There is no excuse – there is never that. But whereas Tabitha, at eighteen, could not comprehend the *staying put*, the choice to stay at Wind Rising and make two more sons with a man like Jack, she can understand much better now. Time has passed indeed, she sees that much. Love may have darted through Tabitha's nets, or mutual love at least, and she has not had children but she has seen enough to know what matters and what does not. They are not young – not these days. She would not say *old*, but she and Emmeline are not young and one day their names will be carved onto stones in the graveyard where their parents are and that will be their lives done with, and gone. They will only be names and a story or two. And what then? That's when it's too late – then and not before. And Emmeline may hiss and she may have spat out *don't you dare* when Tabitha had tried to comfort her in the hours after Tom had gone but the Fishman had said *she is not fully angry* ... He'd said it quietly. He'd talked to Tabitha as a parent might – and, she sees, he had been right.

Anger is Emmeline's veil. Just as she had worn a wedding dress, all those years ago, so Emmeline wears her anger now. She dresses up in it. But it is thin. It is gauze-like and it can be pulled aside. *I will pull it aside.*

They are sixty-five and seventy-two but they are also the girls who played tennis with planks of wood against the lighthouse wall. They shared teacakes. They hung their Christmas stockings, side by side.

It's never too late.

And if a widow can find love again, she can find the sister who used to give her piggybacks, who showed her how a guillemot's egg is tapered so that it can never fall from its ledge; it only rolls back round to its starting place.

*   *   *

Gone?

Hester looks at her brother. She can see a few grey hairs at his temple, and two blue shadows beneath his eyes. She can smell beer on him. Rum.

Yes. Gone.

Where to?

The mainland. Staying with friends for a while, and then ... I don't know.

Are you divorcing?

No. At least, I don't think so. Not yet.

Ah, Nathan ...

He sits on Hester's sofa – slumped, expressionless as if too tired to feel.

Do you know why?

Me, mainly.

I can't believe that. How can it be you?

He swears to himself, under his breath.

She moves closer. *Do you want her back?*

She's left her slippers. They're at the end of the bed and I can see where her heels have been. There are these little dents in them ...

You miss her.

Yes.

How has this been your fault? Have you –?

I don't talk. She said I don't talk and I just ... I never really minded that she lent the tools. I didn't –

What tools? Nathe, I don't understand you.

He looks so sad. He says *I get it wrong. I always get it wrong.*

What have you got wrong? Hester takes his hand. *What? Tell me.* The smell of rum is strong, and she can sense that he is leaving her – that his talk and mind are drifting, in their drunkenness, elsewhere.

The stories ... I gave him shells, to ...

Stories? What shells? Who?

*Shells ... And my front teeth. Remember my front teeth?
It wasn't the quayside. Nope ...*

He is too drunk, too tired. He is a middle-aged man,
but as Hester brings her arms around him and holds him
she feels he is a boy again. They are taller and wider, and
Nathan has not shaved for days so that she can feel his
stubble catching on her clothes – but also, he is just the
same. She is still Hester, who hates her curly hair. *There,
now ...* she whispers.

He had been so fair, at first. She and Ian had been like
their parents – dark, wire-haired, but Nathan had stood in
the yard with a stick for the dog or a plastic spade and his
hair had been yellow – straw-yellow, sun-bright. Not like
a Bundy. Or not at first. In time, it darkened. But sometimes she can see still the ghost of his downy, blond hair
when he walks by her. She can see it now, behind his ear.

*You've never let anyone down, Nathe. That's silly talk.
I do. I deserved it ...
You don't. She'll come back.*

And he does not smell the same, entirely – there is the
rich, animal smell of sweat, the sourer smell of sweat that's
old and there is that half-bottle or more of rum on his
breath, and sheep in his hair. But underneath it all, she can
still smell her brother – leaf tea, Pears soap, the cream
he uses when his hands crack, that soft and indefinable
scent which must purely be him, his own gentle skin's
scent.

* * *

It wasn't the quayside.

She stands in the kitchen, slides the gold cross that
hangs about her neck up and down on its chain. Up and
down.

It wasn't the quayside ... Then what?

Hester shuts her eyes. She tries to see them all as they had been, when all of them had still lived at Wind Rising. Ian is in his early teens; Hester is ten, or maybe more. Tom is toddling, chewing on the end of a rag. And how old was Nathan, when he lost his two front teeth? Six or seven? It happened early. For a long time his smile had two dark gaps.

She goes back to the sitting room. He is sleeping, now. An unconscious man in his forties but also, somewhere, a gummy-mouthed young boy. One day, Alfie will be a pilot or a vet or a spaceman or whatever he may choose, and he might marry, have children, have a row of sports cars or political beliefs, and she may be stunned that her boy has grown into such a man; but he will still be her baby. Still the tot with dinosaur pyjamas. Still the boy who is difficult about eating potatoes. Still the boy who cried when a snowman melted, leaving only a carrot behind.

Hester tucks a blanket around her sleeping brother.

She sits on the floor, at his side.

It was not the quayside. And then – then – it comes. A fear comes, as she sits there. She stares, struggles for breath and a realisation begins to show itself. It breaks the sea's surface as a shipwreck might – as the *Anne-Rosa* rises from the water. This has been buried for so long. It has been buried so deeply but she can see it now and it is dreadful, haunting, black with dripping weed.

This: *something happened to him.*

She brings her face near Nathan's. *Oh …* He'd been so quiet when he'd found two coins by his bed the next day – one for each tooth. He'd thumbed them, sniffed. A sad little face, as if two coins were not enough.

Oh Lord. Be with my brother.

Be with all of us. Each one.

He sleeps on his back with his right hand open, as if asking to have that hand held.

* * *

Six days till the moon is full. It looks down on the island with a sad, kind expression.

Leah sends a message: *have you seen the moon?*

Yes, Sam has seen it. He is walking beneath it.

He treads down the steps that are cut into rock. He unpicks *Pigeon*'s tarpaulin, slides a container of diesel under it. She will sigh, and tell him not to as she has done before – but she is Tom's, or was. *Tom would want me to.*

At Tavey we are lying under blankets, side by side. The windows are open. We have the night breeze on the parts of us that are not covered – arms, toes.

I had always been the one to ask for stories. In my childhood I would gather them, keep them safe. For they filled my spaces, or seemed to; they coloured a world that was, for so long, black and white. It was me, always, who'd whisper *will you tell me about ...?*

But tonight, he says it. He traces my bare shoulder. *How did you meet? You and Tom?*

I am surprised. I twist, look up. *You want to know?*

Of course I do. It's part of you. I want to know everything.

The Blonde and the Bounty Inn

Once there was a girl who had no parents. Or she did have parents but they could not care for her – due to young age, or poor health, or no wish to. She would never know why, and she stopped wanting to. She sealed herself up, watertight.

Others cared for her, as she grew. There was the wide-hipped woman, the woman with hair as black as a crow, the couple who had paintings of saints in every room. There was a house that tinkled with laughter and she – the girl – had liked that house, and had hoped to stay there; she stayed in that house for two years, in the end. But the laughter stopped, in time. The house grew cold, tired. She was passed on, bag-like. She was not too trusting of *care*.

Through woods and cities, by hills and seas – she moved, and she moved.

And she grew older. She became tall, long-haired and she wore a ruby-red stud in her nose for a while. She smoked rolling tobacco – but she stopped when the toothpaste she spat in the sink was brownish, thick. She had friends but none too close to her; she had lovers but none that she wished to settle with. Her favourite flowers were gardenias, for their scent, and her favourite sounds were rain on a roof, a cat's purr and autumn leaves against her boots. She loved to hear good stories. Our wandering, sealed-up soul.

She took a job in a pub by the sea when she was thirty-four.

It was called The Bounty Inn, near the harbour. Its beer garden was right on the edge, so that at high tide the spray might splatter on the tables and drinkers hurried indoors. Maggie would haul on brass handles, wipe sticky tables, carry plates up her arm, smile at every face that came towards her and she'd wear a black apron with *TBI* stitched on it. The apron was longer than the skirt she wore.

Can you see it? This woman?

At night, she could see Parla's lighthouse. As she drew the pub's curtains, she'd see it turn and turn.

Margaret Bell. A serious name.

Days passed, and weeks did. Months.

One day in June. It was a June day as June days tend to be – warm, clean-aired with gulls strutting on railings. The pub's hanging baskets trailed their green. And Maggie was there, beneath them. She was collecting empty glasses – stacking pint glasses into each other so that a tower was formed. It began near her hip, and rose up to her jaw and she held one arm about it.

Then she looked up. Saw him.

A dark-haired man, a red and black shirt. He was standing on the quayside, hands by his side.

She wondered if she'd seen him before and then thought, *no. I have not.*

Later, much later, he will tell her that he knew she would mean something to him – how she held the pint glasses, how she moved her fringe from her eyes with one toss of her head. How she eyed the far islands. How great she looked in that black skirt. *I knew you were going to be …*

Special, was the first word. Then there were other words. *Unique. Loved.*

The one I've been hoping for.

Her shift had ended at nine o'clock. He – Tom Bundy – bought them both fish and chips which they ate on the harbour wall, swinging their legs. She made him laugh. He, in turn, made her say *really? That's true?* He knew so much.

Will you come and live with me?

She had never thought a man would ask her this. And she certainly had never thought she'd ever answer as she did – calmly, looking at him. *Yes.*

*   *   *

You have no family of your own? None? The Fishman looks sad, as he asks this. He strokes her arm – up and down.

No. No family.

Maggie sees the past across the ceiling. She sees the front door of every home. She can feel the different beds beneath her – too uneven, too hard or a frame that creaked when she turned over. All the different landing lights, shining under doors.

I'm sorry.

Don't be. Not for that. I met kind people. It makes you self-reliant, and grateful for what is good. It also makes you wary, I think. I didn't trust enough to stay and so I never really settled down … But then –

Him?

The lighthouse beam moves through the room, and out. *Perhaps I should have known. That it wouldn't last – that he would leave me.*

He hasn't left you. I don't believe they go.

Maggie looks at him. She lifts her own hand and touches his beard, presses his chin with a single fingertip. *Who have you lost? Tell me.*

But of course, he cannot speak of it. Not yet.

It's OK … She nods. *I know.*

Outside, the sheep are settling. They lower themselves into the grass for the night, or against the stone walls.

The lighthouse turns, as it's always done, and as it will always do long after these people are gone.

Thirteen

Nathan dreams of the night he met Katherine Snow. He dreams of the fire that they danced by, the taste of apples when they kissed. But there are changes also in this dream. When she dances, the fire grows too strong and bright to see her, so that all he can see is flames and no dancing Kitty – where has she gone? He can't find her. Only a little flattened grass where she had danced round and round.

And suddenly, a new dream. The old one slides into the other, and Kitty has returned to him but they are not in a field any more. There is no fire and she's not in red. Kitty is holding a finger to her lips. *Ssh* ... she says, coquettishly. She wears a black corset and a jaunty top hat. Then she moves her hand to a curtain that's by her side, says *ready?* And there is a drum-roll, and she winks, and then Kitty pulls the curtain aside so that a stage is revealed and on that stage there is Nathan's younger brother. Tom stands, soaking wet. He shakes weed from his hair and pulls fish-bones from his mouth. He wipes his nose on his forearm, and then looks out at the crowd as if surprised to see it. Nathan is shouting *Tom! Tom!* But he cannot be heard – his voice is too quiet. *Tom!*

The man steps forwards, scans the crowd. He sees nothing that interests him, turns and walks offstage.

Nathan wakes on his front. His arms are braced, pushing him up off the sofa. Where his face has been, there is saliva. His head aches and his back does.

Hester's. I'm at Hester's. He sits up slowly.

Another day of sunshine as he steps outside, and goes home.

At High Haven, he boils the kettle. And as it sings, he sees his mobile phone is flashing next to the fridge. He forgot it, left it here last night and he grapples for it, presses *read* and holds his breath.

WHERE ARE YOU??

Sent last night, at ten thirty.

Nathan sits. He'd wanted it to be Kitty. He'd wanted it to be his wife saying *we are going to be just fine.*

* * *

Hester hears him go, close the door. After this she dresses, makes her way to Wind Rising.

Hello? She stands in the kitchen, calls out. There is no answer: if Ian is not in the house he will be in the barn; and if he's not in the barn he will be out in the fields. Hester knows about farms.

She finds him sharpening shears. He sits on a low stool, and he runs a sharpening stone along the open blades. It is rhythmic, and musical. *It is a sound of our childhood,* Hester thinks – of Parla, and this building. She can see his bald patch. It is like looking at their father, maybe – for he also had this pink hand-span of skin on the top of his head that would burn in hot summers.

Hey.

He looks up. *Hey. OK?*

Hester steps into the barn. *Have you spoken to Nathan? You know Kitty's gone.*

Gone where?

Gone. The mainland.

For her work?

No, Ian.

He is like their father in more than just his baldness – he is like Jack Bundy in his thick brows, in how he frowns at everything, in the way he puts his hands on his thighs as he lifts himself from the stool and winces and Hester sees their father's hands in Ian's hands, too. Short thumbs and lined palms. She thinks *he is like him and also nothing like him – both.* Ian says *for good? Really?*

He doesn't know. But it sounds like it.

Shit. He scratches the back of his head. *I knew they weren't in great shape, but ...*

I know.

They walk outside. Brother and sister – both dark, both stout. The sun is a wall of light that makes them blink, look to the ground and Hester says *he came round last night. He's in trouble.*

Yeah, well. He drinks too much.

He does, I know. But Ian – I'm worried ...

About his drinking? He can sort that out himself.

Not drinking.

The rooster is having a dust bath. They can both hear his claws against the earth and when he shakes his head there is a clap of wattle, which Hester thinks, too, is a sound she knows.

Does he ever talk about Dad?

What? No. Why?

Hester rubs her face, unsure. *Stupid question. We never talk about Dad ... I'm worried because he said things. Nathan. Last night.*

Things?

Do you remember when he lost his teeth? His front milk teeth? He came back with a bloody mouth – remember?

Ian's shrug is scornful, dismissive. *He fell over. On the quayside. Was it the quayside? Somewhere.*

I don't think he fell.

She wonders how they came to be grown-ups, like this – with marriages, and children, and shadows they feel they cannot discuss, even now. It hangs there, this shadow. She can feel it between them. None of them talk about Jack Junior, or only in passing. There are ghosts that press up against the glass of this house and their lives and peer in, and Kitty knew it. Kitty couldn't stand it. It's surely why Kitty has gone.

He said it was the quayside. But he ran back to the house from the north of the island. I remember seeing him. He was coming back from Bundy Head.

So maybe he …

What? Knocked his teeth out at the harbour, and then decided to run the length of the island before coming home? She shakes her head. *I don't think so.*

So –?

I don't think he'd been to the harbour at all. Hester puts her hand to her neck, feels the gold pendant. *I have this feeling …*

The rooster stretches its wings. They are side by side and silent, and yet Hester is sure they are thinking the same thoughts – that the same image and fear is in both of their heads at this moment.

Will you see him? Talk to him?

Kitty will come back, Hest. I'm sure –

Not about that! Don't talk to him about that! You know what I'm thinking, Ian. What if – she leans closer and lowers her voice – *what if it wasn't just Mum? Who got –?*

We'd know.

Would we? Why would we know? Talk to him. Go.
Now?
Yes. Go.
The shears ...
The shears can wait! Go and talk to him. Ask him to
tell you about his milk teeth.*

*   *   *

Ian finds his brother in the garden of High Haven. There
is a rusted iron bench that Nathan sits upon, a bottle of
beer hanging from his hand.

The bench shifts as Ian sits down.

I heard about Kitty.

Yeah.

Think she'll come back?

Who knows? Beer?

No. Thanks.

The house creaks in the heat – the men hear it.

I deserve this, Ian. And she deserves to be happy. I've
been a bastard to her.

We're all bastards sometimes. It is Ian's form of comfort.

Nathan gives a brief, bunched smile. *Yeah, well ...*

They are two brothers whose language to each other is
mostly the farm, and the weather, or sport, but it is rarely
a language that talks of the past or of what they think and
feel. They sit, like stones. Nathan drinks, and when he
lowers the bottle he says, *sure? There's more in the fridge.*

No, you're alright. His eyes are on the bottle's label but
he does not see it. He sees, instead, how Nathan looked,
as a small boy. *How did you lose your milk teeth?*

What?

The front ones.

His brother flinches at the question, as if it is a fly. *My*
teeth?

295

Was it the quayside?

What do you want to know about my teeth for?

Was it?

Jesus. I can't remember. Yes. I tripped.

Hester doesn't think so.

Why not? Has she got divine insight?

Nathan can be many things but he is not sarcastic. *She's worried about you.*

It was the quayside.

Bullshit.

Nathan drinks again. He tilts the bottle right up. When he has drained the beer, he wipes his mouth with the back of his hand, and he gives a single cough, a clear of the throat, and says OK. *Fine. Dad caught me climbing through the wire fence above Lock-and-Key. I was bending the wire to fit through it and he took a swing and got me. You know how he was about those bloody fences.*

Ian sees it. He can see it so clearly. He knows what happened as if he was there – how their father would have grabbed Nathan by the collar, held him whilst the other hand came down against his jaw. *You should have said.*

To who? No point.

To me.

No point.

And Ian feels tired, at that moment. Tired of what they never speak of and have never quite freed themselves of. He is tired of how he himself walls himself up and speaks like his father now and he knows that when Hester was watching him in the barn, earlier, she was seeing the family looks in him – his hair, his hands. *Just that one time?*

Nathan is quiet.

That one time? Or were there other times?

It doesn't matter any more.

There it is. Like the beach when the tide is out he sees it all so differently; what he had thought was a stable and reliable truth no longer seems so truthful. Ian had forgotten about those milk teeth. But now he remembers. He remembers that Hester was jealous of the tooth fairy coming twice; he remembers the cotton wool Nathan held to his gums. And suddenly there are other things: the way Nathan cracks his knuckles; the small scar by his eye which was, he said, a cricket ball. The marks on his arms which he claims are from wire. He doubts them all, now. Ian turns over shells as if each one hides a sharpness.

Did you ever hit Kitty?

Never. I have never hit anyone – not once. But I've still hurt her, Ian – I just chose other ways.

They spend the afternoon on the bench. In the end, Ian goes to the fridge and comes back with two beers. They clink their bottles together, drink.

They talk about the sheep. They talk about the puffins that have nearly all flown now, leaving their burrows to the rabbits and the wind. Also, they talk about him – the bearded man who seems to live at Tavey now and how Maggie is happy in a shy, contented way. *It's good. It's good that she is.* And Ian knows that yes, it is. Tom, then: they talk of Tom – not in the way they've talked of him over the past four years, which has been rarely, and briefly, and as if talking about him would make the loss far worse. Ian talks, instead, of the birthday cake that was shaped like the *Star*, or how Tom tried, once, to ride a sheep. Nathan smiles. He shakes his head, picks at the bottle's label. And Aunt Tabitha passes on her bicycle, waves at them both so that they both wave back.

As Ian readies to leave, his brother looks up. *Never you?*

No.

Hester?

No. *Why did he only go after you?*

I was smaller than you but bigger than Tom? I don't know.

It makes no sense.

Not everything has to make sense.

There is a chill to the air, now. The sky is darkening and the moon is out, and the birds are landing for the night. And Ian's way of leaving is by putting his hand in his brother's hair, ruffling it. He says *she'll come back, kid* – which are his words of love. He might be brimming with it, aching with love for his younger brother and he might be fifty-one years old, but this is his best way, for now, of trying to express it. He is not good at any other way.

*   *   *

Ian finds his wife that night. She is reading in the bath, one foot on the taps. Her hair is coiled up, on top of her head, but there are fronds that have escaped and are wet, now. The bathroom smells sweet – like vanilla.

Can I come in? he asks.

She smiles. She drops the book onto a towel. *Of course.*

He lowers the lid of the loo, and carefully sits on it.

What's up? He can tell she is bemused. *Are the children alright?*

Oh, I think so.

And you? Are you alright?

Constance looks beautiful. He forgets, sometimes, to look – and now he looks. This is how queens looked, in legends, or how the mistresses looked who usurped the queens – flushed, warm, naked, half-smiling – and if he was an articulate man he would tell her this, but he is not. He's a farmer who's seen nothing of the world. He doesn't read books, as she does. *Are you happy?*

She rises from the foam. *Happy?*

Yes. With us. Me.

She frowns, not understanding him.

Kitty's gone. Left.

Constance's mouth opens. She blinks a few times, and then looks down into the water. *Poor them ...* A sound like a moan.

Are you happy?

His wife turns to him. Her gaze is bold, even. *Not always. We never have enough money. I hate smelling of sheep. Sometimes I wonder where my life went – I'm nearly fifty and I love my kids and I love you, but I sometimes feel like I've wasted it. I guess,* she says, *that I am sometimes happy. And sometimes is probably enough.* She rubs his thumb with her own thumb. *Are you?*

He nods. *I have you. I should tell you how I feel more.*

Yes, you should. You never do.

For a while, they are quiet. Then Constance draws her knees to her chest so that the water in the far end of the bath is empty, waiting, and she says very quietly *room for two ...*

That night, in bed, Ian smells of vanilla. He shifts his bulk down under the blankets, and kisses his wife on her ankles. He kisses the damp backs of her knees.

In his own bedroom, Nathan lies alone. He remembers his milk teeth. He had been seven and three-quarters, and hadn't meant any trouble. He'd run home, frightened, clutching them – two hard, bloodied pebbles in the palm of his left hand.

The sea says *hush ... hush ...*

Abigail lowers herself into bed. She has also seen the moon, and it troubles her. It troubles her that, today, she had heard Sam talk about the sly tide that is coming closer; the sly tide makes her wistful, sad.

She also thinks of love. She thinks of her husband, lying beside her, and she believes the love she feels for Jim now is the strongest it has ever been. Their marriage has not been without a raised voice or a little broken china, and once they did not speak for three days; but all the same, their love has grown. Like the plants which send out runners underground so that more of that plant pops up later on, their love is deeply rooted – it cannot be lost and it will never fade. This is love at its best, and most lasting: she would change this for nothing, nothing at all. But she can remember their love's early days. She can still see her shy, teenage self feeling faint and tearful with this *want* – this need, this amazement. She'd look at Jim's fingers, astonished; he, in turn, would feel her fleshy sides with his eyes closed as if trying to absorb exactly how she felt. Early love is … What? Restorative. Extraordinary.

Jim? Are you sleeping?

Not yet.

Do you think there are exceptions?

Exceptions?

I have looked in the book. Maybe the Fishman does not have to return? On a full moon? Maybe there are exceptions, and he could stay? I am thinking of Maggie.

Her husband is quiet. She can see his lips moving; he licks them, as he thinks. *I've heard of no exceptions.*

No … And it saddens her. But Abigail knows this is the way of it, for her mother said so. Mercy had leant forwards and said *what might happen, do you think? If he stayed too long?* A drying out; a yearning. A very gradual death.

Abigail is nearly eighty-four and yet she can still miss her mother. Mercy always counted her children as she kissed them – *one and two and …* – as if checking that they were all still there.

He'll go this Friday, won't he?
Yes, says Jim. *He will.*

* * *

Lorcan is still at his piano. He has been here for an hour and he knows it's late – but he thinks *once more* ... And so he plays from the beginning for the last time, before bed – slowly, leaning over the keys. He is on the third page of music before he plays a wrong note. He gives a single frustrated punch to the air. *So close* ... But Lorcan is getting better. And one day, before too long, he will play it flawlessly.

Rona is tearful, wretched. Her love is turning, darkening. She cracks her knuckles, as a fighter might.

And me? Maggie? The Fishman?
They are in Tavey. There is a single candle – enough to see each other by.
He is like a diver parting the waters.
She is as the eels are – *oh, oh, oh*.

The Imps at the Farm called Wind Rising

Once there were three children – Ian, Hester and Nathan. They lived on a farm with sheep, and high winds. They had hay-seeds in their jumpers and grass stains on their knees. Happy, or mostly. Then a fourth child was born. He was called Thomas and he came like a gift, like the best of all the shells on the shore.

Nathan was the closest in age to him. He liked everything about his younger brother – firstly, how Tom drooled his food or clapped at any music. Later, Nathan loved how he tried to ride the sheep like horses and how he'd go downstairs on his bottom, thudding all the way down. Nathan liked showing Tom all the best parts of the farm – dung-streaked eggs, the bags of grain that they kept in the barn, the warm, gritty patch where the cat had slept.

They played, and made dens. They caught crabs on a wire. And one day a crab nipped Tom on his smallest finger, breaking the skin so that a bead of blood appeared, and Tom cried. His eyes shone, and spilt. He asked *why did it pinch me? Did I do something wrong?* And Nathan said *no, no you didn't* ... and led him home, through the fields.

The crab hurt both of them, maybe. Nathan hated it – seeing his brother fretful, his unsteady bottom lip. The mournful asking of *why?*

To soothe Tom, Nathan told stories. He sang the sea shanties that their grandfather Abelard taught him. He talked of the silver in the fields, and the seals with human hearts. He always told these tales at night.

Nay-than? Are you awake?

Sometimes he'd answer *no*, and turn over; but mostly he'd say, *a story?*

Yes, please.

Some nights, when their father had been drinking, Nathan would wedge jumpers under the bedroom door. Or if it was a stormy sea, he'd open the window so that the sea's sound came in – spray, and booming. One time, when glass got broken in the middle of the night and Nathan heard their mother's frail whimper downstairs, he told Tom *don't worry, it's just the dog*, and then pulled the two seashells down from his bookshelf and clamped them onto Tom's pink ears and said *here. Listen. Keep those on your ears, and you'll hear the sea singing ...*

Tinfoil hats, like aliens. These hats came down over their ears, and muffled sound.

I will keep him safe. Tom, who gave hugs like a starfish in that he'd cling with all his limbs.

Once, Tom – aged six, or no older – woke in the night and padded downstairs. He'd wanted water, but found a broken chair, a smear of blood on the fridge door and their father snoring heavily on the fireside rug. It was too strange, too much. He clambered upstairs, using his hands. Shook Nathan's shoulder.

What is it?

Downstairs ... The voice of a frightened boy.

Ah, said Nathan. He moved over to make room. *Maybe that's the imps, then.*

Imps? A sniffle.

Imps. Like elves. Little people, but they are naughty. They like coming into people's houses at night, and taking things. Food.

Why?

And so Nathan invented them – these miniature, mischievous men. That night, Nathan lay on the bottom bunk with his younger brother snuffling beside him and he talked of these imps with their curled-up beards, their jackets made from leaves and their trousers made from moss, how they hid in old rabbit holes which annoyed the rabbits a lot because who'd want to share their house with them? With cross little people? The imps argued all the time. They'd creep into houses when hungry, or bored. They'd fight over food, kick furniture over, break plates, and make the cat dart upstairs. Nathan looked up at the slats of the upper bunk bed and tried to think of other naughty things that they did – swinging from udders, or plugging a hen so she couldn't lay eggs.

Will they hurt us? Tom was wide-eyed.

No, not people. They are frightened of us. If we stamp our feet they run away.

And they've been downstairs?

Yes. Maybe they came for the last of the ham. But we mustn't talk about them too much. Not everyone believes in them, and we might get told off.

The lies. He knew he shouldn't tell them because it said so in the Bible, but he thought it was better than the truth would be.

Goodnight, Nathan. A drowsy voice, muffled by a pillow.

And once Tom was sleeping, Nathan crept downstairs. He opened the fridge, gave the last of the ham to the cat.

He cleaned up the thumbprint of blood with a damp cloth. He took the bottle from his father, poured the whisky down the sink, pressed the empty bottle back into his father's hand and padded back upstairs to his brother's quiet, unsuspecting snores.

*   *   *

It was what he did. It was what Nathan chose to do as soon as Tom was born – to show him all the good things, and to keep him safe. No playing with wasps, or broken glass. When Tom dropped a biscuit on the floor, Nathan took it and swapped it with his undropped one. Small things.

He loved him. That was the reason. He loved him with a very serious love that was not like the love he felt for the rest. Ian, Hester and Nathan had already seen and heard things which stopped them laughing brightly, and which made them run away when a door slammed – but Tom's laugh was a gurgle, like a half-blocked drain. He wiggled like a worm when the radio was on.

And so Nathan told stories. He told stories that he knew from his grandfather, or was shown in Aunt Abigail's red book. Or he made up his own, when he had to; he made up his own stories because he did not want the joy (that was the word – Tom had been *joyful*) to lessen or vanish as it had for him. He wanted Tom to believe in a better world than the one Wind Rising gave him, and so Tom believed in whales that spoke, the ghosts of sheep, imps, the turning wind and that he'd find, one day, the love of his life – a woman who was worthy of him.

It will be better for you. Nathan vowed it.

He thought *you will never know why our mother wears long sleeves when it's hot.* Or why all four of them would sometimes go to the barn for hours at a time – which was so that their mother could be on her own for a little while, a tissue clamped on her bleeding nose or sitting on the edge of the bath thinking *thank goodness the children have no idea, how lucky that they are in the barn* – and thinking, too, of what could have been for her, if she had chosen differently. Oh, what could have been.

Nathan sits in the dark.

The sun has not yet risen but it will. Before too long, the lighthouse will close its eye, and sleep. Tom, in his early days, called it *the turny light. Because it's all turny. Round and round* …

Now he is dead. He went into the water aged thirty-seven and did not come back out.

What good were the Parlan imps? The shells with sea stories? The fairy tales that said the world was generous and sunlit and worth staying in? What good was the book his Aunt Abigail had shown him in those early days that promised happy secrets and an underwater world? There was no good in it. It stopped nothing, in the end. Of all the Bundy children, Tom was the one who should not have died. He should have stayed for he believed the world was beautiful, and he made it more so by being who he was. He built sandcastles with his niece; he called Abigail *Mrs C*; he might throw his wife over his shoulder and carry her home as a hunter would, so that Maggie would laugh, squeal, slap his bottom and call out *Thomas Bundy, put me down!* And anyone who saw these things, or heard them said *how can he be one of them? From that stock?* All that height, and kindness. All that trust in life.

Nathan vowed to keep him safe, but look. *Dead.*

He closes his eyes. Tonight, he can see Tom's face – the beard, the eyes, the lines by those eyes. Sometimes he can't see his brother, as if the years are fading the memory of him, as sunlight bleaches cloth or paint. But tonight he sees Tom perfectly.

He deserved better. Kitty deserves better, and perhaps she will find it now. Even Rona – *God, poor Rona* – deserves more than this. Who is he helping? Whose life has he ever made better, in fact? Doesn't he let them all down?

Tom. Whose warm, firm body would climb into the bottom bunk and lift the blankets, say Nathan's name. Pyjamas with small tractors on. A clean, lemony smell.

Bad dream?

Yes.

That's OK. Come in.

All that love, and it still didn't save him. All that love and Tom still went away.

Fourteen

Now is the deepest hour of night.

It is the hour of human sleep. They all sleep. Each human is sleeping except one.

Maggie watches him. He lies on his front, with his palms facing down. She knows the grooves of his back. She has moved a single finger down the spine of him, feeling that finger rise and fall as it finds each vertebra, and Maggie has touched the lines on his face – his forehead, his eyes. She has also held his hands, before now. She has tucked her hand into his, or she has wrapped her smallest finger around his own smallest finger and like this they have walked – on beaches, through the fields.

But now he sleeps. And now, by candlelight, Maggie can look at his left hand. It lies beside her, relaxed, with the fingers spread. His skin is freckled here. There are tiny, white scars she has her own versions of; his fingernails have their white half-moons.

She does nothing. She looks, and nothing more.

There ... The mark that he has had, since being found. On the loose flesh between his thumb and forefinger there is that neat, circular mark – no larger than a pencil's end. She saw it at Crest; she has seen it as he's moved his hand across his beard, or held a mug of tea. A scar? From what? What could make a mark like a small, reddish eye?

Maggie has seen blood in water many times. It is not red. In water, blood blackens and it hangs momentarily in the shape it left the body, in the pulse's shape – clouds of blood, a line of them. It is oddly beautiful. Would this wound have looked like that? And what caused it? What briny injuries can leave a rounded scar?

It comes to Maggie, then. By candlelight, she pictures it. She imagines him – the Fishman – moving underwater, pulling his body through the shallows with his hands. Perhaps he parts weed. Perhaps he halves shoals of fish, as he goes. Perhaps he moves through the wreck of *Anne-Rosa* and as he swims with his arms outstretched, his hands pressed together as if in prayer, an eel strikes out at him. One sharp tooth finds its mark; a puff, two puffs of blood.

Or perhaps he is swimming too close to the shore. A man in rubber wading boots stands on a beach and casts out his line; the hook drops like a coin – *plink!* The Fishman is close to surfacing. His left hand leads the way until it feels a cold metallic bite. He flinches, and the line does. The fisherman starts to fight …

She takes his hand, holds it.

Sea … he says, in his sleep.

Maggie smiles to herself. She knows enough: she knows what matters most, which is the tiny things – how he kissed Tabitha's cheek, or cupped a fluttering moth and carried it outside; how he reached for Emmeline's roses but did not touch them as if he could not manage it. The wound? Its making? It will come. His tale in its entirety will come, she knows – and soon.

Nancy decides what colours she will use. She selects them carefully.

And she uses turquoise, yellow, navy-blue, white, an emerald green. She uses her black felt-tip for his beard. She uses silver foil, too – she took a sheet of it from the bottom drawer in the kitchen and she has cut half-moons out of it. One by one, she has stuck these wedges of light onto his tail, so that it shimmers. Her fingers are tacky with glue.

She leaves his face till last. Faces are, Nancy thinks, the most important part.

Carefully, she pushes the felt-tip pen onto the paper in two neat dots – the Fishman's eyes. In red, she gives him a smile.

There! She throws her hands up, finished.

Dee glances down, as she passes. *Lovely. Well done.*

It's for Mrs Coyle, she says. *For when he goes. So it feels like he is still here.*

He is not in turquoise, or navy. He pulls on a T-shirt that has a yellow trim and a hole in it that Maggie does not recognise. It is too tight, perhaps, but it doesn't matter. He looks up and watches Maggie – how she stands on one leg to put on a sock, how she twists into her jeans and gives a single jump.

I know I'm not sleeping with a fish.

No.

Then who are you? Why do you talk of the sea in your sleep?

The sea?

I've heard it. You say 'sea' – something like it.

*   *   *

311

There is the steady squeak of metal in the lane. Emmeline hears it. She kneels amongst her flowers, and looks up. A bicycle.

Her sister lifts her right leg over the saddle as she comes closer, half-dismounting whilst the bicycle still squeaks. Tabitha wears floral shorts that billow, as she rides, and she has pink socks pulled to the knee. A rattle over a pothole. She steps down.

Hello, Em.

Emmeline shifts her jaw from side to side. *Yes? What?*

It has taken her this long to be brave. That's the truth of it – that Tabitha might be the age she is and she might have worked with disease and famine and she might have brought countless lives into the world and held countless hands as their lives have ended but she has been anxious about coming here. To Easterly. To her sister who has had a deep vertical line on her forehead throughout the years of their quiet war.

No, they have never been close. They rarely shared beds as other sisters might, and they were rarely playmates. But still – they have the same parents. The same blood.

Why do we never talk?

What? We talk.

We don't. You know what I'm talking about.

The peonies have long gone. This is, instead, the time of the hydrangeas which bloom like paper balloons, like powdery balls of blue stars, blue light. They have a sound, when the wind comes.

Emmeline gives a hard laugh. *We're talking about this now? Really?* She drops her trowel to the ground. *You know why we don't talk. You.*

Me?

I had to choose.

Choose?

You made your feelings clear, Tabitha. I was married. I loved him.

Softly, *you never had to choose …*

Oh, I did. And I chose my husband because that is what you do, when you marry. You stand by him. Just so you know.

Tabitha wants to say more. Words come to her and sit in her mouth but she keeps them back. The time has long since passed. Instead she says *you do know it was out of love? That I said what I did?*

High up, a gull drifts. *Love? How was it love?*

Of course it was love! You're my sister!

Emmeline is angry, now. *How you spoke to me …*

Was wrong. I was eighteen and stupid. But you had bruises like –

She holds up her hand, stopping her.

They face each other. One woman wears gardening gloves, has her hair pinned neatly into a ball at the nape of her neck; the other shifts in her bright-pink socks, pushes her spectacles back up her nose. The gull calls out. The light is fluid, changing over them.

It feels like they are talking about different people, perhaps. The Emmeline who'd been nursing Hester back then had had hair as shiny as a conker and eyes to match, and her waist was half the size of this Emmeline's, standing here. But the teenage Tabitha was different too – so young, so unaware of what lay ahead of her. Unaware of herself.

Talk to me. I didn't mean to hurt you …

Emmeline looks old, suddenly. It floods her – age, tiredness. By looking down at the flowerbed, she seems to show the skin under her eyes, the hollows in her cheeks, the slight jowls. *I was never going to leave.*

Because you loved him?

Yes. Because I loved him. You haven't married, Tabitha. You don't know –

Tabitha scoffs. *You think he loved you back?*

Don't judge him. Don't you dare when you don't know what Jack had endured. Why do you think he would loiter up at the lighthouse like that? Have baths with us? Sleep in our spare bed? Don't you know what that father of theirs put them through? Don't you dare …

They look at the hydrangeas. There is less than a metre between them, but it feels like a sea that cannot be crossed – too wide, too deep. A sadness finds Tabitha. She is suddenly weighed down by it. *I heard rumours about Jack's father …*

Well, the rumours weren't even half of it.

I didn't know.

No, you didn't. Jack had cigarettes put out on him. He had a pitchfork – a pitchfork! – pushed into his thigh. How could I blame him? When it was all he knew?

Tabitha shifts. She says *doesn't make it better.*

It is like the bones have been taken out of her sister's face, or the blood has, for Emmeline greys and looks down. Tabitha wonders if she has ever talked of this before and she thinks *no, she can't have done.* Who would she have spoken to? She would have had no-one to tell – it was a secret and a huge one and so Emmeline would have put it in an airtight tin like an old piece of cake, kept it out of sunlight. *She should have been able to talk to me,* she realises. *I was the only one.* But Emmeline never could. Tabitha had been away, mending people, when she should perhaps have stayed and mended this person – this one, in front of her now.

They look at each other. They can see their whole lives.

Em, I am so sorry.

And Tabitha does what she has not done for a long, long time or maybe ever. She reaches out. She puts her hand on her sister's arm, holds it. Emmeline does not pull away. They both look at this hand, this arm.

They are together for the rest of the day. They put manure into the flowerbeds, prune the roses down. They do not say much to each other. What is there left to say? It has all been said, and Emmeline had turned when Tabitha had touched her, stepped a little closer. Their first embrace in a very long time.

So much happens that hurts, in life. It doesn't stop, or not for long. Bodies can ache and love can be uneven and kind, gentle men are drowned and never found. But Tabitha knows there are also offered days. There are lives that are saved, against the odds. There are moments like this, deadheading rosebushes next to your sister, who is humming a little under her breath, and who has whispered, whilst embracing you, that she is also sorry, and that yes, yes – she has always missed you too.

* * *

At Tavey, the Fishman stops sawing, looks up. He thinks it will be Leah – he is expecting Leah, for she has been painting the doorframes, the new skirting boards and she said that she would come today. But it is not Leah.

A man walks towards him – sun-lightened hair. The Fishman knows the face but he knows the voice better, for it was this man's voice which he heard before all other voices. On a beach of stones, saying *oh God, oh God. Oh my God.*

Sam. He comes, and he stands with his hands by his side. As if he has no wish to stay long he says *I have to know you're going to take care of her. I need to know you aren't going to hurt her. Are you going to hurt her?*

He looks at the boy's face. It is set, determined. *I promised her I wouldn't.*

Will you promise me?

I promise you, he says – *I will not hurt her.*

Sam exhales. He nods once, accepting this.

You care for her?

Yes. I want her to be happy.

She doesn't blame you, Sam. She told me so – she never did.

But I do. I blame me. I took those guys out in the boat – it was my boat, my life-vest. If you're skipper, you're in charge of everything on that boat, and … His hands go in his pockets. *Every day I'm there again. Wishing I'd done things differently.*

We can all think that. A sheep calls, near them. *It sounds like he was a good man. Tom.*

The best. He'd take me out lobstering. He helped me fix up Sea Fairy *when I first bought her.* He glances across. *You love Maggie?*

The Fishman says *yes. I do.*

And with that, Sam leaves. It was all he came for, all he needed to know.

*   *   *

Ian has not worked today. He slept for most of the morning. When he woke, he went downstairs to find Constance bending down; through the oven's glass door he could see a pie. He went to her, kissed her. *Hello, wife* – smiled.

He went to see his mother and found her in the garden – not gardening, but sitting on a bench with Aunt Tab beside her, both of them drinking glasses of white wine. It had been a brand-new sight. Ian had stared, trodden back.

When had they last sat, like that? Talking?

And he thinks, *not since we were children. Or maybe not even then.*

So it is children he thinks of, as he walks back from Easterly. Nathan had never wanted any of his own. He always shrugged, said *no, not for me* – without giving a true reason. But Ian thinks he knows the reason, now: *a fear of inheritance*. That old Bundy curse.

Tom, too, had mentioned it – children. Only once. One morning in sunshine, outside the barn, he'd said, *Mags and I are going to start trying. For a family. Next month.* And Tom had done his best to be composed, but failed – he'd grinned, blushed, and added *Ian, I can't wait …* And what a father he'd have been. What a mother in Maggie, too. Would their children have been dark or fair? Brown-eyed or blue-? No-one will ever know, now. For that was one of the last conversations Ian ever had with his youngest brother: within a week Tom was diving in to save a boy he didn't know, and in doing that he killed all his future children before they had been made, and their future children, and theirs.

He stands by the fridge in Wind Rising, takes out the milk. He drinks it from the carton, leaning back.

It has become easy to stop seeing the miracle of them: his daughter and son. Maybe he did stop. Maybe he failed to see what they are – unique, remarkable, a fusion of two people and yet their own selves entirely.

As if he has conjured her, Leah walks into the room.

She says *drinking from the carton? I won't tell Mum.*

And he stares. He looks at the woman who stands before him – for that is what she is, now. She has caught the sun. She has filled out in the parts that needed filling – her waist, the tops of her arms, a little in the face so that she looks, he thinks, beautiful. She has picked an orange from the fruit bowl and has stuck her thumb into it. And as Leah begins to peel the fruit she says *I think you should come to Tavey. Have a look.*

I – He has no words.

Dad ... Teasing him. *He's a lovely man! He is! Look how he's been to Great-Aunt Tab and Maggie and me. Look what he's done to the pig farm.* She pops a segment of fruit in her mouth, says *you should come and see it ...*

Everything has changed.

This orange-smelling Leah with freckles on her face. Leah, with cheeks that are round with fruit. She makes her way out of the room, and the man she leaves behind counts his blessings in a way he never has before. He lists what he is grateful for – from this pie in the oven, to his extraordinary children, to vanilla-scented baths with his vanilla-scented wife. *The view from this window. Christmas. Milk.*

The list goes on. It is far longer than he thought.

*　　*　　*

The night that follows this is starless. But the moon, of course, is nearly full and the lighthouse sweeps its beam – so Rona does not need a torch. She knows where the ditches are. She can see enough.

At High Haven, she knocks. She uses her fists – four loud bangs against the wood. There are no lamps on, but his car is here. She scarcely waits before she bangs again.

Still nothing.

Rona bends. Pushes the letterbox. Through it, she can see the hallway – there are waterproof coats, rows of boots and their tabby cat sits on the bottom step. She sees Rona, blinks. *Nathan?* No answer except from the cat.

Rona snaps the letterbox shut. She moves to the kitchen window, presses her hands against the glass and looks in. Then she straddles the old dog cage, tries to open the window beyond. After this Rona climbs onto the bonnet of a rusting car, stands on her tiptoes, reaches up and knocks against the bedroom glass with her knuckles. *Tat-tat-tat-tat-tat!*

For half an hour Rona tries.

She prowls round the house, smacks its walls with the palm of her hand, returns to the front door and tries the handle and throws her weight against it and says *let me IN!* It is no use. The door does not open. No face appears at the window. No footsteps behind her.

She sits for a while, wipes her eyes.

Then Rona walks back with purpose, towards the turning light.

Rona of the hurting heart. We've all had one of those. We have all picked at the seal of things that have been closed against us, and locked.

I saw this from Crest. I had chosen to sleep on my own, that night – and I glanced out of the window as I made my way to bed. *Rona?* I paused. I watched her knock on windows, crouch by the letterbox. She stood like a ballerina on the rusting car.

That was how I knew. How I guessed.

Parlans say *there are no secrets*. But sometimes there are: sometimes, when they are too huge or dark or too painful to be even guessed at.

Like the flakes of silver that fell on silvered nights, this new realisation came down piece by piece. Above all else, it made me sorry. I thought of Kitty, who always peered into my crate of lobsters and praised them for their size or speckled midnight-blue. I thought *does she know?* I hoped not. But as I watched Rona, I felt sorry for her too. For hadn't I searched, also? Pleaded, at night? I had also knelt in mud and called out the name of someone who was gone.

And Nathan? I considered him, as I stood there. I pressed my fingers to my lips and sifted through the feelings – anger, disappointment, an ache for Kitty's sake. But who was I to judge? Or assume I knew his story? All I knew was that he'd saved me – that four years ago he'd waded into water, gathered me, and carried me back to the land in his arms. I'd kicked, sworn and he'd let me. He'd said *I've got you …* as he'd carried me, whilst he himself had cried. And so I knew that he was a good person. *Nathan always has been.* I loved him and felt sorry, as I stood there in the dark.

A blue-sea morning followed. I found a feather on my doorstep – tiny, pale brown.

It was Tuesday. Like the day they found the Fishman, this day would change my life.

I had not loved him as soon as I saw him. But, as with my husband, I had known there was *something*. The potential for love, perhaps – as we might open the curtains and look at the sky and know it could be a clear, warm day. It was a strange knowing. I had laid my head against his chest and felt like I could sleep there; it felt like recognition, as if we'd met somewhere before.

No, three weeks – or three weeks and four days – had not been long. But so much can happen in three small weeks, just as nothing at all can happen in three months or three years, or three hundred years: it is not time that measures love, or measures how much someone has lived. And I had lived more in those three weeks than I had in the four years before it. What life is it, when you are mourning? When you are lonely but will not admit to it? When you are constantly aware of how many things in life are done or made with two in mind – two hymn books in each pew, two chairs in my kitchen; the tea bags I bought from Milton were rectangular, paired, like two halves so that I'd have to split them with a sound like torn cloth;

two rooms in a lobster pot; two eyes, two lungs, two legs, two hands. One mouth but two lips around it.

I have seen seaweed that's been left on the highest part of beaches for so long that it's dried and cracked and looked dead to my small human eyes; and yet the sly tide comes and finds it, and the weed fattens up with water – so it was never dead at all. It was parched, dead-looking. But it had life left in it yet.

I fattened in those three weeks with him. I found my proper shape.

All the small, forgotten things which matter, when you're in love. A song, maybe. Or how a bedroom's curtain moves in and out, in and out. Sometimes I would find him thinking – sitting on his own, staring far away – and I wished that I could paint or write that moment down. He had a legend's face – strong and injured; kind and old. I remember how I led him into the rhododendron bushes near the church, one day. I said *come here* ... Took his hand. And they were like a church in themselves in that they were dark and went up, and up. We stood there, side by side, and we watched the world pass by us, not knowing we were there and it was then that he turned to me and said *I love you, Maggie*. Standing amongst branches and the undersides of leaves.

I remember that we went to see the Coyles. They invited us. We drank homemade lemonade and Jim talked about his old lighthouse days – how the only thing he loved more than that light was *this woman here*, patting his wife. As he did that the Fishman turned, looked at me.

We walked on every headland. We crossed every fence, ducked under every wire. I told him that I'd seen him lift Nancy up, long ago – that I'd heard her wild, delighted squeal, how she'd begged *again-again* – and I took his hand, held it. *That's when I trusted you. Loved you.*

Then? That moment?

That moment.

And we had made love. People marry believing there will be no-one else, in any sense: when I married Tom, I thought there would be no other in every conceivable way. It never occurred to me that I might ever find myself imagining *another* – and so I did not find the walk to Tavey easy, that night. But I knew how I looked in that peacock-blue dress; I knew that I felt, at last, a feeling that was *right*. If it wasn't happiness, it was near it – as a damp chick is not far from a soaring, white-feathered bird.

Him with no name – but we called him the *Fishman*.

The man who held his breath when touching me as if he, or I, might break.

* * *

The dandelion globes start to break apart. The northerly wind is strengthening, and it finds the weeds and blows them. They rise up, and are carried south. They whiten the air, like ghosts.

Maggie walks through them. She turns in a full circle as she walks – looking up, bemused. She wears the linen trousers that are too long, too low on the hips; her silver *M* hangs around her neck.

She pushes the gate, moves past the gorse.

Hello, Fishman – teasing him.

He never knew that humans could be this beautiful.

Gardenia. Lotion. That slight salt smell.

He says *will you sit with me?*

Where?

Here. On the doorstep of Tavey. Looking out at the garden and the dandelion sky.

She sits with her knees bent, and her hands are palm to palm between her knees. Those are the hands, he thinks, that hit him when they first met, when he was standing in the garden and she had clutched at his collar, said *that's my husband's shirt. Take it off ...* It feels like a lifetime ago.

He has seen her in her boat, lifting lobster pots up. He's seen her making coffee, drinking it. He knows how she can close a drawer with a push of her hip, how she twists strands of hair whilst she is thinking and how she tries to hide her laugh with her hand. How she bites her bottom lip, to stay quiet.

He says *I'm so sorry.*

She looks up. He thinks he can see all her grief in her face, all her love and empty days. *You? Why?*

There are stories of phosphorescent seas. There are tales of unicorns and giants that are turned to stone, and there are stories of men – human men – carried out of the earth and placed on the moon where they left their footprints in lunar dust. There are tales of twins who can feel the pain of the other so clearly that it is like that pain is happening to themselves, and there are fish in the darkest depths of the sea that have their own lanterns held out on a stalk, and there are seals that feel our pain, and there are lobsters that mate as humans do – tenderly, facing each other. And which are the hardest tales to believe in? Which are the ones that sound the best of all? Are they all true? None of them?

He has so much to tell her.

Why are you sorry? I don't understand.

In ten seconds or less, it will be different. It will be too late to ever come back to the time when he was a mystery – a man with no story, a man with no name. He thinks how much he loves her – when he wanted to love nothing, when he thought that his own loving days were gone.

Oh, her face.

He takes her hand.

It is not sea.

What is not?

In my sleep. When I am sleeping. The word I say is not 'sea'.

She inhales, holds it. Then she breathes out. *Seal?*

Not seal.

Then what? What are you saying?

The Fishman swallows twice, as if preparing his mouth for the word. And then his mouth says it – his lips, his teeth, his tongue that she has kissed.

Celia.

And so it exists. It sits between them – new, unexpected. She says the word, shakes her head. *Was she a boat? Did you fall from a boat?*

He looks at her sadly. *She wasn't a boat.*

Maggie makes a sound – small, scared.

Hey. He strokes her cheek. *It's OK – it is. Are you ready for this?*

She nods.

Are you sure?

Yes.

You want me to tell you here? On this doorstep?

On this doorstep. Tell me.

*   *   *

He tells it all. Side by side, in the evening sun. There is the smell of sawdust, and honeysuckle, and he does not hurry. He speaks as he always does – carefully, gentle-mouthed. It is a long story. It is a story like no other. His words are gilded with strangeness and beauty, pain and kindness, love and the loss of love. He talks of being under the waves and Maggie listens. She believes it absolutely. Nothing is impossible – not now, not these days.

The man they found at Sye said *I saw you, and I knew you. I felt I recognised you. And I thought that, maybe, you knew me.*

And I did. I did know him. I listened to his story and I fully understood. There was no single part of it which I did not feel inside me as the truth, as possible. After all, what world is this? With no answers in it? It has so few answers.

He told me everything – how dark it becomes underwater, how the lighthouse looks from a night-time sea. He told me how it felt to lie on Sye, how Tabitha had murmured at his bedside that night. He never lost his memory. He always, always knew. And so I asked *why did you lie? Why did you not tell us all?*

He had his reasons. *Who would have believed me?*

Me. I would have done.

But there was more than that. There was a greater reason, and I think I already knew what that reason was. *It's not the tale they wanted. They did not want the truth. It was the Fishman they asked for, Maggie; a fish that grew legs and walked out of the sea.* A shrug, a shy smile. *How could I let them down? These kind people? So it was the Fishman that I chose to be.*

*   *   *

That night, I decided this: that the acts done out of love for another life, or for many other lives, are the best of all. They make the world worth staying in.

I just wanted to be happy, Maggie. For all of us to be.

I loved him. I love him still.

I took his hand and kissed the tips of his thumb and each finger – one, two, three, four, five.

The Sly Tide, or the
Perigean Spring Tide, or the
Highest Tide of all

We had no choice but to know the tides. Perhaps we did not live by the sea as much as others had, in days gone by – no trawling for herring, no days out of sight of land. But an island is water; it is made and defined by the sea that surrounds it. And the tides make an island bigger and smaller; less of a world and far more of one.

Tom taught me that. He talked of the spring tides. He said *it's best to know them, especially with* Pigeon. And so on my calendar I made marks: I ringed, in blue pen, the dates that mattered for the moon and the sea. Sometimes those dates would already be ringed, but for other reasons – and I would smile, feel strange with that. *We are the same.* Woman is moon. Woman is restless sea.

The perigean spring tide. It sounded beautiful but it was far from it. It was the highest spring tide of all – so that it covered Sye entirely. It snaked into the dunes, flooded burrows. It could slip into fields and steal a sheep or two. And it filled Tap Hole to the brim.

When the water retreated that evening, it carried Thomasina out. Her limbs and head hung down. She was pulled ashore by her brother and Jack tried to make her live again. He put his hot mouth on her cold, open one and blew; he pushed down, clumsily, on her broken heart.

*   *   *

Why hadn't she remembered? What made her forget?

They had always known of the *sly tide* – Abigail and her. Mercy Deepwater had told them her tales – not ones from the book but from her own lifetime. Merme was such a flat isle. No hills and no trees, and so when they knew that that highest of tides was on its way they said prayers, lit candles and took all their treasures up onto their roofs where they huddled under blankets and held tight. From their rooftops they watched the sea rising – moving under doors, filling up corners, parting and joining around table-legs. *And we had all that mattered with us – the Bible, our calf, a barrel of herring, the lace from Mother's wedding dress and my best pair of shoes.*

A calf?

Oh yes. She was on the roof before we ever were. That calf was a prim one; she never liked getting wet …

This tide was spoken of, over and over. Tales of babies being swept away in their cradles; a tale of a man swimming after his dog, for he'd loved that dog so dearly, but whilst the dog made it back to land and shook himself as dogs do, the man was gone. Pulled under. *Never trust it*, said Mercy. *You keep an eye on the tides, and know when the sly one is coming. Stay where the grass is. Keep high if you can.*

So yes, Thomasina knew. She knew in the way that she could spell *Thomasina*. She *knew* – just as they all knew that despite the stench and darkness and the inquisitive snouts of the pigs that lived there, the shelters at Tavey were a fine place to hide. Safe and well-tested. *We were never found …*

Yet on the day of the sly tide Thomasina chose Tap Hole instead. Had she preferred it? Felt it was safer? A place that her father was less likely to find?

Abigail winces. *Little thing ...*

She has often wondered how they'd been – those last moments of her sister's life. When had Thomasina remembered? About the highest tide? As the mouth of the cave was lost, underwater? Or as she was lifted up, towards the cave's roof? Or was it as Thomasina pressed her mouth against its single, tiny hole and tried to breathe through it, pushing her fingers into that hole as if trying to widen the rock? Abigail will never know. Nor will she know what her twin's last thoughts had been – if she'd begged *please no, please no ...* or prayed as she'd been taught to. But in the months that followed, Abigail made a choice. She chose to believe that the seals who had loved Thomasina – who'd always loved her – came into the cave that day. They comforted her, sang to her; they nuzzled her wet pinafore. And so Thomasina's death had not been lonely, or tearful, or absolute. *Come with us*, the seals told her – *we will take care of you ...* And so her soul left her body and moved out with them – to the open water, leaving her body behind.

Abigail has tears now. Small ones, in the bathroom. Her husband sleeps, but Abigail sits on the wicker basket where they put their laundry. She holds a damp tissue; she looks down at her blue feet.

She knows this, too: that all the world's stories, all the seals with human hearts and all the falling stars and all the silver in the fields may make the world brighter, and they may bring *hope* back into one's life but they can't erase the things that you wish you'd never seen. You may cling to the tales and they may lift you up – up, up, out of the storm – but it does not mean you can forget it. And didn't Thomasina know that all too well?

Even the Fishman cannot erase the winter's day not long after Mercy's death. Abigail woke to a draught. She went downstairs to find the back door open, and two sets of footprints – marked out in a dusting of snow. Large, booted footprints, and smaller, bootless ones. They led out to the chicken shed. Abigail frowned. She followed the prints, quietly. And as she came towards the shed she heard noises that she did not know – rhythmic, injured, breathy, high-pitched. *The hens? Are they hurting?* And so Abigail put her eye to a hole in the chicken shed's wall, and she can never forget what her one eye saw.

She has heard nothing worse than that whimpering sound, from her sister. The telling of good stories and the loving words of Jim have covered it up, or tried to, so that she no longer hears it – but Abigail knows what she heard.

And she has seen nothing worse, either. There is nothing worse to see. Not even a coffin being lowered; not even a helicopter's beams sweeping a sea that will not give back what it's claimed as its own.

Abigail sniffs.

She had been desperate. She had lost all her faith in the world and had nothing to take hold of. Oh, how she'd wanted those stories of *Folklore and Myth* to be true – the chance for something better than what she'd learnt in her small life. And then there was Jim. Thank God for Jim. Thank God for his glorious words and nervous smile and teenage rash on his chin. Thank God for how he said her name – carefully, beautifully, as one might say *thank you* when you mean it with all your heart. *Jim* … How right that he worked the lighthouse for he was a lighthouse to her, in the end. He was steady, safe, dependable; she loved it when he entered a room. A light, quite simply. Without him, would there have been no light at all? Without him her heart, at least, would have died.

She blows her nose daintily, and stands.

I believe in everything. So that whilst there may have been two sets of footprints leading to a chicken shed, there have also been – thanks to Jim – phosphorescent seas and puffins that talk if you ask them to, and there is the human soul which never dies, and there is a fish that has grown legs and come ashore and so the world remains beautiful. It has the worst of shadows – but it also has the brightest and most remarkable light.

*   *   *

Next door, Jim is awake. He can hear her in the bathroom – the creak of the wicker, her tearful breath. He knows it all. What he has not been told he has guessed at. The sly tide always hurts her; so did the pig farm called Tavey, but that was before it was mended, painted, swept and cared for. Before it had its rusty pig shelters taken out and thrown away.

She comes back to bed, nestles in.

She smells of herself – talc, toothpaste, lily-scented cream.

Jim wants her happiness more than any other thing – more than his own, more than his sight.

Fifteen

I have loved stories all my life. At the start, I chose them because I preferred them – they were better, far better, than what was real. I had no family of my own and so I filled the echoing spaces with tale after strange tale. I used my imagination to feel like I had friends.

Small things, mostly: that a blackbird was singing for me and me alone. That a crack across the ceiling in an unfamiliar bed had been caused by a fat lady jumping, or music played too loud or maybe it was not a crack but a long line of industrious ants who had thought no-one would notice them but *look*, they'd say to each other – *that little blonde girl has spotted us ...* And I'd whisper to the ceiling's crack *don't worry – I won't tell*. I'd see people on the bus and give them names – I would imagine their jobs, the houses they lived in, what they longed for and what they loved. Did they like tea or coffee the most? If they could be an animal, what animal would they be? This was how I lived. I *imagined*.

So I was for stories. I was for stories just as gannets were for balls of silver-flashing fish – I'd crash towards them, gaping. I'd try for as many as I could. And I'd keep them safe like feathers in a vase. For weren't my own tales colourless? Who wanted to know about the different smells of the care system? About counting the steps to each bathroom I slept near, so that I wouldn't get lost in the night? Other tales were better – other people's. Sunsets, dragons, ghosts that said *ooo* … I held them up to the light.

They have been my comfort. My family. My strange nourishment.

And I thought I had heard every kind of story that there was.

But then I heard his. I heard the Fishman's tale – *my* Fishman's. I heard his proper tale and I had no words for it.

* * *

The lighthouse turns until the moon sinks down and the sun, slowly, rises.

I can see them all sleeping: Nancy, with her one-eared bear; Hester whose pillow is lost beneath her curls. Abigail and Jim are side by side, like salt and pepper pots. Her lower teeth fizz in a glass.

At the lighthouse, Rona does her usual morning things – tea, the radio, pre-heating the oven for the quiches she will make. When she looks in the mirror, she sees her tired eyes.

Where can he be? She knows he has not left the island. She knows because Sam and her father work on the *Star* and they know – always – who they are carrying to the mainland, and back. Nathan is still on Parla – but where? His sheep still graze. His rusting cars still flake in his driveway. This cat – their cat, his and his wife's – still licks her paw and runs that paw behind her ear.

Where is he? Why does he not come for me? Or text, or email, or phone?

Rona, whose love is like those rocks she can see at Bundy Head. It exists, and will not stop existing. It is strong, and it can bear any weather, and it is named for him – *my love for him.* And so she tells herself the stories that the less-loved one in a pair will often do: *he isn't well,* or *he is busy,* or *something has happened with his mother and so he must be with her,* or *he is lying low for a while.* She chooses that excuse and tries to believe it.

She carries the tablecloths outside. She squints at the sunlight as it bounces off the courtyard walls. How many days of sun have there been? How many more to come?

Nathan is standing there.

I know it's still early. You're busy. Sorry.

She catches her breath. *That's OK. Coffee, or –?*

No. I –

They stand like strangers. Then Rona softens – a rush of want, and relief, and she drops the tablecloths and comes towards him. She runs her hands down his back, presses her waist against his waist. *Where have you been? I've been trying to see you. Talk to you. Is your phone broken? Is it Emmeline?* She pushes herself onto her tiptoes, tries to find his mouth with hers.

He turns his head. *Let's go inside.*

Yes. Yes.

Inside, Rona studies his face – the brown eyes, the scar by his eye. There are the clear signs of a beard and she knows how it would feel against her chin. He has left her red-coloured, in the past; she has lain, burning from him.

I've texted, and called ... I've been to High Haven twice and you weren't there. Are you trying to be casual? So nobody can guess? Did Kitty –

Rona.

Did you tell her? You must have told her?

Rona. Sharper.

She hears him.

I didn't tell Kitty. She left of her own accord. She left me.

She did? Isn't that … good?

No. He almost smiles as he says this. He sighs, shakes his head. *No, it isn't good. Rona, this has to stop now. You and me.*

She stands, does not blink. Inside her, there is nothing – as if stunned, or scooped out; she feels numb. His words don't make sense.

It has to … We both know it's been the wrong thing. Such a wrong thing.

No, she breathes. *Not wrong.*

It's over. Must be.

A deep, animal noise from her, now. *Why? Why now? Kitty's gone! What's to stop us?*

Because it isn't right, Rona. I still – he sighs, winces – *I still love Kitty.*

But you love me too! I know you do!

Rona, you are beautiful. You are bright and kind and it is a lucky, lucky man who'll be with you one day. But it won't be me. It can't be me.

It will be you. It will be you … She grits her teeth.

Jesus, Ro. I am so sorry. Those weak words. Those words that never sound enough.

Rona turns, grips her hair. In her head she is thinking *how could he? How could he?* Doesn't he know? Surely he knows – how she has doodled *Rona Bundy* on her recipes, folded down the corners of bridal magazines, how she could pick him out of a crowd of a thousand people just by the shape of his ears or shade of his hair or by his scent alone. Doesn't he feel even half of it? Doesn't he, also, look at the place where her mouth has been – the side of a mug or a bottle's neck – and want to put his own mouth there? She does. She has done – with his old teacups. She has placed a fork of his into her own mouth. She has kept the pillow case that he has slept upon – breathed into, rubbed his thick hair against – unwashed and at her bedside, and she has read romance novels in which she thinks *this man is nothing like Nathan* and how the writer has marked down love is, thinks Rona, *nothing like this love, my love for him*; and she had made plans in her head, for so long – she washes her hair on Saturday so that it might be at its shiniest on Sunday, in case he comes when the others are in church, and she has seen Nathan in a dark-red shirt so that Rona has also bought dark red – scarves, a dress, a lace bra – because he must, surely, like the colour? And now he stands here saying *it's not right* as if it's meant nothing, as if it's been a minor event in which no-one had feelings or hopes or proper wishes, and Rona turns back round and says *you bastard*.

Ro –

You love her? Then what have I been? Just fun? A hobby? Did you think it would be rude to turn me down?

No, Rona –

Don't you ... She grabs a tea-towel. With the tea-towel, she hits the side of him – soft, useless strikes with a floury cloth so that a whiteness is left on his sleeve. Flour rises into the air – and he lifts his arms, tries to protect himself against this snapping cloth. He starts to step back. She follows him saying *you used me* as she strikes him.

Rona –

She is crying. Nathan blurs and shimmers. Her eyes spill and she throws the tea-towel away, pushes at him. *You lying piece of ...*

One hard push. She throws her weight against him.

He takes her wrists, says *stop –*

But Rona flings her arms out of his grip – a roar, and a vast, angry gesture of speed and defiance which means that her right arm frees itself, touches air and nothing else, but her left arm, when it breaks free from him, smacks back into the wall – or rather, not the wall but a canvas called *West-Facing* so that there is the brief, tight, echoless sound of a puncture, a tear. The sound stops them both. Both Rona and Nathan stand still. They watch as *West-Facing* tilts left, tilts right, and falls – slowly, impossibly slowly – onto the café floor.

It lands face down. A single *pat*.

Oh God.

They drop to their knees – both of them do. They bend over the painting as if it were a living thing, injured, and their hands are careful with it so they don't hurt it further. *We need to turn it over*, Nathan says. He takes hold of one side. *We'll tilt it. OK?*

They turn it, lift it up.

Rona's eyes scan the canvas until she finds what she knows is there. A tear – or two tears that join each other. She takes her finger, touches it. *Oh …*

What? Where is it?

It is in the bottom left-hand corner. It is a fractured piece of light amongst the darkly painted land. It is white bone showing through the black, glossed vibrancy of muscle or skin and they sit, thinking, with their breath slowing down from the effort of the fight and it is Nathan who speaks, now.

It was wrong to you, too. When I say it's the wrong thing to do I don't just mean for Kitty.

She sniffs. *Shut up.*

Rona stares at the wound. It is small and yet enormous; tiny and yet so conspicuous that it's all she can see. She prods it. Then she moves her finger behind it, finds that if she presses the tear from behind she can close the tear up, so that the land is fully dark again.

I could put tape there. Look.

Will it mend it? Enough?

A shrug. *I'll drop its price a little. Waive my commission.*

You won't tell?

Rona looks at him. She looks at him hotly – hating him. Or hating, maybe, that there has always, always, been three of them. It is not a revelation; it is not a sudden clarity: Rona has always known that it has never been simply her and Nathan on their own. There were three of them with each kiss, three of them in the bedroom, three of them now on the café floor. Always three. Like the bloody lighthouse-keepers' quarters there was always three of everything – and Rona sees that so clearly. She has tried to strip away the long-haired woman with jewellery and her Miss Dior scent, to clear herself of Kitty, but the act of doing this meant that Kitty was, invariably, *there*. She was in the tick of a clock, the crunch of car tyres outside. In every movement her husband made.

You're a coward. And a liar. She says this quietly.

West-Facing. They both look at it but it is Kitty that they see. Her girlish applause when she hears a canvas has been sold.

I never meant to hurt you. Truly –

Well … She looks around, as if to show him what the truth is: a girl crouched on a tiled floor with a torn painting and tear-stained face. *Good job. Well-handled.*

Nathan stands. There are no words to say. All the words are done.

He goes home. He is nauseous, exhausted and he sits down on the bathroom floor with one elbow on the loo seat. *You bastard*, she had called him. And *yes*, he thinks. *Yes.*

He vomits, then. He leans back against the wall.

Then he folds back over the loo, vomits a second time.

Why? Why, for God's sake? How had it happened for eight months or more? It had never been wanted – not by him. Not wanted even slightly. It has only ever been Kitty he has wanted, or loved.

He sits back, shuts his eyes. Rona had been nothing more than another islander until that afternoon in his Land Rover, eight months ago, when she'd clambered over to his side, pressed her hand against his crotch. *I could make you feel better. If you'd let me.* And it had felt – what? Christ, it had felt dreadful – painful, violent, destructive. And it felt *fitting*, somehow. Her mouth pushed against his mouth made his stomach tighten as it tightens now, in sickness; his head had thought *no* and his hands had lifted up as if defending himself but, palms out, they had only rested against her which had made her strengthen even more. He'd thought *I deserve this*: the sickness. The endless gnaw of guilt. It was the punishment that he'd been expecting; it was the warranted outcome for having failed (he always fails) his little brother three years and two months before. It was justice, even. For this is Nathan's understanding of this brutal, unrelenting world: when you err or let down others, you are reprimanded. When you burn the last of the bread in the toaster you deserve the hard push in the jaw, by a hand. When you are slow to shear, or nick a sheep with the blades so that it bleeds and struggles against your knees, you deserve the kick it gives you, and the bruise that follows it – yellowish, and sore. When you bend a wire fence, you are struck; when you spill a pail of water on the floor you are sworn at – *bloody useless boy* ... And therefore when the person you vowed to love and protect since his birth dies, so that you've failed him, you should expect a punishment that is worthy of that failing. *I let him down. I wasn't there when he needed me. I could not reach out a hand or dive in, also.* And so did Nathan seek it? Crave the punishment, almost? Did he seek the worst of punishments, in keeping with his crime? And if so, what was it? That might bring him the greatest sorrow? It was losing Kitty. Nothing else came close.

Katherine.

He wants her back so much; it is like not having air, or not enough air. Each movement is harder.

He sits. Stares at the wall.

Nathan wants to be held, at that moment. He wants Kitty to stroke his hair and say *hush, now* ... Or he wants the firm embrace that Tom used to give, with both of them slapping the other man's back and him, Tom, groaning with the effort of this huge, important, never-ending hug.

* * *

I spent the day in *Pigeon*. Not at sea – not sailing. Just *in* her, as she was moored. I folded her tarpaulin and laid it down upon her; this tarpaulin became my sleeping place. She rocked with the tide. She smelt of Tom and goodness, and I thought of him beneath me – far, far beneath me. The bones I used to see under his skin when he stretched.

I understood this, as I lay there: that I loved the Fishman. And if you love a person, you wish them to be happy. You wish them to be the best that they can be. *He needs to go* – and yes I would be sad; yes, I would sit in Tavey and touch the things that he had touched, and want him back so badly. And the days would feel less than they had done – by far. *But I want him to be happy.*

He had to return to the place he had come from; he was not yet done with it. He had never quite stopped calling *sea, sea*, in the night – and maybe, in turn, he was also being called for. Maybe his old life was singing his name; not *Fishman*, but his proper name.

* * *

In the evening, she does not clear the tables; she does not put the saucepans to soak in the sink.

Rona tends to the injured *West-Facing*. She sits on the floor with her legs splayed and the canvas by her side. She has tape and glue, and she is gentle. Rona holds her breath as she mends it – pushing the torn parts of the canvas back into place, holding them there with her finger as she makes sure the edges meet exactly.

She smoothes on tape. Dabs at it.

There is nothing, she thinks, *I can do, now.*

She returns the canvas to the wall, and stands back. Rona has done her best with it; she wishes she had never flailed her arms at all and that she'd never damaged it but she has done the best she could. *You can't tell.* The tear cannot be noticed; *West-Facing* will still sell and Kitty need never be told of what happened here – that it was damaged by Rona, and that it fell. What good would it do?

Rona does what she has not done for months.

She climbs into her purple car and drives down to the harbour. She knocks on the door of the harbourmaster's house.

Her mother answers the door with her reading glasses on, and her face lights up. *Hello, darling! Are you hungry? We've just eaten but there's plenty left* ... Rona follows her back into the kitchen where the washing machine talks to itself, and there is the smell of casserole, and Nan's felt-tips and crayons are strewn about the floor. And when the tears come, Dee says nothing. She merely goes to her daughter and holds her.

Mum, I've been so stupid ...

Shh, now ... *There.*

Rona doesn't say why. She doubts she will ever say why – or at least not to her mother. How could she tell her parents what she is crying for? But Dee doesn't ask her. She only offers supper, a long bath with lavender oil and a glass of red wine, and when Nancy comes downstairs she shows Rona her best headstand in a way to cheer her up – and it helps. It all helps. Only a little but it does.

By candlelight, he waits. He cracks his knuckles, waits for her. Hopes for her.

She comes. Of course she comes.

She steps through the door, pauses for a moment. Then Maggie takes his hand, leads him to the bedroom where they lie as if one creature – arms and legs looped like rope. They only count the seconds between each sweep of milk-white light.

I looked for you. I couldn't find you.

I was on Pigeon.

I was worried ...

Why?

That you didn't believe my story. Or that it changed how you felt about me.

She looks up from his chest. *How could it do that?*

He strokes her hair. She kisses him – she kisses the mouth that she knows, now, has swallowed saltwater; she kisses the eyelids that have made saltwater of their own. *I know that you have to go.*

I don't want to leave you.

I don't want that either. But you must.

Oh, she knows. She understands it – better than he does, even. She had only ever guessed at the cause of the round, dark scar on the flesh of his hand; she'd imagined the bite of a silver hook or the clamping down of an angry claw. And she had not understood these ways of injury.

But the truth? Now that she has learnt it, Maggie knows that he has a long, long way to go. He has many miles to swim – more than he imagines. He, like the Fishman, cannot stay on Parla; for his skin would crack, and his heart would turn to dust.

He has a journey and he must make it.

I must stand on a quayside, smile and let him go.

*   *   *

In the waters off Lock-and-Key, there is the single puff of whale's breath – a spray, and a settling. The whale's back is a firm, bright, black-shiny back that has been through the deepest of waters and has surfaced into the starriest nights.

Does it come for the Fishman? Is it waiting?

I don't have the answer.

I am looking at my fingers, which are locked between his fingers. It is him and it is me – in our little world of two.

*   *   *

The wind strengthens that night. It grows, so that the sea off Sye is whiter and that bathroom vent at Wind Rising is louder, much louder.

The Fishman notices this wind. He rises from his sleep, listens.

As for Abigail, she is going downstairs the next morning when she pauses, stiffens. *Jim? Are the bells louder?*

Yes, he replies.

Still northerly?

Still northerly. Just much stronger, now.

Nathan finds his brother in the barn. Ian is standing but tucked over, one hand pressed against his chest so that Nathan pauses and then quickens his step. *Ian?*

He does not look up. *Bloody shears. The catch has gone on one of them, and it sprang open ...*

The slice is a scarlet line across a dirty hand. Blood beads and spills. *It's not deep. Come on. Inside.*

In the kitchen, Nathan takes down the green plastic box and opens it. Ian is at the sink, holding his hand under the tap and he says *you'd have thought I'd have learnt by now.*

Here. The younger brother tears the end of a paper packet and takes out a damp cloth and begins to clean.

Ian winces. *Careful.*

Silence, for a time. Nathan dabs around the wound, takes a second cloth and does the same. It is like treating his own hand, he thinks – the same shape, the same lines on the palm, the blackened nails and calluses that are yellow-coloured and rough. How did Kitty stand it? Who'd choose to have such a hand move over her body, for doesn't it catch or graze her? Nathan takes lint and cuts it. He places it on, finds transparent tape.

You doing OK? Ian asks it.

Miss her.

I bet.

Do you want a bandage on it?

This'll do. He turns his hand over, examining it.

Ian?

Hm?

I've done something. Oh God, Ian – this thing I've done ...

There are stories to tell and there are stories not to tell, and Nathan does not know which this one is. He doesn't know. All night, he has thought *what do I do?* This story

is the worst kind; would telling it make it better in some
way? And if so, who does he tell it to?

There was no-one but Ian. Even if Tom had still been
living, Nathan would only have thought of telling Ian and
no other. He could not have coped with Tom's face, when
he heard – the shock and his failing to understand why,
but the disappointment mainly. Oh, the disappointment.
Hadn't Nathan been the brother who he followed, copied,
listened to? *This is how the world is* – bright, with decent
people in it.

It would always have been Ian. Ian, who has no such
beliefs. A farmer cannot believe in happy endings when he
may kill his own sheep in the concrete room at the back of
this barn and pours buckets of disinfectant over the floor
when it is over, washing the blood into the drain. Not
when he thinks that a man with no memory must, instinctively, be a thief of some kind. No high hopes. Never were.

They are still in the kitchen.

I've been having an affair.

Ian looks up from his injured hand. He stares. *What?*

An affair. With Rona.

Rona? Lovegrove? An affair?

For nearly nine months.

Ian can only stand. He blinks several times. He shakes
his head and he forms shapes with his mouth as if to speak
but he does not speak.

It's over now. I've finished it.

Kitty knew? Is that why she went?

*Kitty doesn't know. She knows I'm distant and half-
drunk and we never –*

*Jesus, Nathe! Are you mad? An affair? And with Rona
bloody Lovegrove? She's twenty-four!*

Twenty-five.

The elder man waves his hand, dismissing it. *OK, whatever – it doesn't matter how old she is. Kitty ... For God's*

sake. What were you thinking? And how can you think no-one would know?

No-one does know.

Are you sure about that? Has she told anyone?

No.

Has anyone seen? Worked it out? They will have done. This island ...

No-one knows. And I don't think she'll tell. She's angry, but ...

The kitchen shifts, listening. The boiler ticks.

It is over, Ian.

Ian shakes his head. He does not understand, and Nathan knew he wouldn't fully. But there is, too, a heaviness to him – how he sighs, looks away – as if unsurprised somehow. As if he expects the world to be this way.

I needed to tell someone. I don't know what to do.

Bit late for advice, Nathe.

Kitty. Do I tell Kitty? I want her back, and –

You think telling her will bring her back? Ian almost laughs.

He thinks that if he tells her she will, most likely, never return. She is Kitty – fiery, artistic, who likes to paint a glittery deep-green on her eyelids and who claims that she has travelling blood. She'd hear the truth and hang up. Or slap him – quick, across the cheekbone. No, if he told her he would lose her but at least she would know. At least she would have been handed the truth – however gnarled and corruptive it might be; at least she could make what could be called an informed choice and there would be no lies any more. The truth – like a floor swept clean or the air after a summer storm. There could be new starts; how can there be a new start if there is a lie, or a truth kept from her? Doesn't she deserve to know what happened. What took place?

It would destroy her, Ian says.

But haven't I lied enough to her? Nathan rubs his eyes.

Yeah, you've probably lied enough for the whole island, frankly. But you've got to ask yourself something: who would be helped, now? By telling the truth?

Kitty?

Really? I don't think so. I think she'll hear her husband has been shagging a girl twenty years her junior – a girl who she sees three, four, five times a week, a girl who sells Kitty's own paintings – and not, actually, be helped at all. How could that help her? Nathan, you ...

She'd know the truth, though. She could –

Leave you? She's already left you.

I love her.

Then don't hurt her. For Christ's sake, man. Haven't you hurt her enough?

Nathan nods. But he also knows that if she chooses to return, and if he chooses never to speak of the affair, it will mean a lifetime of that one lie: he will never lose it. He will have to feel the guilt inside him, knowing that she does not know. As Kitty rinses her paintbrushes or fastens a bracelet or scoops up the cat and talks to her, or as she pads through the garden barefoot as she likes to, or as she moves her body over his in a half-lit room and bends down to kiss him he will see the lie, feel the lie inside him. A lie like a death. The weight of it.

But perhaps that's the price. Perhaps that is the cost of it – that he will have to drag this guilt and knowledge through life as he has seen a ewe drag a bramble or a gull fly with twine around his leg; he must feel guilt and endure it for that is better, far better, than Kitty's heart hearing the truth, and breaking apart. It is far better than her ever feeling sad, or less than loved again.

Ian makes tea. He pours the water in each mug, sets the kettle down.

Tell me it is over. Promise me.
It is. I promise.
If she comes back to you, treasure her.
If she comes back to me, I will treasure her. For always.

Later, they both stand in the same way – leaning against the kitchen worktops, one hand in a pocket and with their legs crossed at the ankles. *There is no Bundy curse. You know that.*

You sure?

You aren't like Dad. None of us are like him.

The drink's in me, Nathan says.

Ah – he shrugs. *The drink's in everyone. But it's how we manage it. We break the cycle, Nathan – that's what we do.*

Ian sips; the bathroom air vent rattles. How would it be, if Tom was with them at this moment? He drank tea all the time. He only took a drop of milk and he'd fit whole biscuits into his mouth, and all you can do is manage the absence and how it feels, and try to find good from it. No regret, and no affairs. *Mind you, you'll get the Bundy baldness.*

Nathan smiles over his mug. *No chance.*

*   *   *

I know the island is waiting. We all are. We are counting the days we have left until the sly tide comes.

I know this, and I touch my Fishman. My Fishman, whose true name I know.

And if anyone else knows of waiting, it is Sam – who waits, and waits.

It is all that Sam has ever done – for the past four years, or nearly. For nearly four years he has slept poorly; he has sat by Crest in the darkness and waited in case I might ask, at last, for his help. He has waited so long for an act in which he can make amends, or try to. For *sorry*, to Sam, is not enough. He has tried to say *sorry* – but it felt like air. It felt like nothing, like a faint approximation of what was inside him; as a single chest feather approximates a bird in flight or as a single tap of rain against the glass represents a storm, or as saltwater in cupped hands – mirrored, protected – tries but fails entirely to be an image of the sea.

I will do anything to make this better for you. Anything. Sam wrote this, pushed it under my porch door not long after Tom died. I found it, and read it amongst my tomato plants. And ever since, I know that Sam Lovegrove has been waiting, holding his breath. He's been filling my fuel containers, cutting my hedge, tucking more logs beneath my green tarpaulin without my asking for it. And all this while he has been waiting for the day when I might come to him – serious, gentle – and say *I have something to ask of you.*

I will do anything.

I know he waits. We all do – but Sam waits most of all.

The moon shines through his curtains so that he can see his whitened room. His weights sit, discarded. The powdery baleen of a pilot whale that he found, as a boy, is ghostly at this moment. It looks magical, with purpose. Sam holds his breath.

A blue light. His phone.

It is this, from Leah: *X*. Healthy and vital.

He sends this back: *Xxx*.

*   *   *

There is a candle between us, the Fishman and I.

We sit at the table at the old pig farm. We look at the candle – how it spills its wax, how its flame feels our breath.

For we talk. We plan.

He must leave in two nights' time and we must work out how.

The Fishman asks me this: *what makes a good story? You know your stories.*

I consider this. And I say *it must have happiness in it – people finding it. It must have a landscape that fills the mind, and can be seen so clearly you feel you could be walking there. It must have love. Perhaps a little sadness. And it must have a journey, of some kind.*

The Claw and the Prediction

Once and once only did we walk on Sye.

It was not where we tended to go. If we walked, we went west – over the fields and ducking through the wire fences until we came to the coastal path. In wild weather we'd stand on the headland; at low tide we'd make our way down the wooden stairs to Lock-and-Key where the rubber boots were. *You and those boots* ... I'd pick through the driftwood and Tom would tell me the stories he hadn't yet told, or ones that I knew but had asked for again. We wrote our names in the sand, as children do.

T LOVES M.

Does he, now?

He does. Can't help himself, I'm afraid ... And we'd walk hand in hand.

But one day we were on Sye. And as we trod over its stones, I saw something. I bent down, picked it up. *Look* ...

A claw like no other claw – huge, a polished chestnut-brown with blackened tips and a grooved, serrated edge. *Tom?*

That's a big one ... He turned it over, returned it back to me. And he kissed my forehead as I mourned the rest of this crab that had died – picked at by gulls or crushed against rocks. *This is all that is left of its little crab life ...*

It was then that Tom told me about the crab that can lose its claw and survive it. We were making our way back along the stones. We were not holding hands now but we were close enough to, and he said *here's a little tale for you* ... He described the life of the stone-crab – how fishermen would catch it and pluck off its largest claw before dropping it back onto the sea floor. And, in time, it grew a new claw. It made a replacement for that missing one. *Then it's caught again, and its larger claw is torn off a second time, and it's thrown back where it grows a third ...* I stopped walking, confused. For how did it live? How did it eat? Defend itself? How did it do anything, for surely its largest claw is what defines the crab and ensures its existence? Without it, does it not risk a short and unfair life?

It manages, he said.

But life is better with two claws, I bet ...

Maggie.

He turned. The light was strange, pinkish. He put one hand on my waist and the other hand moved through my hair twice, three times before it stilled.

I want you to be like that. If the worst happens.

I listened to my husband and I hated what he said. I hated it for it conjured up a world in which he did not live, a world he was no part of and where he could not be found. I had married him because I wanted to be with him every day; I wanted to die before he died so that I would never be without him, and I hated the words he was saying – the phrases that started with *Mags, if I die ...* I protested by trying to break free of him, but he only took a better hold and said *but look what I do! For a living!* He sailed most days. He went out in all weather and he might not go far – he might stay near the shore – but when did that mean true safety? He promised he'd always be careful. He promised he'd never take risks in his boat. *Nothing will happen to me*, he smiled – *but isn't it right that we talk ...?*

He wanted me to be like the stone-crab. He wanted, he said, for me to rest as they do, to mend in my own time. *Be sad, but not forever. Grow your claw again ...* And I shook my head. I muttered that if he died I would never grow a new claw, that I'd never want another claw in all my life. I only wanted the one I had now, the love I had in Tom Bundy. I wanted this hand with this wedding ring. *I won't grow a claw ...*

Well, I'd want you to grow one. Just know that – OK? I'd want you to find someone else.

We never spoke of it again. I did not like it – the thought of him gone – and it felt like a new reason to keep away from Sye. I chose to forget it because it did not matter; my husband would never die and I myself would never be plucked, torn, disarmed and cracked open by the impossible news of his death. Like all of us I thought *it won't happen to him*. But such things happen to *someone*, and sometimes that *someone* is him, or it's you.

Boats can rock and men can grow tired.

I have learnt that nothing stays the same. Today might seem the same as yesterday but no day ever is; we may want no changes to ever come, but changes do, in time. They cannot be helped; it is how the world turns. And so I may never have asked for love, or wished to grow a second claw, but these things happened all the same.

It grew outside Lowfield, as I hissed *take it off ...* Not as large as the first claw in many ways – but no less purposeful or real or strong. When I opened my arms and held the Fishman it only felt half-known. It took a long time to remember how certain parts worked, or how to behave with your heart and someone else's heart, and nothing is ever easy. I can't think of anything that has been easy, and a crab, if it could speak, would say the same. But I found love when I thought that it was gone for me. It is beyond my understanding, as so much is. It is stranger than any book could be.

I'd want you to find someone else. Holding my waist on Sye. The whorl in his beard, the life in his eyes.

I wear my wedding ring around my neck these days. And sometimes, when I feel it, I tell Tom *I did – yes. For a while, I did.*

Sixteen

So. All stories have to end. Giants must be turned into stones, Parlan imps must hide by dawn, and notes in bottles have to be read. The lighthouse has to close its eye. And a Fishman must walk back into the sea.

*   *   *

Sam rolls his cigarette on his knee. He pats the tobacco into a line, lays a white filter tip at one end. He begins to roll it, back and forth. Two licks, along the waxed edge of paper – one to the left, one to the right.

He seals the cigarette, lights up.

His phone shudders in his back pocket, makes a sound like a magic trick. *Leah, surely.*

But it is not Leah. It is from Maggie.

It says *you said you would do anything. Did you mean it?*

He sends back immediately. *Yes.*

Across the island, to the far south where the land is flat and fenceless, the Fishman can hear footsteps. He turns at the sound.

They are Tabitha's, and she comes with her hands behind her back so that she walks with a slight roll of the hips and gentle sway. It is how people walk when they have something to say; he knows her mind is elsewhere.

Tabitha wrinkles her nose when she smiles. *Almost done here, by the looks of it.*

Yes. Pretty much.

He puts the paintbrush down. Together they walk through Tavey. He lets her pass through doorways first, his hand near the small of her back but not on it, and in each room the nurse tilts her head back. *Oh, look ...* He watches her as she runs her finger along shelves, feels the sanded, painted doors, and he wonders if he loves her – this plump-bodied, plump-hearted woman who likes her pink wine, and has as many secrets inside her as he does. Story after story. Sadness, tucked away.

Yes, he decides. He loves her. Astute, jovial, a little lonely, wise. He ducked into Lowfield one afternoon to find her dancing to the radio, moving round the kitchen with a loaf of freshly baked bread in her arms as if it were her lover, and it made her look like a young girl with her whole life ahead of her. He'd felt tender, as he'd watched – as if he was the older one. For a moment, he'd watched her dance and sing. And then he'd felt embarrassed for he was watching such privacy, a moment that was meant for no eyes but her own. He'd stepped away. He'd gone back into the garden. He'd waited for a moment before returning to the kitchen – calling *hello?* as he went. Giving her warning. She'd been cutting the bread, when he entered the room.

I think ... She shakes her head. Then, decisively, she says *well, I have an urge to thank you.*

Thank me?

A long sigh. Tabitha smiles. *You don't realise what you've done here.*

He does not understand her.

Surely you've seen the difference. Think of Leah. She would barely leave the house. She would barely leave her bedroom, and now look at her ...

I didn't do that.

Don't be too sure. There have been a hundred changes since you came here, and perhaps they aren't your doing, but they've happened since you came. She shrugs. *I want you to know I've loved having you here.*

He stands, then. He pushes himself away from the dresser and makes his way into the middle of the room. Tabitha frowns, half-expectant. And the man from Sye lifts his arms and he fits himself around her. He embraces her, and she is so small that he has to bend his knees, and he hears her make a sound.

It is a mouse-like sound. A sigh, perhaps. *Oh!*

Perhaps she has not been held for a while. Perhaps she has not been held so unexpectedly, so strongly, and not by a man who is so tall and broad. When their arms soften and they peel back from one another he sees her eyes are shining.

I owe you so much, Tabitha.

No ...! Laughing.

I do. You have been so kind to me.

A breeze comes through the doorway, and there is the sound of a book's pages turning themselves, one by one. Where had he been a month ago? Two months ago?

Tabitha Bright. *Well-named*, she once told him.

She pats his arm and whispers, *it's just what nurses do.*

*   *   *

Sam makes his way up the lane, takes a path that leads past the airstrip and towards The Stash. He sees Maggie, as he approaches.

Thank you. For meeting me.
Sam knows this is what he's been waiting for.

*   *   *

From Easterly, there is a view of The Stash. If Emmeline was standing in her garden at this moment, if she was straightening up from her flowerbed or her small vegetable patch and looked south and east, she would see two figures, talking. A blonde woman and a reddish-blond man. They lean on the fence above The Stash, look down.

But Emmeline is not in her garden.

She has not slept well. She spent the night awake – making tea, carrying that tea back to bed with a cross-word or a romance novel, and turning out the light twenty minutes later only to find herself staring at the ceiling again. Counting the seconds between each passing beam of light. And so today she is leaden. She sits at her kitchen table, with her palms laid down.

I have been unkind.

She knows that for the past month she has avoided Tavey. She has puckered her mouth at the mention of *the Fishman* or *that man from Sye* so that others knew how she felt and might change the conversation to the weather, or the sheep. When she has spied him – black eyes, bright smile – she has felt a weight inside her, a fluttered movement as if she was carrying a child again. Deep down.

She knows her suspicion is unfair. She knows, now (but she probably always knew) that this stranger has not come for trouble or to hurt them all. He has sanded wood, painted it. Emmeline's granddaughter has become the happier, strong-bodied creature that she used to be, and her own three children have seemed closer to each other whilst he's been here – and she doesn't know why, or how. *But I should have said more to him. Over the weeks.*

Yes, maybe. She has been angry and embittered for too long.

Now Emmeline sits at the kitchen table, and what had been anger – what she had formed into anger, as a child forms sand – has gone, and the tiredness that followed it has, also, gone, and what she is left with is pure sadness. She sees the waste. She sees the absolute waste of life that happened in an afternoon sea nearly four years ago, which can never be calculated in any meaningful terms. But other wastes – other wasted lives. Emmeline has always been called *angry*. *So cold, so walled-up*. And yes, she has been. She has been angry for too many reasons to ever count. She has burned because *Sea Fairy* tilted and a boy fell in; she is angry because Tom chose to kick off his shoes and dive in without stopping to think of his own life or the lives of his mother, his family, his wife. And she is angry because she feels, sometimes, as if she's the only one who misses him, as if she and she alone still looks for him on beaches or in the faces of those who step off the *Morning Star*. She feels angry because it isn't fair – he was thirty-seven, and her youngest, and yet she herself is still here when she would gladly bargain with God if He would listen – *my life for his life*. But God doesn't work that way. Even Lorcan says He does not, and she is angry, too, at the death certificate. She is angry that it talks of something she has never been able to see with her eyes – as if that certificate and the words on it are lying words, uninformed. Perhaps she is angry that she has been this angry. It is not the face of grief she had ever thought she'd had.

But then, she was angry before it. Her boxed rage did not begin with Tom diving into the water. When, then? At what moment did it seep into her blood and bones? It is too hard to know. It is hard to know at what point she knew that Tabitha was the favoured one – if not favoured by their parents, then favoured by genes and character.

Fair-haired Tab, stubborn but angelic and without the heavy Bright hips that anchored Emmeline on the windy days. Tab, who could silence the local teenage boys by simply walking past them, whilst Emmeline had to say *excuse me* three times to get noticed in the island's shop: anger had come, she knows, from that. And whilst Emmeline was scraping the sheep dung off the soles of her boots before walking into a house where no-one else had bothered to, Tabitha was on the mainland in her nurse's uniform, writing letters home that were signed with a cheery *bye for now!* and after that she swanned off to save lives in the parched worlds of drought and war. *Quite the heroine.* And if she is honest, there have been days when Emmeline has regretted the choice she made in her teens – to marry a man who could let days pass by without asking her a question or remarking on a single part of Emmeline's own life. *My life* ... Which she had handed over to a sheep farm and the dour farmer in it too easily – too easily. Once, she found a photograph from their wedding day and tore it down the middle. Later, guilt-flushed, she'd mended it: she will never regret – never regret – her children. But if she hadn't married Jack Bundy, what might she have been? Who might she have grown into? Not the farmer's wife. She might have left the island as Tabitha did – taken classes, gone to parties that she only ever heard about from her sister's tales. And she has been angry, too; that low, simmering, unreasonable anger that builds slowly until she almost feared wrapping her hands around a knife's handle and using it against something, anything. She did so many unseen, unthanked jobs. She scrubbed pots whilst others slept; she cleaned the bathroom daily; she wrung the necks of chickens that were too old to lay; she polished school shoes and made five birthday cakes a year when no-one made one for her in return, or even remembered her birthday at all, and she'd hear

Jack Senior say *Emma's not blessed with her looks, is she?* and she'd wash and cook and iron and worm the dog and mourn her dead parents and all the while – all the while – she'd be nursing a headache or a bruise under clothes. So often she thought *they wouldn't miss me. They'd only notice that I'd gone when the laundry basket was full.*

Not true, of course. The children might not have thanked her for their favourite sandwiches in their packed lunch but she knows they loved her and love her still. Sometimes Tom would leave a daisy on her pillow. Other times, Nathan would come to her and cling like a limpet so that she had to prise him off her, finger by finger – *there you go …* They love her and she loves them, and so she can feel guilty, sometimes, about the anger she has. *You raised four happy children by doing what you did.* But still, she could be angry. Oh, how she could be.

It was how I survived him.

It was how I found the fuel to wake up every morning and go to bed at night.

It was how Emmeline stayed in her marriage. How she stayed strong.

Anger was what she knew. And so it was anger she turned to when Tom went overboard. Anger was her help of choice. She went for it instinctively – like the painkillers she came to know did the job, routinely, so that she always bought them.

Her boy. He had always been so happy. In the early days, he sucked his thumb. Once, she found him and Nathan sleeping in the tractor's cab – sharing the seat, entwined so that she wasn't sure whose leg was whose. He'd loved stories. If he discovered something – anything – he'd want to show them, running to Wind Rising with a breathless *guess what?*

She cries.

She wants him back so badly, but she can't have him.

A box of tissues sits beside her. For the next three hours, there is the steady rasp and puff of tissues being pulled from it, and the sound, also, of her blowing her nose. She sobs. It is the sobbing which shakes her, which is rhythmic, almost spasmodic. It is a lifetime's crying, and it flows.

*　　　*　　　*

So she cries. There are damp buds of tissue on the table, on the kitchen floor.

The sun makes its journey from the east towards the west.

Maggie and the Fishman walk on the flat sand. There are the coils of lugworms, the shine of upturned shells. She tells him the names of each weed they come by – channelled wrack, oar-weed. *This is laver, which …* And she stops, unable to tell him more. All she can think is how she will miss him. He knows; he understands this. He holds her against him, kisses her hair and they look out at the water.

I did not want the sun to lower itself, and go. I did not want the moon to come. But who are we to stop it all?

That night at Tavey, we talked of coincidence. And luck – good and bad.

We talked of the world's magic, of all the tiny miracles, and we performed our own warm, human kind of it.

*　　　*　　　*

It is not fully dark. It cannot be fully dark when there are no clouds and the moon is one night away from being as full as a moon can be.

A young woman climbs over the electric fence. She climbs very neatly, in her walking boots.

Walking boots, jeans, a woollen cardigan over a sleeveless top.

Leah Grace Bundy. She walks with her arms swinging, with intent.

Cool air, a strong sea smell. She cannot remember the last time she was walking on Parla this late. It looks small, somehow. The houses look toy-like with their curtains closed, their bedroom lights going out one by one. She tastes salt as she licks her lips.

Past the viewpoint, past the red telephone box.

At the harbour, she finds herself a pebble and stands in front of the harbourmaster's house, looks up. Who is she, these days? She barely knows.

Sam is lying on his bed when he hears it. *Tack.*

He lifts his head.

It comes again. *Tack.*

He goes to the window, leans out. For one small moment he does not know her; he can't be sure who she is. Then Leah smiles. She beckons to him.

What is it? On the quayside, in his bare feet. *Are you alright?*

I wanted to say goodnight to you in person, for once – not by a message on a phone.

She does not look like Leah, or rather she looks like the Leah he used to know. The Leah before.

They do not go far. They walk to the sea wall that shelters one side of the harbour and they climb up onto it. Sam, barefoot, winces – *ow ow ...*

Let's just sit here, then. Save your toes.

They can still see the mainland in the moonlight. A few orange lights cluster at the harbour; further down the coast they can see another town. And to the south Sam can make out the tiny lighthouse on Utta's end. Between all these things is the sea.

She gives out warmth – he can feel it.

I love how the sea sounds, she says.

Still? I reckon I've grown used to it.

What about now? Listen.

They can hear the open water against the sea wall. The harbour's side is quiet, but beneath them in the darkness there is the slop and suck of it. It knocks back and forth.

He says *do you still stay away from Lock-and-Key?*

I haven't been back yet. But I will.

Really?

Yes. Soon. I think I should. It wasn't the beach's fault, after all. And she leans to the side, nudges Sam's shoulder with her shoulder in a gesture of comfort or soft reprimand. *And it wasn't yours …*

Yeah, well.

It wasn't. You need to know that, Sam.

He smiles a little. He cannot help it – he smiles at the fact that Leah who has not left Parla in over three years and who hardly left Wind Rising for most of that time is talking about progression and the future. Perhaps he is dreaming this.

You know she is happy now? Maggie?

It is not a question that he answers. But yes, of course he knows. He knows more than Leah does – more than anybody does. And as he sits on the wall, looking out at the mainland's night-time lights, he thinks *should I tell Leah?* What Maggie has told him? And what will, tomorrow night, come to pass? He could tell her now; he could hint, show her the smallest part of it and let her imagine the incredible rest. *Like orca*, Sam thinks. He saw a pod of them, once – off the side of the *Star*. All he really saw of them was their patch of whiteness – so little in the sea is such a perfect white – and in the days that followed, he'd had to conjure up the rest of them. Their teeth, their eyes.

But he says nothing about it. He can't. He promised Maggie, and he keeps his word.

Do you think he's the Fishman? Honestly?

I love to think that he could be. That's the answer I want.

Leah takes Sam's hand. She reaches across, lifts his wrist out of his lap and places it in hers. It is both shy and bold – he does not know which. And he does not care which. He only likes that she is here – here, in person. Her palm fits against his palm.

They walk to where the lane begins. Sam says *go there on Saturday morning.*

Saturday? The day after tomorrow?

The day after tomorrow.

Where?

Lock-and-Key. The sly tide is coming. It's due tomorrow night. It means there'll be more shells, more driftwood … Who knows what you'll find?

They say goodnight on the quayside. It is spoken – not typed on a small, blue screen.

*   *   *

At High Haven, Nathan turns his wedding band over and over. When he slides it off, it leaves a perfect dent behind – such white skin that it glows, in this bedroom. It is brighter than the wedding ring itself, so that he thinks *I will always be married. We will always be married.*

He dials the mobile number that he knows by heart.

It rings four times. He can feel his pulse in his ears.

It's me.

Nathan. What do you want?

I want you to come back.

Nathe, it's late ...

I love you more than I have ever loved anything.

A pause. In the distance, a siren. He can hear her breath; no answer but her breathing.

Kitty sinks to the floor of a hotel room. She is eye-level with a fraying curtain. She can see the house at High Haven – the blue vase on the windowsill, the tea stain on the rug by the bedroom door. Salt in his hair and holes in his jeans, and Nathan does not talk of love. So rarely has he ever spoken as he's spoken now. Sometimes, she has ached to be touched; but sometimes it has been the words she's been wanting – just the words and nothing else.

Nathan closes his eyes. His puts his hand against his forehead, and in a rush he is holding a towel out for her on a beach, or he is counting her toes after sex – *one, two ...* or he is feeling the draught of air as she passes in the hallway, the scent of the air, or he is watching how she pads barefoot down the lane, or she is dancing, or she is above him with her full, female shape, or she is glancing over her shoulder in a red dress with her shoes in her left hand, swinging as she walks away, or she is marrying him, with perfect skin and a white veil, saying *yes, yes*. And he says *everything is wrong without you. I miss you more than I can tell you.*

A long silence. It is the longest he's known, in all his life.

Good is what she says – *good.*

*　　*　　*

Lorcan once told me there is a season for everything. Moons are thin, and then they are full; tides come in and go out.

We spend our last night together. Me – the widow, the blonde girl with lines by her eyes; and him, the man who came from the sea.

The Nurse and the Wasted Heart

The lighthouse-keeper who knew his sea shanties and who played cards on a green velvet-topped table had two daughters – two Bright girls. One was straight-backed and sharp-tongued, and she married a farmer called Jack. The other – the younger – became a nurse.

At eighteen, Tabitha went across the water. She went to a medical school on the mainland that glinted with needles and scalpels, where the beds were hard and the tea was stewed. Everything smelt of disinfectant. She, like the others, wore a blue uniform. She had to pin her hair back, tuck it under her cap.

New words. *Ventricular, arrhythmia.*

And *love*. That, too, was a new word. It came on a Monday morning in a lecture room – wood-smelling, half-lit. Rain on the windows. Tabitha was chewing on a pencil when the door opened, five minutes late; she glanced across, still chewing. And the latecomer had an armful of books and a rain-wet collar and mouthed *I'm sorry* to the rest of the room. Tabitha lowered the pencil and looked down at the desk. There were many things she had loved, before now. She had loved her mother's roast chicken dinners, and candlelight, and the seals' calling in the evenings, and she'd loved Christmas Eves and her father's peanut jar. She loved how a thin, drab anemone would bloom when the tide came across it – from nothing at all to a broad, open, flame-coloured flower that waved, and waved, and brushed her ankles as she waded out. Tabitha had adored these things – but this feeling was different. It was stronger. Her heart thumped in her chest.

Tabitha Bright woke up, as a woman, in those hospital wards.

By day she took notes. She swabbed, and read thermometers. She learnt how to insert a catheter, and she stroked the veined hands of the old. *Do you need something to take the pain away?*

By night, in her tiny single room, she burned.

This latecomer. This pink-lipped, brown-eyed, honey-scented girl who had sat herself down, brushed the rain from her coat.

It was not what Tabitha expected. She'd not expected it at all. Her heart had not even flinched, till then. All she had known, on the island, was that her heart was sturdy and that one day it would love in its full entirety: she had never known what, or whom. Once, in her early teens, she had felt something like this: a dark December storm had come from the north, and a wave struck the lighthouse tower. It had wrapped itself around the stonework with a boom so deep and thunderous that Tabitha had felt it, under her ribs. Her belly had echoed, and her legs had shaken. And she'd reached out to keep her balance, thinking *what is …?* It was like nothing else she'd known. It was as if something momentous had nearly happened, but not quite. A foreshadowing, perhaps. The storm passed but Tabitha decided that love would feel like that – wise, all-consuming, visceral – when, at last, it came.

She was right. It did feel like that. She'd had to take hold of the wooden desk when this trainee nurse mouthed *I'm sorry ...*

In time, they became friends. This girl was absent-minded, apologetic; she curled her hair on Sunday nights as she listened to the Hit Parade. They shared umbrellas as they ran through the streets, and blew strawberry-flavoured bubbles in the picture house, and when they changed the hospital bed-sheets together Tabitha would think how beautiful she looked, amongst all this white, all this billowing, bridal, unblemished white.

Her.

Who was like a wave, booming. Who turned the drab world into colour and movement and light.

She thinks of her now. She thinks of her now, over forty years on – the person she'd loved and longed to be loved by. But not all things work out.

Tabitha never mentioned it. She never spoke of love. There was no point. The nurse pinched her cheeks before dates with a boy whose eyes were different colours – one brown and one blue. *Have you seen his eyes, Tab? Have you?*

So yes, she knew. No point. It was entirely one-sided love.

Tabitha looks out to sea. She looks out to sea, and feels sad. In the past, she has wished, and wished – but what good does it do? Nothing could have been done. The honey-scented nurse used to take her ponytail in both hands – half in each hand – and pull it, dividing the two halves of hair to tighten the band that fastened it and all Tabitha could do was watch as she did this, before setting off down the ward with the *squeak squeak* of her shoes. Even now, it hurts. That ponytail is as clear as it was, and those rubber-soled shoes still sing. *I am a nurse*, Tabitha thinks – but for this, there are no syrups to be poured onto a spoon, no pills to be placed on the tongue. There is the body, and there is the heart, and they are different things. And whose heart can be ordered? Tabitha's cannot be. The other nurse's heart could not be swayed from its course, or nature. *It was just bad luck* – what else could be said? Hearts are beyond controlling. Wilful, hopeful, wonderful things.

Even the Fishman can't help me with this one. She smiles.

Four decades, or more. It is the only time she has ever felt it – the inner, unbearable boom of love's wave. After it, she left. It hurt her too much to stay, so Tabitha chose to nurse in foreign countries – where she could count the ribs of a child through its thinness, where the only shelter they had from a punishing sun was a square of white canvas tied between trees. It was a tough, tender, relentless business where no-one ever talked of love; love was a luxury, a sideline that had no bearing on malaria or dysentery, on who lived or died. She held limbs where the kneecaps were by far the fattest part, lifted children who were streaming out foul, brown water and doctors would touch her shoulders and say *are you OK? Do you need a break?* She did her best to forget the nurse. Sometimes she did, for there was so much to do. *There are things that matter more than love.* But then there would be sunsets of such extraordinary beauty that she missed her beyond words. *I wish she could see this sunset, or this night sky, or this bird.*

She missed Parla too, in the end. She returned in her thirties – leather-skinned, and wiser – and as she stood on the deck of the *Morning Star*, Tabitha Bright decided this: that there are other loves. There are other fervent, warm, rewarding, long-lasting loves which change lives. It is not just romantic love that turns the world, and if she cannot change her heart, or who it will always truly belong to, she can at least choose to pour a different love into her island life. And she has. She has been an exemplary nurse. She has lifted slick, squawking babies into the salty air, and kissed the foreheads of the frail whilst whispering *I'm here* ... She has developed the knack of injections so that the patient doesn't notice it, and yes, Tabitha does all she can to be a deft, loving, compassionate nurse, as well as dependable aunt, sister and friend.

She feels a thousand loves for other people. And she would not change them. They fill in the spaces, as the tide does.

Forty years on – forty-seven, if she's exact – and Tabitha can still see that mouthed, half-smiling *I'm sorry* and she wonders at this moment, as she's often done, if perhaps it was predictive; perhaps those two, breathy words were not meant for the dozens of students or the lecturer, or the rainy afternoon, but for her. Just her.

*   *   *

No-one knows, of course. Or rather, no-one has told her they know. Perhaps it's been suspected – and Emmeline has drifted near a version of the truth, over the years. *Did you meet someone in Africa?* And Tabitha had merely shrugged, blushed. Her broken heart is known of, but not how it broke, or by whom.

Never married? That question, too, comes once in a while. And Tabitha does not lie. She merely sighs, smiles gently and says *I guess I never found the right man*. After all, it's true – she did not. If there was such a thing as *the right man*, he's never found her and she's never found him.

But that's life, that's how it goes. We can't have every-thing – not always. And why should she, Tabitha, be subjected to different laws to the rest of the world, where crabs get picked up and cracked open by gulls? And those gulls get caught in twine? Some live, some don't. Some love and some are loved in return and if she was never meant to love romantically, equally, then she can at least help the others who *are* meant to love that way. She can, at least, smooth out the pathway for them, turn a blind eye. Take candles to an old pig farm.

She is not the bitter type, and never was.

Worse things happen ... Which is true.

So when Tabitha had stood in the porch of Lowfield and seen Maggie Bundy fighting him, thumping the chest of this unknown man and, later, leaning against his chest, she'd known. Tabitha had stood with a tea-tray in her hand, and recognised it. *Love*. Its wave was wrapping round them, crashing like glass.

Do not call the police. Let the man stay. For she wanted them to grasp this love. To grasp this love and not let go.

Take hold of it. They did. And Tabitha is so glad – on behalf of all the others who were not quick or strong enough, or for whom love was destined to quietly slip by. Isn't it the rarest thing? Never mind the whale migrations, or total eclipses of suns and moons: love that lasts, and is returned in equal measure, is the rarest thing she knows of. What can she say, except *grasp it*? Lift the line gradually. Claim that shining rope as yours, as it passes by.

Seventeen

The wind races, overnight. It loosens the leaves of the schoolyard's tree; it parts the feathers of the kittiwakes which perch on the cliffs between the lighthouse and Sye – white, feathered circles, with a pinkish centre of skin.

The air vent is *tut-tut-tut-tut-tut*.

Pigeon turns on her mooring. She pulls, craving the sea.

Rona is not inside. She does not sleep. She is cold – but she stands barefoot on the grass. The foghorn is beside her. They stand, the foghorn and her, and look out at the water.

She wears her pyjamas. She embraces herself, her hands wrapped round each shoulder.

Every twelve seconds there is a sweep of light.

She asks herself what she loves about this man. She asks herself why it has been him, Nathan, whom she has wanted and hungered for, above all the other men. What had drawn her to him, in the beginning? His looks? His nature?

What Rona remembers is how she saw her parents dancing in the kitchen, one Christmas Eve – no music, just her father's tuneless, loving hum. And what she remembers, too, is the stories she heard when she was small – all the stories of love (always of love) that her mother would tell in the moments before bed, the myths and legends of Parla and elsewhere that involved yearning, and passion, and kind, handsome men who'd lay their cloaks over puddles for beautiful ladies or wait a hundred years for just one kiss. And this island is *this island* – so that when Rona reached her teens, and changed shape, and began to imagine tales of her own in which she, Rona, might be the lady herself, where could she go? On this trapped rock? Surrounded by lobsters, and sheep? And with no boys she liked, no pub, no club. No parties to go to.

No parties at all – except once, there was one. One midsummer night, eight years ago. Rona had been seventeen – not a girl and not a woman, that strange age of both nothing and everything where you feel so alive, and yet are so unsure of how to explore or express this *life*, in any way. Seventeen. Naïve and yet wanting to learn. Wanting to be *wanted*, and to meet that handsome prince. Wanting to look like the woman who none of the islanders knew – curved, scented, hungry-eyed, in a red backless dress. She was casual, hypnotic; her eyes were lined in black. And she was dancing by the bonfire with Nathan Bundy watching her as if he'd been captured, astonished – under her spell.

At that moment, Rona turned her gaze to him. She took her eyes away from the woman in red, and looked at him, instead – at his stare, his expression. How Nathan's lips were parted. How he was not blinking. How he was illuminated by more than just the bonfire's light.

I wanted that. She says this, now. She'd wanted that look, from a man. And so all night, Rona watched them by that fire. She watched (biting her thumb, embarrassed, aware that she should not be watching) how they spoke to each other, how they drank from the same bottle of cider, how the woman danced with her slow-moving hips. Rona saw their first kiss, even – near Wind Rising's barn, away from the fire and only half-lit. The smell of crushed grass; the cool feeling of that grass underfoot … Oh, she can remember it. And Rona remembers how she had wanted to be led into the barn by her hand as this red-dressed woman was being led, and she wanted to make a man look as Nathan had looked the next morning, and as Rona stands by the foghorn she sees that it all began from dreams, from childish longing. From stories that had been told.

That night was better than anything that she'd read, or heard. Better, because it was true: there could, indeed, be meetings of chance which lead to love in a moment. There could be nights that change one's life. She knew this because she *saw* it – with her own eyes, by a bonfire on the longest day of the year. And Rona still knew this when, a year later, she watched as Katherine Snow – bare-shouldered, white-laced, pink-lipped and sweet-smelling – walked up the aisle of Parla's church with a bunch of daisies and gasps in her wake. Nathan had been breathless. He'd stood at the altar, clutched Tom's arm and said *look. Look* … Not believing it.

Since that midsummer's night eight years ago, Rona has hungered. She has wanted the romance that changes everything – the love, the adoration that she had seen in Nathan's eyes. And maybe, somehow, over the months and years that followed, when the only boy who cast a glance at her was Jonny Bundy who smoked too much weed and a tourist (clumsy, overweight, overbearing) with whom she had shared her first kiss, Rona had lost sight of the fact that a deep, fervent love might come, too, from other men – that millions of other men could look at a woman as Nathan had done; not just Nathan, alone. Maybe she'd dropped, without meaning to, the notion that what she wanted was *his kind of love*, so that it twisted itself like an unwell birth into simply *his love* or, even worse, *him*. Maybe, as she'd lain in her childhood bedroom at the harbourmaster's house and dreamt of an adult life with want in it, and infatuation, she brought to mind Nathan's gaze because that was the only gaze she had known – the only clear, unequivocal, remarkable face of love that she had ever seen in her short life – and confused it. *Nathan's gaze* became *Nathan. The love he had for Kitty* became, perhaps, *the way he could also love me.* Maybe all this time – in the most basic of ways – she has got this hugely, immeasurably wrong.

Rona closes her eyes.

All the things she went on to see Nathan do: the kiss he pressed into Kitty's knuckles, the way he'd touch Kitty's waist as she passed him by. How he'd stoop, pick a buttercup and tuck it into her waist-length hair. They were all things that Rona, too, wanted; she wanted a man to do those things to *her*. And because Nathan could do them, she started to want …

I have been such a fool. Such a fool …

But didn't it grow worse? Because then Rona started trying. The mutation took place, so that Rona began to draw his name on the corners of books and onto her skin. And she started to *look* – believing that a wave from Nathan was more than a wave, and if he helped her over a stile she'd assess, fervently, the tightness with which he held her hand or the tone with which he said *careful, now* in case it had meaning to it. And Rona had scrutinised, also, the way Nathan and Kitty moved together, or spoke, or spoke about each other in the hope that there might, one day, be a widening between them, a fracture in the porcelain that seemed so extraordinary and lustrous and bright. For that would mean that he – this man who could love like no other man could – might not love Kitty as he used to. *It might mean that he is ready to fall in love with me.*

Rona winces. *Such a …*

And when did the cracks show? The silences between them, on the *Morning Star*? When did Kitty first start saying in the café *Nathan seems so ... distant ...* When did that begin?

After Tom went overboard. That's when.

Oh ... It is a sound of pain, regret, shame. It is the sound of a realisation which should have come sooner – if only it could have come sooner. If only she had had this airy, night-time clarity two years ago, or four, or six, and so much would not have been done: so much would not have been thought, or said. There would have been, at no point, the hard bite of guilt every time Kitty stepped into the café, shaking an umbrella or taking down her hood or laughing because the wind tried to take her, and always with a musical *hello!* There would have been no wild, desperate reading of messages, deciphering the codes that Rona felt sure were hidden there; there'd have been no small fortunes spent on underwear, online. No deceit, of such proportions. No self-deluded years. And so much less unhappiness – because how has this brought happiness? To anyone? Even when he was lying beside her, in her bed, Rona has never felt happy. His heart was never hers. His thoughts were always of Kitty, and home.

He never loved me. Not once did Nathan look at Rona in the way he'd looked at a dancing, red-dressed woman at a party, eight years ago. Of course not. And that was all Rona had ever wanted. She had only ever yearned to be led by the hand, or to have a buttercup tucked behind her ear.

In which case, maybe I have never loved Nathan either.

And at that, Rona opens her eyes.

There will be few stronger moments in Rona's life than this. There will be very few that she will remember so clearly and with such feelings – awe, regret, relief. And it will be hard, she knows, for a long time to come. She may not have been *in love* – but fondness had not been absent, nor care. And she feels so very guilty, so foolish and unkind that she knows she does not like herself, and may not for some time. *It will be so hard* … How might she move on? How might she stop hurting? She does not know how to start.

And I am so sorry – so sorry …

Rona cries a little. But as she cries, she thinks she hears a voice – so that she turns, scans the fields and the night-time sea. The wind? The water? Her imagination? *It will be alright.* That's what she hears, or thinks she does. Rona sniffs, half-smiles.

She treads across the grass. Climbs back into her still-warm bed.

Rona finds another hour of sleep. She lies on her front, showing the grassy soles of her feet.

Nathan, too, is sleeping. A dream of a small bird tattoo.

*   *   *

Still early, but there is sunlight, now. At the harbourmaster's house, the toast pops up.

Ed butters it. He hollers up the stairs to his son, with his mouth full. *Get up, Sam!* The radio has no good news to say so he turns it off. He has heard it before. He'd heard, too, the shipping forecast which talks of the moon's perigee, and the highest tide of all.

Upstairs his wife is showering. He smells soap, lavender.

Sam!

The *Morning Star* sits, waiting. No black crate on the quayside; no lobsters from Maggie. But he did not expect them. When did she last bring lobsters down? She is busy doing other things these days.

A wavering voice from the attic. *Dad ...*
 He waits, calls again. Sam grasps the banister.
 Ed finds him, says *son?*
 Migraine.
 When did it start?
 An hour ago.
 Right. It's OK. Back to bed.
 What about the ferry?
 We'll manage with three.

* * *

The ferry leaves. It is a crew of three, not four – but sometimes it can happen that way. And the Fishman returns to me. He kisses my shoulder, holds me from behind.
 I say *I'm nervous. This tide has taken lives before ...*
 He rocks me, as he holds me. *The sea won't hurt me. It's had its chance already – hasn't it?*

What else? This: in the house called Easterly, Nathan is sitting on a kitchen chair. He has a towel around his shoulders, and his mother is standing behind him with the dressmaking scissors. *A trim*, he repeats. *Don't hack off bits ...*
 Tabitha is also there. She is sitting on the work surface as a teenager would. She cradles a mug of tea and swings her legs and she is so full of love as she watches them – her sister frowning through her reading glasses, snipping at the hair of her second-youngest son. Yes, she is so very full of love. Why did it take so long? To say sorry to Emmeline, to speak the truth? Why was she so proud, so despondent, so afraid of the talk that took, in the end, half an hour to

have? *But now we are here.* Emmeline snips. Nathan looks at his aunt with an expression that makes her smile: trepidation, resignation, boredom, relief, a little bit of humour, and maybe, for the first time in a long while, she sees in him the smallest look of hope.

In the evening, Ian finds his wife. He has his hands behind his back so that she eyes him, bemused. *What have you got …?*

He has flowers. They are sitting in a jam-jar – daisies, grasses, thistle heads.

Constance takes them from him. She is amazed. *Come here …*

Dee tucks a chattering Nan into bed. *Can we go beach-combing? In the morning? There might be another Fishman washed ashore, or a treasure chest with pearls in, and gold …*

The Coyles climb into bed – the springs creak.

Lorcan plays his nocturne, and he plays it perfectly.

The highest tide comes in. It moves onto the cove at Sye. The pale eye of a dry stone grows smaller and smaller. The water fills the space between each stone so that they shift, rub against themselves. And the water keeps coming – it passes onto stones that have not been touched by the sea for a long time.

Sye grows smaller; then Sye is gone.

And now the parched weed at the highest part of Lock-and-Key feels the sea upon it; it fattens, lifts up from the sand as if saying *at last …* And the waves creep onto the thin grass, under the fence, under the line of lonely rubber boots. Perhaps the boots look down at the water; perhaps they are searching for their lost friends. Lock-and-Key, also, is submerged by this tide.

At Store Bay, the dunes where the giant lived are striped with sea. It snakes down between the dune grass. A mouse and a spider make for higher ground. Sheep bleat, push up from their resting place.

Mussels vanish; the harbour wall grows smaller. The sea stacks look like half their height.

Sea Fairy creaks on her moorings.

Tap Hole fills itself to the brim.

The man from Sye stands above the beach where he came ashore. He is barefoot. He undoes a shirt button, then a second button.

The Lovegrove boy – who has no migraine, who lied about that – lights a cigarette, exhales above his head. The wind carries the smoke to the south. Sam is wearing his oilskins. By his feet, he has a bag.

And me? What of me? What am I doing, at this moment?

I sit in Crest's garden. I am wrapped in a blanket, look-ing at the water. A silver-black sea and a silver moon.

All night I sit there. I whisper *let this work* – to the sky, the sheep, the northerly wind, to the voles that quiver in their nettle bed, to the ghost of Tom or the sea itself or to something greater than all of these things.

And later, too, I said *thank you*. It had been a month of such strangeness and such beauty. So many changes to that small island and to those small lives that spend their days on it; somehow, our lives seemed larger, now.

A *month of stories*, new and old.

A month of hope and wonder, after all.

The Twins, the Fishman, and the Lighthouse-Keeper's Son

Long ago – before the lighthouse was automated, before it was lit each night and unlit each morning by a computer, far away – there were three families that lived in the buildings at its base. Three lighthouse-keepers who greased the hinges, set the weights going, polished the brass and cleaned the lenses that the light shone through. The Brights, the Hallidays and the Coyles.

Jim Coyle was the fourth Coyle to wind the weight back to the top of the lighthouse stairs nine times a night. He had strong arms because of this and strong legs from climbing that winding staircase. He was the fourth James Coyle to have kept it, and he would also be the last.

His old childhood home is part of a hostel, now. The bedroom that Jim grew up in has four beds in it and a chest of drawers. But it also has his initials carved into the paintwork, near the door: *J. C. 1947* – put there in the moments after he'd asked the elder Bundy twin to be his wife and she had said *yes. Yes, I'd like that.* Blushing like a rose, not quite believing that someone might think they could love her forever, or even love her at all.

For Jim had always watched them. Throughout his child-hood, he'd eyed them – these twins from Wind Rising who did not look alike. The eldest was slightly heavy, larger in the lower half, with hair the colour of old hay. The younger twin taller, with hair that streamed when she ran.

No doubt the younger one was deemed the prettiest. But not by Jim – not by Jim, who liked the slow and prac-tical tasks of the day, the care he took in helping his father whose eyesight was going when Jim was still young. No, he didn't love the fast twin; speed is not the friend of a man whose eyesight was never good. He didn't love the flashing, slender mouse of a girl who could duck under wire in a heartbeat; he loved the twin who made her way over stiles very gingerly, using both hands. He liked how she could rest the washing basket on her hip and almost balance it there. A comely, humble, self-conscious girl who liked stories and sewed very neatly, and who noticed such things as the wind direction or the many shades of the sea. *I am like her*, he decided. *We are of the same kind*.

Do you know any stories? I love stories. Sometimes she would pass him in the lane. No, he didn't know stories but he vowed he would find some for Abigail, in time. Instead, he offered her an ox-eye daisy. Later, he gave her a peri-winkle shell – pink, unbroken – that he'd been keeping for weeks.

He hoped, from the start – Jim Coyle.

But then, there was a death. The younger twin disap-peared. The islanders searched their outbuildings, their fishing boats and even the pig shelters in Tavey's fields but by evening they were walking the coast with lanterns in their hands and fear in their bellies. *Thomasina!* Echoing from cliffs.

Jack, their brother, found her. And she was buried in the churchyard with a clutch of ragwort laid on the coffin, for

Abigail always said that her sister had loved yellow – the colour of newness and the sun.

The colour of the sun. Knowing this, young Jim picked stalks of it and looked for Abigail. She had her mourning places – the church, or the sheep fields, or in the dunes at Store where the sand was warm to touch. He would find her, nestle next to her.

I don't want her to be dead. I don't want her to be dead. She sobbed. Or sometimes he found her when she was exhausted from her sobbing, so that she spoke very quietly, blinking reddened eyes. She told Jim of Thomasina's double-jointed thumbs, of how she could whistle between her front teeth. And they began to meet more often – Jim and Abigail. He'd listen, and feel so sorry for her. He'd want to hold her hand.

One day, she brought a book. On a cloudy afternoon, she appeared with a hefty leather-bound book with gold stitching and an attic smell, and Abigail creaked it open in the grass. *It was my mother's,* she told him. *Look …*

Jim looked. He saw the pictures, he read the tales.

I used to believe in all of them. In the Fishman – see his face? But how can they be true? When Thomasina's dead? She crumpled. Stroked the fourteenth page.

Jim even came to love how she blew her nose – with strength, gusto and musicality, which she followed with a hanky's genteel dab.

Jim thought about Abigail all the time. He thought of her as he swept the lighthouse stairs, or as he guided his father's unsure hands towards his knife and fork. He was thinking about Abigail as he reached inside the foghorn to remove litter and last autumn's leaves, and as he retrieved his arm from the foghorn's depths he thought, *I want to make her happier. How can I make her happier?*

An idea came to him, at that moment. A handful of leaves, and a view of dark-blue sea.

Abigail! He found her lying down near Tavey, crying and with pig dung on her knees. *Abigail, you'll never guess ...* And he told her. He told her what he had seen, that morning. He gave her every part of it – the gull's calling, the whiteness of his skin.

She sat very still, bright-eyed. *It was him?*

I think so.

He exists? You saw him?

I saw a man, he told her. *A bearded man, like the one in your book. And a huge, silvery tail.*

*   *   *

It was simple enough. The idea came so neatly. It opened up inside him as if the Fishman himself had been passing by, and he said *tell her that you saw me* ... What harm could it do?

Over sixty years, since then. A new wind is blowing, now, across the isle, and his wife – the twin with the wide behind – sleeps beside him. She is old now, as he is old. Her breath is snuffled, soft.

So he lied about the Fishman. There was never such a thing. Jim does not believe in such stories, or he does not readily. He likes his cogs, his science and maps. He likes what can be *proven* but whilst he might like those things very much – hinges, diagrams – he loves this woman by his side. He loves her more than anything – more than water, or the turning light.

That was the best smile he had ever seen – the one that Abigail gave when she heard him tell his tale. *Really? The Fishman? And if he exists, then ... Maybe ...* A thousand maybes, after that. As if Jim's words had watered a near-dead thing, she flourished, unfurled before him and believed in everything. For if there is a Fishman, what could be impossible? Nothing is impossible. Anything could *be*.

Abigail. With whom Jim shared his first kiss that afternoon, as they walked on the cliffs – timid, awkward. They bumped teeth, smiled, and both apologised.

Guilt? Once, he questioned it. For, after all, he had told a lie. But it was a lie which had stopped her flowing tears. It became a comfort – an offering which she'd taken, grasped, as if he'd offered gold. That lie (that *story*, a far better word) had given her hope, and trust in the world, and it had meant that the sea was no longer the vast, foreboding, malevolent beast it had been. Magic came back to it. Its waves began to sing again.

And didn't it lessen her other, adult sorrows? When she'd discovered she couldn't have children, Abigail had not cried. She'd sat with her hands in her lap and considered it. *There's a reason behind this. I don't know what – but there is a reason.* A decisive nod.

I still love you.

I know. She'd patted his hand. *And I still love you. And it's still a wonderful world ...*

So no – no guilt. His wife is happy. All he ever wanted – from the first moment when he saw Abigail, squatting in the dust in her holey pinafore, using both hands to turn on a rusted tap – was to bring her happiness. A happy Abigail.

Anyway – time and the human mind are powerful, and they are immeasurable when they go hand in hand. The Fishman feels like the truth, now. So many years have passed. Jim has told the tale so often and so vividly that it has come to feel like he *did*, in fact, see the Fishman – the bearded face, the silvery tail – off Sye, six decades ago.

Eighteen

Daylight. Windows glint. The lighthouse turns off.

The dog at Wind Rising stretches her back legs. Lichen shines on the eastern sides of walls. Squares of light edge across the concrete floors of barns.

Loos flush. Backs are stretched.

Alarm clocks click, and burst into life.

Tabitha opens her bedroom window and the salty tang comes in. She inhales. There is a cleaner smell to the morning – cooler – and she supposes there would be; after all, the spring tide cleans out the higher rock pools. It sweeps into caves and hauls out the litter. It carries away the parched weed, the turtle bones, the lost hair-ties and crushed cigarette ends and the dead gull she knows has been lying at Store for weeks. They are gone. Now there is freshness. It makes her smile.

And the wind? She pauses. It is not northerly, now. Overnight, it has changed; the grass flurries in a new direction. The leaves in her vegetable patch are rustling for the first time in weeks. *Westerly* ... she sighs. And isn't that the island's favourite wind? The wind that they prefer? Washing lines tend to be west-facing.

The rhododendrons at the crossroads curve from west to east.

* * *

Leah does not wait for breakfast. She continues to dress and hurries downstairs – pulling on her cardigan, fastening her belt. She ducks outside and crosses the fields so that the sheep rise up, move to a safer place. Once there, they glance back. Their ears switch back and forth.

It is like being a child. This – a summer's morning, damp grass, the excitement of a low-tide beach that she will be, surely, the first to walk on. How old is Leah? She feels brand-new.

Lock-and-Key. She has not placed her foot down on its sand in nearly four years but she will, now.

Down the wooden stairs. There is the line of wellington boots, upended on their fence-posts, and an expanse of beach as bright as glass. And Lock-and-Key is strewn with weed and driftwood, with shells that look white from a distance but which, when held in the palm, will never be white or not white alone. Leah knows this: she has not held a shell for a long time but she knows they are also pink or pale brown or blue-coloured, or they have ribbing of dark grey, or pearly undersides that are a hundred colours or more. All different – each one. The beach has never looked like this – so many shells, so many plastic bottles and rounded glass and rope.

She inhales, sets out.

This is what she knows: that Tom died. That the worst moment of her small life had been standing on a city street with her mobile phone pressed to her ear and her mother's voice saying *I don't know how to tell you this. Darling ...* Leah changed, in that moment. Her physical body – her organs, her blood – changed, and her bones grew heavy and a deep, deep unhappiness soaked through her head like damp so that she thought she'd never laugh, or have a boyfriend, or a job. Or walk on Lock-and-Key again.

But I am here, now ... All these shells; she is walking on shells. She lifts fistfuls of wrack, finds green bottle-glass as smooth as a marble. Also, she finds a crab. It is long dead, but immaculate. Leah crouches, lifts it to see its stalked eyes, its tiny mouth like a door, and she thinks *it is incredible*. It defies her understanding – how something as perfect as this crab exists, how it was made so intricately as to have its hinged legs, its ridged claws, its white underbelly which no human eye has ever seen. It would have made her sad, once. Once this beach would have been strewn with waste and sadness, but not now. Not today. She puts the crab down. She finds the long straps of weed that shine, as if coated. In rock pools there are transparent fish.

How strange that she always thought this beach would make her miss him more, or make Uncle Tom seem even further away. In fact, she feels she could touch him. Or he could touch her; he could be standing beside her and naming the different parts of a crab. He feels all around her – nearer to Leah than he has ever been since he dived off *Pigeon* four years ago.

Lee-loo, he used to call her. *Little Miss Bundy. Niece of mine*.

And just as he feels closer, someone else feels far away. *The man from Sye is gone*. Leah is sure of this – it feels as simple and strong as this stem of weed, or more so. *Gone* ... The sly tide took him. The full moon shone, and so he reached beneath a rock at Sye and found his folded tail ...

She will say he was the Fishman, for always. *But it doesn't matter*, Leah decides, *who he really was*. He *came* – that is what matters. He was the change she'd been craving. He prised the wooden boards down from Tavey's windows and far more besides.

She stoops.

There is a feather here, on the wetter sand. It is white, as long as her forearm. It is muddied, as she knows Maggie likes them – torn, half-bent; its tip is translucent, so hollow that it makes the tiniest sound as the westerly wind blows past. *I will keep it for her.* The smallest of gestures, but she will make it. She will give it to Maggie in the days that follow, to add to her glass vase.

* * *

The nurse leaves her house, pulls the door behind her. She hurries to the old pig farm.

Inside, it is spotless. The floor is swept and the fire is set. In the bedroom, the blankets are folded away. He has washed each paintbrush and laid them out on newspaper; the step-ladder leans against the door. The tools are in their box; the candles are lined up. Tins of paint are sealed, and dry.

Sadness, in a rush. Tabitha wants to find him. Where has he gone to? And how? She reasons, momentarily, that he must still be on the island – he must be, for how might he have left it? No boats set sail last night. And someone would have seen him, surely, if he'd tried. But Tabitha has a small, restless feeling inside her that says *he is gone. Back into the water. Back to …* What?

She has no answers, today. And maybe she does not want them. As she stands in Tavey's garden, the sadness goes away. The day is perfect. The sun is high. She and Emmeline will plant bulbs later – daffodils and snowdrops in the grass verge near the church which will push up like old friends in the spring.

Later, she rings her sister. *Have you seen him?* Just in case.

Emmeline hasn't. She phones her three children to ask them. *Have you seen ...?*

No ... I saw him yesterday.

Not today?

Not today.

No-one has seen him. Rona has not; nor Hester. It is Dee who says, *phone Maggie. Surely he's with Maggie?* But also, just before she hangs up, she says *Tabitha?*

Yes?

You didn't call earlier, did you? An hour or so ago? Only I had a silent call.

Silent?

Nobody spoke. Thought I heard breathing, but –

Tabitha hadn't made the call, and doesn't know who did. But she forgets about it promptly. There are more important things.

*   *   *

In the harbour, the *Morning Star* docks. It drifts towards the quayside, and gently knocks against it. All those onboard sway with it.

Nathan is waiting for this boat. He wears clothes that are clean and pressed; his hair is no longer brushing his collar or half-covering his ears. There is something boyish about him – how he is not sure what to do with his hands, how his feet can't be still.

The gangway chimes, as it is lowered.

One by one, they come: tourists with their backpacks, a man from Say, George, Jonny, a birdwatcher with binoculars knocking against his chest and a guidebook underneath his arm, and as they disembark Nathan steps closer. He pushes up onto his toes and then drops down, trying to see through the railings. He thinks *is she on board? Is she?* For a moment he thinks she is not.

She is the last to descend. Kitty, in a floor-length skirt and hoop earrings that glint through her hair. She keeps one hand on the railing; she puts one foot in front of the other. Elegant, and slow.

I am not there to see it, but Hester is. Hester looks up from the boot of her car and sees them – how they press their hands together, palm to palm; how they seem to say nothing to each other until Kitty smiles, releases one hand and fingers her husband's shorter hair. She comments on it; Nathan nods, bashful. They are how new lovers are – wary, wide-eyed.

Hester watches. She sees her younger brother carry Kitty's bag to the car; she sees Kitty thank him, and consider this man who is careful with the bag as he sets it down. He opens the passenger door for her, and Kitty smiles, climbs in. They make their way back to High Haven.

*   *   *

Ed steps into the hallway, heaves his legs out of his boots. *Hello?* No answer.

Next to the fruit bowl he finds a note which says *Hello you – I'm dropping N up at R's (beachcombing ...) but I'll be back shortly. Love D xx ps S is feeling better.*

He puts on the kettle and the television. In the fridge he finds bacon, and looks for the frying pan. He knows nothing of the Fishman's vanishing – how he has gone like a magic trick, like a dream they all had but have now woken from. But he will, of course. He will.

All of them are looking. They peep into outhouses. They look in the back seats of their cars, just in case. They check that all the boats are accounted for – *Sea Fairy, Lady Caroline, Pigeon.*

Maggie is pale when they ask her. *With me?* She flinches. *No ... Has no-one seen him today? At all?*

Chicken sheds, greenhouses, the old wooden hut by the airstrip, the barn at Wind Rising, the church, the paint-smelling rooms of Tavey. They look everywhere. They call out *Fishman*, over the fields. Milton checks his storeroom. Ian Bundy puts a torch in his back pocket and makes his way down to Tap Hole, and all the other smaller caves – where the only answer to *hello?* is his own echoed voice.

The Fishman is nowhere. He is gone as a mist goes.

Where could he have gone to? Even Emmeline can't explain it. *A bit of a mystery*, she concedes.

It is Nan who finds him, in the end. Nan, who is wearing mismatched socks and a sky-blue dress, and who makes up her own song as she goes. She is running ahead of her sister. She is imagining a whale or an upturned boat or shells you can blow into that make a sound like a hunting horn. Nan trips through the grass, arms in the air.

Then she stops. She wipes her nose on her forearm. *Rona?*

Rona comes beside her. *What?*

Look.

Are they clothes? They look like clothes, left on the grass above Sye, but the sisters are too far away to be sure. So they hurry. They make their way down the path, through the gorse.

Yes, clothes. They are neatly folded. There are jeans with a hole in the left knee, a red and black shirt with a torn collar, a pair of blue socks. Sturdy boots with paint on the toe.

Someone must be swimming, Rona says.

Swimming? With no clothes on?

Some people do.

No, they don't! Incredulous. *Don't be so silly …*

What else could it be?

The younger girl is firm. *They are the Fishman's clothes. He's become a fish again.*

Nan –

She stamps her foot. *It's true! Look at the clothes! And it was a full moon last night!*

They stand there for a while, on Sye. The breeze moves their hair; the waves are white-tipped. And Rona knows that yes, they are the stranger's clothes. He has worn this shirt; she has seen him in these boots. But why are they here? Folded on Sye? She can see no swimmer. She can see no reason for him to set out into the sea, fully naked and whilst the island is still sleeping unless … *Suicide.* A word like a shock. It makes Rona close her eyes, momentarily. *Oh God. Surely not that? Surely?* And yet she can think of no other answer; it is all she has to give.

He's grown his tail? Hasn't he? Half-sung.

Rona makes a choice, at that moment. And she chooses to lie. She looks down at her sister and says *yes – yes, he has.* For Nancy is six and three-quarters. Nancy is chirping, hopping from foot to foot and she believes that the world is a safe, amazing, happy place – and how could Rona change that? With the truth? Rona thinks *let her stay as she is.*

She puts her hand on her little sister's head. She feels the curly hair, the plastic clip with a ladybird on it but Nan is absorbed with a shell that she has found, by the clothes. She holds it to her ear. She peers inside it, as if the Fishman left a clue for her.

I love you, Button.

Don't call me that ...
Come on. Let's take you home.

Rona carries the clothes back to the lighthouse. They climb into the car, drive to Crest and Rona tells her sister *wait here. I won't be long.* Then she makes her way up the drive. She thinks, *my God. What do I say? How do I tell her?*

The yellow door opens as Rona comes to it. Maggie says *come in*, and steps back to let her pass into a neat, clean kitchen with the kettle whistling and two coffee cups on the worktop – as if Maggie has been watching her driveway, waiting for a car. As if she has been expecting this, all along.

Gone. Gone in the way he came – in a way with no understanding, no reason. Gone, so that it was hard to believe that he had been there at all. *And maybe he never was ...* Maybe we had imagined him entirely. Until we saw Tavey with its freshly painted guttering and its mown lawn, the bare earth where the pig shelters had been.

Nathan and Kitty are the last to know. They have turned their phones off. They have drawn their curtains, closed the bedroom door.

They are fully clothed. She sits on the edge of the bed and her husband kneels in front of her. She is stroking his hair as he tells her, slowly, about all of it – the night-time sounds, the Parlan imps, the snuffled sound of Tom as he slept beside him and how the scar by his own eye was not from a cricket ball. And he talks of the love, the guilt. The fear and the love and the guilt.

Why did you never tell me?

He doesn't know. He does not have any answers to give – only a wish to climb into the bed with her and lie beside her. That and only that. And Kitty leans down, kisses his face.

You should have told me. I'm your wife, Nathe ...

I've got so much wrong.

We all get things wrong.

I'm so sorry ...

Do you love me?

He shakes his head in disbelief. *Like nothing else. Like nothing else.*

They undress. And as he rolls over her, he knows what he feels – what he has, what he wants and has always wanted. It is released, in that bed. *I am grateful.* He is grateful that she is here; grateful that he did not lose her when he deserved to, absolutely. He is grateful that despite what he has known, there remains goodness; despite the loss and the lies and the unfairness, there is Kitty and her warm skin. She is here. She is above him. She is a bird tattoo and Miss Dior and a hay barn and a starry night sky and she is the word *wife*, and he is humbled by her in a way that he has never allowed himself to be, until now. How did he ever win her? How did he ever earn her, once? Or deserve this second chance? He will live his life astonished by this.

Gratitude. He can see its letters on the pillow, on the ceiling. He sees *forgiveness.* He sees *luck*, also – all kinds of it – and as Kitty holds him he sees how he tried his best, his very best. What more could he do? He could not have loved more. He knows he could not have saved Tom.

I could not have saved him. The knowledge of it all rushes in like water – clean, cool. It washes everything.

*   *   *

402

It is a strange night. Some half-sleep; some sit, and think of his face. Others walk outside with a drink in their hand and look up at the moon, the distant lights of boats.

In High Haven, they lie like spoons. Nathan's hand clasps her hand – the back of her left hand fits the palm of his, so that their wedding rings find each other with a single *tack*. Kitty bites her lower lip, smiles.

And someone else is smiling, or is about to smile.

Sam wakes. The room is darker – darker than drawn curtains alone. He waits, and waits, and there is a half-second flash. Nancy sleeps beside him. She has climbed into his bed whilst he's been sleeping and she has wedged herself, comma-like, between the wall and his chest. She snores. He thinks *little Nan* … Who no-one expected to come.

When he was her age, he believed in magic. He believed in the Fishman – for a while, at least. And then Sam grew. He became an adult, and discovered adult life. *It takes so little*, he thinks, *to lose it*; grief and disappointment can take one's faith away so easily that you might wake one morning and have none left. He woke, one day, with nothing. No hope, or self-worth. And now?

He knows this much: that Nan does not know love, not yet. She does not know the strength of it, what it can make a person do for another person's sake. *We will risk it all – for love*. And one day she will know this, which is the greatest tale of all.

Sam fits himself against her.

And then Sam smiles. He smiles and smiles at what he has done, into her salt-smelling hair.

The Widow and
the Man from Sye

Once there was a woman – blonde-haired, blue-eyed. She wandered. She drifted from town to town, from job to job, for she had no true sense of home except for what she carried and what she loved – which was skies, books, trees in wind, water, geese flying south.

She had not asked for love, but then she met a man.

She loved how he kissed, and the stories he had; how he called her *Maggie-May*. They married on Parla, and when he held her at the altar Tom whispered *I will love you all my life*.

Nineteen months later, he died. He tried to save a drowning boy, and did – but drowned himself in doing so. Maggie waded out, waist-deep. She ached for him to come back to her, for him to return, pink-cheeked and half-laughing, saying *well, that was an adventure* … later, she ached for his body to be found. She spent hours in church. She lit a single white candle and set it in the porch at Crest as if to guide his boat in. She trawled the coastal paths by day and took to wearing Tom's clothes at night, pressing the sleeves to her nose, trying to find the last, warm, precious, fading smell of him.

* * *

Nearly four years later, a man was washed ashore. On a stony northern beach, a half-naked man was left there by the tide. Briefly, they thought *Tom?* For a moment, each person on that island held their breath and thought, *is it him?* But no. It was not Tom. Of course not; it couldn't be. This man was taller, broader; his eyes were so black that his pupils were lost. Lashes like miniature fans.

So who might he be? This man with no name? For he had no memory of his life before Parla, before the moment he was found.

Old stories shook off their dust. Half-lost, superstitious talk rose out of the dark – sea songs and folklore, bedtime tales. *He is the Fishman*, Abigail said. And whilst most of them looked for better answers, there were no better ones to have. It was all they could find – and all they wanted. A man with a rainbow tail.

Maggie saw the stranger on a Saturday afternoon. She walked into the garden at Lowfield and lost her breath. And in the days that followed, flowers opened. Seals basked on rocks. The old pig farm was mended and secrets were hauled into the light, and the minister could finally play a nocturne perfectly – no wrong notes. Maggie wanted this man to hold her, to fill all her empty spaces. And, very gently, he did.

Hope and wonder, Abigail said. *It's what it says here, in my book.*

Her book also said *he will stay for one moon's turn …*

For the Fishman was meant for the sea. He could not stay forever; he could not stay without end, and so when the tide was at its highest and the moon was full, he went down to Sye. He found his tail where he had left it, shook the tail out. It flashed like foil. It flashed so brightly that it woke the widow who stretched, turned to find him gone.

All day she could not find him. The islanders looked in chicken sheds, and barns. They ran torches into each cave. They looked under every tarpaulin, in Wind Rising's kennel, along and under each pew in the church. And it was only as the day grew old that his clothes were found – stacked in order of thickness so that his socks were on top, side by side.

The news was passed on. They turned off their torches. In the half-dark they trudged back to their homes.

Suicide? Some said so. They could find no other explanation and so they shook their heads and said to each other *it's tragic. He seemed a good man ...*

Or it was an accident, perhaps. For who would fold their clothes so neatly, as their final act? And aren't the currents strong, or quite strong, off Sye? And hadn't it been the spring perigean tide last night which is also called the *sly tide* so that it would have been so easy – so easy – to have been caught out by the water? *That must be what happened ...* After all, he'd not been Parlan: how might he have known?

Or it was the Fishman. Some of the islanders said this, of course. And it could not be denied that his departure was in keeping with the Fishman's story – secretly, on a full moon, having changed the ones he'd met and leaving *there is hope* on the grass, amongst his folded clothes.

*　　*　　*

Strange, what the heart can bear. It can carry grief beyond measure. It can bear a weight that is too great to speak of.

But a heart can't bear the world. It has its limits – even a heart like Maggie's which had thickened with scarring over the years. The Fishman went and autumn came. She trod the coastal paths. She touched the line of rubber boots. She stood on Bundy Head in her anorak and looked at the water – dark-grey and dimpled with rain.

In the prayer book, they found her handwriting; in Crest, they found her packing things.

Sam Lovegrove knew. He was the first to know it, and said *when are you going? Soon?*

She left in early December. She stood at the back of the *Morning Star* in a hard, sideways sleet and she watched Parla grow smaller. Its lighthouse started turning as she moved away from it.

Apparently Maggie lives on the mainland, now. Is she happy? They hope so. They still hear from her – a letter, or text message. She calls Emmeline, sometimes. And they imagine that she lives a quiet, inland life with fruit trees in the garden and the neat, brisk trot of foxes in the lane, at dusk. Perhaps she has new friends. Perhaps she misses the sea but also, perhaps, she does not.

And him? What is the story of him? The Fishman with his breadth and height?

The story, I hear, is this now: that the Fishman thinks of her daily. He cannot reach Maggie in her new inland home and so he stays near Parla, in case she may return. He passes the beaches she has walked on; he rises from the water, watches the people she loves. And some of the islanders think they have felt him passing, on occasion – Leah, Rona, Abigail. Even Nathan, once, as he made his way home, climbed over a stile.

All will be well ... Or I am with you.

They pause, hear it. Smile to themselves.

That is the story they know. They know it because we chose to tell it; we gave it to them like the shells that they have always been hoping to find on the beach. All of us go down to low-tide shorelines to look for the finest treasure of all – curious, coloured, unbroken things; sculptured wood or sea glass or a stone so round, so perfectly round that you suppose it's been rolled by the tides for more than your lifetime. Centuries, even – *if this stone could talk ...* Or we hope that we might find a wellington boot that matches, exactly, another salty boot. I always hoped for that. I'd gather my feathers and my well-travelled shells, but it was boots I longed for. I wanted to find the other half of a matching pair, and hang it on the fence-post by its grateful friend. I wanted to end another's waiting – for I felt I could never end my own. An odd thing to hope for? A boot? It is, absolutely. I have never told anyone of it. Boots don't have feelings, I know that, and nor do the lesser treasures that I left behind. But we all have our comforts. Does it matter if they are childish, or strange? If they are stories or shanties, or our tiny superstitions? Not to me. I think there's beauty in them. I think they are *us* – unique and very precious. They are what help us through the lonely nights and days.

Nineteen

He was nowhere to be found. The days fanned out, and he did not come back. The autumn changed the sky and the leaves and I did not see him walking in the lane again.

I missed him so much that it hurt. I cried, and had no wish to eat. But also, I had known a deeper sort of pain. *I have known far, far worse* – and so I dressed every morning, brushed my teeth, tore two rectangular tea bags apart without finding meaning in it. I took to the old routines: lifting up the lobster pots, treading on a spade to push it down, into the soil. Sometimes I would sit on the doorstep at Tavey and touch the place where he had sat, as if it may still hold his warmth. Once, I talked of unfairness. But I also knew, and told myself, that *this is how it must be.*

At night, I would step out of my clothes and look at myself. I'd stand before the mirror and see what he had seen – my body's flaws, its signs of age. Puckered skin, and softened parts. I looked, perhaps, for fingerprints but there were none to see.

They were all kind to me. One by one, they came – Dee, with a homemade pie; Nathan, with his hugs in which we'd rock, from side to side. Abigail rang: *I'm only ringing to tell you that he isn't dead. You understand me?* And I knew that she believed, absolutely, that he twisted through shoals and skimmed the sea floor. Crested, with the blowing whales. *Thank you*, I told her – loving her. *Yes, yes I know.*

Lorcan came, also. He came with his cool pianist's hands which took my own hands and held them, and I wondered if he could feel the truth through his fingertips – my strange notes, my secret chords. If he did, he did not mind them. *There aren't always answers, Maggie.* It was all he could say and it was enough.

There were times when I nearly told the truth. Nathan came to see me more and more. We'd walk on the coastal path, arm in arm, and he spoke of Tom – stories I'd not heard before. *Oh, he loved you, Maggie ...* And at that moment, I nearly told Nathan all that I knew about the Fishman – his life, his non-death, his real name. But the moment passed. I closed my mouth. It was not a story to tell.

How is Kitty?

She's well. We both are ... I knew that this was true. I had seen them running through the rain not long before with one anorak between them, held above their heads – and I recognised what I saw between them as they ran. And I was so glad for him.

I knew they slept like speech marks and I knew that they slept well.

I shared pots of tea at Wind Rising. Constance poured, talked about the small things that make up a life – the price of fleece, the winter ahead, how the dog was growing old. She made lemon cakes that tasted like sunshine.

You are coping so well, she said, leaning forwards. *Two losses. Maggie ...*

One. I held my finger up. *Just the one. He was the Fishman, wasn't he?*

She'd laughed. *Yes, of course.*
Not gone.

And if I ever doubted what we'd done, he and I, it faded at that exact moment. I will never forget it – how Leah descended the staircase, moved through the kitchen with *hello, Auntie Mags*, how she touched my arm as she walked behind me as if trying to pass a little comfort on. Leah Bundy, in a white angora jumper. Leah, as a woman – beautiful, curved, bright-eyed, adventurous, healthy, hopeful, strong.

Hester would deliver my mail last of all so that she might stay with me a while. Milton would pop an extra something – a packet of peppermints, a magazine, a bar of soap, a miniature bottle of single malt whisky – into my shopping bag, as I stood at the till. Rona knocked on my door one afternoon with a slice of cake – *it's a new recipe. Pear and white chocolate. Would you try it?* And she kept coming to me. She stopped bringing cakes, after a while, so that I wondered what Rona sought or was needing. Sometimes I felt she had questions to ask; she'd linger in doorways, or pinch her lips together with her fingers as if frightened of her words. *Rona? What is it?*

The tears had come. *How did you learn to let go? Move on?*

I never told her that I had seen her, treading round High Haven in the dark. I only passed her a tissue, put my hand on her forearm as she cried and I told her that letting go is not a choice, in many ways. You try to move on, perhaps. But it comes of its own accord, in the end; it happens when it is ready to, and it mostly comes by without announcement or being noticed at all. *I'll always miss my husband. I won't ever be the person I was before.* But one day, you find that a tune on the radio no longer makes you buckle, or lunge to change the frequency; one day a lightbulb dies, and as you climb the step-ladder to change it you think *it's just one of those things*, rather than feel it is symbolic and unbearable, and you do not cry to hear the tiny broken filament when you shake the bulb by your ear. *You don't mend fully*, I tell her. *But you mend enough, in time.*

She sniffed, smiled. *I guess you should know. You of all people.*

Yes, me. Me of all people. Me, who knows too well.

It was Tom that I thought of, in my final island days. I thought of his bones: how we may have clamoured for them – yearned, in fact, to have them so that we could bury them in dark, Parlan soil – but maybe we clamoured so much that we forgot what he himself would have wanted, what he would have preferred. The grass? Never the grass. A man who'd loved the blustery air and the changing light would never have wanted a tomb in the ground. He'd have asked for the resting place he has – tides, storms, weed, the shimmer of scales, the extraordinary silence of the underwater world. *I love the sea because we can never wholly know it*. Perhaps he has come as close to knowing it as anyone will.

And those were the days when I came to believe it was only his bones in that water. Only the shell that held him – not the man he had been. Tom himself was inside me. He was no more on that island than he could be in deserts or forests, and no less. He would be wherever I took him. No more waiting, like a solitary boot; no more thinking *come back, come back*. For I decided, in *Pigeon*, that he had never gone away.

* * *

The brambles at Tavey fattened with fruit. Nancy had picked them, blue-fingered and cheerful. *Look how many!*

she chirped, as she tilted her bucket. *But I am leaving lots for the birds ...*

Then November.

Then gales, and high seas. We weighed down the tarpaulins that kept our firewood dry.

In sleet, I met a straight-backed man. Young, a reddish beard that made him older. He wore a jacket lined with sheepskin with its collar turned up to his ears and leather gloves and we faced each other, smiled. Nudged stones with our toes.

It's within days, isn't it? Your leaving?

Sam who had found his absolution. Sam who knew the truth – the only Parlan that did.

* * *

They were not surprised and they did not try to stop me. I guess they always thought the time would come. I went from house to house, explaining. There were Christmas cards on strings, and dogs by fires. Homes smelt of wet clothes, diesel, salt and cinnamon.

Most knew. When I knocked on the door with a sleet-stung face and a bunched smile they'd say, *ah* ... Yes, they'd guessed that I was leaving; they'd tug the cork out of the whisky bottle or clear the cat off the best chair and say *so what are your plans? Tell us.* And I'd sit and name the things that I hoped for: a new coat that did not smell of lobsters; a trip to a bookshop; a walk in a place with trees. *Beech trees*, I told them. *Oak, maybe* ... I'd find a small job that did not ask much. I'd live simply, safely. Far from the sea.

When I left the house at the harbour I heard Ed saying to his wife, *it's right she goes. New start. She's still young, or quite young ...*

I had spent six and a half years on that island. Nearly a seventh of my life – but in some ways all of it.

* * *

Maggie. Can you see her?

On a December morning, when the sky was half-dark and the sea had ice in it, Maggie moved through Crest. She stood in each room. She looked at the wallpaper, the worn carpets, the curtains she had sewn by hand. She took in views that she'd thought, once, she would always live by – the bathroom's view of the vegetable patch; the kitchen's view of the sea. In the bedroom, she lay down on her dead husband's side.

She did not leave everything there. A box had gone ahead of her in which were the most cherished, larger things: *Coralee*, and his wedding suit, a guide to the seashore that he'd written in, a sketch of them both that Kitty had done, long ago. Maggie's clothes, too, had been taken. But the furniture was staying, in Crest. Where it was meant to be.

Can you? See her?

She is standing there now. She wears a navy-blue coat with a fur-trimmed hood. Her mittens are old; the left thumb is unravelling. By her feet there is a single bag – a rucksack filled with books, photos, stones she has painted, driftwood he'd found and given to her.

Goodbye, she says to the house.

She also says *thank you* to it. For it gave her all the good things.

Maggie pulls the door behind her, hauls her backpack on. The car stays in the drive; *Pigeon* stays rocking in her half-moon harbour. And she walks down the lane from Crest for the last time, past the rusting tractor and past the sheep that are steaming next to lines of hay. She sees the painted words *Wind Rising*, and the rusting car parts, and at this moment Maggie turns very slowly – she turns in a full circle, in the middle of the lane. *Remember this* ... The church, the playground, distant Tavey. The sleeping light-house. All the different rooftops, the friendly chestnut mare.

Still early, but there are lights on at High Haven. Maggie knocks, and Nathan opens it. She says *no long goodbyes* ...

When they embrace, he exhales like it hurts him. She closes her eyes. She tries to soak him up – his scent, his firmness. *I'll phone.*

You'd better. And come and see us.

Nathan. Tom's brother who kept him safe. Who made him wear socks on splintery floors and held shells to his ears.

As for Tabitha's words, they are simple. *We will miss you. Dearest you.*

At the Old Fish Store, the Coyles are waiting for her. Abigail smiles through her tears; Jim pushes himself out of his chair, holds out his arms and says *how about a hug for an old man?* Eyes as milk-white as the moon.

And of course she goes to the church. How could she not go to the church? She lifts the heavy latch that she has lifted so often before. She makes her way to the second-to-last pew on the right-hand side and settles herself there. Cold, in the church. She can see her breath, and it would be dark also if there were not tall, red candles in brass holders – homely, festive. Lorcan loves Christmas time.

She looks down at her hands. The mitten's loose thread.

There will always be stories, she knows that. There will always be the ones that she tells over and over, and there will always be the ones that she keeps for herself and no-one else. And then there will be moments when she lacks the words – when no words can describe it. This feeling.

Tom. The word whitens the air.

I carry you.

She lights a candle. She is sad, and she is strengthened – both.

Sleet, and a wind that has no clear direction so that as Maggie carries her pack to the harbour she has to narrow her eyes and tighten her hood. Her cheeks are pink, and her nose is. She smiles as she passes the viewpoint, for there is no view to speak of today – grey cloud, grey waves.

In the harbour she finds the *Morning Star.*

Ed and Sam Lovegrove are in their fluorescent coats. Nancy waves from her bedroom window. And there is Emmeline: Emmeline stands on the quayside. She wears a green coat and quilted boots and her hands are clasped in front of her – neat, prepared. She does not move when she sees Maggie, but she smiles and says *I wanted to be here.*

I like that you are.

So the men load the *Star*, and the two women who loved Tom Bundy face each other. They say very little but they say enough. *Tom is the love of my life*, Maggie tells her. *Always will be.* And the older woman hears this, gives a single nod. She accepts it because Emmeline understands that things can never stay unchanged; nothing can stay as it always was. Seasons pass. A man who treads water, she knows, will tire. And she knows, also, that Tom's bones may not be safe in a box and easily found but her love for him is. Maggie's love is.

I am sorry. For having been so …

It's OK. And it is.

Look after yourself, Maggie. Find happiness.

You too. I will write. I'll phone.
I'd like that.

*　　*　　*

I think we'd both imagined the moment to be bigger than that. I think we expected tears, or uneasiness. But the moment was small. It was tender, and calm.

Talk of him. Won't you? Those were her parting words to me – as if she feared I'd never speak of her youngest child again. As if I didn't have story after story. As if I didn't carry his heart inside my heart.

I will. I'll never stop.

I boarded the *Star*. I stood at the ferry's stern, leant on the railings. Had Emmeline believed in the Fishman? Perhaps, like some, she hadn't cared who he was, or where he was from – he simply wasn't the man she had hoped for. But perhaps, in time, he became more than that. As he was for the rest of us, he became a change, a gift from the sea when it had only seemed to take away, and he was a chance to say *who knows …? Anything can happen …*

She waved, and I waved.

Parla grew smaller.

Strange – how huge endings can slip by like water when, at last, they come.

The Stranger, Celia and the Night-Time Sea

Tavey is his, entirely. For me, the mere word makes me think *him* – and of our four weeks together. To me, it is not an old pig farm; to me, it is not a house that had, once, splintered wood and rusting troughs in its garden. It is him, and it is loving him. His firm push at the door.

I hear the word and I am in a dress of peacock-blue. I say *Tavey* and I think of the way I'd touch his face, press a fingertip against it as if checking he was real. It is him lifting me into the air, like a child.

And it is a dandelion day.

Dandelions. I kicked through them as I walked there so that their stems broke in half. Their seeds rushed out like water. At Tavey itself, the cobwebs flinched to feel them and my hair grew feathery. The man from Sye had to lift a seed off the tip of his tongue and I can see him doing this, even now– the wetness, his thumb and forefinger.

Not sea, he said. *In my sleep, I do not say 'sea'.*

There are moments that change us entirely. There is no-one on Parla who does not understand that, or has not had their own lives buck and bound from a second or half-second, or less. A man diving overboard; an eye pressed to a hole in the chicken shed wall. A lighthouse-keeper's son saying *I saw something in the water, off Sye …*

Celia. He took my hand. *That's what I've been saying.*

Was she a boat?

She wasn't a boat.

*　　*　　*

I am there now. I am back in my linen trousers that are too long by far, dark at the hem and fraying. He is sitting beside me. We are on the doorstep.

I'm not half-fish.

I didn't think you were.

No? Some people think it. Some seem certain.

Perhaps I imagined it – for a while. I shrug. *I had nothing else to think. But I know you are human.* I had known it all along.

He takes a dandelion seed from the tip of his tongue. And I say *tell me. Tell me your story.*

The Fishman? Who grew legs, and came to live amongst us all?

It is not much of a story at all compared to what was true.

There was a boy from the mainland. He was born in a grey, inland town that had thrummed with factories; once, it had shaken with engines and darkened with smoke and there had been wealth there – wealth, in that town. But by the year of his birth, it had faded. The factory windows were boarded up; the chimneys stopped breathing. There was still pride, or a form of it. But pride was hard to find in the overgrown parks. It was rare amongst the needles in the underpass, or in the bus shelter that had boredom sprayed, like rainbows, on its broken glass.

He was born in a terraced house, with a lawn that was spotted with windfall pears. There was a stream across the road where he fished for minnows with a coloured net, and his father would say *that's a beauty* ... The two of them, trousers tucked into their boots. They'd name the minnows, pour them back. It is a good memory; he smiles, as he talks.

His mother died too soon. Her illness lasted for weeks; she was always sleeping so her son had to close doors quietly, could not throw sticks for the neighbour's dog or kick a football against the garage door. She died before Christmas and was buried after it. *Cold*, he tells me. *There was frosty ground.*

And so his father raised him; his father, who he loved – a whiskery, soft-voiced giant of a man, with eyes so black that they seemed to have no centre; a man who played the mouth organ, put money on the horses, wore a tweed jacket that smelt of teacakes and attics and who watched the football on a Saturday. When his son was older, he taught him the family trade. *See how it's done? Just like that* ... He played cards with his son, liked jazz and secondhand bookshops and he talked of the places he wanted to see one day, but never would for he died in his mid-sixties. His heart gave up – worn-out.

The family trade?

You haven't guessed yet? And he looks above us. He eyes the sanded wood, the paint. *I love it*, he tells me – *making places.* Making and decorating people's homes.

So he could join two lengths of wood perfectly. And he grew: he grew as a tree does – up and up, as if it may never stop. He broadened, matched his father's height and then overtook him. People he did not know would ask him to reach the top shelf, in shops; once he climbed a telegraph pole to retrieve a child's balloon. He was strong from his work, but also he ran. He lifted weights and swam sometimes. As for friends, he still met with boys he'd known at school and he drank with his workmates on Friday nights. He was known in the town – for his size and good manners. And for the smile that was just like his father's, or so they said.

He had his choice of the girls, of course. They eyed him as he passed them; they glanced up at the house that he might be working on. He had girlfriends, but none lasted – a few months, no more. He liked them – *but … I guess I was always waiting.*

For Celia?

She smiles. *To feel certainty. And I was lucky – I knew when I saw her. There are others who wait and keep on waiting but I found her. And later, I found you.*

Celia Jones. No middle name. It was a day like any other, of course – they always are. He'd been working on a house near the town centre and he was pausing for his tea break, sitting on the wall. She walked past him. *Tall*, he thought. *What hair …* And she was walking as if she was happy, as if she'd never been to this town and she was loving what she saw despite the graffiti, the litter that skittered along with the leaves. She seemed to notice everything – the weeds that pushed up through the pavement, the pigeon with the stumped foot, petrol in a puddle, the coins in the fountain that were turning green.

The black-eyed man sitting on a wall. She noticed him, too.

A drink, that evening. Lunch the next day.

Her hair was straight, a deep copper colour that she twisted as she talked. Her eyes were part-brown, part-green. She had recently left a relationship that had made her feel trapped and sad, and so when the black-eyed man remarked that she'd walked down the street looking so happy – *no-one looks that happy here* – her answer had been *freedom! At long last!* A dramatic wave of her hands.

Celia – a teasing word. A word that opened like a door.

He loved the things about her that most people did not know. She played chess. She liked coffee but did not like coffee-flavoured things. She'd jump over the cable of the vacuum cleaner as she used it and he loved that – that jump, feet together. Celia's flat was in a coastal town that she'd moved to, for her brand-new start, and he loved that flat for its mismatched cushions, the beaded curtains, the family photograph in which all of them (parents, a brother, three sisters and a niece) had that copper-red hair. Her smell was hers, like no-one else's – marshmallows, roses, talc. She had some shoes that she had never worn because *they are just too beautiful ... Look at them! How could I wear them?* Gold stilettos; red velvet shoes with a bright-pink bow.

And he loved her beliefs and superstitions: that the end of a loaf of bread is unlucky; that a flame should be snuffed out, never blown; you must greet a single magpie with a cheery *how-do-you-do?* Sometimes, before bed, she would list the things that had made her happy that day, and they were all strange and tiny moments – blue tits eating a sandwich, a sneeze that had its own tune. She loved moths when most people hate them. Since childhood, Celia had believed absolutely that all moths want to fly to the moon.

It's navigation, he told her gently.

They don't just ... want to go there? Shocked, let down.

He loved that she pouted in her sleep; he loved (but never told her so) her unshakeable fear of geese, how she'd grasp his arm near ponds and say *please don't let them chase me*. She collected greetings cards of every size and kind and she'd send them to friends for no reason other than she loved those friends. When she'd drunk too much, she'd sing ballads to strangers – taxi drivers, doormen, an urban fox, a tramp who sang back to her in a perfect baritone. Celia had her own words for certain things – milk was *cow-juice*, a walk round the block was a *bumble* – and she had a theory that you should try to fill your life with people with wrinkles next to their eyes because it means *they've got it right: they've lived and laughed ...* She liked matching underwear and gifts in tissue paper. Poetry – she loved poetry, and read it in the bath. She could, also, be grumpy. Once a month, she would sulk – prod at a cake she'd made, saying *it's not bloody risen. Stupid bloody cake ...* or she'd eye a thumbprint on a window and wail *I just cleaned that!* So no, she wasn't perfect. But her grumpiness never lasted; she couldn't be sulky for long. Her scowl turned, always, into *I'm so sorry* ... and she'd pad over to him for a hug. He hated her crying but loved comforting her – the childlike, hiccupping breath.

Celia. Cee-Cee to her mother. *Silly* to her niece, who was only four.

Cee to him – his own name for her.

I loved the sounds she'd make. When – he pauses. *Is this hard to hear?*

Perhaps. But I understand it. I've felt as he is feeling; I have also loved elsewhere. And I say *it's part of your story. It's OK. Go on.*

He asked Celia to marry him sixteen months ago. They were lying on a picnic rug, and there had been no clouds. *Will you?* She squealed – she would, she would. And not only had they been in love, they had also wanted the same things – marriage, a family, a house with no view of other houses from it, a bath with taps in the middle so that they could lie back at both ends. *A magnolia tree*, he says. *She loved magnolia trees ... I'd have planted one for her. At night, maybe, so that when she pulled back the curtains ...*

I hear it, now – the regret.

He looks down. He steadies himself.

She'd had dreams of a wedding, as most girls do. She hoped to marry in her childhood church, to have her four bridesmaids in a pale shade of blue. And a jazz band in the evening and a firework or two. Roses, on the tables.

That was the plan. But ...

I wait.

There are dandelion seeds. In the fields, a ewe calls out for her lamb and I wait. I wait, but I know. I know what's coming.

She began to feel ill. Aches.

Celia began to bleed more than she should. She ignored it at first; it meant nothing, most likely. But then she bled when she should not be bleeding at all, and she noticed a hardened shape to her belly that was sore and new. Quickly, too quickly, they came to know the smell of hospitals, the noise and size of X-ray machines, the coldness of the room she had her scans in and the look – *the look, oh God, that look* – that the specialist had in his eyes when he came into the room and shut the door behind him. *We have detected a shadow ... Detected* – that word, as if this shadow had been hard to see and the doctors had done well to find it. But it was not hard to see. The X-ray was placed on a box of light, and they saw it instantly: a flourishing, ink-dark bloom of cells. It could, perhaps, be removed but there were other, smaller blooms – her womb, her stomach, her kidneys, her bowels. A rope of ink had started to curl up through her spine.

When they told Celia, she turned, looked at him. She took his hand. She said *I am so sorry*. Those were her only words.

It doesn't take long. Does it? He means for everything to change. For the happiness to be halted and for all the tiny details – a letter, a lost earring, a wasp trapped in an upturned glass – to have a new, horrible meaning. *I thought I could hold her forever. I thought ...* She, who played chess. Who believed moths were in love with the moon.

They were married by the hospital chaplain with her red-headed family around. No jazz band, and no time for rings, but Celia had her roses – a vase of them, still-budded and sugar-pink. They kissed so that their noses touched. *And she still looked beautiful. How could she still look beautiful, when ...?* And her sisters clapped lightly, threw confetti – horseshoes, bells, heart shapes – over her hospital bed.

I loved her more than I'd loved anyone.

Yes.

She died ten months ago. Her family scattered her ashes in a garden with a magnolia tree. On the east coast, where Celia was from.

We talk into the night. Or he does – he talks and I listen, side by side. Our hips and elbows are touching, and we look at the darkening sky. We stay on the doorstep until it grows cool and then we go inside. We draw curtains, light candles. Lie on the bed, fully clothed.

Maggie ... he says slowly. Like he is grateful. Worn-out.

For a while we do not talk. We only listen to the waves, to the sheep in the darkness. He pushes his fingers between mine.

A long, soft silence. But, in the end, I ask *how did you end up on Sye?*

There are as many sorrows as there are people who feel them and there are no rules, and there is no list over which you can hover a pencil's tip and think *yes, that's me; no, that's not* ... I know this because they told me. They – friends, others who have lost their loves – would try their best and I'd listen, but in my head I'd think *you don't understand* – because I was me and Tom was Tom, and who could understand it? Who could truly understand it unless they were also me, and they had also loved Tom, and been loved *by* Tom, and unless they also knew how Tom looked when he placed his forearms on the mattress either side of my head and smiled down? It is solitary. I never knew that till he'd gone. Grief is such a lonely thing. There is no-one in it with you – others may grieve for the same soul, but they do not grieve exactly for what you also grieve. No-one has lost precisely what you have lost. Not exactly, never exactly. We are in it alone.

Sometimes I looked for my husband. I'd pull out drawers, or take down old boxes; I knelt, pressed my cheek to the carpet and peered under the bed thinking *are you there ...?* Was that a form of madness? All I knew was that he was *somewhere* – he had to be somewhere. He could not be gone.

Oh it is wild and it is lonely. It is as if you've woken to a world that you recognise but it has been tilted, somehow – coated, or rubbed down, or made colder or less bright. It echoes where it should not echo; where it should echo, it is as echoless as a single, muffled thud. And grief is not merely sadness, as if sadness alone was not enough to bear. I had imagined the sorrow to be as deep as a well, a howling grief, but I had not imagined the other feelings that have no right to be there, which seem wholly misplaced in a state of grieving – rage, impatience, self-pity, disgust. They come from the dark and rush in upon you so that you snap at good people or you fling food in the bin whilst hissing *what's the fucking point? Of eating?* And eating on your own at a table meant for two? Why would you want to keep going? He was thirty-seven. *He was only thirty-seven* ... And then there is the softening, the hands clasped over the mouth in shock at the fact you thought such things, and then grief returns to the familiar routine – the loss, and the disbelief; the fear at those six words which are *I will not see him again*. And guilt; guilt comes. Guilt, at having snapped like that, at having broken a neighbour's ovenproof dish when they've been so kind as to make a meal for you, the guilt at having smacked a fly a dozen times over until it is no longer a fly, or a fly's body, but pulp, just pulp – a grainy, blackish smear on the rolled magazine – when you could have simply ushered it out of a window as you used to, once. And so you sit down. You close your eyes and feel guilty that you are already forgetting things, and you are frightened, and you miss him all the more, you miss him all the more.

I didn't recognise the things I did ...

He was the same. He tells me this: *I was exactly the same.*

At first, he worked and worked. He took orders, sawed wood, toiled into the evenings until he was told, very gently, *you should go home* ... But at home, he kept working. He repainted things, moved furniture, took books off bookshelves and then put them back on. He'd sand table-legs at four in the morning. It could not stay like that.

Then through lack of sleep he hammered a nail into the side of his hand. No-one could understand how. *How? What the hell* ...? It pierced the fleshy web between his thumb and forefinger – a hole, like a bloodied eye. His hand was bandaged and he could not work; he could only walk the streets – *bumble* – or sit on the sofa and stare at a television screen that brimmed over with face after face but none was the face that he wanted to see. He'd sit on benches, or wedge himself in the corners of pubs where nobody knew him. He went to the café where they had their first lunch together – Celia and him.

He stared at the chair she had sat in, once. Talking of freedom, twisting her hair.

I grew angry, I tell him. *After Tom.*

He nods. *For a while. I was unfair – I thought unfair things. I wanted to know why she had died when there were others who were less kind, less clever, less ...* Dictators; murderers; lying politicians; drink-drivers; molesters; racists; thieves – he kept a list in his head of the people who were *worth less* than his wife, which he knew was not decent or just. Who was he to judge them? It was not his nature; he had never judged like this in his former life. But then he'd pass geese grazing in the park or hear the sound of a vacuum cleaner through the walls, or he'd lift the morning's mail from his doorstep to find mail order catalogues with her name written on them. He'd watch a woman walking by in lavish, high-heeled shoes.

Anger gave way. It went overnight, as floorboards might give way to a weight they had borne for too long. In its place there came exhaustion. A strange fog of tiredness made him lie down as if his bones had been broken, or taken away. For days, he lay still. The phone rang unanswered. He'd watch the line of sky through the half-drawn curtains turn from dark, to grey, to dark again. He only left the bed to drink from the bathroom tap. His hand mended but nothing else did; nothing else got better. How could it? What could heal? Celia's sisters had emptied her flat, and the things that they had given him – *to remember her by* – sat in a cardboard box in his bedroom, as if that was Celia – all she had been. As if her life had been reduced to this: books, a diary, her green leather gloves, a rag doll from her childhood, a hairbrush with copper strands.

Too much to bear, too much to feel.

Too much. It was all too much ... And too much became nothing, in time. As if the body knew it could not bear it any longer, it chose not to bear it and it made itself feel dead.

You don't have to tell me this.
Maggie, I do.

He wanted to be with Celia. That was all he knew. He lifted himself from the mattress one day thinking *I want to be where she is*, as if she had merely stepped on a train or walked down the road. He brushed his teeth. He left notes for a friend that read *I need to get away for a while. Not sure where or how long, but I'll call when I'm back. Don't worry.* It was not a lie; he wrote it without thinking if it was the truth or not the truth. He merely wrote it. He used a chewed ballpoint pen and he knew whose teeth had chewed it. She'd nibble the end, when thinking. Crosswords, or tax forms.

He locked the front door, put the key under the flowerpot.

He caught the bus to the coast where her flat had been. As if he'd dreamt the inky bloom or the white coffin being rolled into the furnace, he knocked on her door, and he felt his blood roar as he heard a radio being turned off and footsteps coming nearer *and I thought I would see her face, Maggie* – he thought she'd throw the door open, flash her wide smile and open her arms to him so that they'd waltz for a moment at the top of the stairs, his mouth pressed down on the crown of her head which would smell of roses, marshmallow, shampoo. But the face was a man's. He wore glasses. A tea-towel lay over one shoulder and he said *no, there's no Cecelia here.*

Celia.

Nor her. Maybe the floor below?

Late evening. He walked along the promenade. He glanced up at the room that had been her bedroom and he could hear her laughing, he could see the whiteness of her skin where it stretched across her hips, and the neat, copper rectangle; he could feel her shift position, turn him over and climb on top, and he could hear Celia saying his name and yet where was she? Not on the promenade. Not in the streets. Not in the off-licence with its strip-lighting, not in the eyes of the women who passed him by, arms linked, and said *well, hello* ... as if they stood a chance. She wasn't in the waste ground where the promenade ended. She wasn't on the beach of concrete blocks and car parts and rusting beer cans.

It's a lonely thing. Grief.

Yes.

Jesus ... I just – he takes his hand off my waist, turns onto his back. *I just missed her. I wanted it to stop being ... as it was.*

It was cold, of course. Perhaps he'd wanted that – the shock of the cold, a feeling that was not loss, for one moment. Perhaps he wanted a physical pain to replace, very briefly, the heart's one that he could not bear – and so he waded into the sea. It came to his knees: his calves looked bone-white in the water. He wanted to see his thighs as white, also, and so he unbuckled his trousers and left them behind. The coldness found his groin, and his pelvis. It was bitingly cold, and yet he undressed as he went – the shirt, the T-shirt beneath it which he'd been wearing for days. He waded on, unable to feel for the coldness. *Celia* ... Who came to him with her hair like a veil that she'd throw back, causing a draught. No stones beneath his feet any more, but she was biting her bottom lip saying *come closer* and he swam into the darkness. The space beneath him. The unbearable space inside.

I wasn't thinking of ... He turns his head, looks at me. *I know how it sounds. But I wasn't trying to do anything other than ... Rest ...* He tightens his eyes. His forearm goes across them.

I think, *like me* – like me, in the garden at Lowfield, where all I wanted was peace from it; all I wanted was a place where I could, for a time, escape the truth, where I could sleep safely and deeply and not feel afraid. I had chosen him, for that safety – his chest, his arms like branches; he had chosen the sea. And who can understand it? Each grief is its own kind.

I push myself up. I move until my face is level with his face. *When I hit you, when I saw you for the first time and I hit you, you said something to me. You said, 'I know.'*

I did. I did know. I understood it.

I was angry with you. Scared ...

I knew that. We wear it, don't we? The loss.

This is what happened in the dark, midnight water. This is what happened to a widower of ten months whose grief and disbelief were so thick and hard to live with that he found himself on a beach with litter and sewage pipes. A full, sad moon overhead.

He swam. But he was not swimming with purpose – no rhythmic kicks or curves of his arms. His limbs moved when they chose to move. He half-floated, half-sank.

I felt my body lowering. I remember that – and so his arms tried harder, briefly. But a wave slapped across his eyes and his mouth was salt-filled. The sea covered and uncovered him so that a silence came and went. And he grew cold, so cold, and his body weakened with the kicking and he knew that he was sinking. It grew colder, as he sank.

His eyes are closed. He is remembering it.

I whisper *what happened next?*

His eyes open. *I kicked. Suddenly. It was like …*
Instinct?
Instinct, yes. My legs just … kicked.

He surfaced like a whale – darkly, with a gasp of breath that came back down as rain. He inhaled with a roar; he turned with his arms, looking for land. *Nothing but water.*

Then what?

A light. It wasn't much. He thought he'd dreamt it – salt in his eyes, or a half-drowned mind. Then a second light. A half-second flash, five times a minute.

You swam? All that way?
No. Not quite.

He tried to. But as the first lines of grey appeared in the sky, he felt something in the water. A soft stroke of his thigh. He gasped, yelled out – *a fish? Weed? A swimmer's hand?* He rolled over to see it more clearly.

Rope, in the end. *Rope. Fraying nylon rope, like twine.* Also, a container of some kind.

So much can be impossible to believe in this world. So much defies all the safe answers and chance is all that's left – but chance sometimes does not feel enough. Chance? This was the ocean. It was bigger than humans can fathom, and he himself was just one man. Yet a floating plastic object passed him, trailing twine.

They wanted a Fishman. It felt more likely than my story. I think the Fishman of Sye was easier to believe.

Him, who I love. I tell him so.
How can you be real? Any of this?
I look at him, thinking the same.

He held onto it. He half-slept, half-kicked. He'd held onto the container or he lolled on it as seals loll. He said her name, as he made his way.

I remember nothing else.

Sye?

Just stillness. And the stones ... And he remembers footsteps on those stones. And a man saying *oh God, oh God. Can you hear me?*

Later, he knows he was carried like a boat.

* * *

I think he was right, all in all. I think the tale of the Fishman of Sye – a fish that grows legs and can walk ashore – was an easier tale to have faith in. The whale that could speak was easier, too, and maybe even the story of the giants being turned to stone because hadn't that been a long time ago? Centuries ago? We hadn't been there at the time.

But this story? This truth? Where could I even begin? Which part of it was the strangest or the most remarkable? That night in Tavey, he slept a deep sleep in which he did not move, or talk – he slept as if, at last, he could. But I stayed awake and I watched him. I watched the candle's light on the wall.

Plastic, and twine? A voice that said *kick*? The fact that a cold, heavy, half-naked man could make a distance that takes a ferry two hours? Or the fact it was Sye that he came to rest on – that dank cove, as slick with rumour as it has ever been with weed?

But the strangest part of it is this: that we found each other. We knew what the other knew; we had felt as the other had felt or was still feeling. I, too, had crawled along the carpet looking for strands of hair as proof of life and I had also rung a mobile phone that I knew could not be answered in the wild, foolish belief that, this time, he'd pick up. We both looked for our loves in odd places. In the windows of shoe shops, or in a boat's tarpaulin. In a single magpie's *cha!*

At first light, when he woke, he said *you're still here?* He thought I might have left him.

Why would I have gone?

Because it sounds like a lie.

The sheep began stirring and the lighthouse clicked off. We pulled the blankets about us, and in that early, dew-damp morning he told me why he'd never breathed a word of this, till now; why he'd never sat a person down and said *I know my name.*

You said you had amnesia.

No. They thought it. Tabitha thought it – and she lit up when she said the word. Maggie, she lit up like a star ...

So it began with her. It started in the nurse's mending room. For on that first night, as he slept or half-slept, he had heard Tabitha talking. She'd whispered – prayed, even – *please ... Let this be the start. Of something good.* And he didn't want to hurt her. He could not tell the truth to her – for how did his truth have any goodness in it? Ovarian cancer in a thirty-one-year-old? A vase of roses that she never saw in bloom?

He didn't want to let this gentle person down.

This nurse with hair like cotton wool.

And there was Leah, after that. Her, and her sorrow. He'd known it when he saw her – for he'd had his own form of it. *It* – she called it. She picked at the blistered paint on the doorframe, chewed the skin by her nails and she said very little for a long time. But then Leah began to tell stories. She began to sweep Tavey, paint its skirting boards. She explained text messaging to him – *see these buttons?* – and tugged nails out of rotten wood and for one small moment he thought that the truth might help her. A story about a slow recovery. But then she'd said *if you aren't the Fishman, I never want to know it.* A decisive nod and then she went outside.

Couldn't tell her, either.

No. I understood.

But he lied for his sake, too. For if he had told the truth – if he'd set Tabitha down on a chair and said *right, here's my story* or if he'd walked down to the harbour and knocked on Ed's door – then he could not have stayed. The tale would have spread; his name would have flown; the islanders would have stepped back from him, perhaps, unsure and alarmed. And his friends on the mainland would have come for him, taken him back to his darkened house and he imagined tests in hospitals, bowls of soup, leaflets pressed into his hands with words like *bereavement* on them and *coming to terms with your loss*, and he'd have been urged into therapy or into a friend's spare room and what *weight* – what a thick, profound hopelessness – that would have felt, to him. He listed these likelihoods. He thought of them at night, whilst the sea said *hush, hush* …

No – he did not want that. Instead, he wanted this island. He wanted the blow of salt. He wanted horizons, such as these. Once, he found lanolin on his hands – brownish grease from a ram's fleece – and he sat in the grass and stared at it, as if this grease spoke of life.

And you.

Me.

I did not want to leave you. I knew that from the start.

And, at last, there was Jim Coyle. Of course. He'd dropped his walking stick and then whispered, urgently, *do not tell the truth – do you hear?* For Jim knew there was no Fishman. He knew absolutely that this man was not half-fish or anything other than a human being who was choosing to lie for his and others' sakes. As Jim had done, long ago. *Stay who they want you to be.*

He told me to look after you, too.

Jim did?

Oh yes. He whispered it. He knew that this would happen.

Before we did?

Long before we did ...

Like a proper fairy tale, the blind man had the sight.

*   *   *

Folklore and Myth. I knew why she had it. I understood why Abigail pressed it to her chest. For as children, we are told stories of magic and unending love. But then we grow and discover that cells divide, that love can be uneven, that loneliness can sweep a man's skin away so that he's bare, bleeding, and feels even the softest touch as pain. We discover that there can be wars, droughts, high-school shootings, a whole new awful reason for the lock upon a chicken shed, and we look for our comfort. We try everything. We miss the world we'd believed in when we were small, unscarred.

I'll be buried with this, Abigail said, patting the book's leather spine.

How we all clung to the Fishman of Sye – as if he alone could save us. And maybe he did, in his own small way.

Joe. His name was Joe. He was a drink of fresh water, after years of brine. He was a shell, left behind. And if I lifted that shell and put it to my ear, I heard a story that defied all human possibility, in which *chance* felt too flimsy to be the proper word. It was – *is* – the best story because of how strange it is, and how impossible it sounded when he whispered it to me; but it's the best story, most of all, in that it was *his*.

He was a note in a bottle, or a lone wellington boot that had found one that almost matched it – almost, but not quite. Is that too trite?

He was a piece of driftwood after a winter storm – unexpected, intricate, and such a smooth, unearthly shape that was like art in its beauty. It was like art in every way. I could not believe it came to me, that it washed up by my feet whilst I was looking out to sea.

How beautiful. Human beauty is the finest kind.

How I wish I could have taken it home, like driftwood, to keep.

Twenty

I send a text to Sam and it says this: *You said you would do anything. Did you mean it?*

And he replies: *Yes.* Nothing else.

He walks up from the harbour and I walk down from Crest and we meet at the fence above The Stash. We lean side by side, look down. The sea has the brown lace of unclean water. It slops against the mossy walls and I can feel its coldness. There is the smell of trapped sea.

Sam's elbow touches mine.

I say *when did you last sail?*

Not since Tom.

Could you still do it? After four years?

A shake of the head, a wry smile. *I'm on that boat again every night. Every night …*

How about Pigeon. *Could you handle* Pigeon?

It is hard to tell a story from the very start, or at least it is hard when the story is ours – Joe's and mine. A tale so full of oddness and absolute chance that most people would hold up a hand and say *what?* Because perhaps we can cope with one wonderful thing, one event of incredibility – but not more than one. Not a tale as strange as ours. I expect Sam to flinch, rub his brow. But he does not flinch.

I tell Sam Lovegrove everything: the meaning of *sea*, the grazes on the stranger's hands, the reason a nail would be flush against Tavey's wood after only two strikes with the hammer. How I feel when I am with him. How I feel now, at this moment. How I am asking, at last, for Sam's help.

The water says *stash*. His hair shines gold.

The highest tide is tomorrow. Didn't you say that?

And a smile passes over him, momentarily. *Yes. Tomorrow night.*

*   *   *

Sam makes his way to *Pigeon* on his own. He goes down the steps that are cut into black rock. He pulls on the rope, brings *Pigeon* in.

He unhooks the tarpaulin.

Oh God ... He crouches down. Sam puts his hands against his chest, takes hold of the boat. *Four years.* He has put notes under her door, sent her messages, sat on the stile in the field by Crest as night comes in for no other reason than to watch over her, protect her and to make sure that if she needs something – anything – Sam would be there. He has listened to the shipping forecasts for her. He has gone online and trawled the sites because she is Maggie – Tom's widow. Tom's wife.

I will do anything. Tell me.

Tell me how I can help.

And now, at last, she has told him. Four years, and here it is.

*   *   *

Maggie crosses the fields. She steps over a stile, moves through the sheep.

The Fishman watches, as she comes.

I found him. I spoke to Sam.

He'll do it?

He'll do it.

She is trembling. *Joe ... Joe, I am so scared.*

He holds her. *Shh ... Strokes her hair.*

Also, Sam goes to the shed. He opens the door of the old boat shed by the harbour, goes inside. He lifts cans of diesel, shakes them. He moves through them until he finds one that is so full he can hardly lift it.

Outside there is *Lady Caroline*. Sam scans the harbour: the black cat is sitting neatly, but there is no-one else. And so he drops down into *Lady Caroline*, lifts the cushioned seat. Another container of fuel is there and he takes it. No-one will notice – and besides, he will replace it, when all this is over in two days' time.

Maggie comes to him. She picks him and the fuel up from the harbour, drives them north. They tread back down the slippery steps and Maggie and Sam fill *Pigeon*'s engine, put blankets, flares, lines, medicines, spare gloves, maps and waterproof clothing into her wooden chest. Maggie wedges plastic boxes of food under the seat, bottles of water and lemonade. *Happy with the boat? See the radio? And ...* She is nervous, unsure. She runs her fingertips over her lips and her frown is deep so that Sam has to tell her *I've got it, Maggie. Don't worry – it's all going to be fine.*

He sticks to the plan, as promised. In the morning that follows, he claims he has a migraine. He's not had one for years, and he is not fond of the lie – but he cannot go on the *Star* today, or stay overnight in the hostel near The Bounty Inn. He needs to be here, for her sake. So he says *I think it's bad ...*

He stays in bed for most of the day, which is no hardship. He needs his strength and wakefulness for the night ahead.

*   *   *

The day passes. And I become anxious. I feel guilty because I know this is a lie.

But he kisses me. And for a moment his breath is my breath; for a short while I have his breath in my lungs and perhaps he has mine in his, and maybe that is how this is. Maybe that is how I must see it, what I must compare it to: isn't the false breath we give to a dying person a trick, of some kind? It is not their own true breath; it is fooling the body. But it is worth it, surely, if it saves the life.

Easy to see, by such moonlight. The full moon like a friend.

I carry his clothes – jeans, the red and black shirt – down to the beach at Sye. I leave them folded on the grass. I tuck the socks into the boots.

And then I make my way to the splintered sign that says *Do Not Use In Wet Weather* and I drop down the steps, two at a time. *Pigeon* waits at the bottom. She bobs, as if eager. Sam, too, is there. He has oars in his hand. Joe stands on the slab of rock, shiny-eyed.

I've known my goodbyes. I have had many, and I've grown used to saying them – I have strengthened against them, perhaps. But not this one. Not now.

I fasten his top button; I smooth down the collar of his waterproof and say *you'll wear the life-vest – won't you?*

Of course. Smiles.

He takes hold of me. Joe brings me against his body and I close my eyes. We do not speak, but I know how he feels from the way that he holds me – tightly, breathing the smell of my hair. I burrow against him. I think, *do not go*.

But I know that he has to go.

I pull back. I say *mend. Mourn her. However long it takes you.*

Joe does not nod, or answer. He puts his hands, very gently, on either side of my face and his eyes move across me, taking in each part – my brow, my chin, the groove between my nose and upper lip. I know what he's doing. I think *he is remembering me. He is storing away the face of me in case we never meet again.*

I hope we do. How I hope.

I make a frail chick's sound.

Hey ... He feels it, also. He thumbs my tears away, says *we found each other once. Wasn't that the hardest part?*

And I soak up his kiss as if it will be my last kiss, for always; not simply from him, but from any man. It is warm, and damp. It is a salted kiss from our island life, our island days and nights.

Sam calls out. *We need to leave, now.*

So they do. Joe climbs down into *Pigeon*. I hold his hand until our arms are stretched out as far as they can be, until we have no choice but to let go. He puts on the life-vest, sits. And Sam rows the boat away from me – out of the harbour, towards the open sea.

He looks at me, and I look at him.

Sam pulls on her engine; I hear the sound, far out.

Pigeon becomes smaller. In time, I lose his face to darkness; I lose the engine's hum until there is no sound but the *slop ... slop ...* of the sea against the mossy harbour walls.

*   *   *

445

A good story would say that the waves were high, that night. A proper bedtime tale would say that the sea was wild, that water raced on *Pigeon*'s floor – up and down, up and down. It would talk of a spray, cold faces, and their voices being carried away from each other by a menacing wind that has no wish for them to be on this water, so late at night. The tale would have that fierce punch beneath the boat as it dropped from one wave onto the other, and Sam would be shouting *woah!* as they climbed up the black, black face of an approaching wave. *Pigeon* would be vertical. The men would look down, see the sea beneath their feet. That would be the best story – two men, one boat and a night-time storm.

But the truth is that the journey is a flat, quiet one. The motor whines steadily. There are waves, and there are a few moments when the boat drops like a handclap and sudden spray finds them. But it is not wild. It is not the sea he knew before.

The Fishman is thinking this. He sits on one side, low down. He says *a month ago ...* as we all have done, and he counts the changes that have come to him in that handful of days.

Sam knows the place that he is heading for. And with the first light of day he can see it – a dark-grey cove with a line of wooden groynes.

With dawn, the sea quietens. The outboard motor seems louder for the silence that is around it. Joe still sits on *Pigeon*'s floor. The water is only a foot beneath him; a cormorant beats his blackness over the flat surface and it is the same height off the water as Joe's eyes are. It is a sight he will keep always, he knows that. The dark bird, and the morning sea.

The cove comes towards them. No-one is on it.

It is not yet four in the morning.

Sam turns off the motor. Everything is still. *Made it*, he says.

They row *Pigeon* into the shallow water. A few yards from shore, Joe rolls up his tracksuit trousers and sits on the boat's side.

Here. Sam hands him a bag. *Food. Torch. Some money – stuff like that.*

The man from Sye takes it, feels its shape. He did not expect this.

What will you do now?

He thinks. *Eat. Rest a while. Go home.*

You have a house? An incredulous smile. *You've got them all fooled, you know that?*

What about you? What will you do?

Fill up the fuel tank and head back. Should be back by nine, if I push it. Get back before the Star.

Sam ... He thinks of what he might say, and finds nothing – only *thank you.*

You're welcome.

You saved my life when you found me. And this ...

He shrugs. *I told her I'd do anything. Who wouldn't do anything for her?*

Joe drops into the water. He has boots slung over one shoulder and a plastic bag in one hand. He wades onto the beach.

Sam watches him go. And then, suddenly, he calls out from *Pigeon*. He cups one hand round his mouth so that his words carry and he says *you'll be talked about in a hundred years' time! A thousand!* And he drops that hand back down into his lap.

They smile at each other. *You will be too, Sam.*

What a morning. What a new day.

Afterwards, Sam eats a sandwich on *Pigeon*. He watches the tiny daybreak things that humans rarely see – the eastern side of every groyne lighting up, gold-brown; starlings flying in and out of bins. *This is my best moment*. It is the single best moment in his life.

He makes his way back to Parla. It is a calm crossing. He sees a seal, and the tucked dive of gannets to the south of him.

Sam moors in the half-moon harbour two minutes before nine.

As for the man from Syc, he thumbs a lift and, later, catches a bus into the town that he has known all his life. He feels a different engine thrum through his bones. He looks at the rough, patterned fabric of the bus seat beside him, where it's been smoothed and greyed from use, and he thinks of Maggie pushing the straps of her dress to one side. He thinks of Maggie showing him the feathers she keeps, in a vase.

He knows he will think of her every day, all the time. Being here does not lessen it. But he knows – as she does – that yes, he had to go.

His house is as he left it – curtains open, the squeak of the gate. His key is still there, beneath the flowerpot; inside there is mail with his name on, a red flashing light on his telephone. Plates stands like gravestones on the draining board. Joe looks around. He walks from room to room. *My old life* … When he knew nothing. When he knew far less than he does now.

There is always hope – always.

He showers, and sleeps on the sofa. *Maggie* … he says, in his sleep.

448

Parla's new dawn. The highest tide has been and gone. The wind is blowing from the west, and the mare stands with her back to it. Shells are lying on beaches; plastic bottles and driftwood have been brought onto grass. *Such clean air* ... They all think it as they open their windows or step outside in their dressing gowns, breathing in the brand-new day.

In a red-bricked house by a harbour, a young girl is singing. She jumps downstairs with unbrushed hair. Her song is her own: *let's go and look at beaches for shells and dead crabs and pretty things* ...

Dee is buttering toast. She says *keep it down*. Sam's *migraine, remember* – and she bites into the toast with a crunch. But Nan still sings and clambers over furniture and she maintains that it's Sye she wants to go to – *where the Fishman was. There might be another one!* She knocks over a pot-plant; a part of the armchair cracks as she climbs on it so that Dee says *fine, I'll take you to Rona's. Rona can take you. How's that?*

They ready themselves, finish their toast, and Dee says *I shall just pop up to Sam, let him know where we're going.* And as she's climbing the stairs towards the attic room, the phone rings. It shakes into life, rattling the china in the cupboard next to it. Dee hurries back to the kitchen, scoops up the receiver. *Hello? Yes?*

A breathing sound. Static.

Dee frowns. *Hello* again. *Who's there? Anyone there?*

Outside, on the quayside, there is a young man with a reddish beard and a diesel smell. He holds his mobile phone. On the screen, lit up, it says HOME.

Sam knows where his mother is. He knows she will be in the kitchen. She will be standing by the fridge with her back to the door saying *hello? I can't hear you* ... Nan, too, will be with her. She'll be hopping from foot to foot saying *who is it?* Who can it be? This mystery caller with no words to say? Like a story in one of her books? Neither will notice as Sam creeps inside.

He takes hold of the door handle, pushes down.

Sam passes the kitchen; he treads up the stairs.

He knows to keep to the wall where the floorboards creak less, and he knows that the cat will be sprawled on the landing so he steps over her, and he passes Nan's room where her bedside lamp is a bright-red heart, and just as he reaches the trapdoor to his room he hears the single *pring* of the receiver being placed back down in its cradle. He looks down. His mobile's screen reads CALL ENDED. His mother, far below him, says *how very odd …*

Sam climbs into bed. And within a minute – less than a minute – Dee comes into his room. Does she notice the smell of diesel and brine? In the room's darkness, does she see the wet hems of his trousers which are lying on the floor or the white line of salt that has crusted on his boots? Is there a fishy tang to the room? Can she hear him shivering?

No. All she sees is what she's expecting to see which is her boy, stirring. His hair is thick from sleep.

Sam? Sammy? How are you feeling?

And he inhales, turns, rubs his eyes. *Better.*

Good. You keep resting. As long as you need to.

OK.

I'm just taking Nan to the lighthouse.

OK.

She closes the hatch, darkens the room.

He will sleep for the next nine hours. At some point, Nancy joins him and they sleep back to back, like two halves of a shell opened out on its hinge.

He wakes in the evening to hear that the Fishman has gone.

You know of the days. You know of the long walks, the little candles in tinfoil cases that I'd light in church, and stand by. I have told you of Nathan coming to me, saying my name as if it were made of glass. He stroked my arm as he held me. *Come to High Haven. Stay with us?*

But I stayed at Crest. I stayed with what I knew. I walked out on the coastal paths and sank into hot baths.

I missed him – I did. I looked out to the mainland and imagined him. But I learnt, also, that I was missing other things. As I snapped a coloured band over a lobster's claw, I thought of fields, suddenly. *Fields? Why fields?* And not the Parlan fields I knew – but deep, green pastures. Molehills and muddy gateways. Cow parsley, waist-high.

And trees. I learnt that I was missing the hand-spanned green of horse chestnuts, or the summer shade of oaks. Beech woods, in autumn. And I missed rivers, too – or any form of water that did not have salt in it: streams, bogs, waterfalls, duck ponds in a city park or lakes so very still that they had their own clouds in. And mountains, and market towns. Orchards and marshland. Crows that winged above ploughed fields.

Inland.

I had rarely said the word. But I pulled back the curtains and said it. And after that, I began to say it more and more.

I wanted where I had come from – unsalted houses, pavements, woods. I wanted a city's dark-orange night sky. What was this? This wanting?

It was homesickness, and like love it grew stronger once it had been recognised.

Enough of the sea, I told *Pigeon*. She was the first to know. *I'll be leaving*, patting her sides. *Back to the mainland, now.*

I left Parla on the *Morning Star* on a winter afternoon. My collar was turned up to cover my ears and I pulled my hat down so that my eyelashes caught its wool when I looked up at the gulls. As Parla grew smaller Sam came beside me. *How does it feel?* he said.

I had no answer. But he stayed there on the back of the ferry with me. We saw the foam beneath us; I saw Parla from the water as the Fishman must have done. And I liked it when the sleet came – the first hard, sideways stones of it so that Sam went into the wheelhouse but I stayed where I was. I felt so alive. Sad, but with a strong heartbeat. Me, with an understanding now of what grief does, and *is*, and how it can slow your own life down so that it is almost lost, also. But my life was still going; I was not dead. And I had to live it fully, for my own and my husband's sakes.

*   *   *

Strictly, I did not lie. I was never asked the truth about that night – *Pigeon*'s secret sailing, or the folded clothes – and so, by never being asked, I never told a falsehood. I merely chose to not speak of all the things I knew. But it is a small difference – I know.

If I ever have my doubts about the *rightness* of our actions, I think back to the morning when they learnt that he was gone. I saw how Nan twirled, sang of magic. I saw Hester widen her eyes, half-smile at the news – *really? Gone? How on earth …?* Leah had shone as she'd searched the outbuildings, and Jim had stood by his bells with a strange, knowing smile. Lorcan had said, *well I never …*

shaking his head, half-laughing, raising his eyes to the skies.

It comes down to this, in the end: each person on Parla was wanting. We had all been wanting, yearning for a change. To hear *there is hope* and believe it – as a pig farmer, long ago, had done.

So, no. There was no Fishman; there never was. But we tried to be him – Joe and I. Together, we swam through the restless sea, raised our tail up to the sky. For we knew about the empty days – how absence hurts, how life flies by, how beauty fades so very quickly.

Happiness – that's all. That's all we were after.

We had wanted happiness again – for us, and for them. And I reckon that excuses any sleight of hand, or any little moon-white lie.

Did it work? Did they stay happy, or happier? When Emmeline had walked away from the quayside, having watched me sail away, did she go back to a warm, safe house? Did she find peace, or enough of it? How does she feel when the word *Fishman* comes?

For it comes. I know he is spoken of. I know that we – him and I – have left such a story that it's told often and when it's not being spoken of it's turning over in their minds, as seals turn as they swim. His tale is remembered when Hester looks at the seven schoolchildren, all cross-legged on the carpet tiles; it is story-time, but what story can she tell them that might be better than what took place on their own island, and not long ago? They wait. Nancy puts her hand up and says *can we have a recent story, maybe?* Which is her sly way of having the Fishman's tale told again.

And his story is in the mind of Dee, as she waits for her two twin boys to come home. They will be different, she expects that – suntans, scars, the glow of new places and love affairs, the hint of accents, maybe piercings, and they'll say *what's new*, casually, as if Parla will surely be just as they left it when it is not, it's not as they left it. *Wait till I tell them* ... She waits on the quayside.

Sea Fairy has been repainted. The barnacles have been sloughed off and she shines.

And the story is not far away as Emmeline and Tabitha eat scones with jam at the lighthouse tea room and smile like children, with full cheeks. Nor is it gone from Constance as she looks at the oilskins hanging in the porch – new, to Wind Rising, but not brand-new. Once, they were Tom's, and then Maggie's – but they are Ian's oilskins now. *His* – as the lobster pots are. She'd never have imagined the day he'd sell lobsters as well as sheep, but life has its surprises. He and Nathan have learnt how to catch them; they bring them back on *Pigeon*. Wide, easy smiles.

Life is richer for Leah, too. The word *Fishman* flits through her mind as she unravels the knot of a home-grown lettuce and she sees how nature made it – how each leaf overlaps the smaller leaf that follows, and it amazes her. She pauses, at the chopping board. She wishes she could tell him, but he is not there to be told.

And Rona? I worried for her. It would be easy to mistrust her for what she did and who she loved – to condemn it. But hearts are oceans in their tug and pull. I imagine the storm of love in her was as all storms are, in that they batter, confuse, shift your navigation away from what you know is the right course and the safer one: I think of it that way. And who was I ever to condemn? How could I? Rona thinks, too, of the Fishman. She thinks of him now, at this moment. The door opens. A man – blond hair, crooked teeth that she sees when he smiles –

asks if he can stay in her hostel for a while. *Photographer*, he tells her – *I hear the light is good*. He lowers his bags, takes off his coat and as he does so, coins fall to the floor. They race under chairs, run across the wooden floors and there are the quick, neat drum-rolls as they drop onto their sides. Rona laughs. The man tries to step on them, arms held high. Later, they kneel side by side with their heads tilted, looking for money underneath the fridge. She is using a broom handle to nudge the coins out. *Did you hear about the Fishman ...?* Rona asks this, as they're kneeling. She tells the story but he is not listening. Instead he is thinking *this girl is ...* What? *Gorgeous. Inventive. Different from the rest.*

And this. There is this, at this moment: Sam and Leah, walking on Lock-and-Key. It is a blustery late-spring day of showers and light. They are not holding hands and they have not linked arms but they walk so close to each other that the sleeves of their anoraks brush. Sam wants to tell her, sometimes. For over a year, he has wanted to tell Leah the truth – the cancer, the grief, the passing plastic container and the silent, full-moon journey *Pigeon* made – for he feels it will amaze her. Wouldn't she stop walking, clasp her hands over her mouth? But when he looks across at her profile, he knows he cannot. Leah is talking at this moment. She talks of countries she would like to see, the poetry she'd like to write, the beauty of that lettuce that she just unfolded and she moves her hands as she's talking. Her hair is past her shoulders now. She is womanly and beautiful and Sam knows he'll never tell her. How she is these days is perfect. She is happy – at last. It is how it should be.

As for Leah? She knows that Sam has his secrets, and she will not ask of them. Instead she kisses him. It is a small, timid kiss, at first. One kiss, which for so long has been a black *X* on a bright-blue screen. The second kiss is not so small.

In time they will travel. In time they will leave Parla to walk in the places that Sam's twin brothers have returned from so that they look up addresses that have been passed on to them, drink in bars where the twins have been. Sam finds the name *Lovegrove* in a hostel's visitor book and it is a strange, good moment – as if the world is, sometimes, small. They duck into temples. They see birds of such colours that they cannot believe such birds exist, but those birds do. They always have. *They have just never flown to Parla*, Leah says.

When they get back to the island, they live together. They move into the old pig farm. Sam gets letters from Tom Bundy's widow on the mainland which always begin *Dearest Sam*, and he writes back faithfully. He describes the sea for her, knowing she must miss it – *silver-flecked* or *dark* or *it is white-tipped – the kind that Tom said he liked.* Or he writes *calm and blue, Maggie. Today the sea is calm and blue.*

I spent my first few inland nights in a single room at The Bounty Inn. The owner remembered me, or partly did. *Didn't you work here, once …?* I nodded, spoke a little. Then I bought a whisky, pressed myself into the corner of the bar near the open fire and saw my own ghost from nearly seven years ago – the Maggie who hadn't yet met a single soul called *Tabitha*, who'd never caught a lobster or walked on Lock-and-Key. Maggie, who had lately accepted with both grace and resignation the notion that she'd never find love, or be loved in return. She knew so little – that girl. And as I sipped my whisky, I looked at the tables

I used to clean, at the velvet-topped bar stools I used to sit on at the end of a night with no knowledge of a man called Tom Bundy, or Crest, or proper loss. No sea stories in me, or none of worth.

We never know what is around the corner. We can only have faith, and try our best. And so I wrote on a damp napkin all the things I wanted. What would make me happy, in the years ahead? What would lessen the sorrow at what had been and gone?

I wrote of bird tables, long grass, woods to walk through, streams to drink from. Contentment and recovery for a man called Joe, wherever he might be. And no seas, no saltwater.

It took a while. But I found most of those things. In the days before Christmas, I saw a handwritten note in a shop window. It said *Cottage to Let. Fully furnished. Rural location*. I rang the number beneath it. And two hours later I was walking down a lane. Cows steamed in the fields on either side.

The cottage was like me, perhaps – worn and tired, but not lost. There was life still in it. And it had its own curiosities – an outside loo where swallows had nested; floorboards with their own old song; windowsills so wide that I lay cushions upon them and read my books there, or wrote, or merely looked out at the frosty garden whilst blowing across a mug of tea. That was a hard winter – snow drifted, and I would set across the fields with a hammer to break the ice on the cows' drinking trough. But I liked such weather. Parla had not seen snow like this. I had not, for years.

I paid my rent to a farmer – a cheerful, whistling man. He called me *Goldilocks*, waved as he passed me. His wife left gifts on my doorstep, as if she somehow guessed my story – rosemary bread, a jar of her plum jam.

I grew vegetables. I sold them in the farmer's shop. I came to work there, too: my earthy hands were shaken by other earthy hands, and I'd cut cheese or slide homemade cakes into white paper bags. I came to know the people who visited weekly for the same things – feathery eggs, whiskered carrots, apples for stewing, their own jars of that sweet plum jam.

And so the days passed.

The days became seasons. Seasons, as they tend to, became years.

*   *   *

We fit the world we are given, as fish grow to the size of the tank they are placed in. And I found my new routines. Daily, I walked through the woods or I'd sit down by the nearest river and watch it flow. After rain, it rumbled; the lower branches dipped themselves in it. I loved the river's moss, and the dainty prints that deer had left behind.

I had foxes in the lane. A tawny owl, nearby.

I wrote to Parla. I'd write to Nathan or Emmeline or the Coyles in their house of bells. Emmeline would sign off with *my fondest love*, and that in itself felt like a story or far more than three words. She told me Sam's news, as if I did not know it; she wrote about the holiday she and her sister would have.

Sam. I saved my longest letters for him. He, without fail, replied to them in his small, uneven hand. And his words took me back to the island. He'd talk of tides and whale sightings; he'd give me the fences that had blown down in the latest gales and I'd read his letters in my sheltered home with my legs tucked up beneath me. As for Leah, he'd describe her in a way that meant I knew he loved her. He wrote of her hands, of the scarf she sank into and how that green scarf matched her eyes.

In one letter, Sam wrote *I think of Joe a lot. Not all the time, but often. Sometimes I think I imagined him – it was all like a dream, wasn't it? But I know he was here. And I hope he is happy, and mended, and well.*

I hoped it too. I put down his letter, looked out at the field of cows.

Yes, I hoped it too.

* * *

We wear it, don't we? The loss? Joe had said that to me. He'd seen my grief when we met in Lowfield's garden. It was what he knew about me before all the other things – my name, or my own story. He thought *she is grieving. She is also missing someone.* And then, *she is beautiful …* Or so he said.

Celia. I have not forgotten her. I never met her, and yet I remember her; I think of her when I see geese, when a moth bumps against my reading light.

Her name joins Tom's. She joins him.

They dance together in another, nearby room.

I knew Joe had to go. He could not grieve with me; grieving needs space, and it needs so much time. And it needs to be *done*; it cannot be trodden round or not looked in the eye. And so when I miss him now, it is softly; it is walking through the beech trees and thinking *how is he, now? Is he strengthening?*

For yes, I miss him, and yes I'd love to meet him again – one day. But what I want mostly, and above all the other things, is for him to mend. To find his own peace, as much as he can.

Sometimes I hear footsteps in the lane, and I walk to the window to see – but they are the farmer's footsteps. Or it is just the trees, or bird sounds. And it doesn't matter that this is all they are.

I live my life. There is a robin which has learnt to eat out of my hand, and there is a stream that I can drink from – crouching, with cupped hands – and I tell myself the truth which is *anything can happen. Who knows what is coming?*

There is always hope and wonder. The Fishman taught me that.

The Woman with
the Inland Life

Once there was a woman who lived inland. She had known, for years, the wild water – the boom, the fizz of broken waves – but she had left that water, now. A coastal life can be too hard.

She came to live near trees. This woman found a house with a wood-burning stove and floors that creaked beneath her weight – and she liked this. She liked the deep, safe silence that came to the house at night; a single branch may tap the window and a tawny owl may call, but no more than that. No storms. No need to rise and go outside to fasten tarpaulins.

No sheep smell on her knuckles.

Whereas once she'd reached into water and hauled up lobster pots, she now sifted through soil for round, firmer things – potatoes, beetroot, radishes. They fell into her metal bowl like rain.

By day, she was contented. But by night, she would hear her beating heart and know that it beat for more than living's sake. For this woman loved a man. She loved a broad, bearded man whose eyes she had seen her own reflection in. And he had loved her, in return; he had held

461

her face in both his hands and said *we found each other once. Wasn't that the hardest part?* And so whilst she called herself *content*, and liked her simple life, she still dreamed. She hoped.

The woman had her friends. She had cows, waterfalls, a hedgehog that slept beneath her compost heap – and these were good things. She loved them. But sometimes she would look at an empty wooden chair and imagine him – older, but still *him* – mended, and sitting there.

She is waiting even now. Not fully, not always – but the dream has never left her. *We might pass in the street one day, or walk to the same bend in the river by chance and chance alone …* He might step into the farm shop, bright with rain. Or a letter may come, signed *Love from Joe.* For *Joe* was his name.

Who knows what will happen? Perhaps they will find each other: perhaps they will not. Perhaps they will find other lovers, in time. But I know this much: that they have not forgotten. Neither of them have. They both talk of the other in a soft voice. They touch the places on their bodies that the other one has touched and they remember their love at strange, sudden moments: a lifting-up of pigeons, or the smell of fresh paint. Anything the colour of deep, peacock-blue.

The end? I know my stories. I gathered them like shells on a beach and I tell you this: no story ends with waiting. That is not a good way to end.

An ending comes when the thing that has been waited for surfaces, at last, or steps down off a bus. An ending comes when a person walks into a crowded room – just one more face amongst hundreds, but she spots him as soon as he enters. She knows the shape of his wrist, his laugh. He knows, too, how she moves.

He says, *remember me?* Perhaps.

An ending like that. Something like that is best.

I am walking down the lane when this ending comes.

It is snowing. It is light, wet snow which settles very thinly on the tops of gateposts and my woollen hat. I carry a cardboard box in my arms. It is late afternoon; the bluishness of winter dusk is not far away, and the cows look darker for it. They watch me as I pass. I can smell the coldness, the wood-smoke. Their sweet hay-breath.

I push the gate with my hip, close it with my foot.

I fumble in my pocket for my key.

There are stories of people who know when change is coming, of an instinct which unfurls in the moments before such moments and perhaps those tales are true. After all, we are creatures; the gulls all came ashore in the hours before storms; the sheep seemed to know when the north wind was due. When Kitty stepped into a flame-red dress a decade ago, she'd had a strange feeling inside her – as if this dress would matter, somehow. *I felt so awake, Maggie! As if …* But me? Not me. All my life's great moments have happened without foreshadowing. I sensed nothing at all before I met Tom Bundy and nothing before losing him; I had no idea when a man was washed ashore. I was stacking pint glasses or pulling on a pair of socks. Or I was making a mug of camomile tea.

And so I am pressing the cardboard box against the wall to keep it there and I'm trying to find my keys in my pocket with my gloved hand but it is hard, in these gloves, so I pull off that glove with my teeth and try again. My nose is cold; I want to put the kettle on.

There was never a less likely moment. He says my name.

I drop the keys. The word stops me entirely. I stay as I am – my glove in my mouth, my eyes on the keys that have fallen. The keys are gold on white snow. I do not turn around.

He says it again. *Maggie ...*

Two years, three months and two days since we said goodbye to each other in a high-walled harbour; one hundred and sixteen weeks since I stood on that slab of stone and watched *Pigeon* grow smaller, thinking *please keep him safe ...* Eight hundred and fourteen days since I last heard his voice, and yet this is his voice. I am hearing it now.

He walks round to face me so that I see his boots, his trouser hems. Slowly, I look up.

His beard is gone. In its place, there is pale, smooth skin and briefly I think *it is not him at all* – but it is. It is him. His eyes are still his eyes; he has the same height, the same warm breadth. He tilts his head and gives a small smile, and that is his smile.

He takes the glove from my mouth, very gently.

Dreams cannot match the good waking moments. The right waking moments are better, by far, and he looks at my face, now – his eyes move over my lips, my jaw, my cold pink nose and he smiles as he sees these things as if they half-amaze him. *Hello, you ...*

We lower the cardboard box to the ground.

His nose is cold too. He no longer smells of brine but it is still him, still his smell, and it is like no time has passed at all – no weeks and no years. No time has slipped by and yet I put my hands on his cheeks as if to prove to myself that he is here with me – that he is not a dream and I am not sleeping. He smiles as I do this. He knows why I am touching him, and it is at this moment that we feel the snow grow heavier. The flakes are falling thickly now, larger than they were. We both look up. A dark-grey sky.

I have not yet spoken. There is too much to say, and nothing – both.

I lead him inside with my ungloved hand.

Once I had believed that the best parts were gone – that the brightest days and nights of my life were over. I had thought that they, too, dived off *Pigeon* on an autumn day six years ago and that the life that remained for me was only half a life. I was wrong. We think we will not mend, but we do. Our scars do not go, but they whiten; our bones fuse back into new shapes that work as well as they used to, or nearly. And there are still bright moments – laughter, friends. There will always be laughter and friends.

I looked at him. I could not stop looking. *You're here. You're in my house.*

I know.

And this: *we only know the foam …* This was Abigail's saying. She gave it to me for the first time after Tom had gone; I had talked of fairness, or unfairness, and I'd asked her *why? Why Tom?* She had no answer, of course. There are rarely answers to give and at first I saw no comfort in these small words of hers. But they brought comfort later, and still do. Who can explain this story? Or any other human story? It is an extraordinary world – full of love, grief, coincidence – and we shall never understand it. We should never try to. We should only be grateful for it. I reckon we should love, breathe, and say *all will be well* and believe it. And we should share our best stories, as often as we can.

That night, we lay down by the stove – the Fishman and I. We moved under blankets, traced the shapes of our new, fixed bones. *How did you find me?*

Sam, he said. *I wrote to Sam.*

Ah ... I smiled. And I reached up, felt the smoothest skin of him. I felt it with my fingers, with the heel of my hand and I whispered as I did this. *Your face ...*

Do you mind it? No beard? I could grow it back ...

No – I didn't mind it. I liked the way he was. I liked the newness of it, as if it was an outward change in keeping with his inner one. Proof, maybe, that he had mended – or enough, at least. I pushed up, kissed him.

Joe. It is like *oh.* It is a breath out, a deep sigh.

And we moved over each other as the sea moves over sea.

*   *   *

He stayed. He did not go away again.

It snowed for three days; for three days we lived near my stove and talked of our time away from each other. I spoke of beech woods, the letters I'd sent; I listed the things we sold in the shop – *hens' eggs, duck eggs, goose eggs, quail eggs ...* – and he laughed as I spoke, laughed into my hands. *Don't stop. Tell me – what else do you sell?*

I also tried to find the words for the rural, inland nights – the restfulness of them, their leafy smell. How I'd thought of him in them. I'd look up at the moon, think *it is the same one* – the same moon that watched *Pigeon* make her way, that glinted on the low-tide sand. That turned my Fishman's hair a silvered black.

He had less to speak of, in some ways. I understood. His past two years had been solitary ones: the walks alone, the reading of old birthday cards, the sudden strike of loss which finds you at the strangest times like waiting at a traffic light or glancing up as a single bird makes its way across the sky. Those long nights spent asking questions of faith. And *guilt*: he seemed sorry for the word. But I locked my fingers between his and told him how well I knew it –

how well I knew the guilt in feeling love again. There is the fear of replacement, which we never wished for.

It does not mean we love them less, I said.

He looked down, at our fingers. *Maggie ...*

I loved – *love* – how he says my name.

This small cottage is ours, now. We knocked on the farmer's door six months ago; he poured us a sherry and he sold the cottage to us with a wave of the hand and a clink of glasses. And so the rooms are our rooms, and the air inside them is our air. When the owl moves through the garden it is, briefly, our owl – Joe's and mine.

It is not always easy. *Being mended* does not mean that we do not miss them; *moving on* does not mean that the faintest smell of marshmallows or being called *Maggie-May* does not lead us into a hushed, grey place where there is not room for two. And sometimes in the moments after sex, as Joe and I lie on our sides, my back pressed into the downy dark of his chest so that we are both looking towards the same wall, the same floral curtains with the same view of trees, I think we both think of the people who died, the ones that we loved with the wild blissful certainty that we'd love no other in all of our days. In the silence that follows, I think of my late husband. In the silence that follows, he thinks of his late wife. And there will always be sadness, briefly. But then he strengthens his hold, stirs against me and I close my eyes against the white wall, that view of bare trees.

We carry them with us, Lorcan said. And we do. We breathe for them, sing for them, soak up the stories that they cannot hear. We think *they would have loved this ...* And we smile for them, on their behalf.

And do we live as they would wish us to? I think so. We have *Coralee* in the kitchen; we grow our own roses against our south-facing wall. Sometimes a family with copper-red hair comes and we walk with them – down to the river, or across the fields to the town. And in the evenings, I walk into the garden and hear the beat of insects' wings, or I see the cows drifting, or I remember how Tom looked on our wedding day. I remember how proud I felt to be his wife. And I hope he knows – I *know* he knows – that I speak of him, I speak of him. He will never be lost or far from me. I tell him that his little crab has grown her second claw.

* * *

I write this story. These words you read are my words – my own. Each night since leaving Parla I have sat down in the evenings, pulled my computer to me and typed of sheep with clotted tails, of churches made from salvaged wood, of bird tattoos and coves called Sye, a house with a bright-yellow door. I've written of people who've had scars or guilt or milky eyes, of secrets so dark that when kept in proper darkness, they are still the darkest part. I've typed of salt and the turning light, and how Tap Hole fills to the brim. Of Tabitha's pearl earrings. Of a red book with gold binding whose pages creak, as they're turned.

I write this tale to keep it. For only three people know of the truthful story of the Fishman and me; only three people can speak of it, and we can only speak of it between ourselves. So it might be lost, one day. When we die, it will be gone. And I do not wish for it to be gone.

So I type – *tick-tick* go the keys. Logs burn and night falls.

And this is for him, too. No stone marks Tom's resting place. There is no monument to prove that he was here at all – that vibrant, kind-eyed, laughing man who met me at The Bounty Inn and, from that moment, changed my life. I find him everywhere, of course. But now, at last, others can. He is in these neat, dark shapes of ink. He is in these cream pages that you lift by their corners, or in the magic of this flat, backlit screen that you hold or lie beside. He is each letter, each space between each word.

I type. But now I will stop typing. I will stand and make my way upstairs to where my Fishman is. He will, I think, be sleeping – the bedside light will still be on and a book will lie across his chest, half-read. I will lift his reading glasses off his nose. I will fold up the book, lean over him and turn the light out with a *click*. I will climb in beside him and feel his warmth – this man who came out of the sea.

The owl calls – can you hear it?

A fox pads down the lane.

And can you hear a lighthouse turning? It is far away from here. It sweeps across the island, and it catches the half-closed eyes of roosting birds, the teaspoon resting on its own. There is the brief, small flash of wedding rings. And at this moment – this moment, right now – a flake of silver is falling. It drifts down, settles in the grass. No-one sees it fall. And it will never be found or seen again but it will always be there – in the long, cool grass near Wind Rising.

Acknowledgements

I'm very grateful to everyone who helped me during the writing of this book: Sarah Bower, Eamonn Flood, Charlotte Kissack, Peggy MacFarlane, Colin McDonald, Tom McAree and all the Clachaigers, Dean Wiggin – and my family, as always. Thank you.